MOONSTONES
FALL EQUINOX

Guardian of the Moonstones Series

Book 1

DEBORA HAINES

Copyright © 2022 Debora Haines

All rights reserved.

No part of this book may be reproduced or used in any manner without written permission of the copyright owner except for the use of quotations in a book review.

Cover and interior layout by Blue Pen

ISBN: 979-8-9861771-1-3 (hardcover)
ISBN: 979-8-9861771-0-6 (paperback)
ISBN: 979-8-9861771-2-0 (ebook)

Published by KnowledgeBox Press

Annicka, you are my Dazzling Sun,
JR, you are my Perspicacious Moody Moon.
And to my parents,
you are my stars that wink to me,
in the nighttime sky.

—With my eternal gratitude and love

Keep me away from the wisdom that does not cry,
the philosophy that does not laugh,
and the greatness which does not bow before children.

—Kahil Gibran, Mirrors of the Soul

Acknowledgments

To each of you, from my Aquarian mind to my Leo heart, I say, thanks for being my friend. You have each been a part of my life's journey and left an imprint on my soul. You know exactly who you are, because as you read these words, in my mind's eye, I can see you smile.

However, some have made invaluable contributions to me in writing this epic tale. First and foremost, my twins who were the first to inspire my imagination when they entered this world exactly during the midnight hour. They were born on the very cusp, just as the sun was transiting from Aquarius into Pisces. I still wonder about their true nature. What is their sun sign? However, in the realm of astrology—one's sun sign is only a piece of the puzzle.

This project started as an astrological guide for parents to help them recognize and nurture that little spirit inside their children. Astrology to my mind is not a science—it is the *philosophy of the heavens*. In its application, it is the *psychology of the stars*. A tool used to encourage each of us to better understand our own nature, as well as the nature of those around us, to become a student of human behavior. It is our life coach who resides in the ether, our tutor who lives in that special place that exists outside over there, in that very space within our reach but not our grasp.

The acumen to learn this ancient craft requires a special blend of mental acuity, cognizance of the arts, and a judicious wisdom. Students of astrology are actually chosen by this discipline, or as in the world of *The Guardian of the Moonstones*—we are *summoned*.

As an eternal student of astrology for the past thirty-five years, the knowledge has helped me through many uncertain times. My teacher Joan Marie Mazza was a wonderful guide, who by using key words, made the astrological world accessible. My hours with Joan brought astrology into my heart and mind, allowing me the freedom of interpretation to create this epic fantasy. I thank you, Joan, with much affection; you were a voice well ahead of your time.

My twins are my "moonstone kids." Moonstone is an art-based preschool located in the heart of the Italian Market in South Philadelphia. This was where I met George Barrick, the school's director. His teachings in all of the different artistic disciplines inspired not only my twins but me as well. Through morning drop off and late evening pick up, this allegorical fantasy started to form and meld. George, heaven welcomed an angel much too soon; you are deeply missed but not forgotten.

To Susan Patrone, my astrology partner, thank you for "talking planets" with me over these many years. Our conversations spanned through boyfriends, friends, husbands, kids, college, workplace drama, and life. To Michael Heierbacher, thank you for bringing all of the scenes and characters to life through your brilliant illustrations. And to my literary sisters: Patricia Lawler Kenet, a true partner in crime, as we shared trial strategies as litigators, and then as authors finding our voices in this current world. Your constant help and suggestions through so many iterations has proved invaluable, as has your friendship. To Nell Whiting, your gift for coining phrases helped to make the "moonstone world" more accessible to the reader, including me.

To Victoria Griffith and her team at Blue Pen, I could not have made it to the finish line without you. Finally, to my husband John, who with the patience of a Taurus watched me slowly traverse this my chosen path, I say to you, directly from my ninth house Mars in Aries—yes, *ahem, I did it!*

Someone who was very special once said during her much too short passage on this Earth, "Sometimes, all you need in life is a good friend." If that truth be told, I am truly blessed.

Thank you,
Prudence George Vespe
My astrological "pen" name

SUMMONS

You are holding a manuscript that tells an epic tale
of two eras,
One in Time,
filled with great harmony and peace,
and the other,
Out of Time,
full of discord and chaos.
Come to know this remarkable chronicle,
when nothing was everything,
and all that is, created thereafter.
Can you hear the echo of a piano note's ring?
Attention!
As of this very precise moment,
extraordinary abilities are *now* awakened within you,
unrealized until this exact placement in the continuum.
Turn these pages and begin to understand
the history these words impart.
They reveal your own power,
as well as those of the heavenly stars charted above.
This quest is yours alone to continue.
Take heed,
and learn these lessons well.
You are *now* aware of the grave perils of this mission.
Time becomes time again only if you succeed.
The prophesied powers now vested within you,
can become a blessing,
a curse,

or another mystery secret.
Help from the heavens will find you,
but you must seek it,
and more importantly, be deserving.
May your journey be safe,
your return swift.
Hereof fail not, due reverence.
You have been expected.

On the seashore of endless worlds children meet . . .

—Rabindranath Tagore

PANGEA

Roughly 300 million years ago there was only one singular landform known as Pangaea. The entirety of Pangea is surrounded by the Panthalassa Ocean. The early formation fo the Tebys Sea can also be seen just off the eastern coast of Pangea. Due to the warmer climate during this time Pangea is mostly covered by forests and desert area. The eastern half of Pangea is slightly cooler than the western half due to the air currents and the rainfall patterns.

STANDING STONES

PANTHALAS OCEAN

PANTHALAS OCEAN

STANDING STONES

Domino44 Maps

PART I

CHAPTER 1

Nicholas

The night before what happened happened, Nicholas sat perched in his dormer window seat. It faced the crystal blue ocean and gave him a great view of the glittering nighttime sky. The sea air on this particular night was energized. It brought with it the distinct smell of salt and change. From this vantage point, Nicholas could watch the moon, planets, and constellations exchanging salutations with the silvery whitecaps for miles and miles of uninterrupted sea. He smiled to himself as his mother's words entered his mind, "Nicholas, this is your sky, your sea, and your very special piece of this planet Earth."

He believed her every word.

The first cool winds of the impending autumn combed the dune grass, while a blanket of wildflowers and dahlias stood firm against the calling of the season. Clearly, some of nature wanted to hold on to the summer sun, while the blustery, chilly gusts indicated the coming of something different.

Nicholas gazed up at the stars, spotting familiar constellations. His luminous brown eyes deepened into a fiery crimson as he peered through his mop of straight brown hair that was perpetually falling in his face.

"There you are, Aquarius, I found you." It gave him comfort to spot an old friend, as the sea and the nighttime panorama were his most constant companions.

Then what happened happened.

It was a brilliant blaze, a rumbling crackle, a flash of sparkling light.

"I knew it!" Nicholas exclaimed as he fearlessly shimmied out through the open window. "I knew it would come. I just knew it!" Arcing across the blackened velvet sky was a shooting star. Its streaking tail was luminous, flickering, and dazzling white.

"Mom, Mom! Hurry, hurry up! Look, it finally came. It's my star, it's my broken star!" Nicholas shouted with delight. "Mom, Mom, come on, hurry up, you have to see it!"

Melissa's motherly instincts had heard Nicholas's words even before they were thoughts. In anticipation, she was already bounding up the stairs to his bedroom. Such a sighting lasted a mere second, and it was not to be missed.

She nuzzled against him on the window seat, her arm going around his shoulders. "Wow, Nic, I see it! Yes, I see it!" she exclaimed, her heart pounding.

Although captivated by the sheer magic of such a spectacle, she still remembered to whisper in his ear, "Make your wish! I just did."

They shared this extraordinary moment, mesmerized by the star's flight.

Nicholas knowingly nodded; now he had a "mystery secret" that belonged only to him. They both followed the star's path, mapping its trajectory with his index finger until it disappeared. With affirmation, Nicholas smiled. "Yep, this is my broken star for sure."

Melissa nodded as a flood of memories took hold. It all seemed like yesterday. As an infant, Nicholas could never sleep, so sitting outside with him on the front porch at midnight became a family

ritual. He loved being rocked back and forth as he listened to the lullaby of the ocean and gazed up at the starry sky. Whether he got his days and nights mixed up, it did not matter because he loved the night with all of its mysteries. He was drawn to it. Even when he was just a toddler, he would stare at the nighttime panorama from his baby stroller as if waiting for something to happen, and he was never disappointed. Whenever he spotted a shooting star, he would clap his hands and point his baby finger up and say, "broken star."

In his young mind, those singular stars that sped across the blackened sky had somehow shaken loose from the bonds of the universe before they fell to Earth. He never stopped anticipating their arrival and, as he grew older, never stopped wondering what their calling might bring.

The crisp voice of irritated exasperation rang into the room. She entered his bedroom, her emerald eyes ablaze with golden flecks. "What is all of the noise about? I am trying to sleep. Can't you see that? Everybody is being so annoying; I can't take this anymore!"

Nicholas's twin sister entered his bedroom with her sleep mask in hand. She was in her usual mood, ready to pounce on any innocent victim who might fall in her way. Penelope stood tall for her twelve years of age. Next to her white T-shirt, her strong tan shoulders glowed a cinnamon shade. She never wanted to leave the beach. She loved soaking up every single golden ray that the Dazzling Sun had to offer. With her platinum-streaked long ash brown hair and those piercing green eyes, she struck a naturally formidable pose. Her fearlessness matched her striking presence.

"So, what is going on?" she demanded. "I want to know."

"You are too late," said Nicholas proudly. "You missed it."

She hated the unmistakable smugness in his voice. "Really? Move out of the way and let me see." It was more of a command than a request. She scurried onto the dormer seat, almost pushing everyone else right out of the window.

"Mom, where did it go? Mom, why didn't someone wake me up to see it? Mom, Mom, why didn't you wake me up? I wanted to see it, but I missed it, and it's all your fault." She pouted. "Now

I will never see it! It's lost forever and nobody knows where it went. It's not fair."

"Actually, that is not true. I know exactly where it is," Nicholas murmured.

"Then you better tell me," demanded Penelope. "Because I *heard* it fall, and it did not sound like all of those other stupid stars you see; this one sounded harsh, like it was in trouble or something. It sounded off key, like when you play that stupid flute of yours." She looked knowingly at her twin with her penetrating gaze. "That's what woke me up. That clattering noise, like a broken alarm clock. It was so annoying. So somebody better tell me because it scared me!" She stood her ground, staking her place and then thought for a second and recanted. "Well, not really. I was not scared at all." Then she murmured ever so faintly that no one could hear the words but herself, "Maybe just a little."

Nicholas remained silent for the moment, and then he met her gaze, eyes burning bright through that thick mop of hair. He knew this particular broken star was different, and it bothered him too. Now Penelope heard its sound, so whatever was going on, it was meant for both of them.

He thought about that for a second. At first, it perplexed him, but upon further thought, he knew it made complete sense. He whispered ever so faintly, out of his mother's hearing. "I'm not going to tell you; I'm going to show you." Then he winked. Penelope sat next to him and whispered something back.

They shared their twin moment.

CHAPTER 2

Penelope

Penelope's assertion that she could hear a shooting star in its flight towards Earth was disturbing. What was more perplexing—Melissa heard it, *too*. She slowly turned towards the bedroom door, reaching for the antique glass door knob; it seemed to glow just a little upon her touch. "Hmmm, that's odd." She shrugged it off, her mind feeling a bit overwhelmed. She turned around, her presence of mind returned to her twins.

"Okay, settle down. This is enough excitement for one night. It's time for the both of you to go to bed. Tomorrow is the full moon, the Harvest Moon, and we will go looking for . . .

"Moonstones," they cried in unison.

"Did I tell you how lucky I am; all I have is a nickel and a penny," Melissa continued.

"We are just six cents," the twins responded to the nightly ritual with rolling eyes.

"We are a nickel and a penny," Penelope said with a yawn, feigning sleepiness, hoping her mother would leave them alone.

"I love you!" said Melissa.

"We love you, *too*," was their reply.

As Melissa closed the door, she could hear them whispering to each other. She called it twin talk; it was a language that belonged to them alone. To the non-twin world, it was just gibberish, like a language from another galaxy. It made them feel special. She sighed. In her eyes, they could not be any more special than they already were. She was proud of them. Their inner light beamed so brightly from within, it reflected through their eyes. She hoped they knew that.

Melissa gingerly crept down the steep narrow stairwell in her Cape-style home, overcome with her own thoughts. The solid yellow pine planks creaked right along with her every step. She was their mother and knew that something was bothering them. "Of course, something was bothering them." Melissa chided herself. She just wondered what they really knew.

She twirled her hair, a nervous habit from childhood as she spoke to herself. "Who is really protecting whom?" She shook her head. "Do *they* know what really happened?" With reproach she said out loud, "Enough with kidding myself; all of this needs to end." Melissa's reprimands seemed to go unheard, as her words floated uselessly upon the air.

Her feelings were filled with a mix of anxiety and speculation. First, uneasy calm, followed by fleeting thoughts of dread. She pushed them all away to the very back of her mind. Tomorrow would be different. This time tomorrow, everything would go back to the way it was before what happened happened. The sun would align in a special way with this year's Harvest Moon, and their family would be back together again. It just had to be. Something would surely present itself. "Come to think of it," Melissa considered, "maybe it already has with Nicholas's shooting star." A voice from very far away gave her assurance, but in the next second that too was gone.

As she continued to make her way down the flight of yellow pine stairs, her children's hushed tones faded into the background.

It was her time now as she made a left turn into the kitchen. Melissa needed her cup of peppermint lavender chamomile tea. She reached for her crockpot discolored with age and filled with the freshly brewed herbs that she had grown in her garden. The brew took but a few minutes to steep, and she took her first sip. A serenity and calmness overtook her; the special blend helped center her thoughts.

She paused and slowly looked around, taking stock of her little home by the sea. It was an old clapboard-style dwelling. The weatherboard was made of split oak, spruce, and pine. Its very steep gable roof had two large dormers that faced the ocean. Although the roof was slate, at nighttime it twinkled purple from the tiny chips of mica embedded within its gray shingles. When sunbeams lit the exterior, the milk-painted clapboards could appear white, but look more closely, and all the subtle shades of the rainbow made their presence known. A person could look right past such magic, but for those who knew the charms of this little abode, its very presence cast a feeling of enchantment.

Her home had an address, located at One Manor Avenue, and was one of the oldest in this little town of Longporte dating back to the eighteenth century. It had, for some reason, withstood the harshest natural elements of wind, ocean, salt, and time. A wedding gift from Melissa's mother, it had been passed down through the maternal side of her family for over three hundred years.

Longporte drew its name from the folklore of a French pirate, Capitaine Longue le Porte, who was a frequent visitor to its shores. Tales of hidden plunder and buried exquisite gemstones never ceased. As the stories passed down through the generations, each resident harbored a secret hope that somehow just such a booty would be discovered. This cape was only one mile long, and at its widest only one-quarter of a mile wide. Surrounded by water, this triangular space narrowed into a point where the ocean met the bay. As the old story was told, the treasure was buried "due east at the point."

At this very pointe, where ocean met the bay, sat Melissa's home. X marked the spot. The steps of the open porch led to a walkway flanked by a field of natural wildflowers, then to the dune grass giving way to the sandy beach. To the right of the pathway loomed large, jutted rocks that formed a wall out into the sea. On the one side, the mighty ocean, and on the other the tranquil bay. Those sarsens stood strong against the march of the ocean. They protected the bay like a sentinel from the dominance of the sea.

The house was perfectly positioned to receive both the dazzling rays of sunlight and moody shimmers from the moon. Melissa was blessed to hear the crescendo of the waves in the morning and the whisper of the winds skimming across the whitecaps at night. The ocean was her perpetual alarm clock. Its constancy reminded her that she was indeed in an extraordinary space that was welcoming, magical, timeless, and safe. This was her special place on this planet Earth that she shared with her family.

The matins hours had begun with a silver-green moon rising from the sea. Melissa opened the screen door to sit on her front porch. It faced the beach. Her flip-flops flicked across the faded wooden planks. The wind chimes nestled in the adjacent magnolia tree whirred an inviting melody stirred by the late-night ocean breezes. An old green spattered rocking chair summoned her to sit and gaze at the nighttime sky. Melissa rhythmically swayed to the cheerful chirps of the yapping crickets. Summersaulting grasshoppers joined the dance in cadence with the late summer evening's fireflies and Luna moths. It was all one big concerto, moving like a clock that kept time for the whole universe.

As the old chair rocked back and forth, she started to feel sleepy and relaxed. The pace of the rhythm did its trick. It created that moment of peace before bed. Melissa readied to get up to go inside but then she heard it. It was that sound again, or was it a snippet of a song? "Come on, Melissa," she chided herself to focus. "It was just the noise of the night, that is all." Then the sound made itself know once more. Melissa stopped to listen. "Oh, that is definitely an instrument playing," she noted. Then she glanced at the wind chimes which seemed to want her attention. Their sudden movement distracted her as she wrung her hands. She started to twirl her hair again. "Who was playing that instrument? Could it be?" The answer left her mind as quickly as it entered and she could not summon its return.

Startled, she looked around—staring, searching, seeking—but all she saw was the quiet of the ocean.

〜

Sleep did not come easily tonight.

Melissa tossed and turned. Her changing thoughts crashed like waves on the shore during a late summer gale. Usually, the ocean was her lullaby with its quiet shushing wavelets, but not tonight. Even the light of the moon was taunting her, as though it was calling her.

"What do you want?" she asked the moonlight. "You must want something, so tell me." She got up from her bed and made her way to the old wooden chest of drawers set in her bedroom. From her childhood she used this old piece of furniture as a step into her window dormer. One of its legs was shorter than the other three, so it tilted back and forth, sometimes even all on its own. She thought the green, lavender, and red hand-painted flowers though worn were still lovely. The old-fashioned pattern calmed nerves just like that rickety old rocking chair and the sound of the crickets outside. This was her home, and she knew its mystery secrets. She nestled in her dormer window seat. Like Nicholas,

Melissa fixated on the visible constellations. She considered the changing season and how it would alter her view of these stars.

Then a deep unyielding sense of guilt engulfed her. No matter how hard she tried to shake that feeling, it was ever-present in this moment. Her twins were in their beds. They were safe. In her conscious mind, she had not an inkling or clue about the disappearance of her twin Gil and the loss of their father Reed. In her subconscious mind, she knew better.

Tonight, she could feel the unrelenting pull of moon, stars, and planets. Their energy around her being was palpable and strong. So she stared back again into the vista of the night, looking for the very same thing as Nicholas. She was waiting for a sign.

Twilight had deepened into darkness, leaving the sea and sky without its boundary line. The horizon vanished, mysteriously disappearing to a frontier yet to be known. It was eerie not being able to separate the two. Her twin Gil always questioned what it would be like to abscond right through that sliver between the two parallel worlds into that space beyond the firmament.

Melissa blinked and refocused her mind. She wanted to concentrate. The full moon was almost upon the Earth, as moonlight and starlight co-twinkled in the waves with extraordinary luminosity. Babbles and bubbles of lighted crystals peeked through the froth and foam. "Pay attention," she told herself, taking a closer look at the cresting surf. "It's right in front of you, look closer." She obeyed the voice inside her head.

Were those glittering gemstones breaking through the swells? Yes, yes, they were. The crescendo of the waves slowed as the swells took their time for her to see its treasure. It was the ethereal power of nature showing itself, making its presence known in the cresting surf. She jumped with excitement, sensing that the surges seemed to obey the power of the moon itself.

"Evanescent and Chance are from the moon. They have power

over the tides," said Melissa, her voice matter of fact. It was a snatch in time, like a snap, but she started to remember. "Thinx and Vespers, those darlings from Uranus, the two of you were always up to some form of mischief, especially at nighttime." Her memory jogged, awakened from a long deep sleep. She knew it; she remembered it all.

A porthole opened before Melissa's eyes, and shapes entered. She rose to greet her old friends from their planets, moons, and stars. Their images seemed blurred. She could see them trying to cross over into her world, traversing through the barrier of time. Then that awful pull, that gut-wrenching feeling enveloped her, yanking her away from her presence of mind.

"No, no! Stop, make it stop," she called in vain.

She tried to fight it because that vision brought her the clarity she sought, helping her to remember what happened a year ago tonight. Then it came, that familiar crackle of energy, forcing her to forget any recollection of those memories, what she most wanted to know. "Come on Melissa, hold on, you can do this. Remember what these moments reveal," she again spoke sternly to herself. It was futile. The pull of the force was fierce and unrelenting. It all slipped slowly away from her mind, just as it had so many times before.

"Next time I will be ready, next time." This promise she made to herself. She looked around for her letterbox where she kept her journal writing paper. The coming of the Fall Equinox would create that moment, this she knew. "When the full moon shows its fullest face, in those precious seconds my opportunity will present, and I will be ready." She spoke the words out loud, wanting to hear the certainty in her own voice. It was a fact.

Melissa fretted a bit, looking around again for her letterbox.

"Where is it? Show yourself." The words of her command floated on the night air. She rummaged through her things in the old chest. An overwhelming feeling of need crept over her. "Why am I obsessing on this letterbox?" That remained unclear, but since those cognitive gaps happened a lot lately, she started to trust her instincts. Tomorrow at dusk she would retrace her steps from the year before and take a leap of faith. Her chance would come and she vowed to make the most of it.

"Here you are." She felt relieved to find her pearlescent writing paper and then grabbed her fountain pen with the purple ink.

Her thoughts then returned to her precious twins.

How much did Nicholas and Penelope know about what happened to their beloved father Reed and their favorite uncle Gil during the last Harvest Moon? It was her perpetual question. The twins knew she was wrestling with something big. She could not hide the strain in her eyes, but tonight she could feel the anticipation that something was about to change.

For a long time, Melissa could feel Penelope's twinges of resentment. Penelope was a fact finder. She had not believed for a second any of her mother's implausible story about Gil and Reed needing to leave for an emergency work assignment. They'd left without saying goodbye. Lame excuse, yes, she knew it, too. Thank God they left her alone with it and did not challenge her assertions on exactly where they had gone.

Heck, Melissa could not convince herself of it, let alone anyone else. She had eavesdropped on them earlier that evening. Their twin talk was not so much a secret from her as they thought since she actually knew their language, too. She was a twin herself.

Nicholas kept Penelope at bay. "Leave Mom alone, will you? Just leave her alone."

"She is getting on my nerves the way she sulks around with that stupid blank stare." Penelope was irritated. "And you are one to talk. How many times has she told you to get a haircut? Exactly. So you are just as bad." She made her point.

"It's been a year—exactly one year—since that last Harvest Moon when they kind of both disappeared. So exactly where are Dad and Uncle Gil? They both left without saying not one word. Does that make sense? Exactly." That was her favorite word.

"And, this is most important, no one has said a word about it. It's like it did not happen. Really? Mom, she must know something, she must.

"And," Penelope was getting really wound up, "how about all those times when she does that spacey thing, you know when she just kind of zones out and gapes looking out at the sky. Like the answer is going to fall right down and hit her on the head or something. It's so annoying.

"And," Penelope's piercing green eyes were blazing, "why didn't they take any clothes with them? Are Dad and Uncle Gil just wearing the same things every day?" She held that fact for last. "See, exactly." Her look was triumphant.

"Penelope," Nicholas countered. "I really don't think Mom has a clue. That is what I think is really bothering her." He tried to push his mop of hair out of his eyes. "It's like she knows but she doesn't know. It's not deliberate anyway. I can sense that." He put his arm around his older twin. "Dad and Uncle Gil are okay, I can feel it."

"Really, what do you know? Everybody keeps telling me how perceptive you are supposed to be. That's all I hear. 'Everybody listen to Nicholas he is *sooo intuitive*. Listen to Nicholas he is *sooo perceptive*.' Really? Well, how about some facts occasionally. They would certainly help! I mean Dad, we know he is really, really smart. He does something weird—that science thing, his particle accelerator cyclotron thingy—so who knows what he is up to. Maybe he is on some secret government mission. But Uncle Gil, he is just a musician. Where did he need to go so quickly just to play the drums or the clarinet? *Really?*"

Nicholas sighed, hoping that Hurricane Pen was calming

down, but no such luck. He knew his sister would someday become a great teacher or a famous lawyer, but in the meantime, he just held on tight as a very determined Penelope continued.

"And Uncle Gil and I were really close; he would *never* leave without saying goodbye. That is the part of the puzzle that bothers me the most—he would *never* not say goodbye to me."

Nicholas could tell her feelings were really hurt, although she would never admit to such a weakness. Penelope rose from the window dormer seat, breaking her tirade. As she paced, she twirled her hair. Uncle Gil was her favorite person in the whole world. She really understood him and he understood her. "I don't like not being able to figure this out! Of course, it's just another one of this family's mystery secrets." She pouted as she nudged back into the dormer seat and opened the window a little wider, taking in a deep breath as she glanced into that space outside over there. "Hey, look at the wildflowers; they seem to be, to be dancing with the fireflies. Oh, could this get any weirder?" She finally exasperated herself. "Now I am getting on my own nerves." Her crescendo like the tides had an ebb and a flow, thankfully.

Expectancy was in the air as an ocean breeze swirled all around them; both could feel it. Everything felt charged and electric. No words needed to be expressed; their twin telepathy shifted into high gear.

Nicholas's broken star and its music were a signal, a sign, or maybe even a calling. But of what? Whether their mother was hiding something or protecting them, those answers would come soon enough. Tomorrow at dusk, the moon would be in its full-face transiting in the sign of Aries, with the sun's position in direct opposition in the sign of Libra. It would be the Harvest Moon, the night the Fall Equinox, a most powerful moment indeed, and they knew exactly where to be at that very second when that precise moment would happen.

They had a plan.

Back in her bedroom, Melissa, too, twirled her broom-straight ash brown hair as she nestled into her bedroom's window seat. She too looked out to the stars. "Gil, you promised to take care of Reed. You always promised me that you would take care of him. Don't let me down, not this time, not again."

Although her mind was burrowed in a quagmire, the music from the ocean commanded her to sleep. This time she obeyed. "Yes, this Harvest Moon will provide the answers to my puzzles and all of those taunting mystery secrets."

CHAPTER 3

Melissa

"*Mom, Mom wake up!*

"Come on, Mom, get up! The sun has been out forever. It's going to be a great beach day and you are not ready," Penelope complained. "Let's go, I want to get there early today. This might be one of the last good days of the summer, and now we are going to be late, and I am going to miss it."

Good morning to you too, Melissa thought. Instinctively closing her ears to the anticipated distracting mantra, she took in a deep breath.

Penelope woke up well before everyone else and, as usual, was barking her orders and a series of complaints from her bed. She was awake, ready for action, completely annoyed, and equally determined to provoke everyone in the house, while still under her bedcovers. It was her morning ritual, beloved by her family.

Melissa was sure that even before the sun peeked its earliest morning rays through her daughter's dormer window, Penelope somehow anticipated it. Melissa was equally confident that she summoned those rays to her each morning and the splendid sun responded to her welcoming commands. One could almost believe that the Dazzling Sun and Penelope shared a private chat about the mystery secrets of the nighttime when the moon took his place in the visible sky.

As a baby, Penelope called it "midnight peek-a-boo" because the sun seemed to disappear from her sight but not from her notice. Nicholas, yes, he might command the panorama of the evening heavens, but the day, the daytime heavens, that was all Penelope's domain.

Melissa waited for the next resounding iteration. "One, two, three . . ." Within the next thirty seconds she heard the refrigerator door open and then slam shut with a shudder. As was her custom, this young girl was determined to push everyone's buttons, including her own.

"Isn't there anything good to eat in this house? I am starving. I always have to do everything myself." Penelope always loved to appear exasperated. Melissa then again counted again in her head *one, two, three* . . . Within the following thirty seconds she could hear Penelope's thumping feet pummeling the hardwood stairs right back to her bedroom sanctuary. The door then slammed shut as she muttered loudly to herself. Penelope's morning ritual was the family alarm clock. It set the coming day.

Melissa smiled as she entered the kitchen, needing her coffee quickly to deal with her daughter's daily exercise that she so loved and awaited. The early morning sun skittled hello across the golden pine floorboards. It felt warm and comforting beneath her feet. She walked towards her old chartreuse cupboard that stood strong like a sentinel against the yellow painted wall. "Good morning, kind sir," she said, addressing the well-worn lime-green cabinet like an old friend. "Yes, today will be a wonderful beach day for sure." The stately cupboard shook a bit as if to acquiesce. Heartfelt rays of sunshine gently hugged her shoulders also in agreement. Its gentle warmth made her feel safe because it was familiar.

The sweet, smoky scent of French roast coffee began to fill the air. She took in the aroma as her fingers touched the crystal amethyst knob that graced the old cupboard's door. She felt a shock of electricity. It startled her for that second, but only in that second. Coffee was the only thing on her mind at this moment in time.

Melissa reached into the familiar spot for her favorite orange coffee mug that was nestled among the kaleidoscope of colorful plates, saucers, and cups. Then she pressed down the plunger of the French press and poured, leaving lots of room for milk and sugar.

She took a sip, sighed, and was ready to start her day. Morning coffee always energized her. Today it bought with it a strong sense of nostalgia in anticipation of tonight's full moon. She took another sip. The dazzling rays of sunrise lit up the lemon-colored kitchen walls. Morning in her sunny kitchen, with those bright and cheerful notes, set the tone for each day.

Melissa turned around and stepped into her living room. She took stock of her little abode by the sea. It was a welcoming place that provided a sense of coziness, comfort, and shelter. All of the colors that identified the morning, afternoon, evening, and night had their place inside her home. It was a color-coded celestial timeclock. The walls were brightly painted, each room a different shade to match the movement of the sun and moon: the kitchen's lemon-lime walls bespoke the early morning dawn, giving way to the dreamy sunset corals in the living room. Electric moody blues marked the vesper hours in the reading room while the cobalt hues of the midnight hour graced her bedroom. Outside the Moody Moon reflected its silvery twinkle right to the milk-painted front porch and electrified the mica chips of the roof shingles, making them glimmer like amethyst geodes.

Yes, each color of the day and night had its own special purpose in her little Cape-style home by the sea, working together in a rhythmic pattern, like a rainbow. She always felt blessed within these walls. Everything was ageless, welcoming, and magical. The antediluvian multicolored glass lamp that hung from the ceiling swung slightly. It caught her attention because the sun's morning light made it sparkle with an amazing clarity. She gave it a second stare, watching it sway.

That's odd. Did it just move? Melissa thought to herself.

Something was different, very different. There was no summer breeze to cause its movement or special rays to cause the twinkle. Melissa started to move closer, seeing something.

"Mom! Mom!!!" Penelope's voice intruded. "Now what are you staring at?"

Her daughter's sharp tone startled her, and Melissa jostled the coffee mug. The hot brew spilled over her hand, interrupting her concentration.

"Mom! You've got that spacey faraway look again. Come on, Mom, cut it out. You said you bought me an everything bagel. Where is it? I was down here earlier and could not find it. Did Nicholas eat it? He eats everything, and that was mine. He knew it was mine and he ate it anyway. It's not fair," she continued, pouting.

"Another thing, where is my lucky purple-and-white striped bathing suit? You know, the two-piece. Did you touch it? You must have moved it. Why is everybody always messing with my stuff?"

Melissa took a deep breath. "It's in your bedroom," she said and thought to herself, *I am sure it's somewhere in that organized mess on your floor.*

Melissa added loud enough to be heard, "If you didn't sleep with that mask on at night, you would see that your room is in a state of complete chaos with bags, books, candy wrappers, empty water bottles, shoes, and clothes just strewn everywhere."

Penelope acted like she didn't hear a word of it as she pelted upstairs and dove head first into the piles of clothes as if digging for treasure.

"Found it," she called out. "Mom, I am ready. Come on, let's go to the beach now."

∿

The three of them hoofed their beach bags and chairs down to the water's edge. The salty air of this beach day was intoxicating. The autumnal equinox was about to happen and the entire universe was acknowledging this night's Harvest Moon.

All three settled into their beach chairs, digging their feet into the cool sand and hearing that familiar wet crunch underfoot. The nippy water lapping back and forth over their toes sent chills to their spines. Within a few moments their body temperature adjusted to the colder temperature of the waves. Reverie descended upon Melissa as she bonded with the sea by listening to the music of the ocean. She closed her eyes and started to daydream back to the time when she and Gil were twelve, the same age as her twins.

September at the seashore holds a certain enchantment. The nights grow a little longer, the temperature a little cooler, and the sound of the waves are more resounding. The return of autumn calls for a new season with new routines. For those who called the seashore their home year-round—like Gil and Melissa—it meant the loss of their summer friends who shuttered up their vacation homes and left. Yes, this splendid beach, sky, and sea were theirs, but there remained a feeling of emptiness until their summertime friends returned. Her thoughts now swirled around as she remembered her brother's vivid imagination that filled the void of those lonely months. Melissa could hear in her mind's eye Gil's endless questions as he stared over the horizon.

"Hey Melissa, what would it be like to travel to other planets in outer space? What if kids just like us lived out there? Maybe they would be those friends who'd never leave us behind."

Her brother was her idol. In her mind, he was such a stark

contrast to her in every way. Gil was endlessly witty-clever and very handsome. He always knew what was going on and what was in vogue. When he was on the stage, his music was electric. All those ingenious pastimes they played as kids, they were all him, his ideas, his games, his wild imaginative world. Like finding sea glass on the beach, that was just one of his favorite pastimes when it was just the two of them. Where Melissa's strength was her IQ, Gil was the one with the high EQ.

After the summer, they would wait until the Harvest Moon in late September and search the beach for different colored sea glass—those crystal gifts from the sea honed from the tumble and topple of the saltwater waves. When washed ashore, these gems hid in the sand, waiting to be discovered. How long did it take for such special treasures to form? Maybe a hundred or thousands of years. Who knew the answer for sure?

The how or when did not matter to Gil and Melissa. Sea glass, to them, was buried treasure, their hidden booty. The plunder from the pirate ships that roamed the sea and shipwrecked right here in Longporte. Did those pirates lose their cache to the power and might of the ocean, never to be found? Or maybe such riches were still buried in the sand, waiting, waiting. This was the stuff of mystery secrets.

In their game, they would pretend that the sea glass that they found were precious jewels worn by the legends of antiquity. They called them "moonstones" because of the way the moonlight made them glitter iridescent on the beach. Gil was always first to spot the spoils of the sea, but it was Melissa who kept them in her pouch. She was their guardian and made jewelry from their brilliant-colored collection. This is what started her interest in gemology and archaeology so many years ago. In Melissa's mind, Earth was one big puzzle to explore, and it was her quest to discover all its mystery secrets.

When their treasure hunt was over, Gil then looked to the heavens and would say to his twin, "See the stars, Melissa. They do not twinkle, they are winking at us." See the moon. You know when it changes its face, that will change our mood. How about we travel to the Moody Moon? We could jump right from this spot."

"No, let's go to Pretty Venus," Melissa would counter. "The Evening Star is my favorite because it was the night's first light. I want to go there first. Just seeing it makes me feel radiant." She would spin around in its glow and pretend to dance.

Gil was always so clever; he gave all those heavenly bodies nicknames, even the ones they could not see through their telescope from the water's edge.

First it was the Moody Moon, then on to Pretty Venus also called the Evening Star, to Dizzy Mercury, next the Dazzling Sun, and then on to Jolly Jupiter, Serious Saturn, Wacky Uranus, Willful Mars, Silent Sedna, Clever Chiron, Wishful Neptune, and Puzzling Pluto.

He even made up a poem about the imaginary friends who lived on those twinkling worlds beyond the horizon:

Moon people must be moody,
like the Ever-Changing Moon.
Plutonians they like puzzles,
because they hide their every move,
Those from the Evening Star,
are enchantingly beautiful,
Those from the Red Planet Mars,
stormy and willful,
Our friends from giant Jupiter,
jolly and bright,
Those from the rings of Saturn teach us
what is wrong from what is right.

Oh my, that Wacky Uranus,
spinning on its side.
The people there are free thinkers,
all-knowing and sometimes wise.
Where is Clever Chiron?
Oh, see the comet's luminous tail take flight,
moving fast like Dizzy Mercury,
ever changeable, witty and bright.
While those from the windy-blue Neptune,
daydream the whole day through,
our friends from the Dazzling Sun,
love to tell us what to do.
Unlike Silent Sedna,
those strong and silent types,
each one forever reaching,
with aspirations,
to touch those glorious and lofty heights.

Melissa was a grown-up now, but sometimes all those ideas still spun in her head. During her most private moments, the child that still lived within her held onto the idea that she did have friends out there throughout the galaxy. The planets and all those heavenly bodies, maybe they did in fact cast a spell over her presence, her thoughts, and sometimes her dreams. The real question was whether these flights of fancy that haunted her had anything to do with the disappearance of her beloved husband and her twin brother.

"Mom! Mom, you got that goofy spacey look again. We are going for a walk."

Penelope's words snapped her back into the present. "Look, there is a ladybug. Hey little guy, do you want to go for a walk too?" Penelope put him on her finger, giggling. "Ugh, go away."

She swished a late summer dragonfly that circled her beach chair. "Let's go, I am getting annoyed, come on." Nicholas was just one step behind.

"Okay, don't wander off too far," Melissa murmured, still wrapped in her daydream, not ready to leave it. Her twins took off as she watched them travel the water's edge into the bright face of the Dazzling Sun. Sandpipers seemed to appear everywhere, hurrying by on tiny feet, as though perpetually late for something important. Always in such a hurry, they seemed to shuffle the twins along. Anxiety took hold when she could no longer see them, but she shrugged off the feeling. The sun felt like a warm hand on her back, her old friend comforting her, telling her everything would be all right. She again focused back on the sea, allowing an array of natural music to lift her spirits. Melissa heard different sounds today, like a flirty flute whose resonance danced above the waves, then the saxophone riffing at the whitecaps. The salty air, too, was seductive and lulled her back into her musings.

In her mind's eye, there he was: Reed looking ever so handsome.

He was standing straight and tall as if at attention. He wore a blue and brown tweed jacket with a crisp white shirt buttoned tightly at the neck. His thin worn maroon tie brought out the purple hint in his eyes that smiled to her through his horn-rimmed eyeglasses.

They'd met by happenstance or so it would have appeared, at the Victoria and Albert Museum in London. Both were completely entranced by what was heralded as a world-famous archaeological find: a multicolored gemstone necklace of unknown origins. Mystery secrets shrouded the object. First the artifact's condition was pristine, timeless, not showing any hint of age. Second, an aura could be seen by some onlookers glowing right above the relic. Those reports however were contradictory, as different viewers identified different shades emanating from the necklace. While some distinctly documented seeing the shade of blue, others saw green, while others saw lavender or even red. What was undisputed was the intensity of the colors in the necklace. The twelve differently colored stones in the bejeweled artifact glowed with a powerful mesmerizing clarity, unusually dazzling even through the thick glass that encased such a prize. What was of more interest was the persistent rumor that the necklace had an energy field that emitted powers. Certain onlookers claimed to feel its energy even through the glass case.

Melissa was a certified gemologist participating in architectural digs all over the world, seeking just such rarities. She was always fascinated by gemstones, their colors, their aura, their power, and their sound. It was her belief that certain gemstones belonged to certain people, and when the bearer wears the correct match, the stones enhance that person's abilities. Likewise, Reed, a nuclear physicist who worked with high-frequency proton beams believed the very same. His theory, yet unproven, was that energies most certainly exist within each gemstone. His mission: how to harness that energy and use its powers as an alternative energy source.

"You must already know that necklace belongs to you," said a soft voice. "I see it gleaming around your neck." Melissa blushed and realized the absurdity of that statement. "Was that a pickup line?" She burst into laughter. Melissa never really had much time for boyfriends and was very flattered. She peered at her admirer, looking directly into his face. Even though he wore glasses, she could see his amethyst-colored eyes smiled back at her. Their connection was immediate. They automatically knew with a mere glance, that each one completed the other. With this shared mutual connection came yet another extraordinary comprehension: the special energies emanating from those twelve brightly colored gemstones, somehow those very special forces brought them together. In that moment in time, there was another shared certainty, that gemstone necklace, no matter how crazy it seemed, did somehow in fact belong to her and no one else.

A dissonant note pierced the air, like a saxophone out of tune. It penetrated the atmosphere and Melissa's daydream, jarring her peacefulness. She opened her eyes expecting something. How much time had passed? Melissa was startled to see the beach was empty. "Penelope, Nicholas," she called out with a fright.

"Mom, what is wrong? We are over here. What is the matter with you?"

They were close by, digging in the sand and building sandcastles. She breathed a sigh of relief.

"Let's get going," she said packing up their things. They turned towards the dune grass heading back up to the house. As she stopped to pick a wildflower that graced their front porch, Melissa paused to listen to the crash of the waves. She was most familiar with this different sound; she'd heard its song before—it was the deep mournful notes of the cello. Its ballad brought with it a sense of foreboding. Melissa knew exactly who sent its message.

Dusk approached very quickly.

Melissa took her time drying the dinner dishes.

Her twins stood ever ready by the screen door; it was time to go.

Melissa felt strangely hesitant, like she was stalling for time. But why? This was the very moment she was waiting for, to go to the beach and reenact what had transpired the year before. Yet she was dragging her feet. Then it came, that sound again. Was it the bagpipes slowly luring her? No, it was surely that cello with its long mournful notes, playing the very same song as earlier.

She froze and thought, *Yejide plays the cello.*

"Mom, Mom, you got that spacy look again. Cut it out. Come

on, let's go!" That was Penelope's command, and although Melissa heard her daughter, she also was distracted with yet another command, coming from another place. Time was taking on a different rhythm. Melissa could feel the shift. It was happening, and she wanted to stop it.

"Mom, Mom, it's already dark, come on." That was a joint order from both Penelope and Nicholas. But Melissa's mind was not her own. She was struggling as the past seemed to envelop her thoughts. Her mind wanted to reminisce. Yes, she could now see it in her mind's eye; it was the necklace, her necklace. Then her mind shifted again to the beach, to remember the midnight magic of the moon turning the caps of the waves into a glistening necklace of vibrant hues. Yes, she could see it very clearly now, her beautiful gemstone necklace floating on the waves; the ocean was bringing her treasure back to the shore, back to her.

"Mom, are you listening? We just asked you if we should bring our telescopes."

"Telescopes, no, not tonight; this Harvest Moon is brilliant like a giant lightbulb. This is a super moon for sure."

"Oh, Mom, we know about the Harvest Moon, the Fall Equinox, and looking for moonstones. We got it already. Now let's go, we are just wasting time."

Penelope was out of patience. She grabbed her school backpack and jacket and headed towards the porch. Nicholas was trying to zip his red jacket, without much success. That mop of hair still covered his eyes. He certainly needed a haircut. He pushed open the screen door with his back, letting Penelope through. He was quick to follow as the screen door seemed to shut itself.

"Hey, wait you two. Wait for me." Melissa's voice was feeble and very faint; her words were soft, almost floating on the air. An extraordinary fatigue overwhelmed her, and a whisper urged her to rest. The ocean joined the effort, lulling her into a trance. The vespers hour had passed, and there was her old friend Thinx trying to tell her something, trying to convey a thought. Could that really be him? Yejide was there too; she was, she was doing what? The old ceiling light was flickering, trying to gain her attention too. Its colors were erratic just like earlier in the day. Their hues twinkled vibrantly. Clarity came to her thoughts. This was Melissa's moment. She fought with all her might; she needed a snippet of time before what was to happen happened. The music was back, along with that soft voice urging to her to sleep. The voice though, it was strangely familiar. Melissa could hear her voice respond. "Not yet, just a few more moments, just a few seconds. I need some time, just a little bit more time."

CHAPTER 4

By the Light of the Moon

Penelope and Nicholas slipped out of the house, quiet like mice.

They scurried to the water's edge, guided by the light of the full moon. Penelope and Nicholas knew it was wrong to be all by themselves on the beach this late at night. However, for some reason they were not afraid. They felt anticipation but not fear. In fact, despite knowing they shouldn't be out, they did not *feel* they were doing anything wrong. They felt free and safe. Most of all, they knew, for some reason, this was exactly where they were supposed to be.

When they got to the place where surf meets the sand, they stood side by side and looked out upon the ocean, seeing it with new eyes. "It's twinkling like ribbons of tinfoil. Watch the moonlight dance on the water." A sudden gust of wind caressed Penelope's face, sending chills down her spine. She hugged her sweatshirt jacket closer, thankful she thought to wear it.

"This ocean looks like shiny black ice, like we could skate right over to the place where the moon is sitting on the water." Nicholas pointed to the spot. Penelope agreed and giggled. That was what she did when she got nervous. No, better said, she was anxious, waiting for something to happen.

When they first came down to the beach, the water had been quietly lapping at the shore in a very slow rhythm. But now, the waves were encroaching closer and closer to the pathway that led to their house. Penelope knew that the powerful full Harvest Moon would bring the tides up the beach, but this seemed rather sudden. The wind, too, was now kicking up spirals of sand that started to blow around her legs, stinging her face. The sound was terrifying as the beach started to hiss.

She looked at her brother with trepidation as they braced themselves against the elements. Their eyes met. She questioned him without saying a word, knowing his response. Nicholas had come for his star, and there would be no turning back now. She, too, was steadfast.

The howling wind was incessant, its dissonance unnerving her. "Penelope, grab my hand," shouted Nicholas just as the wind sent them both tumbling into the sand. They tried unsuccessfully to shield their faces from the sting of salt and sea. Clutching each other, they tried to stand their ground and not be taken away by the ever-rising tide or lost in the turbulent whitecaps.

"Nicholas, what's happening!" she screamed. Violent waves soared above the surf, growing dark and fierce. The wind shifted over the water and the surface began to roil. It churned and churned, awakening a sleeping ocean that fiercely guarded its secret treasures. Nicholas was not sure, but strangely he wasn't afraid at all. He wanted to see just what his broken star was bringing to him, so he, too, watched and waited.

Then it happened just like that.

A geyser abruptly sprouted up from the maelstrom, sending up a spiraling cyclone with its glinting funnel. Crystal droplets the size of walnuts poured down. The sea was spraying a cache of its cherished possessions upon the sand, and they fell with a soft pat, pat, pat all around them.

The twins were wide eyed filled with wonderment.

The storm was over as quickly as it began. Just as oddly, the sea now swished softly towards the sand as the whirling wind

settled into a gentle breeze. But the moon, she still blazed a pure white light, illuminating the evidence that something wonderful had most certainly just happened. The sand was aglow around them, lit from below, and the colored stones glistened in every direction like a moon dial.

"I bet this is what Mommie and Uncle Gil were talking about," said Penelope. "These must be those moonstones they used to collect. Look at the pattern they made on the sand. It looks like a treasure map."

"Penelope, no, I think these are real moonstones," Nicholas said pensively. "Can't you feel their energy? It's like they are pulling at us. These are not just sea glass, no way." Tentatively at first, and then with more confidence, Nicholas reached into the sand and picked up a clear red one. It pulsed as it nestled itself in the palm of his hand. "It feels warm, just like the sun." He felt a comfort emanating from it, as if the stone wanted to be with him.

Penelope moved down the beach to a brilliant blue stone. It, too, fit perfectly in her palm. "Oh, this one feels cool and soft." She could not help but lift it to her cheek. The energy from the stone deepened, and she too felt something else; it was a clarity to her thoughts. Giving her stone one final caress, Penelope put it gently into her backpack and rose to take the red stone from Nicholas's hand for safekeeping before going to find another.

"Here is an exquisite green one," she called out as she combed the beach, spotting it along with various colors. "It feels really strong, like it's powerful. Oh, and here is one that must be a pearl, although I have never seen one so big. Oh, it's cool and it feels liquidly but it's not."

They ran across the sand, gingerly picking up all the gleaming stones that jutted out of the sand: an opal that danced with all the colors of the rainbow, a diamond as big as a doorknob with red fire in its center, a turquoise that smelled of sage, a lime-green stone aglow with the bright tones of summer, an onyx embedded with the hues of fall, an amethyst that reflected the color of the night-time sky, and a garnet that smelled and felt like rich mahogany.

"That makes for eleven stones so far," said Penelope who was keeping count. Nicholas was still very busy in the hunt for the furtive stones, so much so, that he almost stepped on one. A clear violet iolite lay at his feet, waiting to be found; it was the twelfth stone. As he bent down to pick it up, a kaleidoscope of color emanated from the gem, and a beam of guiding light seemed to point towards the rocks.

"It looks like reflected starlight," said Penelope. "And its beam is pointing in that direction. Wait, I think this violet thingy is telling us where to go. This must be a sunstone, giving us direction, just like those stones that guided the ancient Viking mariners across the seas." Her curiosity distracted her, but not Nicholas; his mind was now on only one thing.

"It's pointing directly towards the rocks."

In a flash, Nicholas sprinted, his feet spraying the sand and forming a cloud of sparkling dust that trailed behind him. "Penelope, I found it, I found it. It's my broken star!" There it sat nestled within the twinkling sand, right by the rocks at the point. That very delineated X at the spot where the ocean meets the bay. He looked triumphantly at his twin.

"Told you."

"Hey, wait for me! You promised!" She dashed behind her brother who seemed to know exactly where he was going, and he did. Buried deep from the impact, sitting in a crystallized colored sandcastle, sat Nicholas's broken star. Actually, it looked like two rays of something pointed, like narrow pyramids sticking out of the beach. The points were not made of glass, but they did not look like they were made of anything familiar either. Its substance was another mystery secret.

After a long pause, Nicholas finally bent down and very carefully began to sweep the surrounding sand away from his star.

"Wait, are you crazy? It could be some dangerous space thingy stuff." Penelope tried to stop him, but an invisible force kept her hands by her side.

Nicholas continued to dig. Gradually, more colorful pointed rays revealed themselves, twelve to be exact. Nicholas reached under the star and pulled the rest of it out of the damp sand. His broken star was now free. He held it up for Penelope to see. Even though the star was only twelve inches across, he used both hands to hold it. The star was light like a feather, so light that it might have blown away in the wind that whistled softly around them.

"Oh, I have seen this shape before," Penelope said almost reverently. "It looks like a Moravian star, like the ones we see hanging on trees at Christmas. Only this one is solid, no opening for a candle."

"No," said Nicholas, "actually this is called a dodecahedron, a stellated dodecahedron to be exact. We just learned about it in our science class."

"Well, whatever," said Penelope, getting annoyed; she hated when he sprouted out facts. After all, that was her domain. "Anyway, this one fell from the sky." She felt better getting in the last word. "Here, let me see it. It looks like a colored glass snowflake. The very same twelve colors of the moonstones we found on the beach are reflected in the star. There is one shade in each point. Oh, wait, look at the center, it's an optic white. Here, let me see it closer. Give it to me."

Penelope grabbed for the star, wanting a closer examination.

"No, it's mine," said Nicholas.

"I just want to see it up close, that's all." A petulant Penelope attempted to grab it right out of her brother's hand. Nicholas moved back a second too late, still caressing his star. Penelope's sweater jacket caught one of its points, and his broken star tumbled out of his safekeeping and thumped ever so gently on the sand.

"Now look what you did—you broke my star."

"No, I didn't, it's fine. Anyway, it was all your fault. I told you to let me see it!"

Nicholas was distraught as bent down and sat on the sand, hands around his head. Penelope sheepishly leaned over his shoulder, still wanting a closer look. As she stared, she noticed that the star was not broken; it was more like it had opened. The solid crystal center was now unlocked.

"Hey Nic . . ." The sound of her voice became lost in the resonance of a high-pitched flute, and then *bam*. Lightning bolts in a dozen colors flew out of the broken star's center: red, green, yellow, silver, gold, blue, lavender, bronze, turquoise, garnet, purple, and violet. In the next second, the bolts swirled around the twins, lifting them higher and higher through the moonlit sky.

Penelope was thrilled to feel like she was flying. Nicholas dared to look behind him and immediately wished he hadn't. The beach was gone. Only the quicksilver gleam of the whitecaps remained visible down below. Wonder replaced fear, though they didn't know which was which, or what was what, not anymore. The rainbow bands of color arced up around them and over their heads until they found themselves cocooned inside a sparkling capsule of colored lights.

And then everything was quiet.

The roar of the ocean grew more and more distant until it faded to the whisper inside a seashell. It was a deep soothing silence that Penelope and Nicholas had never experienced, and it brought a sense of peacefulness. Penelope closed her eyes to the natural jingle of the chiming wind. A moment later the fluttering sound of a flute danced through the air. Then the deep mournful sound of the cello greeted the flute, along with the reverberating cascade of the harp and the sophisticated sounds of the French horn, all coming together to join the dance. It was a song of anticipation, the announcing of a foretold adventure.

"La, la, la, bum, bum, bum," Penelope hummed along.

Something was going to happen; the music was building up to a magical static.

"Hey, my heart is beating to the rhythm of a hand drum. Bah-bump, bah-bump, bah-bump . . ." Nicholas kept his hand steady over his heart.

Then came the echo of a piano note's ring, a tambourine jingle, the clinging clash of a cymbal, a busy banjo strumming, and the distant call of the bagpiper's song. The twins were both spellbound by the serenity of the music.

It was the hum of harmony.

Penelope was pleased that she could share the special sound with her twin.

Ding, the resonance from a triangle being rung jarred them both back into attention. They opened their eyes.

"Ouch! Stop pinching me," snarled Penelope.

"Just checking to see if this is just a dream. I . . . I just want to be sure."

"I keep telling you, we can't be having the very same dream. Now cut it out and leave me alone. You are being so annoying again." Penelope was being petulant and would have none of it. They were on an adventure for sure, and she wanted to be the first to puzzle this mystery out.

Just then, the colored bands that swirled around them changed into blazing lightening bolts, and they could hear the crackle of its energy. *Zoom*, they furled straight into a velvet blanket of midnight blue. Twinkling stars were suddenly upon them, brighter than ever before, as were the planets, comets, and asteroids that whizzed around them radiating colors and an orchestra of sounds.

"Maybe Nicholas was right," she thought grudgingly. "This must be a dream."

Whoosh!

They first flew past the silvery Moody Moon, then onward to Pretty Venus, the Evening Star. When up close, she glowed the very softest shade of mellow yellow. "Night's first light, wow. Look at how beautiful she really is," whispered Penelope.

Next stop, the red planet: Willful Mars. "Well," commented Pen, "so this guy does have an angry pulse after all."

Then a sharp move in trajectory, as a sort of spaceship of sorts veered around seemingly headed back towards Earth. "*Whoa!*" they both screamed with delight. This was quite the roller-coaster ride. Nestled within this wheel of color, they clung to each other, not exactly sure if those crystal bands were solid and not really wanting to know either.

One fact they knew, this colored cloud of dust could sure move. "*Wahoo!*"

Slipping back past the extraordinary radiance of Venus's softest gold, they careened straight towards the Dazzling Sun. A huge inferno of orange-red gases roared into their field of vision. "No, no, no!" Nicholas breathed softly as Penelope clutched his jacket even tighter. They both just stared ahead awestruck at the massive furnace. Penelope's scream was fueled by adrenaline as they contacted its surface. Strangely enough, there was no heat, warmth, yes, but no hotness, not even as they passed through the very heart of the star. And then came the clash of the cymbals, accompanied by a swirling orange lasso of luminosity. It made them feel snug and safe.

Whiz!

Now back into the void of velvet darkness space, but it wasn't true darkness; it was speckled with stars awash with light. As they continued to sail around towards the Milky Way, they realized they were actually seeing the entire solar system, their larger home. Each planet, comet, asteroid, moon, and nebula seemed so close. Time seemed not to exist. They had no idea how long this magical ride was taking—maybe an hour, a day, or a million moments—they had not a clue. Then just rising over the moon's surface, they saw it, the serene blue-green orb of the planet Earth.

"Home, we are headed back home—I mean Earth," said Penelope looking at the blue-green jewel in a much different light, with new eyes. "Look, see the jetty, that's our stretch of beach. Oh, Nicholas, see our house, the roof its twinkling amethyst. It's like the mica in the chips are our runway lights, beckoning us home."

Ever so gently, the glowing starship touched the sand. Slowly, the dancing colored lights that had surrounded them dimmed and faded. Nicholas and Penelope slowly looked around them. Could it be that nothing had changed?

Immediately, Nicholas looked for his broken star. It sat there, right in the sand where he'd left it, poised now on three of its points and still softly glowing.

"Yeah, it's still here." Nicholas gave a sigh of relief. His voice was high and shaky. "Penelope, what is going on? Do you think that we are somehow on an amusement ride? That's it, we both just went on an amusement ride."

"That's what you *think*," she shrieked. "You actually think that we were just on an amusement ride? And you are supposed to be the intuitive twin? The super smart one, *really?*" She did not have time for this ridiculous train of thought, not now anyway.

"Okay, Miss Know-It-All, then I guess we just did share the

very same dream. All because we went on the beach, all by ourselves, and looked for moonstones!"

His words hung in the air and landed upon Penelope, making her see the facts in a whole new light. "Hey, you suppose this is what happened to Dad and Uncle Gil? Maybe they came on the beach with Mommie, and they got scooped up just like we did, but they were not returned home like us."

"That's just crazy. Why not Mommie? She was with them, and wouldn't she remember something like this? Come on, Penelope, that does not make any sense, not even a little bit of logic. Everything with you always needs to make some sense; don't change now."

"Sense, why should that matter? How has any of this made sense at all?" She was now really wound up. "Who knows what just happened. It's sheer craziness, but I still want to figure all of this out. When we do that, everything will be okay. I promise. I just know it."

Nicholas just shrugged; arguing any further was futile. "Let's just go back home. Mommie must be worried. We should have never left her alone and come here by ourselves. We should have waited for her."

He then went to move his feet, but they were firmly planted in the sand.

"Penelope, I can't move my feet; my legs are frozen in place."

"What are you talking about? Now you have gone crazy, too. Ugh, you are getting on my nerves again." She went to give him a shove, but alas, she too was firmly planted in place. "I don't think we are supposed to leave this beach." Her voice took on an alarming pitch as she struggled against her invisible captor.

"We must be having that same bad dream. We woke up, and now it's back," wailed Nicholas.

"Stop saying that because it does not help. It does not help at all." Penelope's soliloquy was interrupted by a strange but familiar voice

"Enough, stop bickering. I have been waiting for you both for a very very long time."

"Mom, Mom, it that you? Mom, we are so sorry we left without you, but at the time it seemed the right thing to do. Mom, it was like we were exactly where we were supposed to be." They both implored. They were relieved to hear their mother's voice.

"How did you enjoy the dance of the stars and the song of the universe? Have you learned the rhythm of the tides and the tempo of the wind?" Again, the voice sounded so much like their mother. But no, maybe not.

"Nicholas, you must stay still, your broken star was set free from the bounds of the universe to tell you, brave Nicholas, and your sister, curious Penelope, a very important story. And to ask something very special of both of you as well."

"Show yourself. Who are you?" Nicholas feet were now set free, and he spun around to see the speaker. Why did the voice sound so much like his mother? Yes, there was something different in the timbre—maybe mellowed with age—but it was still his mother's voice. "What do you know about my broken star?" Nicholas challenged her. He would not allow some voice to talk about his star, no way, not even if it did sound like his mother. There might be some trickery here.

Feeling bolder now too, he still looked for the source of the voice, wanting to understand.

"What story? Whose story?" Nicholas stood his ground. "We have a story for you too: Once upon a time there were two twelve-year-old twins who nobody messed with—you got it."

His fists were clenched and he stood with a swagger that he

didn't quite feel. "Do you know where my father and my uncle Gil are? *Do you?* Is that the story you want to tell us?" His fear was interchanged with bravado, and it seemed he could not hold on to either.

In this moment, time seemed to pass very slowly in a deliberate sort of way. "No, Nicholas, no, I think this story will begin and end a different way." That response came from Penelope; it was in her most very certain voice.

It was a matter of fact.

CHAPTER 5

Honora

Once again, everything was quiet, still, and tranquil.

It was as if the star, still balanced on its three points, was the source of the calm. The twins approached with trepidation, staring at its pearly grey surface as it continued to glow. What was the source of its radiance? Was the voice coming from the star? How could that be?

As they grew closer, they strained to hear the crunch of their feet on the sand or the whistle of their breath on the wind, but they heard nothing. Their world was completely void of sound. As they slowly advanced, the star seemed to sense their approach and appeared to grow larger, its light growing stronger and brighter.

And then, aah, the pure sweet notes of a flute, and a cello playing a low and languid melody in counterpoint. The light within the star pulsed with colors again, as its now-open center seemed more like a window. Nicholas and Penelope leaned forward to look inside. Music rose around them. String instruments and woodwinds joined the flute and the cello in a melody that filled their hearts with excitement. As another and then another instrument joined the concerto, more colors swirled and whirled.

It was the hum of harmony, the orchestra of the universe.

"The colors match the music," Penelope gasped after a moment. "Watch how the greens soar with the sound of the violin's arpeggio."

Nicholas, too, could feel the colors and the dance that competed for his attention. Each instrument had its own color. The pirouetting shades swirled about, first red, then green, yellow, silver, orange, blue, lavender, topaz, turquoise, garnet, purple then the palest violet. They showed themselves in that very order, in a balance of both color and sound.

"Penelope, look how the colors match the frequency of the instruments. Listen to the wavelengths of light and the wave of the instrument's sound. It's all about math, the dance of math!" he exclaimed.

The open center of the star became more luminous, blinding them, and then the intensity dissipated, forming a crystal pothole that allowed them to see into the eye of the prism. They peered inside.

Taking shape before them were two figures, a man and a woman with hands outstretched towards Nicholas and Penelope. Once again, a rainbow-like glow coalesced around this man and women, encircling them in distinct rotations. Pen knew that the bands of lights formed an astrolabe. Nicholas also took notice. "Look, Pen, it's an armillary sphere, just like the one on Dad's desk in his study. Remember how he showed us the movement of the stars and the planets in the solar system around the Earth."

Their father loved to study the stars and math. Hadn't he always said, "Remember, the universe tells us its stories in light and numbers, while human beings tell the same stories with words'?" Those words were from so long ago, or so it seemed. Upon hearing them, they felt his presence. It was a sign. It was a message. They both knew it. Their father Reed was somehow nearby; he was close. He was telling them something. Nicholas heard Penelope's thoughts. He admired his twin sister's gumption, her moxie, and most of all, her determination.

"Dad, I got this. I promise. I will follow the facts, just like you taught me. I will not let you down."

He gave his sister a wink. "And you will, Penelope, you will."

Then the music's tempo took an uptake, its song enthralling. The hum of harmony seemed to encircle the man and the woman. The softest yellow light, the mellow yellow of Pretty Venus glowed around them. Nicholas remembered his mother telling him that the goodness in a person's heart, that light, shone from within.

Meeting their gaze, he now understood.

The couple slowly turned their heads and smiled, that welcoming joyous smile of relatives seeing a loved one again after a very long time.

"Who are they?" Pen's brow furrowed. "Do we know them?"

Nicholas, deep in thought, responded to her. "I don't know, but they sure seem to know us."

"That's what it seems like to me, too. That's strange right?" She was puzzled.

"Penelope, Nicholas."

With a jolt, the twins jumped back from the star. It was that voice from before, the voice that sounded like their mother's. It startled them out of their peaceful trance. When they blinked their eyes, the couple had vanished. An emptiness crept in, leaving them feeling very alone again. A deep longing swelled up in Penelope's heart. If she could only see those faintly familiar faces again, even if only for a second. But they were gone.

A cool mist formed as a crystal cloud began to envelop them. The roar of the ocean and wind vanished, and the sounds of the music grew very faint. Gradually, the beach was completely obscured by the vapor, and they could only see each other as vague shadows in pearlescent whiteness. They were not exactly afraid, but not so confident either. Disoriented, yes, that would best describe it.

Penelope drew Nicholas closer. "We are not on the beach anymore."

"No kidding." Nicholas instinctively pulled Penelope's hair.

"Ouch! What is the matter with you?"

"Well, I just wanted to see if this was real or not," Nicholas countered, as he dared not say the word *dream* again even though she knew what he meant.

"Cut it out; you are getting on my nerves again. Pay attention."

He smiled. "Well, I was just checking to be sure."

Penelope had no time for her brother's antics, not now. She wanted the facts, not his feeble attempts at humor. Even though much to her chagrin, they both came to the same conclusion, albeit in two very different ways. At least he did make her laugh. That secret she kept to herself.

"Well, someone *did* call our names, right, Penelope?"

"Yes, I think so. Or maybe not. I am not sure of anything in this moment." Penelope lamented. "I don't have a clue. It's all just too weird."

As if in response, another shadow began to coalesce in the mist. Gradually Nicholas and Penelope could make out yet another figure. Her aura was lavender and opalescent, tinted with many hues of indigo.

Again, a frisson of recognition ran through the twins. They had seen her before, hadn't they? No wait, it was her voice they recognized most, but it had blended with the sound of the sea and wind. The harder they tried to pin down a memory of her, the less they could remember. Even though they could see her face, they somehow knew they would never remember what she looked like. That was a fact, they both acknowledged.

A gentle breeze caressed her silver-streaked hair, allowing it to drift across her face. She appeared to be a tall women with erect carriage and noble bearing. Her countenance was imposing with her long regal nose and wide high cheekbones. Yet she stood light on the ground as if poised to float away. Her eyes, the color of pale blue ice, sparkled with mirth. They complemented the silver tones of her hair. Her skin was smooth, luminous like that couple in the sphere.

A mesmerizing smile spread across her face. They could feel her warmth, and it was directed towards them. They knew it. She too knew them—and better said, she understood them inside and out. How did they know this? Because they could actually see her thoughts.

"Are we dead?" they both asked in unison with a gulp in their throats.

"Dead, of course you're not dead, don't be silly," the voice said with a tone of assurance.

"Okay great, so then we are still alive," stammered Nicholas.

"Oh yes, very much alive."

"Is this a dream?" Nicholas continued.

"*Stop* with the dream," Penelope said automatically, then paused, just needing to be sure. She looked directly at the woman and asked. "Well, *are* we in a dream?"

"No, this is most certainly not a dream, my dears."

Penelope now having clarity knew there could only be one answer, but Nicholas beat her to it.

"Okay, so you must be an angel." His eyes were wide with amazement, and he was afraid to even say the word.

The women threw her head back and laughed heartily. "I have been called many things down through the ages, Nicholas, but I am most assuredly not an angel. See, no wings."

She pirouetted and held her arms wide. Her robes rose in

billows of lavender with flicks of indigo blue. Silver flames danced along the edges. Penelope took special note of the sparks that flickered from her gown. Of course, what she just saw was impossible, but who really cared at this point. Nothing made any sense, not anymore. That was another fact.

"Wait a second, you called me by my name! How do you know my name? Who are you anyway?" Nicholas now was more curious than scared.

"Please do not be afraid. I have known you both forever. I am, if anything, your great, great, great-grandmother, but there are too many greats too count. We share the very same genetic code. Genealogy as you might say, or is it DNA?"

Penelope, the fact finder, had had it with all of this. Her twin might be intrigued, but she would have none of it.

"Oh, so you are our great-great-great-*grandmother*! Right. Time to wake up and for you to go away. Go away! You heard me, go away!"

The entity's presence remained.

"You are not listening. I told you to *go away*." Penelope persisted then snapped her fingers. "Wake up, it's time to wake up," she now commanded herself.

"I thought you told me this *wasn't* a dream. Now you think I am right." Nicholas felt smug.

"I think who cares if we're in a dream or not. It's time to get out of here and find Dad and Uncle Gil. How we get there doesn't matter; all that matters is that we get there. I just want to go right *now*! Pull my hair or pinch me; I want this to be over. No more colored lights that dance to music, no more crazy lady claiming to be our great-great-great-grandmother, no more amusement rides. Just tell us where or how to find our family." She'd enough of the puzzles, enough of the games, enough of the mystery secrets; all she just wanted was answers.

"What about *your* moonstones?" Honora's clear voice pierced the surrounding air.

"Moonstones? Wait a second, you just called them moonstones. Only Mom and my uncle Gil call them that, oh yes, and us of course! How do you know about moonstones?" Penelope's eyes narrowed; suspicion crept into her voice and fearlessness into her stance.

Honora countered, straightening up to her full height and towering over Penelope. A strong scent of lavender filled the air. She didn't look threatening but rather as if she carried a majestic air of great knowledge and power. A long, low melancholy note from the cello filled the air, and her robes deepened now to indigo.

"Yes, moonstones." Her voice sounded sad, in tune with the cello's message. "Our family's treasure and burden for in time and time out of time. There are many moonstones but only one set of the Latter Twelfstanin. Those twelve stones must be returned by you, my dear Penelope."

"Returned by me? Right." Penelope was incredulous.

"Yep. There are twelve moonstones. We gathered them from the beach tonight when my star broke free and found me." Nicholas felt he, too, had a role in this summons.

"Yes, dear heart, I sent your star on its way to you, and to Penelope her set of moonstones. There are many sets of wondrous gems, but you, Penelope, were chosen to guard over the Latter Twelfstanin, whose tale is long and must be carefully taught. You must listen carefully to understand." Honora took a step closer. "It is my story, but not mine to tell."

"Why us? Why now? And why are you here now? Where are we?" Penelope needed some answers to feel safe.

"Here is where we are right now. We are *not* there. We are not hither nor yon. We are neither coming nor going. We three are here together now."

Penelope's mother loved these word games, she not so much. "What is that supposed to mean? Riddles are not fun when there are no facts with it."

Penelope was annoyed while Nicholas stared out into space, deep in pensive thoughts at her words. She could feel her sense of infuriation rising and shot her brother a thought. *You better be really paying attention and not that stupid daydreaming you do all the time.*

Honora heard Penelope's thoughts but moved on.

"It means, my dear, that where we are is neither here nor there. The point is we are together, and this time is for us to talk. You have much to learn. You both have been summoned. We need your help."

"Our help *really*? You need our help." They both scoffed. "Can't you see that we are just a couple of kids." They both felt too confused to be scared, bewildered by this talk from a mysterious stranger. Now this entity or whatever, whoever, if ever she really existed, was saying she needed *their* help.

Crazy lady. They could both read each other's minds.

"Wait a second, who is 'we'? Oh no, are there more of you?" This was said in unison. "No way! Let's get out of here!"

Honora took on quite the professorial pose. "Yes, of course there are; don't be silly. You saw that man and women when you looked into your broken star. That is my daughter Esme and her husband Mikai." She huffed. "You better start paying better attention." She looked right at Nicholas.

"So, where are they? Are they going to pop out of nowhere, too, just like you do?" he asked and then he thought to himself, *I hope I'm not arguing with some apparition or something. That would be super stupid.*

Frustrated at the twins' distracted yammering, Honora snapped the edge of her luminous robe in their faces. The jolt of scintillating indigo silenced them for a brief moment. "You will meet them soon enough, but that's not what I am here to talk about with the two of you."

"You need to understand about the twelve moonstones that I sent to Penelope; nothing else is more important in this moment."

"What about my star? Are you going to explain that, too?"

Flames flickered from beneath her garment. Honora was exasperated. "*No*, just the moonstones."

Penelope reached for her backpack, making sure they were safe. "They are amazing," she gushed. "I have never seen anything like them before. They feel, well, they feel almost like they are alive."

"They are, in a way of sorts, so be very careful with them and hold them most precious. You will need them to succeed." Honora was trying to get the conversation back on track. This was getting harder than she thought with these two.

"I am so confused, my head hurts," Penelope said as she held her forehead. Curiosity had erased their concerns and ignited a need for answers. Questions began to pour out of her:

"Do Mom and Uncle Gil have moonstones too? What about Dad? Why is he even involved in all of this? What about Uncle Gil? What does he have to do with any of this anyway? And why did that star come to Nicholas and not me? What exactly is with the twelve thingy you talk about? Why is it my responsibility? Why do Esme and Mikai seem so familiar? Where does the music come from? Why do I hear it? Why does one color match a certain instrument when it plays?"

Nicholas interrupted the tirade. "*Why us? Why are we here now with you?*"

Honora swirled her robes, creating a wind tunnel about her personage. It caught the twins by surprise and garnered their immediate attention.

"Because you are a nickel and a penny; that is why you were chosen. You are just—"

"We are just six cents." It was Penelope who responded, considering the reference to their nightly family ritual. "So you *do* know our father, mother, and our uncle? What else do you know about my family?"

Honora raised her hand. "Always inquisitive, aren't you? Those incessant questions suit your personality. You have a scholar's mind, Penelope, one well suited to finding answers and, dare I say, at times forcing solutions."

Penelope stopped for a moment to consider her words but, with a quick intake of breath, measured her response. "That is not an answer, just another word puzzle. Where is my dad and my uncle?"

"Enough Scholar Pen! You must promise to start listening in a very different way. Not just with your ears, but with your mind and heart. You have so much to realize and then to understand. Your usual quickness of mind might not always serve you best in this space and time. There are always facts and answers beyond what is in front of you."

"That is the nature of math and science." Nicholas again quoted his father. Penelope was quiet in this instance. It brought back to her mind so many learning sessions with her beloved dad. She often had twinges of jealousy that Nicholas seemed to get to the answers first using intuition as opposed to proof of the facts, but her father always encouraged her.

"Penelope, remember, getting to the answer is fine, but proving that answer is just as important. When you and Nicholas work as a team, there is no conundrum beyond your capability to solve. No mystery secret will ever elude your ability to find the facts and get to the answer you seek."

Nicholas was once again reading her thoughts. "Dad was right

Penelope." She smiled at her brother. It was a special twin moment, and then, one second later she pounced.

"Cut it out. Stop reading my thoughts. It's so *rude!*"

Nicholas laughed as he shook his head. "Penelope will always be Hurricane Pen; that is a fact you can count on."

"And you will always need a stupid haircut!" Penelope got on his case.

Honora just stared at them, puzzled by their behavior and not amused.

Mon Dieu! These Earth kids are impossible. They can't seem to stay focused on anything, not for one second, she thought to herself.

"Attention!" Her voice was piercing. "I am here as your guide. I'm to escort you to your new school."

The twins looked as her, more skeptical than before.

"Take us, take us to a new school. You really are a crazy lady. You think that you are taking us to a new school. Right, really? What kind of school—some spacey school? With people, or aliens, or whatever you are, who just walk around in stupid circles and talk in ridiculous riddles like you do. You think we are just going to leave with you, just like that? What about Mom?" barked Nicholas. "We can't leave her; we won't leave her. It would be like Dad and Uncle Gil all over again. No way."

A lovely smile seemed to spread upon Honora's face, and it seemed magically to give them some clarity as she placed her arm around his shoulder. "You are kindhearted, Nicholas, wanting to protect your mother. You, too, have an exceptionally gifted mind very different from your twin. You think with your soul. Between the two of you, we have a scholar who studies facts and an intuitor who understands patterns and things beyond what's in front of him. You will have equal need for each skill set, I can assure you."

Both Nicholas and Penelope could recognize their father's sentiments, even if the messenger was this . . . whatever she was.

"You sound like our dad. He always said that." They both welled up. "And now Mom . . ."

"In this moment—in time and out of time—I can promise you that my dearest Melissa, your mother, is safe. Very much protected by the other forces that surround her. That promise I have kept."

"What did you just say?" Penelope was paying attention. "So there *were* some promises you failed to keep," Pen said in almost demanding tone. "So now you tell us that you don't always keep your word? How are we supposed to trust you?"

Nicholas nodded. His sister was right, but he was still curious to know more, intrigued by thoughts of what might be next.

"All of this—whatever this is—is really your problem, not ours." Then Nicholas dared to ask, "So, why should it be so important to us?"

Honora swirled her robes, turning a much darker ominous shade of dark blue. The flames danced dangerously close to them.

"It was important enough for my dear Melissa and Reed to respond" was her curt response.

"And our uncle Gil," added Penelope.

"That is a different matter, and story, certainly not for now."

"All we want is our family back together again. That is all. Your story, your problem, all of this, it seems . . . well, it seems not real and it's not fair to us," Nicholas countered, hoping for more of an explanation.

Honora swirled her robes again, turning them a dark cobalt and creating a nasty swishing sound. Even her voice changed, lowering an octave or two. Her point was made. She was trying to scare them, or at the very least get their attention.

"You have been summoned, and it is up to you to answer the call. You have a choice. There will be much for you to do and to learn. The decision is yours to make. If you accept this challenge, look inside the star and it will guide you to your destination, but only if you acquiesce to this mission. If not, then I will take my leave of you."

Then, in a tone barely audible, a remorseful tone, they heard her whisper almost to herself, "We must not fail, not this time, not again." Honora then centered herself, making eye contact with the twins, and raised her voice. "But know that time is not our friend, not yours and most certainly not mine." She murmured to herself, "Not anymore." Then she moved her head as if she heard something that she did not want to hear. "My time here grows short. I must ready to leave."

The twins stared at her for the moment. "Leave? You can't just leave, not yet!" Penelope exclaimed. There were so many things on their minds. They spoke to each other in their twin talk. For how long, they did not know because time did not seem to be real anymore. There was one burning question on their young minds, a question with an answer that might be too frightening for them to hear. They both felt she knew the answer even if she chose not to say, but they knew she knew. They felt it.

"Will we ever be able to get home?"

Honora's eyes grew misty and then crystal clear. "I can promise that extraordinary gifts and talents will be awakened within you, unrealized and unrecognized until this moment. Take heed, as you both will be met with unexpected challenges if you undertake this quest. You must learn to live the unexpected."

Nicholas and Penelope hoped for a different response. They did not want to live the uncertainty of their promise. Then came the calling of the French horn, a song of anticipation. The cool icy mist was back, enveloping Honora; even though they could see her face, they could not remember what she looked like. This they already knew.

Suddenly their minds became oddly focused. They were not afraid. Why, they did not know. They were changing, no longer just two twelve-year-old twins who lived by the beach. They were becoming something special. This lady, crazy as she must be, most certainly knew their mother. What mattered to them in this space in time was that she somehow also knew their father. Maybe Honora's mission for them was to replace something called the Twelfstanin. That was her problem, not theirs. They had a very different intention if they acquiesced to this calling. Their objective was simple—to find their dad and their uncle Gil and bring their family together again. That was all they cared about, and that was their promise they made to each other.

They winked at each other and followed the directions given. "So be it."

They approached Nicholas's broken star, their minds in concert with each other. They giggled out of nervousness; both of them needed a distraction. Although they were not sure how real any of this was, they were willing to go along with all of it. If it was a dream, they would now wake up. If it were something else, then let the adventure begin.

Penelope could not help herself imitating Honora. She theatrically swung around with a dramatic flare, tilting her head as she spoke. "So, all we need do is look inside this little star and . . ." She did not get the chance to finish. When it happened, it was in a mere split of a second. Where once the star's center was closed, it was now open, looming as large as the doors of a cathedral. The low notes of a cello swirled towards them, and the violin sang so softly that they leaned forward to hear its song. With a burst of pure white light, the misty landscape vanished, and they were uplifted.

Their quest began, with the snap of a finger, in the blink of an eye, taking them from a moment "out of time," to their new beginning "in time." They soared at the speed of sound, then accelerated to the speed of light, and as they looked straight ahead, they flew right into the very heart of Nicholas's broken star.

PART II

CHAPTER 6

Esme

E verything was perfect.

Esme and Mikai were given the mission to stand guard over the Solar System, and like the one who came before them, they pledged to never take away any gifts bestowed upon this creation. This was their vow to Honora and now their promise to keep. It was all wondrous to see and protect: the whizzing sound of Mercury's pathway, the beauty of Venus, the night's first light, and the red ferrous iron terrain of Mars. They loved the brilliant fury of the Sun's rays and the ever-changing face of the Earth's moon. They rejoiced in the lopsided movement of Uranus, the chilling winds of icy blue Neptune, and Saturn's spectacular multicolored rings. They looked on with awe at Jupiter's big bright audacious presence in contrast to tiny Sedna, whose existence was almost silent. They loved the mysterious transit of Pluto and the unpredictable excitement of Chiron's pathway. As guardians, they even loved what they could not restrain like the wild and uncontrolled asteroids, the blaze of the comets' tail, the myriad meteor showers, and the Sun's explosive eruptions.

They watched each movement of the celestial bodies from the giant portal window inside their home, a ginormous spaceship that was called the *Sphere of Comets*. It was an immense stellated dodecahedron that twinkled against the blackness of a dark velvet sky; its twelve-pointed crystal color wheels rotated clockwise and counterclockwise. Esme and Mikai lived in the very heart of it. The spacecraft's presence could be invisible, if so desired, and too, its journey silent.

This massive transport was like no other, as the great ship's power source was organic in its nature, derived from the enigmatic element known as Jxyquium. Its designation on the antediluvian elemental tables that were designed by the ancients was a simple JX; any other information was secreted away in trepidation, to conceal the very knowledge of its power—veiled, buried, hidden, and yet to be discovered throughout the continuum of time.

The sheer energy derived from the JX was unmistakable, its vim viscerally felt by any entity who passed within the orb of its force. Emissions from the element were empowering. The strength of its energy could embolden each recipient in ways that were familiar to them and in ways that were not. Such gifts were yet to be learned and then hopefully controlled. Again, its origin, just like the understanding of its omnipotent power, remained a most protected mystery secret, only known to a select and chosen few. The beginnings of such knowledge, too, were of shrouded origin, a puzzle, passed down through the millennia only by a secret code of riddles.

Access to the JX was also an enigma as it was encased in a protective canister. Its sheath was fashioned of pure Xyzanium, the strongest material known in this universe. Designed to be impenetrable as it was fashioned from a time long ago, by those who came before. This protective encasement was most deliberate to ensure that the element's power was not galvanized by those who sought to be empowered by exposure. All known sources of the element throughout the ether were depleted. The only known supply was housed and protected within the *Sphere of Comets'* center portal, or so it was believed.

Mikai and Esme guarded it closely.

When visible, the *Sphere of Comets* looked like its namesake. Its movements were directed by the rotational energy generated by each of its twelve spinning color wheels. Each tangent sparked a special hue, creating a spiraling ball of hues that twinkled against the cerulean backdrop of the cosmos.

From here, Esme listened to the hum of harmony. The song of the universe, with the music of the ether. The sound that meant all was well, all was peaceful, and all was as it should be. It was the resonance of perfect music—the spinning of the planets, the pull of gravity, the force of a dying star and the birth of a new one, the whiz of the comets and the fall of the meteorites. The sum of it all created an aria. The vibrations were ever unfolding, expanding, and yet whoever heard this solar system's song felt it was just for them.

Twelve colored beams vividly flashed around Esme's neck; the source of the splay of colors was her jeweled necklace. Esme smiled as she looked at her husband. Yes, they loved their task to guard over this solar system, but what they loved the most above all else was their children.

"Mikai, the children are calling."

"Which ones, Esme?" he asked.

"It's all twenty-four of them, our twelve sets of twins. They love to play this game of contacting us, all at exactly the same time." She shook her head, smiling.

Mikai grinned. "For this antic, they always seem to be coordinated and on time. Not so when it comes to practically anything else."

She touched her bejeweled necklace, each gemstone a present from her beloved husband. It always brought the same feeling of wonder. This gift came with a story and a purpose. With the birth of each set of twins, Mikai presented her with a unique colored jewel, a gemstone. Each set of twins wore the duplicate stone. It could be used as a means of contacting their mother whenever they wanted, a tele responder of sorts. Accessing each gemstone's powers needed to be carefully taught and skillfully executed. The true breath of each stone's powers still were yet to be recognized by each of her children, although some who were more intuitive knew about those mystery secrets.

She beamed, thinking back to the birth of their first set of twins. Wink and Catriz, her little starters were born on the planet Mars. From their very first wink, their personalities were willful and headstrong. As babies, they had an athletic build, berry-colored skin, large warm brown eyes, and thick dark hair tinged with red. Because they moved so quickly without looking, they always hit their heads. When they were born, Mikai gave Esme a transparent form of carbon that was the hardest mineral yet known. It was to be called a diamond, a most highly prized jewel, and it was the first precious gemstone in her necklace.

Harmonious and Domenica, her little doers, were born on a tiny planetoid named Sedna. They possessed a shy, quiet sweetness and a soft melodic voice. Even their baby cries sounded like a melodious aria. Blessed with an incredible strength, olive-colored skin and soft curly hair, they loved to be held and snuggled. Esme received a beryl, colored green by the element chromium; it matched the color of their eyes. This extremely valuable gemstone was to be called an emerald.

A lemon-lime peridot was the third prized stone in Esme's necklace, given to her with the birth of Witt and Clarity. Her little informers were born on the quick spinning-dizzying planet Mercury. From their first moments, Esme noticed something very special about them in addition to their constant smile. They could not hear. Despite this, they seemed to always know everything that was going on around them. As they got older, they used hand signals to communicate with one another. Mikai crafted their birthstone gems as earrings that enabled them to perceive sounds with an extraordinary clearness.

Next came Evanescent and Chance, the entertainers, who were born during the fullest face of the third planet from the Sun's only Moon. Their skin was luminescent, and their eyes matched the silvery green cast of the tranquil sea. Happiest when their moon was waxing, fretful when their moon was waning. Upon their birth, Mikai placed a single grain of sand inside an oyster filled with lustrous aragonite. It formed a beautiful gem to be known as a pearl.

If each necklace has a crowning jewel, Esme's was a piece of corundum laced with chromium to enhance its deep reddish purplish glow. The resulting asterism: the star ruby. Courage and Olympia, her little leaders, were their fifth set of twins. From the moment of their birth on the star called the Sun, they had the power to bring rays of sunshine into the lives of others. They were tall and broad shouldered with dark wavy hair and wide-set eyebrows. Their eye color changed just like the Sun's rays, from a warm golden hue to the cool dark fury of a sunspot. Like any ruler, they loved to tell their subjects what to do. Fortunately for them, their stuffed animals and wooden soldiers always stood straight at attention, awaiting their commands.

The sudden movement of the comet Chiron's luminous tail caused a problem during the birth of their sixth set of twins Fastidious and Tien. Their son Fastidious's leg was severely injured. As babies, their hands, and their fingers in particular, were magnificent to behold. So Mikai made rings from the firmament, using the color of the sky and the deep blue sea. This beautiful shade of cerulean blue matched the color of their eyes and accented the tawny tone of their skin. This most precious gemstone was to be known as a sapphire. They were also very smart and loved to correct their brothers and sisters, so they became known as the teachers.

Esme continued to reminisce, but Mikai's words interrupted her wistful trance.

"Esme, Esme, the children are calling," Mikai said, putting his hand in hers with a look of loving affection. "What's wrong? You seem, you seem very distracted."

Esme smiled as her pensive mood slowly slipped away.

"What? Oh, yes, they are calling at once. Our daily ritual," she said, collecting her thoughts. "They will want to do a million things before their lessons. A plea together with a united front usually gets them a day off from school." Esme laughed as she gently let go of her charmed necklace. As she did, she thought just for a second that there was a slight change in the sound of the universe.

~

It was barely noticeable at first.

Esme did not concern herself with a missed note of the flute, or the skipped beat of the drum, or even a dissonant piano chord; that was nothing to worry about because the nature of the universe moved constantly, ever folding and unfolding. So a single discordant note would not disrupt the serenity that was the Tao of their existence. The intermittent cacophonous sounds persisted; Esme knew this was different and knew what it meant.

The realization of what might be going on seeped into Esme's thoughts, and a feeling of dread began to take hold. She moved those thoughts to the very back of her mind, as any mother would. She had her children, her twelve sets of twins, and that was what she held most precious. She looked at Mikai, her golden eyes gleaming and moist. They stood side by side looking through the prism of the porthole.

"Finally, it is happening. I can hear it, at long last, it has begun. After all this time . . ." She paused.

"Are you sure the time is now?" Mikai was dubious, seeing his wife waver just a bit. Any hesitancy was very much out of character. "You seem . . ."

Esme turned away so Mikai could not see her frustration. "The wheels of time that will set the future have been triggered." She continued, her tone still ambiguous, almost oblique. "The end of what is to happen, I do not know. That still remains very much uncertain, as the future shifts, but I can feel the coming of change." Esme knew she sounded equivocal, and that did not suit her. But she, just like her children, needed to live the uncertainty of what time had in store for them—all of them.

"Do you think what we see, outside over there, is what was foretold?" Mikai pressed his wife.

Silence was her response.

Through the porthole of the *Sphere of Comets* they both could see across the galaxies through to the Cluster of Hercules. A large dark void, surrounded by ionic crystals presented, wanting to be seen. Slowly looming, just beyond the very outer edges of the Milky Way. Against the cobalt velvet background, the ultra-high energy cosmic rays that surrounded it pulsed, and although silent, Esme could not help but wonder if its very presence could *somehow* create such a change in the sound. But why, how? Such thoughts were from the corners of her mind, hidden in her faraway past, where she fervently wished for them to remain.

"Esme, do you think . . ."

She twirled her hair, childhood habit, and interrupted. "There are only two entities who might know that answer, one of them for sure, the other just as unsure."

"Now you sound like your mother, Honora, who likes to talk in riddles."

Esme remained evasive. She then murmured, keeping those thoughts close. *So you may think, but to know that answer, my dear husband, is to uncover Maman's mystery secrets which she guards ever so close to her heart.*

"Honora and your father will make a swift return to the *Sphere of Comets* from Varuna. Your mother will try to handle this all on her own though her powers are no longer what they were. They are so greatly diminished."

"Maybe, that might very well be, but her determined will, that firm resolve of destiny and purpose," Esme's confidence was returning, "is never to be underestimated—not ever."

Mikai knowingly nodded. *Oh, don't I know about all of that determined will of both of you.*

Esme, like her mother Honora, was Concordaie, the peace-keepers of the universe. They were great warriors who also could hear the orchestra of its sound—the hum of harmony. Their resolve always fierce, indomitable.

"So, as you said, the summons will begin." Esme was matter of fact.

She closed her eyes again, touching the dazzling charm neck-lace that adorned her neck. In her heart, she knew this was the moment of her destiny, the reason she had been given the strength to bring all these children to life. Mikai was quiet, very quiet for a long time, and then he slowly turned to his wife, seeing her hand upon her necklace. He was of the Quintessence, the seers. They continued to share memories of their children's entry into the universe.

Esme reminisced as she stared into the precious opal charm that Mikai gave her with the birth of their seventh set of twins, Beau and Gracious. Their home was Pretty Venus, also known as the Evening Star. Their gemstone was indeed unique as its play of color represented the color spectrum of the other twelve birthstones. Beau and Gracious thought that each time they kept one of their sibling's secrets another color was added to their opal's milky white face. To keep all those confidences safe, they hid their opal inside a golden locket. Esme called them her little charmers with their amiable smiles, rosebud lips, and dimpled cherub cheeks.

The eighth set of twins were her little investigators, Mysterious and OnyX, born on the planet Pluto. From the moment they opened their eyes, Esme gasped at the intensity of their fierce glare. Their eyes had an opaque center with surrounding bands of bronze, hazel, maroon, and topaz that looked like a puzzle. Mikai fashioned a gem from the mineral chalcedony, a gemstone that would match both the force and concentration of their gaze. It was the eighth stone on Esme's necklace, called the black onyx. Their birthstone, just like everything about them, was mysterious.

As Esme's fingers moved to her ninth gemstone, she could not help but laugh out loud. She remembered that, as infants, Sage and AlexSandra loved to put their big toes into their mouths. They would ask who, what, when, and where but never listened to the answers. They always jumped to conclusions, thinking that one of their brothers or sisters had gotten more presents, more candy, or more attention than they had. They were Sage and AlexSandra, her little adventurers who were born on the biggest, brightest, jolliest planet in their Solar System: Jupiter. Their gemstone, just like their eyes, was a deep greenish-blue shade of cyan, a mineral that came to be called a turquoise.

Her two Celestial Task Masters came next, Yejide and A'dept; a garnet was their gemstone. The soft reddish-brown hue of this stone matched the color of their eyes and enhanced the strong beauty of their mahogany-colored skin and hair. Esme called them her adult children. One of their gifts was as they grew older, they would become younger. They came to the planet Saturn, knowing many of life's lessons as they passed through the tests presented by each one of Saturn's colored rings during their birth. Their favorite thing in the whole world was to have a plan of action, not just for themselves but each of their siblings as well.

Next came her little daydreamers, Vespers and Thinx, number eleven. Their appearance was quite unlike any of the others, as their looks weren't startling. They had medium height and build with ash brown hair and eyes. However, nothing was ever quite as it seemed with these two. As babies, while everyone else went to sleep, they stayed up all night. Why? They loved the colors of the night. As for their ash brown eyes, a closer look deep into their center would reveal a twinkle of purple, the same color as their amethyst birthstone and the hue of the evening sky. They were born on the planet that traveled sideways, Uranus.

Esme's last jewel, her twelfth, held a very mystical story for a very numinous pair of twins, Excelsia and Skye. They were born on the windy-blue planet Neptune. They could easily be forgotten due to their quietness and inability to see. Just for them Mikai created a special jewel that had the property of pleochroism. This enabled their eyes to see different colors from different positions and beyond and through what was in front of them. Their hair was long, platinum blond and flowing, and their crystal eyes would sparkle like the colors of a bright clear day: the palest violet, pink and blue—the Northern Lights. They spoke very few words, more content to listen and to learn. Their birthstone was an iolite, a sunstone, and they were known to their siblings as the seekers of what was to be.

Esme grabbed onto her necklace ever so tightly. She could not think anymore. Her head started to hurt. She looked over at her husband but did not want to hear his thoughts.

"Esme, you know the plan, and the promise," he said with resolve.

"Mikai, they are so young for such a test," Esme responded.

"Our children will surprise you; more importantly they will surprise themselves and each other." His voice was filled with a knowing affirmation.

"Let me ask them first. It is important that each one of our children recognize that they have a choice as to whatever their role may be."

Esme took leave with an open mind and heart knowing her children as only she their mother could. She wanted to take this burden from them; she wanted to go through the tests, trials, and tribulations, not them. That would be so much easier. But Esme knew better than anyone, that she too had promises to keep.

The summons was upon each of them. The time to begin was now.

CHAPTER 7

Summons

With a touch to the diamond gemstone on her necklace, Esme moved through space. Her destination was the red planet Mars, the home of Wink and Catriz. When they saw their mother's warm smile, the competition for her attention began as their voices tripped over each other.

"What took you so long? We contacted you, like, a forever ago." Wink was stamping his feet, at first his voice echoing above his twin's, but not for long.

"We've been waiting and waiting, and just so you know, it was me who called you first, not him; it was my idea," Catriz retorted, daring her brother to answer.

His response was a mad dash. Red ferrous dust splayed in her direction as Wink's berry-colored cheeks were flushed. He raced towards his twin. "Ha! I just ran sixty yards in less than five seconds."

"Oh, that is so wonderful, my dear." Esme could not help herself but to compliment him as he strutted.

"Yes, maybe, but I can beat that time," Catriz boasted, but not loud enough for Wink to hear. She winked at her mother. Esme adoringly winked back; it was their private signal. "I love your new embroidered headband; it covers that tiny scar above your eyebrow."

Wink struck an athletic pose, ready for action. "What about my new red and black headscarf?" Large reddish-brown eyes peeked through his dark mop of brown hair. The tips were tinged with crimson. "Mine covers my scar, and it keeps my hair out of my eyes, too." He won this round.

"Patience, patience, my dears, you both must take turns," Esme responded, but she was not quick enough.

"Wink hates to take turns. I at least try," said Catriz. She sashayed with a determined march as she walked towards her mother, giving her a quick little kiss. She was built as solidly as her brother and also carried herself with the grace of an athlete.

"You are both winners," Esme stated assuredly as she looked into two sets of doubtful eyes.

"Really, we are?"

"Yes, of course, you are my two firstborn, correct?"

"Oh yeah," they both chanted in unison, doing back flips and cartwheels. Their confidence quickly returned. "We are number one. We are number one."

Esme took the opportunity to interrupt their chant. "I need your help."

"I will do it."

"I can help."

Their words of enthusiasm tripped over each other.

Esme put up her hand to silence them. "Thank you, my darlings. Gather what is most precious to you, and hurry. You need to first return to the *Sphere of Comets*. Then we will discuss what is happening."

A fleeting thought crossed Esme's mind, and it bothered her. She turned to her firstborn. "Bring the JX with you."

"What?" Wink asked almost in disbelief.

"Maman, did you just say to take our tetrahedron with us? The canister filled with the JX?" Catriz was in astonishment.

"Yes, bring it, we will place it in the floating chamber with our dodecahedron that powers the *Sphere of Comets*." Esme could hear the sound of her voice but was not sure why she would ever consider such a request.

"But what will power life on our red planet if we take the JX?" Esme winked.

"Do not worry," she said uneasily.

"Why? Are we not coming back?" Wink and Catriz looked imploringly at their mother. "We don't understand. You always told us to protect our planet's JX, always to guard it and keep it safe. Now we are supposed to bring it with us to the *Sphere of Comets*. We never had to do that before. We don't get it." Two pairs of deep brown eyes with a tinge of red bore down on Esme; she needed a diversion.

To distract them, she then handed them their very favorite treat, cherry-flavored lollipops. The trick worked; they devoured them.

"Just remember to always keep your gemstone close to your person." Again, she heard her own voice but was not so sure of the source of the message.

"I will," said Wink, bearing down on his candy.

"I will," said Catriz, hoping for a second if she finished hers first.

Wherever this mission would take each of them, it would be fraught with uncertainty. Esme needed to adjust to that feeling, the very same way her children would need to learn and to trust themselves.

As she took leave of her firstborn twins, she could hear the beat of the hand drum. It was something the twins from Mars always did when they began a task or when they were anxious.

As she looked at the second stone on her necklace, Esme shared her motherly confidence with the universe. "My twins from Mars are willful starters, but they will need to learn so much before this task is finished." She knew those words of wisdom applied just as much to herself.

She moved quickly through the surrounding heavens until she heard the faint aria of the violin. "Onward to Sedna." She called out to the universe as she pressed the emerald beryl ever so close to her heart as she mapped out her quest in verse . . .

Onward to Silent Sedna,
Out there in space so far,
listen for the aria of the violin,
where my Domenica and Harmonious are.
These 'doers' need to plan ahead,
And often say, 'let's not.'
To get them moving,
a gentle kiss,
then, onward with the plot.
It is their love of home and habit,
that makes them careful not to roam.
The bequest of strength their special power,
art and song, of course, their tome.
Though patience is their middle name,
they can be pushed too far,
they might erupt, like Vesuvius
with a temper that can reach the stars.
Lack of confidence, their secret weakness,
until you ask or need,
and then those on whom you can depend,
will often take the lead.
An emerald beryl is their charm,

their color springy green,
they get things done
through the sheer force of will,
because they like a team.

Onward to Dizzy Mercury

Witt and Clarity's speedy home,
they know the business of the universe,
but never quite their own.
My 'informers' will keep a journal,
of all that comes to pass,
and assure me, they will do all they promised,
not just do what's fast.
Always witty-clever,
and ready with a smile,
but their incessant sense of restlessness,
makes their siblings just go wild.
They buzz around in banjo circles,
feet never quite hitting the ground,
and just as quickly, talk with their fingers,
and need not make a sound.
Lemon-lime are their colors,
like a bright fresh summer day,
and since they are so newsy,
they cause nothing but delay.
The secret to their magic,
besides their adorable personality,
tis the gift of hearing sound,
but with a bit of help, naturally.
Is it those twinkling earrings?
Of yellow-olive hue,
a charm to help them just slow down,
and remember what to do.

They need to learn to listen,
like Evanescent and Chance, you see,
to trust their intuition.
Because whatever will be, will be.
Onward to the Moody Moon
To hear the bagpipes song,
and watch my sentimental softies,
entertain the whole night long.
Evan and Chance step dance and pace,
to the rhythm of the tides,
it is their power of intuition.
that should be their source of pride.
But these two are my worry warts,
In all the galaxy,
they need to learn to trust their feelings,
their hunches come naturally.
When they play their grown-up games,
the parent they will always be,
But when things go wrong,
it's a frosted cupcake
that calms them down,
as they hold their tummy, you see.
They need my constant 'bravos,'
and that of siblings too,
You may not like their moodiness,
but can trust them through and through.
Old spirits create the legends,
and this will be their task,
to pass down through the ages,
both mythology and the facts.
So, look inside their soul-filled eyes,
luminous pearl of the sea,

they depend on those from the Dazzling Sun
To lead them supportively.
Onward to the Dazzling Sun
Where happiness abounds,
it is the realm of Rage and Olympia,
I know where they can be found.
They hold their court of cuddly toys,
telling them all what to do,
and if they receive their devotion,
hugs and kisses will be your due.
Their royal escort is a lightening bug,
their pet a fleecy little lamb.
A game of tennis anyone?
Sunflowers picked by hand.
Within their golden aura,
they possess a special trait,
born with the gift of wisdom
yet even kings and queens must learn to wait.
To earn respect of others,
you must learn the ways to lead,
and learn to share the accolades,
This inspires others yes, indeed.
A ruby amulet worn over their heart,
they strike a regal pose,
bright red, hot orange are their colors
and of course, a brilliant gold,
Royal wardrobes, lavish parties,
they sometimes lose their senses!
And who, but Tien and Fastidious,
try to keep them unpretentious.
Onward to Clever Chiron
Catch the comet's luminous tail,

to the abode of Fastidious and Tien,
their methodology helps them prevail.
Busy sewing, cooking, Feng shui,
mixing potions too!
They can nit pick and be critical,
Do you have something for them to do?
They love a schedule of small tasks;
it is important that they feel needed,
But don't ever tell them 'not to say,'
as that will go unheeded.
Their eyes the deepest cerulean,
to match their sapphire ring,
that protects them against illusion,
and many other things.
Fastidious works the Kendo sticks,
to make up for his weakened limb,
A setback? No, it gives him strength,
agility to his kin.
They need to learn from Beau and Gracious
compliments to express,
and know that each will have a time,
to outshine all the rest.

Onward to The Evening Star

To the land of the night's first light,
where the aura of Pretty Venus casts,
enchantment to those in flight.
Ahhh! Here's the charming duo,
practicing their tai chi,
Or are they juggling? Playing the flirty flute?
Or whirling hypnotically.
What is everybody else doing?
They certainly need to ask,

77

They need to know what the 'in crowd' does,
Where is my partner, fast?
They are certainly the most exquisite,
for all the world to see,
but their failure to take a stand,
Causes such disharmony.
Yet, they can be most powerful
of all the twins so far,
born with the gift of persuasion
yet uncertain, oh yes, yes, they are.
Beau and Gracious are their names
I am sure you know by now,
but do you know, how they keep mystery secrets?
Inside their spinning locket, that's how.
Therein their opalescent charm
Tourmaline milky white,
remember beauty can be fragile,
so, hold your gemstone tight.
They need to learn from Mysterious and OnyX,
the importance of independence,
and to recognize a most special gift,
the power of transcendence.

Onward to Puzzling Pluto

Where X, they mark their spot,
of dark, cavernous, zigzag caves,
let's see what's under that rock!
Welcome to the world of Mysterious,
and yes, the world of OnyX, too.
To their world of mystery secrets,
just act like you never knew.
Tell me, did you catch their glare?
I am sure you would remember,

Or the intensity of their stare?
That seems to last forever.
What else but the power of levitation,
could be their special gift,
endowed with the power for Reiki healing,
and there is more, yes more than this.
Yet another unusual talent
upon these two bestowed,
is the ability to read maps and puzzles
And to find what no one knows.
Is it their treasured talisman?
Worn banded around their wrist,
it is more like the call from Sage and AlexSandra
That keeps them curious.

Onward to Jolly Jupiter

A planet big and bright,
These two love to tell everyone,
what they think—wrong or right.
Nothing is ever quite enough,
not even sixty moons,
I am talking about Sage and AlexSandra,
Who else would you presume?
They ask a lot of questions,
about things they already know,
and when you try to answer,
they just say, "You already told me so."
They think the grass is always greener,
on the other side,
yet they themselves are lucky,
and are often full of pride.
Tap dancing, soccer, the high jump,
their legs are very strong,

but the ability to see far and wide,
this gift is theirs alone.
Sage fancies himself a wise man,
AlexSandra proclaims she's a star.
They are the best of storytellers,
oh yes, oh yes, they are.
They stand majestic as the mountains,
listen to the proclamation of the horn,
Optimism and foresight are their strengths
jumping to conclusions is their scorn.
Sage and AlexSandra do not believe,
they need a gemstone to succeed,
The confidence they keep about their person,
makes everyone take heed.
Onward to Serious Saturn
Where my Celestial Task Masters do reside,
busily planning from their Tree House,
without asking when or why.
Yejide and A'dept have the most amazing power,
the ability to make time stop.
They get very annoyed with their siblings,
whether it is deserved or not.
"It is important that you both have faith,
in your own abilities,
old as children, young as seniors,
that is how it will be, you see.
Focus on your siblings' strengths,
and not their weaknesses;
each one of you will need the other
before this mission finishes."
Is it their garnet trinket
that makes Saturn's rings stand still?

Or the way they play the cello,
quiet, soft, and nil?
Why not ask the only two,
who will answer them for sure,
The twins who think that only they,
know the answer, we implore.

Onward to Wacky Uranus

To the land where "everything, know we,"
Vespers and Thinx will tellingly ask,
"Now, don't you sooo agree?"
And while you may try to respond,
to a question so absurd,
they'll jazz with that tilted harp they play,
while getting on your nerves.
And then with deliberate audacity,
they put gemstone glasses on,
and seemingly laugh right along with you,
and wonder if you catch on.
For Thinx and Vespers live in the world
that is waiting yet to be—
searching the heavens for a clue,
the future one may never see.
Ahhh!
They love the vibrant colors,
of the nighttime sky,
magenta, black and crystal blue,
they love astronomy, cards, and math,
oh, and astrology too!
Don't ever doubt their power to know things,
that might never-ever seem true,
they see tomorrow differently
from the likes of me and you.

Is it their amethyst amulet,
that bestows the gift of prescience?
Or is it the call of the wind chimes
who whisper to them in silence?

Onward to the windy, wish-filled blue planet; to the forgotten twins who surreptitiously touch all. As she approached, Esme swirled to Neptune's powerful winds, hearing the rhapsody of its chime.

Onward to Wishful Neptune

In a land far away, a mystical prince and princess lived. They were enchanting to behold yet warmhearted and sentimental and always enveloped in an air of refinement, grace, and glamour.

They loved with all their heart and knew the secret of how to love and be loved. Some of their favorite things were swans and butterflies, cotton candy and dandelion puffs.

In their presence, you could hear the wind sing a lullaby. They were flirtatious and changeable and loved to play dress-up games. So, from each day to the next, they could be someone else. And when they told tales of adventure or wonder, you could never be sure if the stories were true or just some nocturnal fairy tales that children loved to hear before turning off the light, to say good night and dream.

They had the power to bring serenity to the mind and the gift of magical thinking. Their names were Excelsia and Skye.

"What are you two snickering at?" Esme asked as she appeared, still touching her iolite gemstone on her necklace.

"Oh Maman," the two addressed their mother dramatically, "we are giggling at Thinx and Vespers. They always make us laugh. What makes it so great, when you laugh at them, they laugh right along with you."

"Yes, they can have their confident moments, well sometimes."

Esme shook her head and mused to herself. *Especially when they figure things out before the rest of you.* Then she, too, started to laugh. "You two also make me laugh, but in a very different way." She paused and then corrected herself. "You both can make your each and every emotion quite contagious."

Excelsia and Skye just smiled. Even their smiles were enigmatic—did they just agree or not?

"Maman, all of our brothers and sisters have already arrived at the *Sphere of Comets.* Of course, they are looking for you. Evan and Chance are becoming frantic. They're both holding their tummies and looking for food."

"They will be just fine; they are so much more powerful than they know. That lesson will apply to each of you."

Excelsia turned to Esme, her eyes sparkling. "We already got our container of JX ready for you to bring back to the *Sphere of Comets.*" She handed the icosahedron casket to her mother. "You can put it with the other strongboxes that you took with you from each of our brothers and sisters when you visited them."

Skye interjected. "We could not help snickering at Domenica and Harm not wanting to give up their JX-filled cube, and then Witt and Clarity not remembering where they hid their JX-filled octahedron container."

"Oh, and you had to bribe Wink and Catriz with candy to get their tetrahedron." CeSe started to put her hair in a ponytail.

The giggling continued.

Esme just stared and marveled at the two of them.

"How did you know about bringing the JX? Was that your thought that entered my mind? Was that your premonition that each of your brothers and sisters take their home planet's JX with them to the *Sphere of Comets?* That thought, it puzzled me, but now I am beginning to understand."

No response was their response.

Though born without the gift of sight, Excelsia and her twin Skye saw far beyond what vision offered to the others. It was uncanny.

With a theatrical wave of her hand, Excelsia embraced the power of the wind. "Maman, the atmosphere on Earth will be most beneficial. It will enhance the well-being of each of us in many ways. Is this why ZR and Honora chose the third planet from the Dazzling Sun as the special place? Does the planet Earth have an unlimited supply of the JX? It that why we're all going there? Will all the answers to our family's mystery secrets be revealed there?" She looked to her mother for confirmation.

Esme stood frozen in fear that any response would somehow reveal such confidences that were not hers to share. The answers were not clear even to her, and she was not prepared for this conversation.

"Your father and I do not know." She knew it was futile to be clever with these two. Their powers of magical thinking were still maturing but ever-present. "Know that every gift in the song of creation has its limits—this applies to everything and everyone."

A gust of wind changed the direction of her thoughts. "My time here on Neptune is growing short." Esme turned her face to meet the gusting gales—it felt good to feel the softness of its breezes in stark contrast to the dread of its call.

"Of course," said Excelsia, sensing her mother's mind, "but first, please come to the pond and see how lovely Tuuli glides across the water!" Her tone was imploring, knowing the time to leave was upon them. "She stares at her reflection all day, just daydreaming with her best friend Spar. So, for now, let's visit and see what a silly trumpet swan she is."

Oh, how will my companions miss their time here on our windy-blue planet! *Just like the two of you,* mused Esme always amazed at the foresight of their thoughts that moved to places beyond where even she, Esme, had learned yet to venture.

"Spar! Come please. Please come now and take us to the pond." The magnificent platinum steed appeared, so much like CeSe and Skye, seemingly out of nowhere. Long mane flowing and nostrils flared, CeSe held him close. She whispered ever so softly into the ears of the great stallion, his ice blue eyes blinked. *We are all going on a great adventure, and we cannot succeed without you.* Spar snorted; he understood.

"Let's join Tuuli on the pond," whispered Skye.

Using the magic of the midnight air, Excelsia and Skye commanded the wind, making the pond's water freeze. Esme took her place beside her son and her daughter. Their platinum hair was long and flowing, their crystal eyes were sparkling, and their clothing glistened with metallic blues and pinks. It was the colors of the clear winter sky. Their iolite toe ring twinkled.

The three moved upon the ice, enchanted as they skated to the music of the planets, stars, comets, and moons. As they twirled and whirled upon the water's icy crown, magic abounded with twinkling hues in bands of crystal colors.

A twelve-faceted crystal formed: it was the *Sphere of Comets.* The colors of the twelve-pointed star hummed as it opened, to receive, at last, the two who knew so much but shared so little, the twins from Wishful Neptune.

CHAPTER 8

The École des Etoiles

I t felt like they were flying, then spinning, then tumbling or maybe suspended in space. Spellbinding rainbow-colored lights surrounded them; the orchestra of the entire universe enveloped them. A new awareness now created within them, and their senses were heightened. Yet they were unafraid.

Just how long were they in the star's porthole? They had no idea. Time seemed adjourned, on hold in some way; they could sense it. The twins landed ever so softly on their feet in a large circular cavernous room. The intensity of the colors and sounds dissipated, and their vision slowly adapted to their surroundings within the spectrum of the star's center. First, they could see their hands materialize, then each other, then everything else came more clearly into focus.

Penelope was at a loss for words. Nicholas was at a loss for thoughts. This was a whole new experience.

They pinched each other to check if they were still in that same dream. Neither woke up; it was the status quo. Shapes began to appear, then shadows and some blurs, but slowly these ethereal shapes resolved themselves into recognizable objects—people or entities of sorts. Masses and masses of them bustled about everywhere in the circular commodious space. When they felt their feet firmly planted on the ground, it was time to take their first step. It felt good to firmly touch down, so they took another.

"We need to find that crazy lady, Honora," said Penelope.

"She better be here. She seems to come and go all over the place," replied Nicholas. "That lady is never where she is supposed to be."

Their search proved impossible, as the interior of the star was incomprehensible to them in size, space, and activity. They had no idea which way to turn or where to go. As the enormity of the place enveloped them, they felt diminished, swallowed by the swirling mass. A panic began to arise in them both, as the thrill of the adventure seemed a thing in the distant past. Figures swept around them, sometimes glancing at them but mostly just dashing by. The twins were oblivious, adrift in the seas of perpetual movement.

The echoing sound of hurrying feet, swishing garments, and babbling voices was all around them. They assumed the voices were speaking, but they understood nothing. Everything seemed frenetic but not chaotic, and they could sense a rhythm and order to the sounds. It was not the cacophony one might expect, but it was oddly musical. Here and there they heard the snippet of a piano or a violin. Yes, this song, had a beat, a rhyme, a rhythm, a purpose, so it actually calmed them.

Even the air was different; it crackled with energy, like it was filled with high octane. Each breath gave them a feeling of exhilaration. Even the scents had a clarity of presence—crisp, clean, and not overpowering. Certain people had a very distinct floral scent; some smelled of a rich mahogany, while others smelled of fruits and spices.

"Nicholas, look up!" Penelope finally found her voice as she pointed towards a group of objects floating near the ceiling. What might have been panels or dividers spun and pivoted. The louvers moved in a clockwise direction; each panel was a distinctive color and marked by a different glyph.

"There are twelve of them. That is a closed loop as they move around the room. See how each is marked at thirty degrees," Penelope noted. " It's a perfect three hundred sixty-degree circle in this room."

"Well, we have twelve differently colored moonstones, my star has twelve points with each of the same twelve colors, and there are twelve colors of those moving louvers that match the very same colors as your moonstones. I wonder if they're all connected to that Twelfstanin thing or whatever she called it. We need to learn more."

"You *think*?"

"I know" was his response. "It all must be related somehow."

"Really, you just figured that all out. You better start to pay better attention."

Penelope turned slowly in a circle with her mouth agape, staring at the panels. "Those glyphs, they must also correspond—color, panel, glyph."

"Well done, the both of you," said a voice from behind them. "My greetings to the fact finder and the empath. We have been expecting you."

Startled, the twins whipped around to see who had just addressed them. It was the women they'd seen inside the star. Her tone was soothing, clear, and strong. They faced a smile that let them know it was all going to be okay, and they welcomed it.

"I am Esme, Concordaie, daughter of Honora and ZR. You have met my mother, Honora." Esme took a pause looking at her newest guests. "Yes, she is quite dramatic, in her own very ethereal way, but don't let her fool you; she is very powerful, even still."

A blur approached them at an amazing rate of speed. It resolved into a man, the same entity that was with Esme in the porthole. He swept up to the twins to introduce himself.

"My name is Mikai. I am Quintessence, husband of Esme. We have awaited your arrival, welcome. Your first official introduction to the *Sphere of Comets* must be overwhelming, but it will feel like home soon. We promise."

Neither Nicholas nor Penelope could speak, at least not out loud, but their twin telepathy was intact, and they had much to say to each other.

So now we have three of these crazy people or whatever they are, with titles and who knows what, and living in this big circle, spherical bubble of colors. They think it's our new home? Yep, it's time to go to sleep and wake up back in reality before they make more promises that they can't keep.

Esme smiled. "Of course you feel that way. We completely understand." She then gave them a wink. "I am a twin, too."

In that very second, the twins realized that they could hear their minds, too. They took a closer look at this couple and acknowledged some special bond that could not be explained.

Nicholas spoke first.

"I am Nicho, of the planet Earth. That is spelled like Nicholas but without the *las*. This is my sister—"

"I don't need you to introduce me," said Penelope. She thought her brother sounded like an idiot; she would do better, of course. *Nicho is Nicholas spelt without the las. Really? You should be embarrassed. I will do much better.* She used her twin telepathy to convey her thoughts. Nicholas waited for her new name.

"Hello, my name is . . . my name is Pen." She knew she sounded as lame as her brother, but if Nicholas was giving himself a new clever name, well so would she. Well, she tried anyway; it was hard to be witty on the spot.

"Well then, Nicho and Pen, welcome to our home, the *Sphere of Comets*. In your world, you would think of it as a really big spaceship. It's a very large version of your broken star. We are now in its center and twelve corridors extend from this center point, each in a different hue to correspond to a constellation. You correctly called it a stellated dodecahedron, I believe."

Esme and Mikai both approached them in a familial way. The twins still remained stunned by their mere presence, their allure, their enchantment, their warmth. They were both magnificent to behold. Esme was tall, broad shouldered and stood strong with a sense of purpose. Her eyes were liquid gold, her skin also glowed with a radiance of polished bronze. She made them feel safe. They felt that same sense of security they got from being with their mother. But it was her stance that was of particular note. Esme's carriage, how she comported herself, was like Pen's, always with that purposeful pose.

Mikai's presence was subtler yet more intense, but not in the physical sense. Oddly enough, he reminded the twins of their father Reed, both having those wisteria purple flecks in their eyes.

"I hear your thoughts, remember?" Esme smiled "We will have time to get our genealogy all sorted out. And, yes, on Earth you call it DNA—that is your genetic code language. And yes, again to your next question."

Nicholas smiled with chagrin, looking sheepish. He wanted to know more about Mikai, but his mind was again diverted in another direction. "It's hard to stay focused with so much going on." Mikai nodded as if he understood him.

Panels seemed to be moving everywhere, on the ceilings, on the walls, and between rooms: constant movement. Esme put her arms around the twins and ushered them down a very long corridor, off the center round circle; it seemed to have a purple glow. "It is time for you to meet the others; they, too, have been summoned and await your arrival."

Just then, the louvers parted, and the twins found themselves in a yet another room. There, twenty-four sets of eyes all cast gazes directly upon them. A cacophony of twin gibberish ensued as the group saw the two newcomers.

Nicho and Pen had their own feelings. They spoke to each other in twin talk as well. "Look at them" said Nicho. "They all look really peculiar, don't they? I mean, look at what they're wearing. They look like they're dressed up for Halloween or something. What are those goofy costumes? Are they pajamas or what? Are they cartoon characters?"

Pen responded. "*Shhh*, I think that is their native dress. Quiet, they will hear us."

"*You're* worried about them hearing us; just listen to them, its sounds like a bunch of babies whining. Oh boy, are we in trouble."

"Why? Now what's wrong?" Pen was impatient.

"Listen to what they are saying. They never saw kids like us before. Don't you hear them? They must have grown up in this bubble or someplace like this nowhere place. Either that or they are just really weird."

"No, Nicho, they just look like a bunch of kids, like they could be in our new seventh-grade class. They don't really look any different from us, save the costume or whatever they are wearing. Besides, we promised we would help."

"Help, help whom? *Them*? Help them do *what*? This is a real joke. Okay, it's time for us to wake up and for this bad dream to go away." Nicho's face started to show his frustration. "How long are they just going to stare at us? They are acting childish," Nicho said as his face reflected the anger he felt.

"Enough with these games, Pen. You want to puzzle this all out, fine, but I am tired of the one-piece-of-information-at-a-time thing. All these mystery secrets continue. Who is going to help *us*? Think about that for a second."

"Well, we made a promise to Honora, remember." Pen stood firm.

"Oh, right, we made a promise to that crazy lady from the beach who said she knows Mommie. Tell me, Pen, do you remember what she even looked like? Because I can't remember a thing about her face, not even a little bit. Where is she now? Tell me, where did she go? I want Mommie!"

"I know, Nicho. I am scared too. No, I am not. Well maybe just a little, but even so, we made a promise." Pen took a deep breath. "And Mommie would want us to keep it. *I* want to keep it."

"Okay, well maybe if they just stopped looking at us. I thought they were supposed to be brothers and sisters. They act like they are all a little estranged from each other, and they are strange. Do you get it?" Nicho was cracking himself up, although a feeble attempt.

"Not funny, little bro, not even a little bit. And take a closer look, it's like seeing double."

"They look like a box of crayons, red, red, yellow, yellow, green, green, orange, orange," Nicho continued.

Esme and Mikai stayed silent for what seemed to be an eternity, listening to the twins from Earth grapple with all the new faces in the room. Esme moved a little closer.

Pen looked at her and gasped. "You are wearing my mother's moonstone necklace!" How can you have the same necklace?" Before Esme could respond, a boy pushed his way through the rest of the twins. His mop of dark brown hair was held back by a red headscarf; his coal brown eyes had a red twinkle dot right in the middle.

"Hi, I am Wink."

"Ummm." Penelope gulped. "Uhhh . . ." She could not help herself, staring at a huge diamond in the middle of his forehead.

"Is your name Ummm or is it Uhhh?"

"Uhhh" was Pen's response.

"Nice to meet you, Uhhh; this is my twin Catriz. Is that your twin brother?"

Nicholas looked at Penelope dumbfounded. Never was she at a loss for words or a sassy remark, not once, not ever. Was she sick or something?

He reached out his hand to Wink. "Hi, I am Uhhh Nicho."

"Hello, Uhhh Nicho," Wink said.

"No, it's just Nicho. My name is Nicho. And that is my sister Penelope. She is not herself right now." He shook his head, completely bewildered at his twin acting so completely stupid in this moment.

Pen glared. "No, I am fine. No, I mean, hello, my name is Pen." She roused from her stupor, furious with her brother for using her full name—Penelope seemed ever so fuddy-duddy in this moment.

"Hey, I like the name of Penelope, but if you like Pen, then I like it, too." Wink was now the one starting to babble.

Catriz stepped in with a grin and a roll of her eyes. "Welcome to the *Ecole de Etoile*. We've heard everything about you and have been looking forward to finally meeting you." She had the same deep berry-colored skin as her twin and was dressed the same as Wink, a red leotard of sorts, with an emblem or, no, it was a glyph. Nicho affirmed her thought. The glyph and color each matched one of the panels they had seen earlier in the big circular room.

Pen sized Catriz up. She could tell she was really athletic from her strong and purposeful stride. Penelope kept a mental note not to get in her way. Her diamond also gleamed in the radiant light of the room, giving her an elegant demeanor.

"I was the firstborn on Willful Mars," said Wink, getting ahead of Catriz, pushing her aside. Catriz played nice and let the slight go this time.

Dragging her eyes from these two who started the introductions,

Pen cast a glance around the room. Each set of twins looked just as dramatic as Wink and Catriz. All of them had a distinctive air, a grace about them that was both ethereal and enigmatic. Yet there was a vague sense of similarity about them too. Suddenly a thought dawned.

"Hey, have we ever met before?" Pen blurted out.

"Perhaps," Wink replied with a wink while sweeping his hand around the room.

Esme approached. "These are all our children. We have twelve sets of twins, and as Wink likes to say, he and Catriz are our firstborn."

"So, who is the oldest? They all look the same age as us," said Nicho, thoroughly confused.

Esme laughed, and the ripple of her voice cascaded around the room. "You will need to suspend your concept of time, Nicho. Time does not have the same meaning here as on the Earth."

"Well, how old are you?" He was not letting go of the question.

"Well, in your world time, let's say about 100 million years, but compared to those of the Coterie, I am pretty young." Esme turned to the other twins. "Pen and Nicho are from Earth, the third planet from the sun. Courage and Olympia, come say hello. Earth relies on your warmth to sustain it."

Two very regal-looking beings approached, both brimming with the air of authority. A brilliant star ruby badge was worn right over their hearts; their leotards were a golden orange. Their build was different from Wink and Catriz, wider shoulders, more angular with dark wide-set eyes that were flecked with gold, wavy dark hair, and a radiant olive skin tone.

"Hello, I am Courage. You may call me Rage if you so choose, and this is my sister Olympia. We rule the star you call Sol, born in the constellation of Leo. Maman calls us her leaders."

"Oh, no you don't, stop being such showoffs. Cut it out. You are guardians of your birthplace just like the rest of us," came a sassy voice from the crowd. "The only things you rule are those toys of yours." Pen could see the girl's long black braided ponytail bobble as she spoke, shaking her head to make her point.

Nicho just laughed. He liked that sassy voice; it reminded him of someone close to him.

Pen's reaction however was quite different. She was puzzled, looking out upon myriad faces.

Mikai caught the look and realized the Earth twins still needed to understand that yes, all twenty-four of them were brothers and sisters. "This is all strange for you now, I know. Each of our twins was born on a different part of the creation that you call your solar system. In it, the sun is the engine that drives life on the Earth. Each set of our twins is responsible for their home world. Courage and Olympia guard the star you call the Sun. Wink and Catriz protect the red planet Mars, and so it goes."

"Wait, you are talking about the zodiac?" Pen was shocked as the puzzle pieces were slowly coming together.

"Indeed, Pen, indeed." Mikai seemed proud at how quickly she had realized the connection. "You are a part of a most wondrous family. Here, now you will learn how it began. Try to remember that you will realize your full potential soon as extraordinary abilities will be awakened within you, unrealized and unrecognized until the right moment."

Esme saw the shocked confusion on their faces. "It all sounds so impossible, doesn't it?"

Pen was undeterred. "So, we are going to a school? Honora told us that, and Catriz called this place *Ecole des Etoiles,* The School of the Stars. What do your twins learn about here?"

"Well, they learn a lot about your history, cultures, and traditions, but for now, you need to learn about ours. Honora told you a little about how the Earth and this Solar System began. I serve as its Guardian; I hear the hum of harmony. We can watch your Earth through the portal window in the center of the *Sphere of Comets.*"

"You must have been watching for millions and millions of years."

"It's like I said, our time is different from your time, but we are coming to a point where our two parallel worlds will need to meet once again, yours 'out of time' and ours 'in time.' An alignment of the sun, moon, planets, and stars will be coming soon."

"You mean in your world, correct?" Nicho mused.

"No, I mean in both of our worlds." Esme was firm. "You will have much to learn. Please know that we have waited a long time, and you have been expected. Classes begin tomorrow. You will come to know about the Clock of Perpetual Motion, the regulator that controls the past, present, and future. You will come to understand about the power within the Imperium and the mind games in the Tunnel of Infinity. You will also learn about our ancient races: The Coterie, that is our parliamentary ruling body; the Concordaie, our peacekeepers as well as the guardians of the hum of harmony; and the Quintessence, who are our teachers, the keepers of our souls, and our spiritual guides. You have already seen the Great Chamber of the Ancients where the Coterie resides. There are six women and six men in the Coterie. Each member represents one sign of the zodiac; the panels marked with the glyphs move just like the constellations. No one sign has greater weight or prominence over the other. My father, ZR, is a member of the ruling council."

"We, I, have a mission with the moonstones." Pen clutched her backpack; she had almost forgotten about her prized jeweled possessions.

"Yes, you do," Esme replied.

"So, I see you have a necklace made of our twelve moonstones; all twelve stones are there." Pen was trying to figure this out. "My mother also has a set of gemstones, but it was somehow lost. Do you know about that, about my mother's, that is? Why would she have one too?"

Mikai offered clarity. "Yes, I gave Esme those gemstones with each birth of our twins. There are several sets of the gemstones, but only one set of the Latter Twelfstanin."

Pen again reached for her prized possessions just to double check.

Esme lifted her jewels so that Pen could get a better look. "I use my necklace to talk to them. See, if I touch the diamond, I can reach Catriz and Wink." Pen watched the diamond flash.

"You know, our parents met when they were looking at a necklace just like yours; it was at a museum. Our mom is a world-famous gemologist and our dad, he studies the energy in matter." Nicho was proud of his parents.

Esme gave a slight smile and murmured something they could not hear. "Let's settle in for a moment and rest. You have been through a lot, and this is a lot to take in."

"Do you sleep on this spaceship?" Pen suddenly felt over-whelmed with fatigue.

"Yes, we do. Please follow me." Esme led them to another space that had twinkling lights on the walls and ceilings. There, in the room's center sat what looked like two large mushroom puffballs. Pen hesitated to sit, fearful that the ball of puff or fluff would en-velope her. As she got closer, it almost seemed to breathe.

"Please, don't be concerned, my dear. The Sphere is a living thing, as it is powered by the element JX. We sustain it, and it sustains us. You are definitely in a state of sensory overload, so try to rest. Sit and settle; you will see how comfortable it is."

Reluctantly, Pen edged into the soft white mound. Immediately she sank into what she thought had to be the softest, coziest chair in the universe. She could sense the presence of something familiar and felt at ease. No more questions for now, she looked over at her brother, who seemed to share her sense of contentment. The twinkling lights started to dim in the softest way as she sank more deeply into the chair. A peacefulness took hold, and she surrendered to the heartbeat of her new home—the *Sphere of Comets.*

Nicho was quiet for a long time, keeping watch over his sister. Then, after Pen drifted off, he almost inaudibly asked the question that had been on his young mind for some time.

"So, who is responsible for our home planet? Who is the guardian for our planet Earth?"

Mikai paused and looked at his young face, but before he could respond, he heard his sigh and soft snore as Nicho fell into a much-needed slumber.

"That answer, dear boy, will be for another time."

CHAPTER 9

A School Day

It was such a good dream.

Nicholas snuggled into his soft mushroom cloud; it fit him perfectly. If he could only stop that ringing in his ear and the annoying voice that kept pestering him.

"Wake up! Come on, we need to get moving." Pen gave him another hard nudge. "It doesn't matter what is going on, whether we are on vacation or on an adventure, you can never ever get up, *never*." With one more solid push, Nicholas was dislodged from his nest. He groaned and started to snuggle back down into the incredibly soft, warm, inviting bed that fit him so perfectly.

Then he bolted upright, realizing this was not a dream. "What is that noise?"

"It's not noise; it is the sound of a French horn; it must be reveille, or something. You know a *wake-up* call. We need to get moving. No, *you* need to get moving. I'm ready."

Nicholas watched Pen pace around in the softly lit room. He was surprised to see her wearing a one-piece bodysuit that looked like silver except when it didn't. "Just what color is that?"

"The color changes with my mood. When I am not around you to irritate me, it's multicolored."

Then he realized. "Of course, there must be twelve colors on that swirl of a pattern. What else is new?" He shrugged to himself. Wait, she even changed her hair, now it was up in a ponytail, or maybe back with a headband. In any event, it was now completely off her face. Her step was full of energy, and she almost broke into a run as she exited the room, moving down the corridor. Nicho could see that kid who winked a lot and wore the red bandana. Wink was waiting for her. He just shook his head and said very quietly to himself, "Some things never change. There goes my sister; she sees a guy she thinks is cute, and she is right there bossing him around."

"Oh, Nicho, there is a sweatsuit for you to wear; it's over by what now looks like a chair." She returned his look with a wink. "Put it on."

Nicholas muttered to himself, "I am not wearing any multi-colored sweatsuit, no way. I will look like a popsicle."

Esme's gentle voice suddenly came into his mind, although he could not see her. Her tone softened his mood. "Nicho, everything you will need to freshen up is here for you. Right in there. Would you like your hair cut?" He noticed the mop of hair perpetually in his eyes, considered it but decided against it. Nicho nodded to everything except the haircut. A shower, an electric toothbrush, and a blow dryer—all he needed to do was walk through some kind of chamber. It was warm and fast, and it felt really great. When he got to the other side of the tube—done. Yep, he could do this routine everyday for sure. Now, he was hungry.

Less than one minute later, he was ready and very impressed with himself. He put on the new sweatshirt and admired himself. *I mean, where else in the universe can you get ready in less than sixty seconds? Breaking down and wearing a simple sweatshirt isn't so bad,* Nicho mused. The base color was cobalt, like the color of the midnight sky. He succumbed to the twelve splashes of colored rings on the front. What was the use in fighting it? "When in Rome, do as the Romans would do," Nicho muttered, knowing he needed to adapt to this new situation—new world. Besides, this new unearthly fabric felt like a second skin: soft, cozy, and comfy. He looked at his new colored pants, picked them up and sighed before putting them back down. "Maybe later." He turned to look at the pants again and reconsidered. "No, no way."

Then that same bugle call filled the halls again. Ugh!

This time Nicho moved quickly as the panels that surrounded his sleeping quarters started to move into different configurations. He looked for his sister and spotted her now talking to another entity. This one wore glasses and was dressed in purple. Nicho made his way towards Pen to introduce himself to yet another male twin from another who knew where. *Does she need to meet everyone on the first day?* Nicho was exasperated, but he always felt that way when he needed to eat.

Suddenly, Esme's sweet voice made its way to their ears. "Come on, you two. Classes are starting; just follow the line of colors through the corridor."

"Classes? What about breakfast? Don't these people eat up here?" Nicho held his stomach and heard it groan.

A panel pivoted open. Nicho and Pen found themselves in a room buzzing with conversation. All the twins were in the same class. Pen made a mental note. *We are now twenty-six, not so many, same as my school homeroom.* Esme made sure that the Earth twins had assigned seats, placing them somewhere near the middle. Nicho and Pen twin-spoke to each other, forgetting everyone knew their language. Lots of eyes just glared at them.

Esme laughed. "Being new in a school is not easy, but sometimes especially with this group. You will find it will have certain advantages. Many situations are yet to unfold when my children will get to know you better; just be patient."

"Attention, class, my name is Professor Jais. I am a member of the Quintessence."

"Yes, we all know, you are the fifth essence." The class snickered but kept a respectful tone.

Jais continued without being the least bit phased. "There are others like me in this realm, some of you sitting among us now." Sets of eyes looked around. "Ahem. More of that for later, because today we will talk about astrology, astronomy, and mathematics."

A very loud groan permeated the air.

With an eloquent wave of his hand, he silenced the class. "Enough of the childish behavior." He spoke with an air of distinction. His thick spectacles obscured his eyes, but yet those unmistakable wisteria-colored flecks could be detected. Although diminutive in size, his aura and strength of spirit were quite powerful.

"Who does he remind you of, Pen?" Nicholas asked, intuitively knowing the answer.

I see it too, responded Pen in twin telepathy. *I read about the Fifth Essence, but does this Quintessence mean the same thing?*

I get the feeling it means that and a whole lot more.

Suddenly Professor's Jais's voice came directly into Nicho's mind. *Pay attention, young man, this is class time, and yes you are correct, yes indeed.*

Professor Jais cleared his throat again to get the class's attention. "Ahem. We have newcomers with us today. Nicho and Pen from the planet Earth. They are from a time out of time as we all know. Please try to make them feel welcome after our learning session."

A hand was raised. "So, exactly what is this Quintessence?"

"Ah, yes, Pen, the twin from Earth, the one who asks all of the questions. The Quintessence are a group of seers who are teachers, clairvoyants, astrologers, empaths, and yes, much more. As I just told your twin."

"Do you mean astrology, as in what is our sun sign?" It was Pen speaking up again.

Professor Jais chose not to respond, at least not directly. He continued to address the class.

"Now, let us distinguish some ancient truths about three subjects that are interdependent upon each other, and *do not* get their sound justification on Earth."

Suddenly, with a wave of his hand, a vision of a man dressed in Renaissance garb and using a telescope appeared as a backdrop on the wall of the classroom. His telescope pointed upward to the nighttime sky.

"Nicho, look, it's Galileo," Pen whispered, and he nodded. No introduction was needed for the twins from Earth.

Jais continued as he touched the avatar to become more lifelike and vivid for his students. He looked so real to Pen that she reached to touch his clothes.

"Astronomy is one of the oldest sciences. Here, we see Galileo Galilei who is known as the father of observational astronomy. As you can see, those scholars on Earth used astrolabes, armillary spheres, and telescopes to study all the visual phenomenon of space. Math, always math, of course was the common denominator. I like to call astronomy the math of the sky. It is the science of understanding coordinates, their physical placement in the cosmos and beyond."

The class became very quiet.

"Since the dawn of time, all beings, including earthlings, have studied the nighttime sky, all wondering about the celestial objects therein. The planets, moons, stars, galaxies, constellations, comets, black holes, and nebulae were all objects of wonder. Today, we will concentrate only on the skies of the Earth so Nicho and Pen can appreciate our unique knowledge of their world. We will discuss all phenomena that occur outside of Earth's atmosphere. We will examine motion, position, and properties of those bodies as seen from the prospective on Earth. More simply, what can be seen from their vantage point, what they see when they look up, outside over there."

With yet another touch from his pointer, the avatar was replaced with lifelike impressions of Earth's ancient civilizations like the Babylonians or the Mesopotamians. The students watched those figures staring at the nighttime.

"I like this class," Nicho said, impressed with the display. But Pen was not so much.

The professor continued.

"On the planet Earth, the curiosity about the cosmos goes back to the earliest time of the planet's history. Pen, Nicho, your ancient ancestors looked to the heavens and sought to understand their purpose in creation. Careful observation over the millennia allowed them to draw conclusions about the effects of these celestial bodies on mundane things like the tides and the planting cycles. The ancients also grouped the stars into constellations that reminded them of pictures of familiar things. So, the Ancient Babylonians gave us our current system of the zodiac, naming the constellations they identified in the sky.

"The word astrology means the study of the stars.

"I like to call *Astrology* the *Philosophy of the Stars, Planets, Moons, and Constellations*. This discipline looks beyond the mundane aspects. It is the recognition to the entirety of the energies of the universe that surrounds us. It is the study of the patterns in human behavior, personality traits, and reactions as reflected by the energies that existed during the moment of birth. Astrology is not about predestination or one's charted destiny; quite the opposite, it is rather about influences, inspirations, and encouragements from the energies of the cosmos on our day-to-day experiences.

"To interpret the influence of the energies at the very moment of birth, we use the positions of these heavenly bodies in that exact moment. The study of astrology is just one way to tell a story. A story that can be interpreted throughout one's lifetime. Some call it an outline of our character, a shaping of our attitudes in our journey of understanding ourselves, and the nature of those we choose to gather around us. Some potentials and tendencies are to be nurtured, and some may need to be tamed. Awareness and recognition are the underlying keys. Be ever mindful and remember above all else that each of us can shape our destiny through free will. We are always in control of our pathway."

Professor Jais cleared his throat to make that point before moving on to the next subject. "Ahem. And now on to mathematics. Yes, math is the language common to both disciplines of astronomy and astrology. Does this make sense?"

Nods and muttering of yes met his question, although not all seemed so confident on the subject matter.

"Good, let us proceed."

In a snap, the envelope of louvers seemed to melt away; even the spaceship walls disappeared. The students were positioned out in the cosmos itself with only the velvet cobalt ether around them. Twinkling stars were everywhere, and a map of the constellations materialized out of the air.

"Wow." Nicho was awestruck as he held tightly on to his spiraling desk.

"I can't believe what I am seeing." Pen almost shrieked as the floor disappeared out from under her feet and her seat soared upward. She deftly caught her pencil midair.

With an ionized pointer that suddenly appeared, Professor Jais twirled and swirled upward to identify each of the constellations on the charted map that now circled and sparkled around the classroom. The ambient light was dimmed with only the starlight to illuminate the lesson. Pen and Nicho were mesmerized, thunderstruck by being what seemed to be learning right out in the center of the cosmos. It was exhilarating.

"Let us now all look at exactly what they, the ancients, witnessed during their careful watch of the nighttime panorama. The word zodiac comes from a language that was spoken in ancient Greece on Earth. In its earliest form, the word means small animal."

The class went wild with excitement.

"So this was why it was called the *Ecole d' Etoile*," Nicho mused. He once caught his professor's glare to be silent, or better said, he heard his admonishment.

Attention, your attention please. Professor Jais then levitated even higher into the backdrop of a blanket of twinkling stars, propelled by what could only have been the air around him.

"This is how the earthlings developed their astrological calendar. Think of it as basically a circle, a full three-hundred-and-sixty-degree circle. This is pure mathematics. Note that the elliptical is equally divided into twelve sections to correspond to the twelve months of the year, each arc equally measuring thirty degrees."

"Just like those panels in the great room with all of the glyphs. Those symbols must match the color and the astrological sign I bet," Pen blurted out.

"Yep," Nicho echoed, deducing the very same. "Just like each set of twins always wears a certain color. Do you think they get tired of wearing the same color every day? Do you think they have other clothes or just wear the same thing every night?"

"Not funny, not funny at all, and you are getting on my nerves again," Penelope grumbled. "You sound once again super stupid."

Professor Jais, however, was elated, ignoring the last comment. "Excellent analyses from our new scholars from the planet Earth, well done. These ancient disciplines require what you call on Earth a *sixth sense,* a gift of the Quintessence.

"For now, let us settle ourselves. Look around at the cosmos and try to reimagine what the ancients saw and deciphered in the nighttime celestial sky."

All twenty-six sets of eyes stared at the star-clustered blackboard that encircled them. With the oohs and ahhhs continuing, they held on tightly to their desks and seats as those two spiraled upward.

The professor's crystalized baton rocked into the heavens, pointing to the golden elliptical pathway that formed around the room, heading towards the first constellation in the astrological calendar.

Aries the Ram

"The zodiac year begins with the Spring Equinox on or about March 20, as the Sun begins its transit through the constellation of Aries. Close your eyes, now blink, and now open them. What do you see?" The class looked at the constellation with new eyes.

"It looks like a *ram,*" the voices shouted. Professor Jais was pleased.

"Now, Catriz and Wink, tell us about your constellation sign, your birth planet and you."

Suddenly against the backdrop of the dark velvet glimmering sky, Catriz and Wink were catapulted up high, centered within the configured stars of the ram.

Wink began, "So I, so I–I–I am firstborn . . ."

"Twin, yes I know, I know. I was next remember? " Catriz finished his sentence and winked.

Laughter erupted.

A waving hand appeared. "I–I am the most athletic. I am going to run as fast as I can, I am going to—"

Then another voice from the class added, "Trip. That is what you will do, because you never watch where you are going."

The sassy female spoke. "Then you will need an even bigger headband to cover your newest gash."

Wink laughed very easily. "Hey, you are making fun of my twin. Cut it out!" With a good-natured wink.

"Yes, I *do* like to be first, but this is something you don't know. I got into a lot of trouble when I slipped down to Earth and I showed them fire. You know, I can split atoms, and I can get all that energy out of those little invisible things. *And* I was the first to learn that trick—I am talking about visiting Earth, that is."

"No, no, I was the first to teach them that trick, that was me!" It was Catriz who would have none of her brother's boastings. "Not you!" She then adjusted her head wrap and thought about her next words—"*It was I.*"

Their diamond headbands glistened against the red. Wink winked at Pen, and then he winked again at her. She looked away quickly, not wanting everyone seeing all of the attention he was giving her. Catriz dramatically rolled her eyes and in twin telepathy said, *Stop winking at her, you look super stupid!*

Taurus the Bull

"Ahem. Let's now move to the next thirty degrees of longitude moving into the month of April, to the constellation of Taurus. What does this cluster remind you of?"

"A bull" was the collective response.

"Now let's hear from Domenica and Harmonious, born under the sign of Taurus the Bull."

"Oh yes, the strong silent type," someone yelled out.

"Oh, that's right, they are *shy!*" yelled another.

"Yes, those shy, shy super twins." The whole class started to laugh.

"You better watch out," another voice. "Watch out for their tempers."

"Remember how when they slipped to Earth and got caught because they overstayed their allowed time." You could now hear more laughter erupting.

"And they had to make up some crazy story calling themselves Remus and Romulus."

Hoots could be heard all the way around the class.

More clatter continued. "They complain all of the time about having to do all of the hard work, wonder if that is why . . ."

Nicho and Pen looked at these twins from Silent Sedna, with their thick muscular physique, light brown wavy hair, olive skin, and piercing green eyes. They both wore beautiful neckerchief chokers with brilliant emerald gemstones.

"They look like two marble sculptures up there. Do you think they talk?" Pen asked.

"Do you think they talk; they look like two sculptures up there," was the response. The sound of Pen's very own voice came echoing right back to her.

"Hey, who just said that?" Pen's head snapped around looking for her imitator.

"Hey, who just said that?" the imitator continued. Then one of the beautiful marble statues moved, adjusting her emerald pin. She cleared her throat and gave a timid smile.

"That was, um, a perfect imitation." Pen laughed as the two pairs of green eyes locked. Domenica gave a nod.

"Ahem." The professor was getting viscerally annoyed with the banter. Then completely out of character for the Taurian twins, a voice, clear and strong wanted to be heard, and not the professor or anyone else would stop this kind of determination.

"Excuse me," Harmonious added fiercely, looking directly at Clarity, Catriz, Thinx, Gracious, and Skye just to name a few. "Some people start more than they can finish. We end up finishing what everyone starts."

"Oh, here they go again, complaining!" It was a collective response.

"Cut it out, don't get them mad, it's not worth it," Beau interjected keeping the peace, just in case. "Go on, Harmonious, we are all paying attention to you now, we are all listening." But before, Harmonious got the opportunity to speak . . .

"Our birth planetoid Sedna, swings though the solar system effortlessly, so very quiet, you don't even know she is there. Her orbit is serene and cautious, just like us." Domenica continued to use Pen's voice as she spoke. Everyone laughed, including him, at he approached Nicho and Pen with his hand extended.

"Hello, twins from Earth, welcome to our team," Harmonious said in a beautiful melodic tone.

"I really like these two," said Pen.

"They have a quiet sense of humor, get it?" Nicho amused himself.

"Still cracking yourself up, I see."

Gemini the Twins

Whiz! Zoom!

"Enough, please some manners and wait to be introduced," Professor Jais pivoted left and to the right, trying to keep up with the whirl of conversation.

"Ahem. Let us move another thirty degrees along the elliptical, to the third cluster in the constellation of Gemini; to the ancients it looked like a set of twins."

"Look at those two, showing off how fast they are," came that sassy voice that Pen and Nicho heard before. This twin wanted to be noticed.

"Well, for once in their lifetimes, they are on time." This was said by another voice that also sounded familiar.

Pen was sympathetic. "Aren't they the twins who guard Mercury? They can't hear, right?"

"They can hear plenty, and they know everyone's business but their own. They report back to Maman, the little tattletales. See those peridot earrings; that helps them hear; it gives them one of their superpowers. They use their hands to communicate with each other because it's quicker than talking. It's *so* fast, all any of us can hear is the hum of their conversations but not always their words." Pen looked about because it was that same sassy voice talking to her again.

In the next nanosecond, Pen jumped. The Gemini twins appeared out of nowhere and gave her a friendly push.

"Hey watch it! Do your feet ever touch the ground?" Pen asked.

"Not if we can help it." Witt laughed.

"Nice to meet you." A smiling Clarity held out her hand. Her blond hair bobbed about, as her lemon-lime earring brought out the color of her light green eyes.

Nicho could feel her cheerful spirit. Witt flew past, giving him a brotherly bump too. "Welcome." Nicho responded with a smile and a fist pump.

Professor Jais was clearly annoyed by all their frivolity.

"Enough. We are moving along the elliptical path to the Summer Solstice; on your Earth, it's the longest day of the year. Remember, many stories, myths, and folklore became associated with such astronomical events like the equinoxes and solstices. Those who studied the heavens drew conclusions on how the beginning and end of each season affected what happened in their lives. It is critical to note—"

The sound of the French horn filled the air.

"Ahem. It is time for your next class. Remember, when we

finish the journey along the elliptical pathway, we will have completed a full year's cycle. The name given to that crossing will be called a zodiac."

Suddenly, the backdrop of space disappeared. Everyone, including their desks, seats, pencils, and notebooks moved back down to their prior placement. A circle formed around them of what looked like padded walls; the floor underneath changed into a rubberized mat.

Suddenly, Esme stood at attention directly in the center of the room.

"Guardians of Mars, Sedna, Mercury, the Sun, Chiron, Pluto, Jupiter and Saturn, come to the center please." Nicho and Pen thought they knew what Esme's voice sounded like: ever so sweet, gentle, soothing, and motherly in tone. This voice was so very different; it was a voice of command, authority, and power.

CHAPTER 10

Strengths

The eight sets of twins gathered in the circle.

"Ready, combat positions," Esme commanded.

"Oh, here they go. I hope Maman does not call us in combat class. Someone always gets hurt when this starts," said a luminescent twin with a worried face. "We love watching your beautiful blue-green planet, swirling with white clouds as the Sun rises in the morning." Evanescent blushed.

"You are guardians of the moon." Pen knew that to be a fact.

Chance, her twin, moved closer. "Yes, brilliant. We were born on your closest celestial neighbor. How did you know?" he asked with a bashful smile.

"Your skin shines like the light of the full moon on the water, and your eyes are silvery green, the color of the sea." Pen's power of deduction was growing even more acute. She felt confident.

"You two are what our mother Melissa on Earth would call old souls, as the expression goes," mused Nicho, picking up their essence.

"Some say we are changeable, like our home world, but it more like we are just—"

"Moody, that is the word you seek, you are moody." Another twin, this one wearing purple gemstone glasses, joined their little foray. "Their nature is just like the different phases of their birth planet. You see how the moon affects your world; well, it seems to affect them the very same way."

"They are so emotional." An unknown voice interjected and was ignored.

"We were born under Cancer the Crab; nice to meet you. I am Evanescent and this is my twin, Chance," she said a little shyly.

"When we get nervous, we get hungry." Chance hugged his belly. His luminous pearl moonstone was in the center of his belt. As he laughed, a mop of ginger colored hair shook with him. "Like now, we don't like to fight. See how they align with their sparring partners; some of my siblings actually like that sort of stuff."

"I get that." Then Pen spotted one of the most exquisite beings she had ever seen standing aloofly on the perimeter of the circle. Their eyes met and in the next moment he was there besides her.

"Hello, I am Beau, and this is my twin Gracious, we are the guardians of—"

Nicho interrupted. "Pretty Venus, Night's First Light, the Evening Star. I have watched your pale golden glow in the nighttime sky forever."

Dimples abounded around both smiles. *So they like to be recognized.* Nicho took a mental note.

Beau reached out his hand to greet them. They stepped ever so lightly, in a very feline manner. Pen just continued to stare. *Wow, these two really look different, more androgynous than the other sets of twins, almost too beautiful to behold with their cinnamon-colored skin and hypnotic lavender eyes.* Her conversation within her mind was interrupted by her brother.

"What is that scent?" Nicho asked. "Is that wild primrose or lavender?"

"No," said Gracious, "it's gardenia."

"Wow, it's intoxicating for sure, almost . . ." Nicho did not finish.

"Alluring, right?" It was that same twin who wore the purple eyeglasses. "Who could ever fight with them? They would just charm their opponent to death."

Yep, these two are charmers for sure. That appeal could even be dangerous, Nicho thought, keeping his feelings to himself.

"This is Thinx," said Gracious. "He and Vespers are some of our brainiac siblings, but then again they were born on Wacky Uranus." Laughter abounded. The twins from Wacky Uranus laughed at themselves, too. "Yes, our birth planet spins on its side, so we call it Wacky Uranus. We can be loose cannons sometimes, much to everyone's chagrin."

"So," deducted Pen, "if you are from Uranus, you were born in the Constellation of Aquarius. The same way those two from Pretty Venus were born in the Constellation of Libra."

"You must be very clever," responded Thinx.

He looked directly at Pen, who gasped. "I know what you are going to say: we have that purple dot in the center of our eyes."

Just like our dad, Pen wanted to respond, but now, in this moment, she chose to just listen. Answers would come in their own time. Nicho might not have that purple twinkle to his eye, but Pen easily detected the power of Nicho's intellect reflected in Thinx's gaze and knew he too could be easily distracted, just like her brother and her dad. When she looked at Thinx again, she knew his mind was already a million miles away; their conversation was over as soon as it began. Pen started to feel more connected to this group. Sure, they were different, but maybe just the same as any other twelve-year-old kids.

"They love the nighttime sky, just staring, watching, dreaming, and thinking."

"Interesting that you seem to know so much about them." Beau's smile was so alluring, Pen found herself losing focus.

"They remind me of my brother," Pen managed to say.

Gracious watched her twin flirting with Pen. So she instead focused on Nicho. "Among our brothers and sisters there are those who like the mental fight; there are those who like to take up the sword. You understand the difference, don't you?"

"Sure, I do, well, maybe not." Nicho was caught mentally off guard by Gracious. "I am not afraid of anything if that is what you are trying to say." Nicho regained his composure. *If this was a mind game of sorts, bring it on.*

Gracious just smiled at him. "Touché."

She then flaunted her beauteous accessory; it looked like a locket. Pen could not help but stare, forcing her concentration back to the world around her.

"Is that your gemstone?" Pen was curious.

"Yes, our opal has a milky white face. The display of colors you see floating from within the stone, those colors belong to our siblings. Whenever they tell us a secret, the color of their gemstone goes inside. It is where we keep their secrets safe."

"Is that some sort of locket?" Pen asked.

"Yes, it is; this is called a spinning locket."

Then they started to do tai chi. Their movements were flawless, in perfect balance with each other.

Nicho looked at Pen. "What are you thinking?"

"I think, maybe just a little too *perfect*; no one always smiles. It's so annoying."

Nicho laughed. "Only you would find a problem with someone who smiles."

"But what they do, it's not just a smile; it's so charming it's like some sort of drug."

"I know, the problem is I like them." Nicho just shook his head.

"Me too," said Pen with a note of irritation. "And their brothers and sisters tell them their secrets, so—"

"Align," Esme gave the command.

"I am ready for anything, anything," Wink yelled out. He was first, of course.

"You better be," said that sassy girl with the jeweled braided ponytail. With lightning speed, her leg rose and high kicked Wink who sailed across the room.

"You go, girl!" yelled Catriz. AlexSandra responded by running up the side of the wall for her next hit.

"Hey, fight fair!" Wink shouted.

"No way, you better look out." AlexSandra proceeded to flank her opponent; another entity made their way over to the Earth twins.

"Hi, I love to make new friends. I am Vespers. You already met my twin Thinx."

Nicho extended his hand.

Vespers turned to Pen. "My brother is over there, probably just staring at the stars. Looking for an answer. We do that a lot, but you already know that."

Pen nodded and then in the next moment realized exactly what Vespers just did. She called her out. "Hey, how did you know that I was looking for Thinx?"

"Oh, because I just had a feeling." Vesper smiled; her amethyst gemstones twinkled on the corner of her eyeglasses.

"So, you are Quintessence, too?" asked Nicho.

"Yes, *we* are," Vesper responded looking directly at him. Nicho took stock of the female twin from Wacky Uranus. She was non-descript, like her brother, of medium build and height. Her hair was ash brown, like the color of her eyes, save that wisteria dot in the center. Yet standing close, you could feel electricity or static energy. Their presence could most certainly be felt, even though their physical stature was not imposing.

"Thinx, pay attention! We are still in class you know." He slowly turned back to view the action, smiling, not the least bit offended by his mother's admonition. He never paid attention, or so it would seem.

AlexSandra gave Wink another shove with her high leg kick, but this time he recovered with a somersault.

"That first one was just a lucky kick. I am ready for you now."

"You always say we are just lucky; I say, we have more skill than you." She was taking none of this for granted.

Vespers pointed to another warrior type anxiously awaiting his turn against Catriz. "That is Sage, born on the planet Jupiter."

"So, they are Sagittarius," added Pen.

The only difference between the Sagittarius twins was how they wore their hair. AlexSandra wore her beaded braids in a ponytail, and Sage's braids were worn long over his shoulders. Their turquoise gemstone was attached to an ankle bracelet prominently displayed whenever they used their powerful legs in combat against an opponent.

"Their talents are many," said Vespers, "but like Witt and Clarity whose hearing is most remarkable, theirs is their gift of sight."

"They look kind of amazing," noted Nicho. Their cyan-colored eyes against their deep copper skin made them look magnificent.

"It's funny how each of you has a very different but distinct look, yet save for your wild eye colors, you are all very human like. Each of you could so easily have been born my birth planet Earth. It's almost like . . ." His thought remained unfinished.

"Here come the next set of challengers. You have met Domenica; she will spar with Fastidious, born on the comet Chiron." Vespers became their personal tutor.

"Oh no," wailed Pen. "This can't happen, no way. Those two from Sedna are like Herculean strong, and your brother Fastidious walks with a crutch. Tien, too, she looks so gentle." Pen was in horror as to what could happen.

Vespers laughed out loud. "You mean it's the other way around, don't you? Poor Harmonious and Domenica. Just watch this duel. This is a battle of brute strength versus agility." She and Fastidious assumed combat positions.

"Fastidious is a master user of the kendo shinai, not only to walk but as a weapon of deterrence. Maman pairs us like opposites to learn the different combat styles."

Another student came over to introduce herself. "Hello, I am Tien. I was born on the comet Chiron, while it was transiting the Constellation of Virgo."

There was a sense of ceremony or properness to this twin, as Tien formally outstretched her hand. Pen immediately noticed her beautiful long fingers, so well defined.

"Your gemstone ring is exquisite. It is known as a Star Sapphire, correct?" Tien nodded, visibly pleased with Pen's knowledge. "Our mother is a gemologist, so we recognize its rareness. Your gemstone has the quality of a star asterism."

"We will get along well; you seek to learn. Now, pay close attention to my brother's movements, learn how to use another's strength against them in hand-to-hand combat."

Nicho watched the sparring match closely. Such a mismatched pairing was hard to believe knowing the superior strength of the Taurians. Fastidious moved astutely, deftly avoiding one of Domenica's thunderous blows, his straight shiny black hair flying about his tawny skin. "Wow, look at him maneuver!"

"Look at the fierce determination in his eyes." Pen observed a pair of coal black eyes that were darting throughout the duel. The color of the firmament was deep in its center.

"Ah-ayah!" Fastidious made his first contact. Soon thereafter, the Taurus twin was pinned to the ground and the match was finished.

"Olympia, OnyX, center please. Make your marks in the ring's center," came Esme's command.

"Now this is an exciting match of personality. Their skill sets are evenly matched in strength and coordination, but ego and pride, they too can be determinative attributes," said Tien.

Thinx and Vespers nodded as they watched OnyX take command of the center of the mat.

"Oh, my tummy hurts again. I do not like seeing these two fight against each other. It's never over fast." Chance moaned. "I hope this time one of them just calls it a draw."

"No chance with these two," said Domenica. "You know how they are, and we all know how fiercely they fight."

"You met Courage earlier. He and Olympia were born on the sun and wield its power. OnyX was—"

"Let me finish telling them about *my* twin and be the first to say some of us don't trust you. Everyone is acting nice, but we did not ask for you to come, nor do we need your help. My name is Mysterious. We were born on Pluto; we call it Puzzling Pluto because we solve puzzles and our own problems."

Pen looked up knowing the comments were meant for her ears.

"So, you must be the Scorpio twins . . . well enough said." Pen was fearless. "Oh, by the way, nice gemstone bracelet, black onyx, right?"

Pen could feel the intensity of her stare but was not backing down, no way.

Nicho whispered, "Smart move, avoiding that gaze. Another set of those crazy eyes. They have an opaque center with bands of bronze, hazel, and maroon. I think it's a celestial thing, space eyeballs."

"I don't care about her eyes; I am not getting bullied by her."

Suddenly OnyX levitated right off the floor, while Olympia generated sunspots to throw him off balance. Their combat maneuvers had a visceral effect on everyone watching.

"Wow, this is really becoming interesting." A few moments passed. "Is it getting hot in here? Hello, anyone, everyone. It's getting really really hot in here. Does anyone even care? Hey, we are going to all burn up!" Nicho felt the urge to panic as the heat became unbearable.

Suddenly both opponents fell backwards, hitting the rubberized surface hard.

"If you are going to be so bold to use your powers, you need to learn how to control those gifts while conserving your energy," Esme warned. "This is not the Earth, where the Jxyquium (JX) is in unlimited supply. You both need to learn to pace yourselves to not exhaust the force this spaceship has to offer."

"Adept told them both a million times what to do. They never listen." Thinx was always so much more aware than he was given credit.

"He's right, and I am tired of hearing about it again." That same sassy voice with the ponytail agreed. "Either those two are stupid or just being annoying. We are able to control our powers, but you two can't because of your big egos."

Tempers flared all the way around the penned space.

"Enough!" Two very serious-looking twins emerged, making their presence known in the center of the crowd. Standing so resilient with a powerful and deliberate stance, their siblings' grunting quieted. The female moved towards Nicho and Pen, extending her hand. Her skin was the color of mahogany, and their woolen textured hair was worn braided to keep it off their faces.

"Hello, I am Yejide, and over there is my twin; his name

A'dept. We are disciplined in all things and plan our actions with a schedule."

Nicho felt as though he knew these two, or at least their purpose. "You seem so, so—"

"Adult-like. Maman calls us her adult children. We were born on the planet Saturn, while transiting the Constellation of Capricornus," A'dept said as he extended his hand.

"Are you familiar with the Rings of Saturn?"

"Yes, of course, they are amazingly beautiful."

Nicho was intrigued by these twins.

Yejide proudly stepped forth. "There are seven major rings of various hues. Before we came to the *Sphere of Comets*, we needed to pass the challenge of each colored ring. They were tests of endurance. Some of the ordeals were mental, and some were physical. We succeeded in our trials. Our gemstone garnet is placed on the tops of our spine as a testament to our strength of mind and body."

"May I get a closer look at your gemstone please? It must be of special hue." Pen examined the garnet. "So, your color is a mixture of the red of the sun and colors of our birth planet Earth." Pen was starting to understand the gemstones' significance and how the energy of that stone was transferred to the bearer. She thought of her dad and his philosophy on the energy of all things and its effects on those who were exposed to their aura.

Nicho, too, started to understand the nature of this new world. "Your sign offers the gift of time. That is why you appear older though you are actually young, right? I would guess that your body grows younger as you grow old." It was not a guess; he could feel the truth of the answer that was right in front of him. He approached them.

"Hello, I am Nicho. I am of the Quintessence."

Suddenly the song of the wind chimes filled the air. Everyone seemed to know its meaning. The Aquarian twins were ever-present and continued to be their guides. "So, Thinx, there seems to be a lot of different instruments that signal different things. Does this mean we are going to another classroom or meeting someone new?"

"We each have our favorite instrument to play. Art is learned in all the spheres of discipline: painting, drawing, sculpting, dance, music, poetry, and so on. It's something we learned from watching your world. The importance of the arts is greatly recognized here. We strive to educate the mind, the body, and the soul, and that is what art brings to each of us. Some of us are better at certain things than others, of course. Take the art of music for example; you should hear Domenica play the violin, and OnyX play the saxophone. They are amazing."

"You learned from watching us? Or could it be that our world's past has somehow learned from yours?" Nicho mused. "Your mother said that I needed to learn about 'time.' As time is different here from as it is on our Earth time. I am starting to understand."

"The nature of infinity is a puzzle and a game. Does the music of the chiming wind remind you of Earth? I asked Maman if I could play that music for you. It is a song of affirmation. You are of the Quintessence with a very high JQ in that discipline; this we do know."

Nicho was astounded by the stunning creature who just accosted him. Pen could see her brother's face from behind the curtain of her long flowing platinum hair. This entity had a tall willowy figure; her body seemed to float upon the very air. She rushed to Nicho's side to understand why he looked so dumbfounded.

What she saw left her awestruck as well. "Who . . . who are you?" Pen managed to say.

Thinx again ever-present by Pen's side interjected, "Don't let their eyes freak you out. They are blind, but they see so much more than the likes of you or me ever could."

"It that a riddle?" Pen was not in the mood for anymore puzzles.

"No, they see by reflection. Look, you have met all of us. You know we each have crazy-colored eyes; theirs are just a little more crazy so to speak."

"No, they have kaleidoscope eyes; that is a little more than a little crazy I would say." Pen, like Nicho, had the very same reaction. *Just when we start to feel like these kids are normal, this stuff happens.*

"Let me make a formal introduction." Thinx minded his manners. "Pen and Nicho, please meet my siblings Excelsia and her twin, Skye. They were born on the planet Neptune while transiting the constellation of Pisces."

The Neptunian twins glided over to them in a very theatrical way.

"We have visited your Earth many times. See our toe rings— our gemstone is iolite that contains the property of pleochroism. Iolite is from the Greek word *ion;* that means violet. Your Vikings used this gem for navigation as a polarized lens to track the sun's position. I gave it to them. Oh, you can call me CeSe if you like." With that she disappeared.

"They don't say much," said Thinx. "But, remember one thing; whenever they do say something, you need to listen to them. We have all learned the hard way to pay attention to their prophecies and trust their truths, no matter how bizarre their words may seem in the moment. They will never let on or respond to questions about how much they know, but they listen to *everything* in the quietness of their minds."

Just then, another instrument played, but it was not the soft music of the chiming wind. No, it was something much harsher. At first it seemed like the clash of cymbals, then the full spectrum of the piano joined the Tenebrae.

"Nicho, that awful sound is back. Something must be terribly wrong." Pen knew it well; it was the hum of discord.

Just then CeSe seemed to materialize right beside Pen and whispered into her ear.

"Remember to trust—" She then just as quickly disappeared in a blue/pink crystal mist.

CHAPTER 11

The Trial of Honora

Hear ye, hear ye! Come all to listen.

"It seems like everybody here knows exactly what is going on," Nicho said, exasperated once again. "I feel as if I'm being left in the dark here; it's like we are supposed to know what's happening, and we really don't. We are strangers among these people or whatever they really are."

"Everyone seems nice enough, well, at least most of them. Why? Do you think it's deliberate? Do you think they are not being truthful?" Pen asked.

"The jury is out on that."

"Jury, that's a strange word to use." Pen shrugged.

As they left their celestial classroom inside the spaceship under the stars, Pen could not help but take one more glance at the majesty of it all. She wondered just where all of this would lead. Truth be told, it did not feel at all like a dream anymore; no, they were on an adventure. What remained scary was the ambiguity of it all, the lack of clarity. Pen was brave and fearless always, at least that is what her friends at school always said—but this was so different. The lessons learned here would have a profound impact on everything. That much she knew, but how would it all end? It was hard to live the uncertainty.

"Let's keep up, Nicho." She wanted her brother close. They followed the group back into that large circular space where they first entered when they went through the portal of the *Sphere of Comets*. It was the room with the pulsing panels or the Talking Panels as she had come to learn. What did Esme call it, yes, the Chamber of the Ancients. She remembered there were twelve members of the Coterie, and the twelve louvers that moved strategically around the circumference of the circle.

"This feels so much different from the first time we were in this room. Before, it looked more like an open auditorium with people all milling about; it now has a different, more formal feel." Nicho was taking in all of the energies. "Look, everyone has an assigned seat too. Check this out, Pen."

Each set of twins sat in their designated places, in front of the panel that matched the color and glyph on their garments. "Something is about to happen: something important for sure," Pen agreed.

Nicholas and Penelope watched as various bystanders settled on sets of benches. Wink left his seat and approached Pen, still obviously smitten with her, while she was obviously smitten with someone else.

"Can *somebody* please tell us what is going on?" Pen was exasperated.

"We are gathered here in the Great Chamber of the Ancients to answer the call for the resolution of the question." Wink was quick to reply. He wanted to be the first to describe the order of events that would take place.

"So, like, what exactly is that?" Pen was intrigued.

"On your Earth, this might be called a trial by jury. It is our way of resolving issues. There are no penalties here, just questions are asked, answers are weighed, decisions are made, and matters resolved. Here in this chamber, we learn to listen."

Nicho did not like the sound of what he heard and was about to say so, but then Vespers approached.

"Nicho, just be still and really pay attention. We learn to listen here in a different way, not just hear the words, but try to understand what is truly being said, and see past what is apparent. Look beyond the facts." Vespers' demeanor turned a little ambivalent. "This is not easy for any of us; don't let any of my siblings fool you. We are all a little scared and not sure what to do. You and Pen will be a part of the group that makes the decision in the resolution. We will all need each other's guidance." With her explanation given, she just disappeared.

"*Us,* what do we know? They want us to make some kind of decision. Are they kidding, or just crazy?" Pen was livid. "We have no idea what is even going on, let alone are we able to determine the result. Hey, Nicho, we are back in that dream again."

Nicho nodded. "That's for sure. Just when you start to get just a little bit comfortable with all this wild stuff, these . . . these creatures just drag us into something else that has nothing to do with us. Yes, it is time to wake up." He pulled Pen's hair.

Thinx then turned to her and took out a cloth to clean his eyeglasses. He looked right into Penelope's eyes, and she gasped again for about the tenth time. He really reminded her of her father. He smiled because he knew what she was thinking.

"You need to sit down; you two are *always so in* the way." The beads in AlexSandra's ponytail hit Pen in the face as she brushed past her.

"You are *always so* rude." Pen was quick to react. AlexSandra just kept walking towards her seat.

"Is she always like that?" Pen asked.

"I think your Earth word is sassy, and yes, she is always like that." Thinx smiled.

Nicho looked at his new friend imploringly. "All of your siblings seem to have visited Earth at some point in what you call "in time." That was not so hard to figure out, because of the Earth-like way they all look and act. Yet, you and Vespers seem the least familiar to me. Did you never visit my Earth? Or did you not play a part in its history? I am just curious because I can't seem to place you at all, not in the way you act, not in the way you think, not in the way you comport yourselves. Can you tell me why?"

Thinx put his hand on Nicho's shoulder. "Well done, Nicho, well done. It is really quite simple. The explanation is this: From your perspective of Earth time, my sister and I are of the future. We are of your Earth's tomorrow."

Another clang of the cymbal resonated throughout the *Sphere,* and all was called to order.

Professor Jais, with all eyes upon him, gingerly moved into the very center of the forum. Pen's and Nicho's focus shifted to this Chamber of the Ancients as they moved their eyes. For the first time, they realized that the Talking Panels slowly orbited about the space.

Thinx, again, was there to explain. "Yes, they are in perpetual motion, the panels, that is. The Coterie are the twelve members of our ruling body. It is always six men and six women. It is our form of government, as you would say on your Earth. Watch how the rotunda moves; the only space that stays stagnant in the epicenter where Professor Jais now stands. Each member of the Coterie sits at the spherical-shaped table that moves with the constellations. No one sign has greater weight or prominence than another."

A collective *shhh* was heard, accompanied by a look of admonishment.

Professor Jais opened the forum with the following statement: "We are seeking by questions and response, a resolution of the Tale of the Twelfstanin. My name is Jais. I am of the Quintessence." Then he gave the pronouncement.

Hear ye, hear ye! All come to order.
To those of whom this matter concerns, may you please
take your assigned position in these proceedings. If there
is anyone here who is of interest from this point forward,
may ye show yourself.
If those of interest who heretofore have not expressed their
truth, ye may remain silent.
These proceeding will now commence.

With the pronouncement came the moment of pause for anyone to assert their interest. Then a sound not quite like any other caught everyone's attention. The huffing sound was rhythmic, almost like someone was panting. At first it seemed far away, but as it grew louder and louder it seemed to come from all around. All the twins were turning their heads to look around the room, to find the source of the strange foreign whirling noise.

Clarity and Witt were waving their hands frenetically, the sound too painful for their ears. It was a B-flat note, registering at fifty-seven octaves lower than a middle C on the piano. It was the hum of discord, the hum of disharmony, the hum of chaos, the reverberating sound of the Black Hole—a low persistent beating whirr.

Oddly enough, all twelve members of the Coterie remained unflappable. They knew who or what exactly was coming. Their demeanor expressed concern but not fear. Professor Jais held fast, not moving from his designated spot, his voice strong, firm, and clear.

"Who shall serve as the seeker of the truth?"

In a horrific blast of heat and light, the Talking Panels stuttered, signaling an unwelcoming reception for whoever was now anticipated.

"Nicho, do you feel that unrelenting coldness? How could that be? There was just a horrific blast of heat. It is so odd not to feel any warmth from such a blaze of fire." Penelope was shivering.

"Pen, you know what. It's not just that the temperature that has dramatically dropped; the room suddenly feels empty and cold, like we are in a void."

The unseen presence coalesced into the shape of a man and proclaimed, "I am Ahreman, Lord of the Black Holes. I will serve as the seeker of the truth."

Loud jeers and hisses spread throughout the chamber.

"You have not a place in this forum; you are neither Coterie nor Quintessence nor Concordaie. You are unwelcome, but this you already know."

"I challenge your assertion of my birthright. My powers are second to none when compared with any of your elderly and waning Coterie. I sought a seat on your very council. My rightful place that I have been denied this past millennium."

Noise erupted throughout the forum; it was difficult to discern support from opposition.

Nicho's and Pen's eyes were spellbound. This was a most beautiful creature who stood before them, the most striking that they had ever seen. His gleaming charcoal black hair was long and flowing. His robes, a most magnificent coat of many colors, billowed around him from the gust of his entry. His entire presence was heavily adorned with resplendent gems. His eyes were two opaque sapphire orbs, rimmed with cassis-colored liner that evoked a lack of emotion. He did not blink, and neither the whites of his eyes nor iris nor pupil could be seen. They glinted like nimbus thunderbolts and invoked fear. It made his face expressionless, and that induced uncertainty. His cheekbones were high with a touch of rouge in contrast to his translucent skin tone. His lips were painted deep dark cherry with nails of the same reddish purple. Not only was he stunning to behold, but his voice was soothing, melodic, and almost hypnotic. He was mesmerizing.

"He looks like a movie star," said Pen dreamily.

"Or maybe some old burned-out rock star," said Nicho, who was not so impressed.

Jais continued, "Who say—"

A lone voice was heard from the rotunda table, interrupting the professor. It was hard to discern who it was. The Talking Panels moved adjacent to the head table where the Coterie sat; such movement made it difficult to identify the interrupter.

"He, Ahreman, Lord of the Black Holes, has a right to be heard in regard to his place among us. Is not one of those who banished him to the planet Eris now at the very center of this inquiry? Is she not, at the very center of our resolution of the question before us? So, say he."

Jais looked for the source of the interruption and to the Coterie for guidance as the ruling body.

Another voice spoke: "Our laws dictate that we only need a party of one to address the question before us. Jais, you are Quintessence and serve as the monitor of justice. What say ye to Ahreman's request?"

Thinx whispered to Pen, "So, on Earth in your jury trials, the judge would be like Jais; he serves as the monitor. Ahreman is asking to be what you would call the prosecutor—the seeker of the truth."

Pen nodded; she understood. "Who defends the accused?" She was interested in learning every detail of this process.

"That would be the defender of the truth, who has not yet shown themselves. Any witnesses called to testify are the sayeurs."

"But who makes the final decision?" asked Nicho.

"We do, or those the most affected by the turn of events in the resolution of the question. We, all my siblings and I, were asked to go on this mission with you. So, since we are the most affected by the summons, we make the final decision. It is up to each of us to decide. Remember, we have free will to decide our future. This is always the way, here."

Jais was reluctant to obey the ruling of the Coterie, eventually relenting but still concerned about who was the source. "Ahem." He cleared his throat and continued.

"So, we call Ahreman to speak to the resolution of the question and serve as seeker of the truth."

The creature approached, taking Jais's place in the epicenter. The professor was not happy to relinquish the forum.

"I call ZR, husband to Honora, father of Esme, to say his truth."

ZR stood to address the crowd. He was Coterie and so remained at the rotunda table, moving to a designated thirteenth chair that remained empty up until now. He was almost translucent, due to his age, but his voice rang with power. As he began, the chamber became ever so silent, a sign of great respect to his position among them.

"In the beginning, there were just the two of us, Honora and me. And so it was that we were sent into this place, a void, where time and space were to begin by the one who sent us. When we arrived, we found an empty gap of darkened velvet, devoid of sound.

"As the first guardians of this place, our task was formidable. We were imbued with instructions on how to begin, and we promised to follow them explicitly. Please indulge me here, it been such a long time that I would like to remember the plan entwined with music, as it was made for an orchestral sonnet:

And so, the first creations
were called the stars,
that twinkled to the echo
of a piano note's ring,
And a certain star
Called the Sun,
dazzled to the clash
of the cymbal's bling!
Dizzy Mercury frenzied
to a busy banjo's strum,
while Pretty Venus shined
to a flirty flute's hum.
The Moon,
waxed and waned
to a moody bagpipes' song,
and Mars' red face pulsed strong
to the beat of a hand drum.
Saturn spun its rings,
to the serious sound of the cello,
while Jupiter's French horn proclaimed,
"Hey, I am quite a jolly fellow!"
Neptune whirled wishfully
To the music of the chimes that sing in the wind,
Uranus tilted on its side because
an electric harpsichord made it spin.
While Pluto's path became a puzzle,
to the jingle of the tambourine,
aah, its passage is a mystery secret,
not wanting to be seen.
Watch out for Clever Chiron,
its comet tail radiates just like a beam,
the triangle's vibration makes it scamper,

it's everywhere it seems.
Listen for the aria of the violin,
Sedna's pathway so silent!
In comparison to the clamor of the rest,
its passage must seem quite ironic.

"And as each heavenly body moved with a defined resonance, this orchestration became the song of the solar system. This was the hum of harmony, and all was well.

"In the midst of this sound, and because of this sound, life forces flourished on the planets, moons, asteroids, and comets. The shape, size, and systems of all living things varied, but they all required one very special and unique element that would be come to be known as Jxyquium or JX.

"After our first task was completed, we as the guardians were given yet another assignment: to watch over a blue-green jewel called Earth, the third planet from the star called the Sun. To this planet many special gifts were given, an almost unlimited abundance of the elements hydrogen, oxygen, carbon, and nitrogen making its air pure, clear, and rejuvenating, and a special cache of Jxyquium, to ensure its future.

"So it was that both Honora and I used most of our energy to finish this task.

"We were never told the fate of all we guarded, never told the purpose of our task. What we did was based on faith in something greater than ourselves. We presided over this universe until we could no longer go on, and we then appointed new guardians to take our place. We chose Esme and Mikai. The responsibility of the solar system was given to them, and they too promised to watch over everything with goodness, just as we had promised.

"It was then decided that the time had come for Honora and me to go far away, in search of a new life. We renewed our promise to the one who sent us, not to take any gifts from these creations, especially the blue-green orb. Due to our age, our mere presence would cause a depletion of the limited resources to sustain life. We knew the JX to be limited, but we were unaware of the quantity that was meant to be safeguarded. We chose to retire not just from this place, our home, but from this solar system and went far into space to a planet called Varuna. It was in the Quaoar and beyond, and that is where we chose to live out our remaining years."

"And Honora," Ahreman turned and took a step closer. "What of her?"

ZR looked directly at Ahreman with an unflinching gaze.

"Honora is Concordaie and was given one more special task known only to her, but you know all about that, don't you?" Contempt sharpened his tone, and condemnation filled his eyes.

Ahreman just smiled. "And who say I to you, may I ask?"

ZR stood firm. "You are my son Ahreman, twin to Esme."

Nicholas and Penelope sat transfixed for a moment unable to fully grasp or comprehend the story they'd just heard. They got their bearings soon enough to both blurt out.

"No way! *He, is Esme's twin*? No way?' They were both stunned.

"You have fully met your question, with satisfactory response. ZR, you may return to your rightful place at the rotunda table as a member of the Coterie."

Jais as monitor of justice continued. "As the rightful seeker of the truth, ye may call your second sayeur."

Ahreman's robes swirled about him, making his presence even more enigmatic as he declared.

"I call Honora, to pose questions on the Tale of the Twelfstanin. How they were lost into the cosmos, and of her two failed missions to replace them back into the Clock of Perpetual Motion, the regulator of time."

Time had stopped, at least that is how Pen and Nicho felt. "What is going on? Is she in some kind of trouble or something?" Pen was worried and perplexed.

"I told you she was a crazy lady. It sure looks like she makes trouble for everybody, not just us." Now, in this moment, Nicho really started to pay attention, not liking any of these so-called proceedings. "I hope this isn't a kangaroo court."

Honora appeared, her lavender robes, hanging about her personage like a mantel. As she moved into the center of the forum, the normal whoosh from her garment was absent, her movement barely audible.

"Who are ye?" Ahreman asked her to state her identity to the court.

"I am Honora, a member of the Concordaie, a warrior and a peacekeeper."

"*She looks so frail,*" Pen spoke twin talk into Nicho's ear.

"*Yep, oh boy are we in big trouble now. She can't help herself— let alone us.*" Nicho's train of thought was interrupted by a set of kaleidoscope eyes that suddenly appeared next to him.

"Remember, we understand you; your twin talk, it is our language too. Be very careful, Nicho and Pen, all you meet here, know now, they're not your friends."

Once again, Excelsia seemed to float away.

"Another mystery secret, these riddles do not help, not at all. They seem content to say words, but without one fact to help us puzzle this out. Yes, Nicho, we are in some big trouble here." Pen was getting uncomfortable again, and like Nicho not trusting anyone here, not anymore.

Jais entered Nicho's mind telling him to be quiet. He gave Pen the same signal. They both needed to pay attention in this very moment.

"Who, too, besides ye, will speak on your behalf?"

Honora cleared her throat. "Mikai, husband of Esme, and Penelope, daughter of Melissa and Reed." Honora's response was clear.

Penelope could not believe her ears. "Did she just say my name? Did she just say that I will speak on her behalf? No way! She made a mistake. That is it; it's all one big, very big mistake. She doesn't know what she is saying. Yep, Nicho, we are most certainly back in that dream. That lady *is* really out of her mind, and yes, we are in some big trouble if she needs me to help her." Pen didn't care who heard her; she was nearing her limits.

Oddly it was Nicho who now took a different path to approach the situation. "No, she is not crazy, eccentric yes, but not crazy. I know that I call her 'that crazy lady' but something is not right here. Pen, this is a puzzle just for you. There is a reason that it's you. Remember when we play card games at night, during the winter when it's too cold to go outside? You know how when you think you might lose, you want to stop the game and want to deal another hand. And Mom, what does she always say to you?"

She looked at her twin, hoping he would finish her thoughts, and he did. "'You got this, just take your time, don't jump to conclusions, and learn to listen, not just the words but the truth of it. *The hand is not over, play it to the finish.*'" She stopped to reconsider.

"Pen, we need to learn how to live this uncertainty. How to take the risk of betting on ourselves and no one else. We need to know that *we* can do this thing, whatever it is. That is what Mom and Dad would want. That is what they taught us."

She nodded but not with enthusiasm. *How did Nicho get this smart? He is such an idiot sometimes.* She admonished herself. *Who cares, it doesn't matter, not right now.*

Professor Jais, as monitor addressed Honora. "Call you first sayeur."

Mikai entered the epicenter of the forum to tell his tale in the resolution of the question.

Honora approached Mikai; she seemed even more diminutive than before. "Who say ye?"

"I am Mikai, of the Quintessence. We are the seers, the professors, the teachers, the astrologers, the rulers of the ether. We possess the power of the fifth element and have the gift of the sixth sense."

"So you claim," spat Ahreman.

"Enough, you will have your time to speak." Jais warned Ahreman and nodded to the sayeur.

"What say ye about Honora and ZR? What say ye from your gift to ascertain the energy of the soul?" Honora asked.

Ahreman interrupted again. "Objection if you please." He looked with contempt at Jais. "Are we just supposed to believe a member of the Quintessence because they seem to think that their word is superior to everyone else here? Is that not against the very essence of our way?

"Agreed," said Jais. "Testimony is weighted on the evidence and how it's presented. No one has more privilege or entitlement because of their characterization at birth."

He turned back to the witness and cleared his throat. "Ahem, you may continue."

Mikai faced the crowd, undaunted by Ahreman's jeers. "Earth was their blue-green jewel."

"Please tell us about whom you refer. Identify who is 'their.'" Jais interrupted for clarification.

"I am talking about Honora and ZR and the Earth. It is the planet with the most precious of gifts: its air, its atmosphere, and its abundance of JX. It was the culmination of all their, I mean, Honora and ZR's powers, all of their gifts. Esme and I were told that Earth was created for some purpose well beyond what any of us could ever know. Neither we, nor Honora, nor ZR were ever told the reason for its existence. Our task was that we were to guard and protect it above all else."

Mikai then continued. "So, we were given a mission by the two who came before us." He nodded to Honora and ZR. "That task was to guard over this solar system, and we, like Honora and ZR promised to never take any gifts from all of this that was fashioned. We watched each movement from the window portal inside our home, the *Sphere of Comets*.

"From this place, we listen for the sound. The pitch of the movements meaning all was well, all was peaceful, and all was as it should be. It was the sound of perfect music—the spinning of the planets, the pull of gravity, the force of a dying star and the birth of a new one, and the whiz of the comets and the fall of the meteorites; they all work together in harmony to create an aria. The sound was ever unfolding, expanding, and yet whoever hears it, feels that it is a song just for them. This is the hum of harmony."

Ahreman stood up, clearly outraged. "Enough, we all know this old and tired, well-worn story. What say ye give witness to? Nothing so far. The same myths and folklore we have all heard over and over again."

Mikai stood firm. "That is just it; this is the very reason why we, not you, were given this guardianship. You, brother-in-law, have always had an empty cold heart; that makes you unworthy of such a task."

Mikai was surprisingly quite fearless in his reproach of Ahreman.

"Hey, Pen, Mikai has got some real guts to stand up to him. That guy is one very scary dude," Nicho whispered, forgetting that the circular room enhanced every sound.

"Shhh" was the collective response from the crowd. Nicho sheepishly bowed his head and paid attention.

"We remember when we said goodbye to them before they settled on Varuna. That is when they entrusted us to keep their promise, and I asked them for the last time. Please tell me again, what were the first things that were created?"

"Ah yes, the stars."

"And tell me again, what did the stars sound like when they twinkled?"

"Of course, just like the echo of a piano note's ring."

Mikai once again addressed Ahreman. "You, Ahreman, my brother, were given your own very special place. You were given all those very same instructions to look over and care for what was given to you. And look what you have wrought: a black hole that is devoid of warmth. As the Lord of the Black Holes, did you listen to its dismal sound? Did you feel its cold void space filled with the darkness of your spirit? That is why Honora and ZR did not entrust this Solar System to you. Because you are a taker, and all of this would cease to exist if placed within your care. That much they most surely knew. That much we all knew. We each know the true source of your power, why your capabilities are so beyond each of us here; it's because you have taken every element from your given place and left it empty and unable to support any life but your own."

The silence in the room was deafening.

"So, say ye," Ahreman spat, "but what of Honora, did she not try to do the very same? Did she not try to drain every ounce of JX from the third orb from 'their blue-green jewel' as you call it? That which is the very same act you so accuse of me?"

"No, that is not so; you know I am of the Quintessence," Mikai continued.

"I remember her parting words to us. They repeated to us what was told to them, from the one who sent them, the one to whom they made them promise such a long time ago."

141

"A child comes to life,
their star disappears from the heavens.
When they pass on, their star reappears,
where it will twinkle forever."

"'Look for us in the cosmos' she said. 'It will not be long. You will recognize our twinkle.' Then your father ZR added, 'And remember us too, whenever you hear the echo of a piano note's ring.'"

Mikai fearlessly continued, although his voice was choked with sadness. "You are nothing like your parents. Esme is your twin, but you are unlike her too; but you already knew that to be true, know that better that any other entity: you are nothing more than abomination."

That allegation found it mark. Although Ahreman's ferocious rage was perfectly controlled, the power of his hatred was overwhelming. Those present in the *Sphere of Comets* could feel the great ship's heart silently whimper, wounded from his want of revenge and retribution.

CHAPTER 12

Consequences

Bedlam ensued as Ahreman continued to let the sheer power of his rage be felt by everyone present in the chamber. It was a pure display of the depth of his might and supremacy, and it was working.

"Order. Order." Jais called the room to order, attempting to stem the wave of discord that was taking over, but to no avail. Such admonitions would prove futile.

"Recess." He then called a break in the proceedings to regain some measure of control before proceeding.

Even the air was strained and tense. Nicho and Pen could feel the change in atmosphere, and it left them both feeling very vulnerable. "Okay, Pen, if this is a dream like we think it is—like we already know it is—it's time to wake up now and go home." Nicho's powers of empathy and intuition started to overwhelm him. He needed to learn how to control the abilities now awakened within him, learn to disconnect with the emotions in the room. Everything was so new to him. He could feel the presence of Professor Jais's cognizance trying to help calm his mind. He looked to him for affirmation, and the visual connection made him feel better, but in strengthening their empathic link, Nicho became aware of the depth of Jais's own concern. It scared him.

Pen, however, was not ready for this adventure to be over, not yet. Yes, the fun was all gone, the playfulness and the learning had come to an abrupt halt. The sound of discord now filled her ears from Ahreman's anger, and all that remained was that low persistent dismal flat note that emanated from his very being. She was not happy with her so-called special gift to hear the hum of harmony, not right now anyway; it sounded more like the hum of misery.

Nicho's voice again entered her thoughts. *Pen, let's try to get out of here or try to wake up. There is a feeling in this room of unresolved anger, hatred, and vengeance. I don't know who is right or who is wrong, but we need to leave them to their own history: past, present, and future. We don't belong here. They are not telling us something, and something that is really big. What is really going on here?*

Pen turned to look at her brother to comfort him but instead saw the answer. Nicho jumped at seeing her face. The green in her eyes glowed widely, specks of gold were blazing, almost piercing. "No, not you! Hey, Pen, look at me, how did you get those crazy eyes? No, not you, too." He was half hoping, half not, as he stood up to stretch his legs, but his sister just sat there like a statue, frozen in place.

"Pen, what's the matter with you?" His sister's expression worried him. "You like you just saw a ghost! Cut it out. You *know* you are not the funny one."

Then in that very moment in time, a most familiar voice in the whole universe filled his and Pen's ears.

"Hey, Penny Candy! I have missed you!"

Pen gasped for air. Nicho now understood, not only her state of shock, but all of the foreboding it would bring.

"It can't be! But it sounds just like him." Pen stood up; she needed to get a better look. Her heart skipped a beat or two as she looked frantically around the space, trying to find the source of the voice, *his* voice. Then she heard that whistle, that ever so special sound that would make everything all right.

"Uncle Gil," she shrieked as she spotted him across the great room. "Uncle Gil, thank goodness you are here. Oh, how I've missed you." Pen ran towards her uncle and flung her arms around him. "Now everything will be all right. Nicho, Nicho, look who it is! Uncle Gil is here. He is here for us."

In Nicho's present state of mind, he was looking, hoping for someone else. He immediately did not share his sister's sense of elation, no way. Although he wasn't sure what it was, he had a sense that something still was not right. That suspicion got the better of him.

"What are you doing here? Where is my dad? Where is our father? Why isn't he with you? What happened to him." It was Nicholas this time firing the questions.

"Hey, Bud, let me rub that mop of hair of yours out of the way so I can see your eyes." Gil reached out to give his nephew an affectionate hug.

It took Penelope a second to realize that her dad was not right behind her uncle. She, too, was taken aback. "Hey, Uncle Gil, where *is* Dad? Why isn't Dad with you? Dad is with you, right?" Her voice was now panicky.

Gil held his niece close to him. "Hey, he is safe, I promise. I need to go back to get him. He somehow got locked in that inner chamber that troublemaker Honora created. It's all her fault that our mission got messed up. Reed got lost in the crazy Tunnel of Infinity and then somehow got stuck in that inner chamber. I really tried to warn him, and I tried to get him out, honest I tried." Gil turned to look at Honora. "I am going to spring him loose next time we go into the tunnel. I know the way; I led him there—that was me, I was first. I am coming on the next mission, to help you. That is why I am here, you know, to help with your mission."

Pen looked at her uncle, confused. "What mission? What are you talking about?"

"You just left him there to die? You just left him behind!" Nicho cried out, incensed. "You got out and left our father there alone!"

"No, no dude, no way. You have got it all wrong. I would never leave my favorite brother-in-law behind. It was all her fault, that one. I keep telling you, it's because of her, that Honora. Ahreman saved me. If not for him, I would have been stuck in there, too, right with Reed. It was really scary, a really bad scene." Gil looked at them beseechingly.

"Ahreman saved me, man. He is a really great dude. He got to me just in time before I followed your dad into that inner chamber. That is where your father got stuck. I tried to warn him, but he would not listen. He insisted on getting a closer look, you know how he is; he wanted to understand what was going on in there. Those walls . . . they just closed up. Yep, that is exactly what happened. Just like that, it happened. It's because that crazy old lady is nothing but trouble. Nothing but trouble, I tell you. It's all her fault because she made some big mistake a long time ago. It was her fault in the very beginning, and it is her fault now."

Gil paused and then started to whistle and tap his pocket. "Ahreman brought me here to help you guys," he said, not making any eye contact with his niece and nephew, then turned his face away from them.

Penelope felt confused and let down. She really loved her uncle, and she knew they understood each other. In her mind, he was simply the best, so clever, so cool. Her mom, she just adored him. She loved to talk about him, how he could play any instrument by ear, and how people always thought he was a movie star. Yes, he was that good looking, always that epitome of coolness in every way. He was so unlike her mom, who was brilliant, world renowned in her field and all of that, but lacked that kind of aura or charisma. She had her own great qualities, for sure, but lacked his presence and sense of fun. They were more like opposites. However, whenever her mother spoke of her younger brother, she always felt the need to make excuses for his shortcomings and failures. Her mother would say, "Of course, he loves to be admired; everyone loved him. How could anyone not love him?"

Melissa understood that when the lights of the big city started to fade, and his star did not rise as high as he wished, she knew how that was hard for him. "He is so talented, so clever, always so much ahead of everyone else. None of it was his fault; his time will come again, I just know it.'"

In Melissa's eyes, Uncle Gil could never do anything wrong. She admired her rambunctious younger twin, who was so unlike herself. She lived through his stories of the music scene on the East and West Coast. Tales of late-night music gigs with all of the greats, hobnobbing with the rule breakers. Everything was always so much fun when Gil was around. Melissa always said she felt as if he was everything she was not. Unbeknownst to Penelope, Gil felt the exact same way about her mother, that she was everything he was not. However, with him, it caused nothing but resentment and bitterness that he kept bottled up inside.

"So, you are telling us that Ahreman saved *you*, but not my father?" asked Nicho, still feeling a little skeptical.

"I told you it was too late to get your dad out of that place. That is why I am here, dude; I am here to help you guys. I am here to find Reed. I am here to help you and Penelope put those moonstones back where they belong."

"The moonstones! I almost forgot about them, with everything that is going on," Pen exclaimed.

"So exactly where are they?" Gil asked.

Penelope instinctively held her backpack closer to her side. "They are right here with me, where they will stay until they go back to their proper place."

"Well, why not let me help you with that? I can keep them safe for you. You know you can trust me; that is why I came for you—I came to keep you and those stones secure. You have to be careful you know; you can't trust anybody here." He started to whistle again.

"Well, Honora told me to keep them close, until they are rightfully returned." Pen checked her backpack again, just to be sure.

"Ha! Of course she told you that. Don't you get what is going on here, Penny Candy? She wants to get you on her side. She is just trying to con you. She has everyone fooled, but not me, not anymore. If you listen to her, your dad will never get out of that place. If only my sister were here, she would tell you who to trust. Melissa would tell you exactly who to trust." He shook his head incredulously, still not looking at Penelope as he continued. "Gee, I thought you and I were special to each other, Penelope. I thought we really got each other. Thought me and you were tight, guess not. Guess I made a big mistake, coming back here and trying to help my favorite niece." Gil looked dejected.

Penelope got upset. Those words coming from her favorite uncle caught her off guard, and her feelings were hurt. "No, Uncle Gil, it's you and me, just like before. You are my favorite person in the whole universe. I am sorry, here, just let me—"

Suddenly, within that very moment before Pen could finish her sentence, a clapping sound interrupted her train of thought. The *tap tap tap* grew louder and louder and louder. The sound reverberated and spun around the rotunda. A whirlwind of the steady drum beat sound grew more furious and overwhelming. What Penelope then saw, she could not quite believe—not with her own eyes, not even here on the *Sphere of Comets*. Suddenly, everyone and everything seemed to move very slowly, like it was all in slow motion. Slower and slower until each and every thing was frozen in place. Time had stopped.

"Nicho, Nicho," she called to her twin.

"I know, Pen. Everything is getting impossibly weirder, and I can't believe that is even possible up here. It's as if time has been suspended for everyone but not for me and you."

The two just stared at what was surrounding them, the absolute stillness of it all. "Hey, Pen, how come we're not?"

"What do you mean?"

"Well, I mean, how come we are not frozen still like everyone and everything else? Look at Professor Jais's tea; he spilled some of it, and it's just hanging there in midair. Not hitting the ground, just suspended in motion, just like he is."

Pen was transfixed by what she saw, but as the fact finder, she knew there was a reason. She looked for her first clue.

"Hey, Nicho, look at those two twins from Serious Saturn; they are up to something for sure, and they are not affected by this . . . whatever this is. See, they can move."

"And those twins with the kaleidoscope eyes, it's like—"

"Yes," Pen could not contain herself; here was her second clue. "They are controlling the wind inside this space. They created the whirlpool of air, to make the clapping sound more powerful. Oh look, she is staring at me, that CeSe. She is *really* staring at me. Should I wave at her?"

"Are you crazy? You want to know if you should wave to her? We are in a time warp, and you want to wave to someone who seems to have the power to control the wind, or the air, or whatever this is up here." Nicho looked at her imploringly. "Please don't become as nutty as everyone else up here."

"Talk about what is right in front of you. Look here comes that Yejide. What does she have in her hand? It looks familiar, doesn't it?"

Nicho rose to greet her, and in an awkward way extended his hand. "Hi, I am Nicho; we met before."

"When we met before, you were Nicho of the Quintessence. Has that changed?"

"No . . . I mean yes . . . I mean, my name is Nicho."

Yejide's smile was warm and welcoming; she knew that Nicho was smitten.

"You and your brother Adept can make time stop, right? I am guessing that is your Saturnian power. How do you do it? You slip between the two worlds of in time and out of time? That is amazing! That is super, super cool!"

Pen started to roll her eyes at her besotted brother, who sounded super stupid again for the one millionth time; then, she saw it and bolted right out from her seat.

"Hey, that's my mom's. You have our mom's letterbox. How—I mean where did you get it? Our father gave that to her as an engagement gift. She keeps her most precious belongings in that box, like letters from Dad, and, and . . . the sea glass that she finds on the beach." Penelope's eyes welled up. "Is she okay?"

"Your mother Melissa, she is fine. Please do not worry about her; we promise she is okay." Yejide assured her. "Help will always be close to you when you need it the most, like right now. This is for you." She handed her the mahogany box. "Keep your moonstones safe inside it, but for now hide this in your backpack. This is our mystery secret, okay."

Penelope ran her hand across the well-worn wood, and for the first time, she noticed the hand-carved glyphs. Of course, now she recognized them immediately because of the corresponding markings on the Talking Panels.

Yejide, the twin who always had a plan, moved very close to her and whispered in her ear. "Remember you can trust—"

Suddenly, in that very second, time began moving forward again.

"Hear ye, hear ye, all are called to order." Professor Jais's tea spilled onto his robes, as he continued trying to gain control of the room.

Nicho just shrugged. "Hey, another thing, what was Uncle Gill saying to you? It seemed intense, not like, well not like, you know, he is always kidding around and being funny. He was acting strange, tapping his pockets, and whistling."

"So, he always whistles," Pen responded.

"No," Nicho retorted, "he only whistles when he is nervous about something."

"Oh, Nicho, not now. Why can't you just see what is right in front of you? Why do you always need to look through everything? It's Uncle Gil. He really loves us."

Pen looked at her brother. Nicho looked at his sister. Enough was said.

"Ahem."

The monitor of justice then called for the next sayeur.

Honora took to the center. "I call Penelope, of the planet Earth, third orb from the Dazzling Sun."

All eyes now were secured on Penelope as she approached the center of the forum.

"What say ye?" Jais asked.

"I say the truth as I know it to be."

"You may continue." Jais nodded for her to proceed.

"My brother Nicho and I were summoned here to go on a mission. We made a promise to help restore the Latter Twelfstanin to the Clock of Perpetual Motion, the regulator that controls the time: past, present, and future. My brother Nicho was also summoned. His broken star is the stellated dodecahedron."

Ahreman approached. "And who told you all of this?"

"Honora told us."

"And just where are the Latter Twelfstanin?" he queried.

"Right here with me, and it is my purpose and promise to return them to their rightful place."

Ahreman's snicker grew to an uncontrollable laugh. "So, Honora told you it was *your* obligation to return the gemstones that control the past into the Clock. Did she tell you how you were to accomplish this monumental task?"

"No."

"So, she gave you *no* instructions on how to return the stones, just that they belong somehow to you." He continued to move around Penelope in a circle, his blank eyes ever-present on her countenance. "Please correct me if I misstate your mission as you call it. You must somehow return the Latter Twelfstanin to their rightful place. Is this your testimony?"

"Yes." Penelope remained unflappable.

The crowd murmured with conversations that seemed unfriendly to her ears. Even the members of the Coterie just stared at her with a look of incredulity.

"And please tell me, where are these most precious stones, the Latter Twelfstanin?"

"Here, they are right here in my backpack. I was told to keep them with me for safekeeping." Those moonstones belonged to her; that was a fact; she knew it wholeheartedly. She would not be deterred, not by anyone.

"Who told you that there were to be only in *your* possession?" Ahreman's question came with a sneer.

"Honora, it was Honora who gave me that instruction." Pen's voice was clear and firm amidst the jeers and speculative remarks from the onlookers. "And that is exactly what I intend to do," she proclaimed. "Are we finished?"

As Penelope rose to return to her seat, she held on ever so tightly to her backpack. As she left the witness space, she was careful not to make eye contact with the jury of her peers, especially *him*.

Ahreman dramatically swung his robes for effect as Penelope walked by him. He must not know he was dealing with a seventh grader who knew exactly how to play this game. Sparring with him was not so bad, she thought.

"I now call Gil Val as the next sayeur." Their uncle Gil walked slowly to the stand, his shoulders a little slumped. He then looked at Penelope before he gave his testimony.

"Do you know this *child*?" Ahreman asked him to call attention to Penelope's youth.

"Yes, she is my niece, the daughter of my twin Melissa Valiquette and her husband, Reed Winterbourne.

"Yes, and what say ye here?"

"I came to help Penelope because I knew she must be frightened by all of this. She is not from this world; she is not *of* this world. Honora was grasping at straws asking Penelope and my nephew to do this job. The very task she herself failed at again, again, and again. A problem, by the way, that was completely of her own making. Look what she did to my brother-in-law, Reed. Penelope and Nicho's father got lost in that maze she calls the Tunnel of Infinity. It was Honora who led us into that terrible situation. I managed to escape, but poor Reed got trapped in that inner chamber. That is all because of her folly, once again. Where is my sister Melissa right now? Why didn't Honora ask Melissa to finish this mission of hers? Why did she just ask my niece and nephew and not their mother, who by the way, knows exactly what happened."

"Do you know why your sister is not present?" Ahreman asked.

"Yes, I do. It's because Honora knows that Melissa would never follow her again, not *ever* again. So now she is using my innocent niece and nephew to finish her dirty work. I am here to stop this travesty."

Ahreman gave a small nod, seemingly satisfied with this answer.

Gil then turned to Honora.

"Haven't you caused my sister enough harm? She has already lost her husband and now you seek to go after her children? I know about that first mission, how you misjudged Melissa's pregnancy, and how you did not know how that tunnel would affect her because you did not know how time works in that bizarre place. Did you share with my niece and nephew the facts of your first failed mission? How my niece and nephew were born in that Tunnel of Infinity inside that crazy maze, or is it a labyrinth you created? That very place where only you know the secret entrance to the inner chamber. She almost died there."

Gil took a deep breath, clearly upset.

"Then you come back years later to ask for her help again. To ask for her help in a situation that you created but do not have the power to fix yourself. Because you made a mistake, because you broke a promise, and because you flung those stones right into the cosmos. I know that you can't enter that chamber because of what you did. Yeah, I know all about that. I know you are corrupted and how you can't put those stones back because of that taint. Did you tell my niece and nephew that, too? No, I bet you didn't. I am lucky to have gotten out, just in the nick of time. Ahreman saved me, and he tried to save Reed, too, but it was already too late."

The room grew deadly quiet. Murmurs were soft and low. Confused thoughts could be felt everywhere.

Ahreman approached the sayeur. "Thank you for your honesty and the courage to come forward. We are so sorry to hear of all of your sister Melissa's sacrifices on behalf of my dear mother's folly."

"Objection." Nicho stood up and spoke loud enough to be heard. He immediately turned red faced and sat down.

"You've been watching way too many lawyer movies," Pen said to her twin.

Ahreman ignored the interruption. "Now, I, as the seeker of the truth call my last sayeurs, Camillus and Tamzin, to tell the Tale of the Twelfstanin."

These twins approached the center of the forum with swagger.

"Say ye the truth," demanded the seeker of the truth.

"Sure, that is what we do, we tell the truth."

"Who say ye?"

Camillus spoke first. "We are the guardians of the planet Eris. Daughter and son to our father Acerbus the ruler of Eris. Although our birth home was located in this Solar System, we do not acknowledge this placement."

Tamzin continued. "We were there when she threw those stones into the cosmos. Our father knew of Honora's treachery. He sent us to spy on her, because she kept going back to that place called the Imperium. He told us to watch her and make sure she did not do anything wrong. Because we are little kids, she never saw us behind her, and we slid down that cosmic string right behind her. Yep, she is so out of it, she is an old lady for sure. She didn't even see us."

Camillus broke in. "Yeah, and we nearly got killed when it almost closed. She attacked us, and she is so old she kept missing us and then one of her bolts hit that clock and some stones fell out. She went crazy and tried to kill us. We ran away. We were only trying to protect that old clock. We didn't want to steal anything. We were so scared; we are lucky to be alive." Camillus got very choked up and hugged her twin brother.

"Right, Tamzin?" she asked and her twin just nodded.

Ahreman then went up to his young warriors and put his arms around them as they disappeared into his flowing robes.

"I, Ahreman, seeker of the truth, rest my case on the resolution of the question."

Professor Jais looked solemnly at Honora. "What say ye as the defender of the truth? Have you any words of witness to this testimony?"

Gravitas shone in Honora's face; her voice somber in tone, she started her story slowly. "Just one last time, I promised myself. Just one last time. That promise I broke, and yes I broke my promise to the one who sent me. The one who showed us exactly what to do." Honora's gown swirled perfect shades of lavender and blue that looked like the firmament in the heavens.

"We all know that story," Ahreman said.

She stared down at Ahreman with a fearless ceremonial stance. "I am Honora, Concordaie, keeper of the peace and warrior for justice."

To a captive audience, she turned and spoke. "My crime is one of hubris. With the passing of the time, I felt the hum that brought serenity, the spheres that brought such exquisite beauty, and the JX that brought power were my right, and in my mind, so it came to be. I accept the transgression of my folly. I created the Omnis Tempus to correct that very temptation. To ensure that such a wrongdoing would never happen again."

She seemed to grow in height, and her presence larger, stronger, and more majestic.

"Only those who are pure of heart can enter the Omnia Tempus. Only those who are chosen have the privilege of entry. The chamber will recognize any falsity or weakness of spirit, of that I made very sure."

Honora turned her eyes to Penelope and Nicholas's uncle.

"So you say Gil Val, that Reed entered the inner chamber of the Omnia Tempus by accident? Is this your testimony before this tribunal? You say that he was trapped, and you tried to save him? You say that Ahreman saved you from being locked from within the sacred inner chamber where the Clock is housed. Do you still claim these words to be true?"

Honora paused, waiting for Gil to reply. It was a long wait.

"Hey, Pen, look at Honora; there goes those crazy eyes that everyone seems to have up here. She looks mighty scary right now." Nicho was amusing himself with his observations until he looked at his sister. He was taken aback as Pen gave him an admonishing look. Her eyes were now once again piercing brilliant green with gold blazing lightening bolts. *Oh boy, am I the only normal one left up here?* he asked himself. He did not want to know the answer.

Gil started to move about in his seat, unconsciously tapping his pockets.

"Yes, that is what I said."

Honora stepped so very close to his presence. "I say you have given false testimony here. You were not allowed to enter. I say you could not enter and did not enter. I say that Reed closed the wall to your very presence."

Murmurs could be heard throughout the great room.

"Ahem, order please," Jais called out.

Honora continued, "So, I need to ask others to help me in this one final undertaking. Not because I failed in my missions but because I broke my promise to the one who sent me. That is my shame to bear, and that is enough to disallow my entry. But I, too, have promises to keep, before I pass into the twinkling stars, promises made before your time, and promises yet to be. I will keep them, *all of them.*" With that last promise, she disappeared and vanished into the ether.

Everything and everyone in the rotunda, even the Talking Panels, were silent in those moments that ensued.

Professor Jais slowly took to the center once again.

"We have completed the resolution of the question. We will now seek time of reflection. The question: Who should lead the third mission to restore the Latter Twelfstanin to the Clock of Perpetual Motion. Shall it be Honora or Ahreman?"

"We will deliberate in our chambers, and may discernment be your gift."

With that, the forum emptied.

~

The deliberations for the resolution of the question had begun, but not everyone was so engaged. Meanwhile, on the far side of the *Sphere of Comets* two enigmatic figures hovered in a clandestine conversation.

"That petulant niece of yours, did you handle her?" Ahreman was not in a good mood.

"Of course I did; she trusts me completely." Gil started to whistle again.

"I am not so sure about that. She started to remind me of that sanctimonious sister of yours. Melissa always thinks she is above everyone. I did not like that imp's lack of respect." The glint in his opaque orbs started to form an ominous shape.

"No way, come on, she is just a kid. She did not mean anything by what she said. She is confused. She told me she was really scared of you."

The thought that he invoked fear in Penelope appeased his anger.

"You don't understand how it is. She is my niece. We get along. Dude, she won't follow Honora. Penelope knows how my sister feels about me. She would never ever go against Melissa, no way."

"Maybe so, but that clever nephew of yours, he thinks like his father. That means that he is going to be a problem, just like Reed. Did you take care of him too?"

"Don't worry about him," Gil responded. "Those two will stick together. I can promise you that; they will stick together like glue. Nicho follows Penelope's lead. It was always like that."

Ahreman saw the pathetic irony in Gil's thoughts.

"Really, just like you and twin sister Melissa, eh?" Ahreman gave a sinister chuckle as he took a step towards Gil.

"Leave my sister out of this, okay? She has been through enough. Isn't it bad enough that Reed is struck in the tunnel place and can't get out? You made sure we all got separated in that maze. And your mother, Honora, she made sure that place is loaded with tricks and deception. We all got turned around, even Melissa and, boy, that never happens with her. Now, she doesn't know the truth about what really happened. My sister Melissa always gets to the bottom of things; she is tenacious like that. It's what made her famous. She keeps digging and trust me, she is no one's fool. You cast a spell preventing her from what she does the very best in the whole world—finding answers."

The mood in the corridor shifted, moving to an even darker place.

"Oh, now you are getting soft. Do you feel guilty about all of the pain and misery you caused your sister? Remember, you played a big part in all of this. I will not let you forget it." Ahreman sneered. "We are close to getting everything we both want, very close."

Gil shifted his stance to avoid that penetrating gaze. "Penelope will not let me down, no way."

Ahreman's mood grew very dark and brooding. He crowded Gil's space.

"What is the matter? I told you I got my niece under control.

What are you worried about? We went over this a million times." Gil started to whistle again.

There was a moment, when that meddlesome Jais called a recess during the proceedings, that things seemed a little hazy," Ahreman countered. "It's when you had your little sentimental reunion with that niece and nephew of yours."

"What are you talking about? The whole room was chaotic because you lost your temper. That is what I remember. Nothing went wrong. Why are you getting paranoid?" Gil shook his head trying to avoid his contact. "Hazy, no way? Maybe your mind is getting hazy."

"Watch what you say, Gil Val. Step very carefully with me. I just hope that sister of yours is not trying to reach those kids of hers. Sometimes I feel like my spells are being worked against me by some unknown force."

"Melissa, she has no power, no way. She has no idea what is going on. I would know; I am her twin. You have nothing to worry about with her, absolutely nothing. Nobody has your power, no one, so who could even try to mess with you, dude?"

"That is what you keep telling me. Maybe I should have just silenced her forever when I had the opportunity. That would be one less thing to worry about as she is quite unnecessary in my plans."

Gil got dangerously close to his benefactor, fearless in the moment. "Wait a second. No one was supposed to get hurt, no one. You promised not to hurt her. You promised me that you don't want to hurt anyone. Remember that was part of our deal. My job is just to keep them out of your way, and I am. I've got them all under control. You don't have to worry about Melissa, Reed, or the kids. In the end all they care about is each other." Gil's voice evoked some assurance. *I should know that better than anyone.*

"I said as long as she, that sister of yours, stays under control.

I said as long as everything went my way; I said as long as I got exactly what I what. But something happened in that rotunda, maybe just for a second, a mere moment, but I know that something happened. I felt it; there was a shift in the energy. And it better not be that sister of yours doing something I don't know about." Ahreman's tone was lethal.

Then it became velvety, seductive, and mesmerizing. "Gil, you are my friend, my only friend. You know how much you hate your goody-two-shoes sister. You never had to say it, I knew it, I sensed it. I understood it. You have a sister who is always right, like Esme. Your sister who does everything correctly—your perfect brilliant twin. You know all about your twin, the very same twin who makes excuses for you all the time, who feels sorry for you, who really is embarrassed by you—that twin sister. Now you feign to care about that Reed, another censorious creature, pompous and morally condescending. It seemed you had no problem leaving him behind. Or better said, you left him to do what you, once again, failed to do. That is our little mystery secret, eh Gil?"

Gil nervously tapped his pockets.

In the next second, Ahreman's mood changed again. The very air in the room became cold as did his countenance. His visage morphed as his two opaque orbs turned a dark cobalt hue, streaked with shards of white-hot lightening. His eyes bore down on Gil.

"How soon you seemed to forget about that sister of yours. Hmmm, so let's chat about your famous beloved twin." He spat.

"You know your twin, the one who looks at you with pity and sorrow. That twin who never really wished you success. That sister who was so glad when you returned to that little town in the middle of nowhere by the sea. Was it not the very place your whole entire life you despised and always wanted to escape? You were always wanting to run away from the mundane life it promised, vowing never to return. How very nice it must have been for you to come home as a complete failure. Just in time to babysit those twins of hers. How convenient indeed that must have been for her. You gave Melissa and Reed their perfect opportunity. You made it so easy for them to traverse the continents, going hither and yon to bolster their own reputations. You helped them at home so that they could do their research all around the world, going on adventures time and time again while you just languished in that little town by the sea. We are talking about that *that sister*. Correct me if I am wrong." He turned swiftly to leave, his robes flicking of fire and metal. "Maybe you need time to think, reflect and remember." His voice was chilling, empty, void of emotion.

Gil stood there with his shoulders slumped. He softly murmured, "Dude, you don't understand, you don't understand anything, and you really don't know my sister. You do not know anything about her. My sister really loves those kids; I mean she really loves those kids. Best to leave her alone."

Then he started to whistle as he walked back to the great chamber. *So do I,* he thought but kept that truth to himself.

CHAPTER 13

A Journal Entry

Meanwhile, throughout the *Sphere of Comets*, all the twins squabbled.

The answer to the resolution of the question as to who should lead this perilous mission brought with it some very lively debates. Each twin in their own special way paid close attention to the questions posed, the veracity of their testimony, the evidence presented, and how authentic the witnesses were.

As Pen followed the facts, Nicho followed his intuition. It seemed their distant cousins followed very much the same process and pattern. The astrological signs known for their superior IQ, who embrace the elements of earth and fire:

Virgo – Tien and Fastidious
Taurus – Domenica and Harmonious
Capricorn – Adept and Yejidi
Leo – Rage' and Olympia
Aries – Wink and Catriz, and
Sagittarius – AlexSandra and Sage

approached the issues more like Penelope. They focused on the facts, the tangible evidence presented, and still did not agree with each other's assessments.

"But she was given the power first, she was the first chosen," Tien and Domenica pointed out. This is how each of the female twins from Chiron and Sedna viewed the evidence by the tangible facts.

"Yes, but she failed in her two missions," countered their brothers Fastidious and Harmonious.

The celestial planners of Saturn also teed off against each other.

"Honora, she always had a plan and fulfilled her mission." Yejidi stood firm.

"But she lost the stones because she did not anticipate the interlopers." A'dept would have none of it, no excuses for the explanation offered.

"Ahreman is at the very height of his powers; those powers are second to none." Wink and Courage were impressed thinking him the most powerful. A trait held most precious to these Leo and Aries twins.

"Yes, but there are reasons he was not allowed on the Coterie." Catriz and Olympia countered their respective twins.

AlexSandra interjected her voice. "The Coterie, really, are so old. Ahreman is the Lord and Ruler of the Black Holes; he does not need their inferred power; he has his own." Sage agreed with his twin.

"I think he is a real creeper," said an unidentified voice.

"No, I think he looks kind of dreamy, like those famous people on Earth, you all know the ones they make such a big fuss over. He looks like a movie star," said another.

"Ugh!" several grunts. "He looks *spooky*!"

Those signs known for their superior EQ who embrace the elements of water and air used more of an intuitive approach like Nicho:

Pisces – Skye and CeSe
Aquarius – Thinx and Vespers
Gemini – Clarity and Witt
Cancer – Evan and Chance
Libra – Beau and Gracious
Scorpio – Mysterous and OnyX

saw things differently. They listened to the facts as presented by their siblings but focused more on the genuineness of the evidence presented, as opposed to its veracity. It was about the bigger picture and how they felt as the witnesses spoke.

Interesting enough, it was Gil's testimony that caused the deepest divide amongst the twins.

"I don't trust him, I don't like him, I think he is a liar." Mysterious was holding no prisoners with her comments on Gil.

"You say this because his way of presenting himself is foreign to you, especially the way he nervously whistles. Yet, he loves his niece and nephew. You can feel that energy; it's very powerful. They have a strong familial bond," OnyX countered.

He has a great voice and seemed like a lot of fun—so very Earthlike. I really liked him. It's no wonder that Pen loves him so much, he must be the most fun uncle ever. Clarity spoke in sign language and she sounded like she had a little crush on Gil.

"You got that right. We got stuck with Uncle Ahreman." That voice was really disguised to sound just like their Uncle Ahreman. Everyone oddly found that weirdly funny.

Oh, you would say that, Witt signed, showing exasperation, *but you know that whistle of his did not sound right at all. If anything, it sounded quite chaotic; it was disturbing to my ears.*

"Agreed." It was Beau from Pretty Venus. "My spinning locket went wild as he spoke; it was very energized while he gave his testimony. He is keeping a lot of mystery secrets, that is for sure."

165

Excelsia from Wishful Neptune swirled about her siblings. "You are all right about their uncle, and at the very same time, you are also so very wrong."

"This Gil, their uncle, has promises to keep and promises to break. All still unknown, even to him." Skye then joined his twin; their whirling seemed to invigorate the air itself, helping their siblings with a renewed boost of vitality.

"I am really worried about Grandmama Honora. At times she seems so frail, and then at other times not. Her powers, they wax and wane just like our moon. Suppose this mission will prove too much for her? So much of her power already dwindled. What if, at the very moment that she needs all her vim, there is nothing left?" Chance started to rock back and forth holding his tummy.

Evanescent looked at her twin, her misty eyes the color of the shimmering sea when the moon casts its most brilliant light. "Is that not why we are called to help her? Are we not our most powerful during the fullest face of the moon during this equinox?"

Up to this point, Nicho and Pen just listened.

"You have been pretty quiet," Pen queried Thinx. "It's very unlike you and Vespers; you always have a thought or two or three to share. What's up?"

"I would feel better if Skye and CeSe did not chose to talk in circles." Thinx looked perplexed and very annoyed.

"The problem is," Vespers said as she joined their conversation. "I don't think they really know any more than we do. I don't think they have the answers as to where all of this is supposed to go. Part of our task is to live with the uncertainty of this mission and with its outcome."

"That is what is bothering me, why I don't want to offer my thoughts. It's because we are all right, and we all wrong. There is always an answer. Like in math, there is an order, a pattern yet to be revealed. In the end everything is math." Thinx was deliberate and determined.

"Yes, and we each have a free will." Vespers looked to her twin. "Maybe we need to daydream on this and look to the stars for a clue."

That mischievous twinkle came back into those wisteria-colored eyes. "There is always an answer, yes, always an answer. A clue yet to be discovered. Maybe that answer is not for us to decipher." Now he looked directly at Pen and Nicho. "Maybe that challenge is for you."

"Come to think of it. It is only the two of you who remain without expressing your thoughts on who should lead this mission. Why is that? It is that you can't make up your minds, or you do not want to share your thoughts?"

Nicho was first to speak up. "It's because we still feel like we are outsiders. Like it is not our place to make this monumental decision, and maybe we still don't trust you."

"Yet you are here among us, chosen just the same as each one of us. Our Grandmama and father Mikai spoke. Your uncle gave witness. Your father Reed is missing. Your mother Melissa was summoned for the first two missions. It would seem that you are both very much indeed entrenched in the fulfillment of this task. Both of you, just like each of us, have promises to keep."

With that the twins of the future born on the planet that spins sideways, turned and left Pen and Nicho completely to themselves.

Pen took charge and spoke in twin telepathy. Mere words could never adequately express her feelings. She turned to Nicho, her green eyes ablaze.

He is right, you know, we need to get more into this game. We act as if we are on the sidelines, but we are not. We have been keeping everyone at arm's length; maybe that needs to stop.

Okay, I get what you are trying to say, Nicho silently replied. *So, what do you think about who should lead the mission?*

Oh, that answer is easy; we go with Uncle Gil. Pen breathed a sigh of relief, not expecting her twin's response.

"What? Are you crazy?" Nicho exploded, his voice thundering around the room. "No way! We can't go with Uncle Gil and that Ahreman guy, no way."

Pen stood up facing her brother. The quiet shared moment of twin telepathy was over, and their voices echoed around the great chamber. "I knew you felt that way; I just knew it. That is why I did not want to say how I felt. You were always jealous of our closeness. You were always envious that Uncle Gil liked me the best, better than you."

Nicho shook his head. "What are you saying? I can't believe what you just said to me. What if Mom heard you say that? How would she feel?"

Penelope could hear the hurt in his voice.

"Come on Pen, you are the puzzle master, the fact finder. Think about this as a puzzle, a conundrum of facts, some clear, some vague. Let's play this brainteaser out to the finish just the way Dad taught us."

Penelope just stared at her twin, shocked by her own words.

"Penelope, Mom and I knew that you and Uncle Gil were tight. We were happy for both of you. She knew how different she was from him, but she still loved him. Mom adored him for all the ways he was different, and she was happy that you found someone who understood you too. I'm more like Mom. I love Uncle Gil, but we are nothing alike, not in any way. We were all happy for you, for the both of you."

Pen needed a moment. It wasn't that she was at a loss for words, it was more that she needed to find the right thing to say. With a gentle tone, she said, "I know that, Nicho, of course I do. There are things about Uncle Gil that are bothering me too. Like, where is Dad, and why did he leave him behind? I mean I know he tried to explain it. He said he got stuck in that time tunnel thing that Honora created, but why didn't he try to tell Mom?"

"I bet he could have gotten to Mommie through that crazy lady Honora. Time and space are still impervious to her. Somehow, she is still able to do whatever she wants, and she asked the three of them to help her, so what happened between her and Uncle Gil? Neither of them are saying," Nicho puzzled out.

"That's really bothering me, too. Why didn't he try to get to her and let her know what happened? He had to know that Mom has been worried sick about the both of them. Can you believe all of this happened because of that game they played on the beach, looking for those stupid moonstones?" Pen then jumped at a sudden realization.

"Moonstones, yikes, I almost forgot all about them. There is so much that has been going on, like, almost too much. It's hard to keep track of what is really important. Good thing I put them in that letter case that Yejidi gave us for safekeeping. Grr, I could just scream."

"Well, it is good that we are having the exact same dream, Pen. This way we can keep track of everything we are supposed to do like"—Nicho counted on his fingers—"like go on a secret mission to save the world; find the moonstones and keep them safe in Mom's letterbox, because somehow that box will be a safe hiding spot; watch time stop, watch time start; find our lost uncle, oh wait, check, we did that. So, what's next? Oh right, find our lost dad, we can't forget about that—you know all of those little things we need to do before we wake up. We should make a list."

"That is what she asked us to do, I remember."

"Who?" asked Nicho.

"Mommie, don't you remember? She said to write everything down."

"There must be some hocus pocus about the box too, another mystery secret." Nicho was on a roll.

"I wonder what all of that was about everything slowing down and Yejidi giving us Mom's letterbox. What could Mom's engagement gift from Dad have to do with what is happening now?" Pen reached for her backpack. "Yeah, that was pretty weird."

"Yes, but now we can actually tell all of our friends that we were in a real time warp." Nicho laughed and could not help himself. "You know this is all just a dream, right?"

"It has to be. *Whew*! Thank goodness this is just a dream . . . just one really crazy, wild, never-ending dream." Penelope started to unzip her backpack. "Drum roll please. *Hear ye, hear ye, attention please*—watch me as I put the moonstones into Mom's letter case for safekeeping." The show was on, and it brought a welcome break.

"Yes, just like Yejidi told you to do. Just like when she made time stop in the spaceship." Nicho started to crack himself up again with the ever-changing turn of events in this *Sphere of Comets*.

"How about Professor Jais's tea, floating in midair, and then it landed on his coat anyway." Nicho started to slap his leg in laughter.

Penelope giggled at the memory, too. Nicho did make her laugh. Just then a thought popped into her mind. "Nicho, do you remember when it seemed that time started to slow down?"

"Like, how could I ever forget that one?"

"Did you get to look around at everyone, at their facial expressions?"

"Sure, a bit but I was more overwhelmed by that sensation of time slowing down almost going backwards. What did you see, Pen, or who did you see?"

"Well, I saw Uncle Gil's face. He was looking directly at me. Now his face is directly in my mind's eye."

"So, what is bothering you about what you saw?"

"Nicho, I know that I am not as good as you are at intuiting people's feelings, their emotions, what they are thinking and all of that you intuit. But I do know what I saw on his face."

"What did you see?"

"I saw, I saw fear."

Their moment of jest and frivolity disappeared as quickly as it came. The air turned somber, as did the twins.

Penelope stroked her hand over the letter box. "It funny how I never paid attention to all of the hand-carved glyphs. I never felt the softness of the wood or noticed that it smells of lavender. Just having this reminds me of home."

"Me too, Pen, me too," Nicho added wistfully.

Penelope opened her mother's box. She gathered her moonstones from their hiding spot inside her backpack and as she started to place the twelve precious gems back inside the box, she gasped. "Nicho, there is a letter here, inside the box."

"What? No way!"

"There is a letter here inside the box, and it's on Mommie's stationary!" Penelope insisted.

Nicho was incredulous. But there it was, a folded sheet of his mother's special journal paper. The paper was luminous with an opalescent cast in the very softest shade of wisteria. A gift from their dad to their mom on her last birthday.

"We have to open it and read what is says," Pen quietly whispered.

"You think so?" Nicho was not quite so sure.

"I know so," said Pen.

JOURNAL ENTRY

Ephemeris

The planetary positions are as follows:
It is the Harvest Moon and the Autumnal Equinox.
The Sun is in the Constellation of Libra
at 00 degrees latitude and longitude.
The Moon is in the constellation of Aries at
00 degrees latitude and longitude.
Both the Sun and the Moon are in
direct opposition in the celestial sky.
It is a time of awareness in the tenants of astrology

To My Precious Twins,

As children, you would always tell me stories.

They are neither stories from books, nor ones you made up in your head.

Your stories were always so very real.

And me, I believed your every word.

Why?

Because I am your mother.

Nicholas, you are my intuitive one.

When you speak, you want me to look directly into your eyes, and of course never interrupt your train of thought.

Your presence suggests a theatrical energy, always to be interpreted.

I'm never really sure what you are thinking, knowing that you keep so much to yourself. But I do know that your reflections are well beyond the obvious, beyond what is in front of you, and well beyond what others deem you capable of knowing.

And yes, because of your extraordinary sense of intuition, you will always prove them wrong.

Penelope, you, my very dearest, are my fact finder, my puzzle master, my fearless leader and most importantly, my firstborn twin just like myself.

When you tell a story, you remind me of a rosebud opening.

The more questions I ask, the more you bloom, color rising to your cheeks fueled by your enthusiasm. During the funny parts, you get so very excited that you laugh and wave your hands around to better express yourself. If my attention should dare to drift for a mere moment, your piercing green eyes with their golden specks blaze. So, I know to listen very carefully to your every word and respect your thoughts. You know exactly what is in front of you, you know what you see, hear, and feel: you are confident, fearless, and spirited. Yes, oh yes, you are.

Penelope, you need to be heard. Nicholas you need to be understood.

So, now it is my turn to share my story with you. A story that has a most unique beginning on this most extraordinary night but is without an end. You must learn to trust these words, as I trust yours.

As I write to you, my heart is filled with sorrow because I—no we—failed you.

I know that in this very moment in the continuum of time, you are in grave danger, aware of the challenges that confront not only you, but that threaten the very existence of this Earth—its past, present, and future.

Yes, I know.

Penelope, you heard the music and the hum of harmony, but do you truly understand and respect the power of its discord?

Nicholas, this will be your charge: to be steadfast with your sister, so she does not rush into this mystery secret headfirst.

You must promise me that.

Your father, Uncle Gil, and I, we, too, made promises that we could not keep, sadly, not even to each other. I wonder why? Why did they summon us three? Did they not know the divination of our own charted stars? Or was it our own hubris? Or maybe our pre-destination? Or maybe we each fell victim to the choices we made?

Now, I wonder if the answer, too, will remain elusive.

This calling, your calling, will be fraught with uncertainty, so be most curious, brave, and valiant, but above all else, always seek the bequest of discernment.

Trust the gifts that have now been awakened in both of you and remember above all else to always have utmost confidence in each other.

My mind is clear at this moment, as there is a celestial time gap in the rhythm of our parallel universes with the onset of this full moon. The cosmic string on the pendulum of perpetuity has allowed me these precious moments. The Tunnel of Infinity for some puzzling reason has not closed. So, I am grateful for this help from the heavens, although I do not know the answer why this is so.

There is a piece of the puzzle for you to remember in this compendium of time because you have learned about infinity, both in time and out.

Within my mind's eye, I went to the beach to find you at the very precise and singular second when the anonymity of the night changes into the clarity of the day.

I remember the power of the wind and the sound of raindrops that awoke me from a very profound deep sleep. My unconsciousness was willed by another power, but I too, have some strengths known to me as I write.

Though groggy, I knew where to focus, so I looked out through the blurred stained-glass window in our living room and spotted you both by the water's edge. I tried with all my might to steady my breathing. From what I could see, you seemed fine, but this time I needed to be sure. I hurriedly made my way to that place where the ocean meets the land.

My presence startled you because you were both immersed in thought and looking intently at the horizon. You both stared at me in disbelief, like you were wondering whether I was real.

Then came your mischievous twin smiles.

I gathered you both to me. I needed to feel that we were together. All was silent in our walk home as we listened to the raindrops splash the gravel pathway, my umbrella opened wide above us. Then, before I could ask any questions, both of you began telling and telling like the wind before a storm.

"Just tell me everything," I said. "We're together now and we love each other. There's a lot of power in that."

As we turned from the beach, a déjà vu overtook me. I knew exactly where you had been and knew exactly what had happened.

Penelope, I can watch you move your lips but am unable to hear your words.

Nicholas, I can feel the vim of your JQ. I try to hold you close, needing your powerful energy for clarity, because a more formidable force is now compelling my mind backwards into confusion. Its command is overwhelming my awareness, trying to wrench me back into my own subconscious thoughts, distorting my perceptions.

The excitement in your voice, Penelope, ushered me back for a brief second, but even that was not enough time to tell you, to warn you—

You, my puzzle master, then interrupted. "Mom, do you know I have the very highest JQ?"

"No, actually my JQ is much higher," countered Nicholas.

"Yes, yes, but not as high as—"

"The Tunnel of Infinity is now closing, I can feel its power and taking with it my presence of mind, my cognizance with it. Just remember to trust—"

CHAPTER 14

Verdict

Deliberations were over.

Professor Jais received the notice that each twin had made their individual decision on the resolution of the question: *Who Shall Lead the Mission of the Latter Twelfstanin's Return to the Clock of Perpetual Motion, the Regulator of the Tick of Time.*

"Ahem. All ye come to order and may each of those most affected by this resolution of the question come forward to cast their say."

Each set of twins stood vigilant by the Talking Panels that represented their astrological sign, and the constellation of their birth. Nicholas and Penelope stood in the background, hoping their votes would be of little significance.

The first twin set called was Catriz and Wink, guardians of the planet Mars.

"How say ye?"

Wink in a clear strong voice said, "I vote that Honora lead our mission."

Catriz, also in a clear strong voice, cast her vote for Ahreman.

And so it went that each twin was called upon the cast his or her vote, finishing with the twins from Wishful Neptune.

The votes were cast as follows and divided evenly:

Honora received a vote of twelve nods to lead the mission: Wink, Domenica, Witt, Evanescent, Courage, Tien, Beau, Mysterious, Sage, Yejidi, Thinx, and Excelsia.

Ahreman also received a vote of twelve nods to lead the mission: Catriz, Harmonious, Clarity, Chance, Olympia, Fastidious, Gracious, OnyX, AlexSandra, A'dept, Vespers, and Skye.

All eyes turned towards the twins from the planet Earth. Penelope, keeper of the moonstones, the Latter Twelfstanin and Nicho, rightful guardian of the stellated dodecahedron, the star of the present.

Penelope and Nicholas stood up together, as everyone waited with bated breath to hear their choice. They turned to each other to confirm the decision they'd agreed upon, and pandemonium set in, spreading like wildfire around the rotunda.

Gil ran over to his favorite niece, shocked by her decision.

"Penny Candy, please tell them you made a mistake. You really did make a huge mistake. Just tell them you changed your mind, tell them before it's too late. Tell them the right choice and hurry." Panic was in his voice and fear in his eyes.

"No, Uncle Gil, it's you who made the big mistake. You broke your promise to Mom. You promised to take care of our dad and you didn't."

"You got it all wrong. I tried to save him, your dad, but he would not listen. You know how smart he is, Reed; he thinks he is always so ahead of everyone around him. He thought that he figured it all out. I pleaded with him to just go along, that the forces in play were much too powerful, but he would not listen. I could not help your dad, but I protected your mother. I got Honora to get her out, to bring her home to you. I did it; it was me."

Gil took in a deep breath. "Your mother." He shook his head. "She, too, just like your father, so dogmatic, and ever vigilant. She gave me a really hard time about going back. It was that Honora who put a spell on your mom, to make her forget. It was her. Now, you need to listen to me, I'm trying to protect the both of you."

Pen was upset but stayed firm. "I think the only person you are trying to protect, Uncle Gil, is yourself." With that, she turned away, seeking camaraderie in her distant cousins who had made the same choice, a decision of their own free will: to trust Honora to guide them through this mission filled with uncertainty.

Fourteen of them had chosen Honora as their leader. They huddled together, looking over to their brothers and sisters across the rotunda. It would be the first time in their young life they would not be all together.

"It will be weird not to be with Harmonious," said Domenica, her voice a little sad.

"I feel the same way," said Sage. "I am so used to AlexSandra's sassy comments, I will feel kind of lost, without her too."

"And what is a queen without her king?" Olympia could not help herself.

Wails of lament could be heard among all of them, mixed with good-natured jibes about each of their loving but very annoying foibles. Of course, they had grown rather fond of each other's idiosyncratic eccentricities. They loved each other for those differences.

Esme shared her concerns with Mikai. "For them this is something completely unanticipated. I don't know if they can go on this mission without their other twin. I don't know if they can deal with the separation."

Mikai looked out into the cosmos. "Well, maybe we rushed to judgment when we assumed that their vote of Ahreman meant they would not follow Honora. We should ask each of the twins to tell us what they want to do, not what we thought they might want to do."

Everyone was gathered into the forum awaiting instructions from Esme. Though mostly quiet during the proceedings, she now strode with deliberate purpose to the epicenter of the great chamber of the Coterie and smiled at what she saw.

Twenty-four set of eyes stared back at her. "So, I guess now it's all twenty-four who are going, yes? Well, not exactly," she spied Pen and Nicho, "as we now have twenty-six." Her heart swelled with a mother's gratification; she was so proud of all of them. "Let's get this mission started." Esme knew just where to begin. It was a drum roll of assignments as she called out the names of each twin:

"Adept and Yejidi, my planners, you know everyone will look to you for some semblance of discipline; make sure you have a solid plan and follow it through together.

"Tien and Fastidious, my teachers, your job is to instruct them in all the things they will need to know. This Earth is not the same Earth each of you visited throughout your stolen times or your quick secret visits." Esme gave them that look that only a parent can do that says, *yes, we know exactly what you were up to.*

"Thinx and Vespers, please pay attention; staring at the stars at midnight might prove to be selfish. Your siblings need your knowledge and powers of intuition, so be right here in the present. You will promise to try, correct?

"Wink and Catriz, try to be good sports and let others go first, even if it's just once in a while. Do not rush or dive into situations headfirst; there are many dangers to face. Be ready to control your powers as well as your impulses.

"Domenica and Harmonious, try not to complain all the time. Just get the job done, as you always do, and remember how much your siblings depend on you. I am depending on you too.

"Witt and Clarity, try to slow down and not drive your siblings crazy. Remember you promised me, your mother, that you would keep a journal. Make sure you do; in this moment in time, it's more important than you know.

"Evan and Chance, try not to worry; your moods have more of a dramatic effect on your brothers and sisters than you realize. Your powers during this full moon will increase a thousandfold, so be ready and willing to embrace those abilities.

"Courage and Olympia, lead with your hearts, not by giving orders. By living up to your namesakes, others will follow you effortlessly, and remember what the sun brings, especially with the coming of the dawn.

"Beau and Gracious, your EQ is most extraordinary. Spread your special charm when everyone will need it the most, and that moment will come, that I can promise you. Keep your siblings' secrets safe in your spinning lockets. They will need to know those thoughts are kept precious and safeguarded."

Then Mikai spoke up as he took special notice of the twins from Puzzling Pluto.

"Assure me that you will go easy on your brothers and sisters. You don't have to live up to your name, Mysterious. Your powers even here in the *Sphere of Comets* are most intense. Remember control, control, control. The atmosphere on Earth will influence your abilities the most, especially when you first enter its atmosphere, as you will quickly recognize. Know that your siblings need you more than you realize. They can feel the vim of your energy, but they can also feel that you always know more than you offer. It's upsetting to them. You must learn to trust them, and in this circle of trust will come the moments of the completeness you seek. Believe me, even Wink and Catriz will learn to go second if you are forthright."

That last comment brought a rare moment, and OnyX and Mysterious, they could not hold back a smile, albeit a small one.

"And what about us, saving the best for last?" AlexSandra could not contain herself.

"Maybe." Esme paused for effect. "Settle down and learn to listen. Your power of sight will be most enhanced, but it is your gift of luck that will be most needed." AlexSandra started to open her mouth to contradict her mother. She stopped short.

"And remember, the grass is not always greener on the other side, as you both so like to attest. So, it's most important that you believe in your own luck. Remember that everyone will need that little bit of luck, and that is your gift on this mission."

To CeSe and Skye, no words needed to be spoken. They understood their roles.

With that, Esme suddenly soared in height, her liquid gold eyes glistened with power, and her bronze skin glowed with might, her very countenance brimming with the authority of command. She was Esme of the Concordaie, warrior and peacekeeper. Her open arms lifted high above her head, encircling her hair of copper streaked with silver, platinum, nickel, and iron. Her robes swirled about her presence shimmering of the very same metallics of every element. The air was charged with ions that mixed with her presence, as bolts of colors flickered about her very essence, but the sound of silence emerged, as she spoke, the atmosphere grew still and quiet.

"Go forth." She roared. "We are so very proud of each of you in undertaking this quest. Now you live the uncertainty of your promise to the one who sent you and to each other. May your journey be safe, your return swift. Hereof fail not, due reverence, you have been expected."

With eyes now focused on the Earthly twins, the pure tenor of her melodic voice echoed throughout the Great Chamber of the Ancients. "Pen and Nicho, I can promise you two things—your time, it will come, and you will not fail. Help will be at hand if you seek it."

Her magnanimous smile gave them courage. "Go with faith in your own abilities that are now awakened within you, unrecognized and unrealized until this very moment. Learn your lessons well. It is now the time for a new adventure."

A clap of the cymbal met her command, along with the horn, the drums, a trumpet, and other instruments—it was the hum of harmony, the orchestra of the universe playing just for them as they began their mission.

The great spaceship, too, obeyed as it readied for its task. The large stellated dodecahedron—the twelve-pointed star—hummed and purred with it portal open. Then the center of the star closed, and each set of twins took their place in this assigned queue for takeoff.

Wink and Catriz from Willful Mars wanted to be first, of course, so they flung themselves into the radiant red mist, tripping as they entered, giving themselves yet another tiny scar.

Domenica and Harmonious from Silent Sedna forcefully plowed their way into the glittering green haze.

Witt and Clarity from Dizzy Mercury, not daring to be their usual late selves, frenziedly darted into the twinkling yellow fog.

They were followed by Evan and Chance from the Moody Moon who took their usual circuitous route into the luminous pearl vapor, still worried of course.

Courage and Olympia from the Dazzling Sun charged flamboyantly into the opulent orange gust.

Tien and Fastidious from Clever Chiron moved most methodically and carefully into the shimmering sapphire spray.

Beau and Gracious from Pretty Venus hesitantly entered the incandescent opal rays, watching to be sure that everyone else was doing the very same.

Mysterious and OnyX from Puzzling Pluto stealthily moved into the gleaming topaz smoke, of course not wanting to be seen, in stark contrast to Sage and AlexSandra from Jolly Jupiter, who most boldly and with great panache entered the resplendent turquoise puff, wanting everyone to see.

Yejide and A'dept from Serious Saturn, prudently and with caution, moved into the gleaming garnet queue, just as planned of course.

Thinx and Vespers from Wacky Uranus aimlessly wandered into the flickering amethyst beam.

Excelsia and Skye from Wishful Neptune decided to swirl and whirl while they glided into the sparkling iolite cloud.

Nicholas and Penelope stood back waiting to be assigned a color queue.

"Hey, you need to hitch a ride." It was Yejidi.

"Sure do," said Nicho as he jumped in right behind her.

"How about you, Pen? Want to be first to land back on Earth?"

Pen laughed. "Why not!" She winked at Nicho as she hurriedly made her way to be first with Wink and Catriz.

"I guess this is the middle of our story."

Nicho and Pen exchanged a wink. "Yep, it is. Not a dream, right?" They both laughed.

The tinted mists then crystallized into vivid lines of saturated color. Everything was complete for takeoff. Each tangent began to spin in its own direction, until a celestial armillary sphere formed.

In the next moment, the *Sphere of Comets* let go of its precious cargo, hurling them towards their destination, the third planet from the sun. As each bolt of colored lightening blazed across the mica velvet space, the heavens applauded with a celebration of lights.

As Mikai watched the sparkling encasements blitz like comets to their ultimate target, he reached for Esme's hand. "Our children were given a choice without a choice, direction without direction, and asked to keep a promise without a promise in return."

"Yes, it goes something like that." Esme reached for her gemstone necklace and imparted a final word of motherly advice.

"Each of you is blessed with extraordinary gifts. Use them wisely and remember the true secret of your strengths will be found in your love for one another. Now search for the Circle of Stones that houses the Imperium."

As the encasements traversed the heavens, in this very instance of time, as least for the moment, each planet played its own unique instrument in perfect harmony, and the universe sang its beautiful song.

PART III

CHAPTER 15

Tale of the Twelfstanin

A cool mist coiled around Honora's feet as she glided down the cosmic string. The ethereal intergalactic thread connected two worlds, the one outside over there, and the other was her destination. She calculated her entrance perfectly, the portal's opening precise and finite. The location of the elusive mystical doorway needed to remain a mystery secret, this she knew. Her access was dictated by the change of seasons with a unique alignment of planet and sun. The Dazzling Sun was readying for just such a transition; its presence in the sky was moving towards the season of fall. The autumnal equinox was imminent, the time for entry now.

Honora's feet touched down. The energy from the cosmic string still crackled around her as she hurriedly walked forward. Her lilac robes dusted the rich, lush grass, still damp from the late summer rain. There was an urgency in her step, as she had an air of furtive haste. Clearly, she was supposed to be somewhere other than here.

She paused to center herself and inhaled deeply. She knew all of the mystery secrets ensconced around her and wanted to take in everything it had to offer. She remained upright like a statue, her eyes tightly closed, fists clenched. The whole of creation revolved within this most extraordinary place, which was zealously protected by a massive Circle of Stones. She then slowly opened her eyes and looked with certainty at the protective sarsens, confident in the formation of its impenetrable 360-degree loop. Guarding this designated sanctuary's precious treasures was one of her promises to the one who sent her. A pledge she vowed to honor.

Here, within the walled domain of the Imperium, the four fundamental forces of nature intersected with the conjoined energies from the planets, stars, and moons. Even the very air within the protected enclave was unique. Elemental combinations in their purest forms inhabited this space. Ions of oxygen, nitrogen, carbon, and hydrogen bonded freely, uninterrupted by human or celestial intervention. Such an inimitable atmosphere was a most extraordinary cache, but one more treasure remained. It was a secret whose very existence needed to remain an enigma. The rarest, most potent naturally occurring element known in the universe was also very present here. It was the element Jxyquium (JX). Never to be recognized on the periodic table because the existence of its very presence was meant to remain forever unknown throughout the continuum of time. Its life-giving energies and abundance of pure power was best left as a confidence known only to a precious few.

The Imperium's creation was predestined, identified at the very beginning when this particular solar system was fashioned. The blue-green orb, third from the blazing heart of this galaxy, was the chosen place. It would be called the planet Earth. Then, an unanticipated wondrous gift was also bequeathed to this unfathomable locus of power. The hum of harmony resonated off the rocks that shouldered the enclave. The sound, the harmonic pitch of each planet, moon, asteroid, and comet could be heard right here, as each heavenly body moved around its Dazzling

Sun. The orchestra of each sound maintained a song of perfect synchronization and balance. It brought serenity to those empowered to hear its song.

However, there was more.

She, Honora, was entrusted with one final task, to find a home for the Clock of Perpetual Motion. Yes, it was the timepiece that regulated time itself. Where else but within the absolute safety of this hallowed space should the clock that controlled the very tick of time reside? To her mind, it was the perfect place. Within this Circle of Stones, time itself would be shielded from forces that hungered to usurp its power. Placement within this impenetrable sanctuary would surely ensure her promise to safeguard the past, present, and the future, now and forever.

This she fervently believed.

Honora knew of the natural endowments bequeathed to this place. She also knew that her once-limitless powers had met with diminution. She knew that the mere presence of an ancient such as herself would draw unlimited amounts of purest energy from this potent haven, thereby, depleting its most guarded limited reserve. She knew, too, such abuse, that kind of taking, like all gifts in the song of creation, had its limits. All of this she knew, yet she did not desire to acknowledge the truth of it.

The time had come for her to retire, to go into that space just outside this solar system and live out her remaining days on the tiny planet Varuna, in the Quaoar. This was the one promise she could not keep. With all of the passing of time, she had deemed the Imperium to be her very own special place. She coveted the sound of the synchronized pitch of harmony, and yes, the ability to absorb the unique elemental energies that the Imperium offered her. She believed these gifts were her right as their protector, that she was entitled to them.

Unfortunately, spies tracked her returning to this most secret place. They stalked her coming and going, seeking to learn her secret for entry, so that they, too, could access its unique offerings.

"Just one more time," she foolishly promised herself. "Just one more time."

Honora set out again, recklessly seeking her "one last look." She promised herself this would truly be the final time she'd hear its sweetly humming music or feel the vim of its perfect pitch. She would never again watch the balanced beauty of its spheres: twelve gemstones moving counterclockwise to control the past, twelve gemstones moving clockwise towards the future, and a resplendent stellated dodecahedron to control the very present. This was the Clock of Perpetual Motion, that regulator of the past, present, and the future, the very tick of time itself. Honora had vowed to protect it—it was her last promise.

She continued to breathe in, even more deeply than before, standing even more erect, her palms opened wide as she slowly swirled, her robes gently swishing. "Ah!" she silently whispered, and her body was lifted high above the epicenter as she twirled with precision and grace. The absorption of such amalgamations empowered not only an ancient, such as herself, but all forms of carbon-based life.

A tingle crept down her spine, as she realized that the crackle of energy closing the portal had lasted just a heartbeat too long. She willed herself to the ground, breaking free of the ecstasy that she sought. Honora spun in shock and screamed in horror. Rushing towards her were twins from another time and place, the dark void. Somehow, they had slipped along the cosmic string directly behind her, risking their own oblivion upon the portal's swift closing, but apparently, they felt the rewards of such risk outweighed its peril. Or so they were told.

They dashed left and right around her, and Honora, recognizing her folly, blindly lashed out, blasting first one and then the other, hurling bolts of pure energy to protect the Clock. Alas, the agility of youth was their gift, the slowness of age her millstone. Nimbly, they ducked and dodged, moving ever closer to the precious sets of gems. Intent on their mission, they evaded her attacks and wasted no time in fighting back. She was caught off guard, her powers and skills no longer omnipotent, but this they already knew.

She pivoted and sent another bolt towards the male. This time, she made contact. He landed with a thud against one of the massive menhirs of the circle and slid to the ground. She readied to aim a killing blow but whirled back, distracted by the hum of discord that filled the air with dissonant mournful notes.

Her delay proved fatal, as the other twin had already reached the Latter Twelfstanin, the counterclockwise gemstones controlling the past. Ranting incoherently, the female twin dug an obsidian blade at the very nucleus of the Clock, trying to extricate the stellated dodecahedron that controlled the present.

Honora focused on the invader, her energy poised to obliterate. She never saw the wounded twin's bolt, green and sizzling as it hurled towards her, slamming into her back just as the volt of power erupted from her hands. It was a misguided flash. She missed her target, but the invader too was distracted; that gave Honora one last opportunity.

She spun and hurled yet another electric blue lightning beam, this time at the Latter Twelfstanin. Honora hit her mark. The gemstones scattered from the Everter's hands, taking their own flight through the ether, then diffusing into the cosmos. In the crisis of the moment, it seemed the right maneuver of choice, but then the effect of her action made itself quickly known.

"No!" she screamed, as the rhythmic tick of the Clock of Time began to falter, the stutter of its perfect balance stammering.

Slowly, the horror of it all dawned—without the past, there could be no future.

Whirling around, she sought the evil twins, but they too, were gone, probably trying to retrieve the scattered gemstones. They had no idea the futility of their quest. Honora now turned her focus to what remained of the Clock. Staggering painfully to her feet, she stumbled towards the ruins of the tick of time. Her one last thought was to somehow suspend its workings, to create some form of stasis to give herself an opportunity to rectify the grievous error of her conceit.

Madly she searched the land near the Imperium's protective stones. She then spied a slot canyon in the distance. Honora hurriedly conceived a plan to hide the ruined Clock. She decided to create an impenetrable chamber to house it in suspension. Hastening into the canyon, she ran to the point where the cliffs of the rift nearly blotted out all sky. The heavens should not see this ruination, not now, no, not now. Not until all was made right again.

There, inside the canyon's narrow maze of solid stone, she swept her arms wide and willed an inner sanctum into being. The Omnia Tempus was walled with pure Xyzanium, the hardest substance in the universe, impervious to even the power of the Concordaie. She camouflaged its entrance to look like a wall of solid rock. Then she created a single panel with a Key of Access that would be known to her and one other.

Summoning her last remaining strength, she staggered back to the scene of devastation and slowly levitated the tangled mass of time, guiding it through the maze of the slot canyon into the hidden chamber, thereby creating the Tunnel of Infinity. Anyone foolish enough to traverse this labyrinth would be confronted with trickery and delusion, thus, further ensuring the Clock's protection.

She thought through her folly. Without the Latter Twelfstanin, the gemstones of the Past, the very future could be stolen. So, with all of her last remaining powers, she summoned the very energies from the Imperium itself, all the powers of the fundamental forces of nature, propelling pure waves of powerful electromagnetic beams into the ether and beyond. The sheer magnitude of those relentless currents created a rip in the continuum of time. From this point forward, two parallel worlds would exist, one "in time," the other "out of time." Both timelines would concurrently exist until the Latter Twelfstanin were returned.

The severity of such a cosmic rift came with a severe cost, as this division brought with it dangers yet unknown to begin. A passageway out of the Black Hole was created in that single nanosecond, permitting ultra-high-energy cosmic particle beams to escape its gravitational hold. The planet Earth was their destination. It would take one thousand millennia in Earth's time for the beams to enter this solar system, but in the realm of infinity, it was a mere instant.

Honora now understood the enormity of her folly, the cost of her imprudence.

It now was her burden to restore what was, no matter what. She accepted the challenge and took flight with firm resolve.

Time was no one's friend, not anymore, but she saw for a mere second, a brief glimmer of hope in what could be the possible future, and in that, accepted with faith, the uncertainty of her quest.

It had begun.

CHAPTER 16

Pangea

Thump. Thump. Thump.

Twelve crystal landing pods exploded into colored clouds of cosmic dust.

To an outsider, it might appear as if a small shower of meteors lost their way and landed by happenstance on the third planet from the Dazzling Sun. Their journey had rocketed them across the cosmos, unerring in its path to a particular cluster of sarsens. Emerging from their mini cocoons with caution, they rose slowly with trepidation, their legs wobbly and vision a bit spotty. They were unsure of their new surroundings, wanting to take stock of this very special place, the subject of the legends they had learned about in their history classes at the Sphere of Comets, now they were here. They'd landed in the very center of the Imperium.

A moment of profound silence descended upon the group. They instinctively turned to the other to make sure they were okay—a nod, a smile, a wink, and then a loud *whoop* echoed off the large boulders. Yep, they'd made it.

Earth was a very different planet from whence they came, a new world. Of course, each of them had stealthily snuck through

the time portal of infinity, interfering with the course of myriad civilizations, but those moments were stolen snippets in the tick of time. This visit was different.

Strange little creatures buzzed around their heads, while small furry ones hopped over their toes. Some larger animals meandered over to sniff at them, too, just as curious as those little ones. The air of Earth's atmosphere brought with it new smells and sounds. All the space travelers felt a sense of wonder and amazement. A resonance in the distance met their ears; it was an earthly vibration yet unknown to them. Maybe it was more of a sensation, or maybe a roar, or a crash and then an echo. It was soothing to hear, almost rhythmic.

Chance and Evan beamed with pride at the splash of the ocean waves. "Yes, we know from our home, the Moody Moon, its melody can be quite hypnotic and lulling. It's one of our special gifts, creating the tide of the ocean. Listen closely to its music."

Some then ran to see the source of the splash, while others crouched down to study the grass, or a nearby tree or a flower. The beauty of Earth's nature was exhilarating.

"I thought they'd been here before," observed Nicho. "From their stories, it sounded like their visits influenced cultures all around the world. Now, they seem to be going on and on about everything, like they've never seen any of this before."

Pen just nodded. "Gross, that one who always has something sassy to say, just put a cricket into her mouth. Ha! She had that one coming, and *ew,* she just swallowed it. Hey, good news, they have seen a mountain before, that is a start." Pen laughed.

"Up there, in that spaceship sphere, they seemed so much more together; now, down here, they just sound like a bunch of regular kids." Nicho shook his head. "They are all arguing with each other, again, and boy do they complain a lot, about everything."

"It's so annoying. Well, maybe we should say something," Pen suggested.

Nicho shook his head. "And say what? They all think they are super special, with their superpowers, super stuff. Problem is, right now they sound like super crybabies. I always got the sense that they don't think we are one of them because we are different. Look at them all huddled together and squabbling. Another thing, where is that crazy lady Honora? She always seems to be somewhere she is not supposed to be."

Pen shrugged and shook her head in agreement. "Yep, or never where she should be, like right now here with us. Then she seems to pop up just in the nick of time. So hopefully, she shows up real soon." In the next second, Pen now annoyed again, looked over at the celestial twins. "Gosh, do we sound like that when we bicker?"

Nicho laughed. "Hope not. Some of them are nice, but some of them need to get over themselves. I got news for them. They are on our turf now, and now it's their turn to feel lost and alone. They will ask for our help sooner or later—if they ever cut the cry baby stuff out, that is."

"They really do not listen to each other. Oh, they really do whine," Pen said, quite matter of fact. Nicho looked, grinning. *Of all people, look who is talking.* But he kept that thought to himself.

"So, let us get started." Wink and Catriz's voices joined forces with Courage and Olympia. Any and all suggestions were met with zero encouragement from their siblings.

"We are not taking orders from any of you." Those sassy twins from Jupiter would not hear any of it. The twins from Pluto took an adamant stance without a reason, just wanting to be difficult.

"Let's try to get along," implored Beau and Gracious.

"Oh, that is easy for you to say; you two never make up your minds and start nothing but trouble when you play this goody-two-shoes game of yours. We need to have a plan." Yejidi was in no mood for them.

"Oh sure, you make some plan, and then who does all of the hard work? We do." Domenica's temper was erupting, "Don't you dare say that is not true."

"Let's just go home. I want to talk to Maman," wailed Evan.

"Then you should just go home. We have much to learn, and your energy is not helpful." Tien spoke quietly but with purpose.

"You are distracting all of us when you mention quitting and wanting to go home."

The twins from Wacky Uranus were completely detached from their siblings' plight, as they were too preoccupied with their own. "Ouch! Something keeps pinching me." Thinx yelped.

"Me too," moaned Vespers, as she grappled at her clothing to stop the itch. "It's making a buzzing sound, but I can't see it."

"You made a promise, too, you know," Excelsia reminded them. "We need your powers of intuition and *your attention*." Vespers and Thinx looked at her knowingly; they stopped fidgeting and gave her a nod.

As CeSe floated away, they could hear her parting comment. "And whatever else you might know that you don't feel like explaining—like those ionized currents that swirl around your bodies when you are inside the circle. Remember, you are of the future, so your help is invaluable."

They smiled good-naturedly at the sentiment, knowing she was right.

Just then, Nicho looked over at the boulders that stood around the Imperium. "Hey, Pen, look at the placement of the silhouette in the circle. The sun's shadow has moved from when we first landed; it's gone from high noon to three o'clock p.m."

"Oh no, you are right. Time is moving again—Earth time, that is," Pen noted.

"It's just like what Dad and Professor Jais said, 'It's always all about math.'"

Growing up at the seashore, they learned as toddlers how to make a sun dial by sticking your popsicle stick in the sand. Just like a clock, they were able to tell time by the sun's position in the sky. Pen and Nicho gave a little strut, a wink, and a high five. "So, we have to teach them about how to tell time on Earth and use the Imperium stones to do it." Pen was smug with knowledge in this moment. Now they were dealing with Earth like know how, on Earth time.

"'And to let them know that 'time is not our friend,'" Nicho said, quoting Honora.

"Not anymore," Pen finished his thought.

In that very second, Witt and Clarity appeared next to them. In this Earth's atmosphere, they signed at such rapid speed a sound emitted from the movement of their fingers, just as if they spoke with their mouths.

Hey, what's going on? Their agility had also increased, as they moved so quickly their feet did not hit the ground. *Why does everyone look so glum? Did we miss something? Aren't we all here? Look what we found: these two very cute little creatures. They go yap, yap, yap. They are like the animal version of us! We have found, as you say here on Earth, a pet.*

Meanwhile, pandemonium reached a threatening level with some who were not in such a good mood, like Mysterious and OnyX. Their response to the Gemini twins was wordless, but the energy of this new place made them feel overloaded and out of control. Their mother's words reverberated inside their heads but to no avail. The colored bands within their eyes blazed and the intensity of their stare was so forceful, it caused the boulders to shake. It was as if they were trying to move those very sarsens that encased the Imperium itself. Their siblings looked on, wondering how to stop their madness.

"Cut it out." It was Wink who bolted towards them. Yejidi quickly blocked her brother's advance. "Not now, they are not themselves, and you *will* get hurt." Their delirium of power only increased as the large Circle of Stones rumbled dangerously, joining the whirl of fury. "But we do need a plan and we need it now!"

It was Thinx who accessed CeSe's thoughts. *They need to feel the energy they derive from their own element—that of water. You are Pisces, they will understand your vim; only you and Skye can reach them in this moment.*

With a soft whir of the chiming wind, the twins from Wishful Neptune caressed their siblings in melodic song and soft breeze. The subtle movement of the wind and purr of the bells bellowed off the rocks. It got the twins from Puzzling Pluto's attention, giving way to a moment of comfort. It gave them pause to control their abilities that were yet unrecognized.

"Whew!" was the collective response.

All of this uncertainty of what to do, how to do it and when to do it took its toll. This was very new to each of them. It was a rite of passage, to do things without the direction and approval of their parents and teachers. It was frightening to know that their own worst enemy could be themselves or, worst yet each other.

Then, just in the nick of time, above the clatter, came the perfect sound of a fluttering flute. Beau and Gracious adhered to their Maman's words, "Do what you do best."

They both stood poised and alluring; with a sweeping wave of their arms, they began to move like whirling dervishes, working their magic, exuding their charm, and creating an aura of peace and meditation. They both gave a nod to Pen and Nicho.

"So, we did our part. It's your turn to do something. This is your home. Think, and do it fast," Gracious offered. "This mood will not last forever, and my brothers and sisters are still really upset and scared. This is all quite novel for us. I guess we all know how it felt when you visited our home in the *Sphere of Comets.* Now it is our turn to feel out of place." Even her imploring voice was captivating.

Nicho and Pen were also a little dazed by her magnetism but felt, for the first time, like a real peer to each of them. Pen then took charge and let out a loud whistle. It actually worked beautifully and got everyone's attention.

"Let's all go back into the Imperium and get organized; we have a plan."

Yejidi gave her a high five.

"We do?" asked Nicho. His tone was filled with incredulity. Pen, green eyes ablaze gave her brother a withering stare. "Well, yes, maybe . . . I guess." He started to pay attention.

As they all gathered inside the circular wall of monolithic stones, Nicho thought out loud to himself. *Okay space, there is no way you are just a sundial and a landing site. No way. There must be something more, a lot more. And I going to figure out all of your mystery secrets.*

Pen looked at her twin with affirmation. *Yes, you will, yes you most certainly will. That is a fact I know to count on whenever you focus.*

She turned towards the group. This was her time now.

"These specific glyphs were deliberately carved on each stone for a purpose. This is not a coincidence. Unlike the Talking Panels that were in a constant motion in the *Sphere of Comets* these large limestone sarsens are permanently placed. So, yes, there is a reason with a definite function."

Nicho inferred an astrological theory to the boulder's precise placement. Like Vespers and Thinx, he too was a student of the nighttime sky as such ancient knowledge of astrology, the study of the stars, was a gift that belonged to the Aquarians. *We heard you needed our help.* Thinx and Vespers approached him. *No words of explanation were required with these two.*

"Yes, we do need your help," he said loud enough to be heard, "and a few other of your siblings." Tien and Fastidious acknowledged their cue.

The twins from Clever Chiron were endowed with the power of collective intelligence. Their assignment was to teach the ageless science of astrology to the group. Tien entered the very epicenter of the Imperium to address her siblings.

"Let's start with what is so special about the placement of the sarsens."

She most carefully straightened her outfit, pressing out any hint of a wrinkle. Fastidious too checked himself for any speck of dust.

"On a natal astrological chart, picture a wheel with twelve spokes." Tien looked to Skye or CeSe for their help. "Could you please use your power of magical thinking to recreate an image of this wheel, and a frame to outline each home so to speak."

CeSe theatrically waved her arms and brought the colored outline to life. What appeared directly above the sarsens was a crystal circle with twelve spokes. Within the spindles was a color-coded overlay with each one of twelve colors marking each house, starting with the color red, right through to the color iolite.

Oohs, aahs, and wows were the collective response. It was quite beautiful to see Tien's explanation come to life.

"Wink and Catriz please stand within the red space assigned to your stone inside the Imperium. This is known as the first house, also known as the ascendant, your placement on the astrological wheel. Note the radius that forms this house is directly due east from the epicenter of the circle," Fastidious instructed, using his kendo shinai to point at the boulder with the red glyph marking of the sign of Aries.

"Remember," Tien continued. "The zodiac is a set of constellations in the orbit of the Sun's pathway through the twelve fields of stars. As we know from Professor Jais's class, each astrological sign has thirty degrees, so that is the degree for each of the twelve houses." She paused to address a Neptunian twin.

"CeSe, please light up each of the houses so that each of us can take our rightful place." A quick wind chime was heard as the space above the stone circle glowed.

"Fastidious, can you please direct so as to ensure correctness of everyone's placement?"

Cling, clang, bling, ding, jingle. The sounds of the triangle resonated as Fastidious enjoyed annoying his siblings with his favorite instrument. It marked the completion of the zodiac circle—all twenty-four of them stood at attention, wanting the clinking to stop.

Tien, looking very professorial and equally annoyed, put up an open hand into the air then closed it into a fist. Silence ensued. "So, as we further explore this ageless science, it is important to remember that the portal to the Tunnel of Infinity only opens and closes during the winter/summer solstices and spring/fall equinoxes. We can remember that Honora testified that she entered this space using the cosmic string during the Fall Equinox. The exact timing of that opening, however, remains her mystery secret.

"To continue: During the spring/vernal equinox on or about March 20, the sun moves from the 29th degree of Pisces, the twelfth and last sign of the zodiac, to 00 degree of Aries, the first sign.

"During the summer solstice on or about June 20, the sun moves from the 29th degree of Gemini to the 00 degree of Cancer. This is always the longest day of the year in the Northern Hemisphere, where we currently are.

"So, for the Fall Equinox, Earth time is about September 20, when the sun passes from the 29th degree of Virgo into the sign of Libra at 00 degree.

"During the winter solstice, on or about December 21, the sun moves from the 29th degree of Sagittarius into the 00 degree of Capricorn. This is always the shortest day of the year in the Northern Hemisphere."

"Enough," a sassy loud voice shouted loud enough to echo around the stones. The outburst was met with murmurs of agreement. "We don't need any more astrology lessons." It was a totally exasperated AlexSandra. "We need to know what we should do next, and what some others plan to do."

Fastidious, always polite, just bowed to her while he smiled to himself. Tien was unhappy to be interrupted, but she did not relinquish her place in the center. She cleared her voice, giving further direction. "We now need to hear from Pen and Nicho. Sometimes, we learn more by the questions we ask than the answers we seek."

"*Finally!*" was the collective response.

Pen looked at Nicho, grabbing her backpack, keeping her treasures safe. She stood fearless as always. "I am out of here. We have our own mission, our own promises to keep." Pen was not putting up with any of this nonsense. No way.

As she walked away from the Imperium her voice was filled with resentment and it was clearly heard. "So, to each and everyone of you, I say, go do whatever you need to, and just leave us alone." Her eyes were ablaze with indignation.

Nicho applauded her resolve and admired her determination. "You know, you are starting to look like them, with those crazy eyes and all, and sound just like them, too."

"*Really?*" Pen glared at her twin. "All of this astrology stuff has nothing to do with our mission, those big boulders, that stupid circle, none of it. Remember, we have our own mission, *our* mission, to find Dad." Pen paused to take a deep breath, and her voice grew quiet as some apprehension seeped into her tone.

"Now what?" Even that crazy lady Honora has disappeared." Pen continued to walk away from their group. "Where is she, huh? Exactly, nowhere to be seen. This is not going to work out. Look at the facts."

Nicho tried a different tactic. "Sure, I know what it looks like; they are all lost, and we are lost too—no Honora, no Uncle Gil, no Dad, no anyone, or anything—and the equinox is almost over.

I get it, but one thing, and it's meant for you. That letter from Mommie—she is telling us we make it back. We make it back, Pen—me and you. We do."

"So, what are you telling me? We have to start to trust them."

"Penelope, you said yourself, they are like a bunch of new kids, like in our seventh-grade class. We can't do this alone. I know you want to, but they are really just like us. We need each other in this. You think they don't feel the same way. The way they are learning to trust each other, we've got to learn that too."

Pen thought hard on her brother's words. "Okay, I guess now is the time," she said, just like that. "I'm not happy about it, but it's time to get moving and go with it, wherever it goes."

She walked most deliberately and slowly to the epicenter of the circle. Still a little hesitant, she pulled the wooden letter case from her backpack. The moment had come to empty the precious cargo into the circle's center. As she opened the case, the twelve moonstones tumbled to the ground, glistening and gleaming just as they did at night on the beach. In the very next second, each gemstone vaulted skyward, hopping, and bobbling in the air.

"Wahoo!" Pen jumped back, eyes wide in wonder and awe. "Hey, you guys, settle down!" she said playfully to the stones. Each moonstone seemed to have a mind of its own—hurling, twirling, and bobbing like a group of twelve protons, neutrons, and swirling electrons. The pathways of the gems were color-coded beams of lights that hovered over the epicenter of the Imperium.

"These are the stones of the Latter Twelfstanin," Pen said proudly as she watched her moonstones spin in midair right above the group.

A resounding gasp could be soundly heard among the twins. "Wow, they are wondrous!" and "Hey, where did you get them?" was said twenty-four different ways as they all scampered to reach the stones.

Wink and Catriz were the first who tried futilely to grab the red centered diamond, but it stealthily alluded their grasp. Next, Witt and Clarity, even with their amazing speed, made an unsuccessful attempt at grabbing their lemon-lime gem, to no avail. Then Thinx and Vespers reached for their amethyst gemstone. "Ouch! What is that feeling of pins and needles? First those little buzzy things are biting us, and now some static vibration that we can't see is around our birthstone; that stings us, not fair."

"No one can touch them, no one but me," instructed Pen.

"What are you saying? That no one can touch them but you, really? We don't think so." Twenty plus voices erupted, demanding answers as they all tried in vain to grab their colored moonstones. "We all have the matching stone, so they are ours too."

Nicho had had it. "Cut it out! You are all wasting time. You, no I mean *we*, don't have much of that left; the sun will be setting soon, and we need to figure this all out. We all have more questions, a lot of them. I know that, and we might never know all the answers, but we do know our roles in this mission: Pen and I are to return these stones back into the Clock. Your task is to defend the planet Earth in a different way. How or why, we do not know, but arguing about the stones is not helping."

The wind blew through Pen's hair, alarming her. "Time is moving. We need to really all work together; if not, then all will be lost." Her voice had softened.

"May we?" It was Fastidious and Tien again. "Let's try this again if you please. We know that we now have some additional energy above us; let us see how it helps."

"Pay attention," came a commanding voice. "We need to finish."

Tien's soothing voice again entered their space. "Some of us have been endowed with the gift of thought transference either cognitively by the air signs, like Thinx and Vespers, Beau and

Gracious, Witt and Clarity, or through intuition by the water signs like Evan and Chance, Skye and CeSe, Mysterious and OnyX.

"Let's all sit in our assigned spaces within this wheel. Everyone, please close your eyes and try to clear your minds. Focus your inner self and await the knowledge that seeks to come your way if you allow it to. Breathe deeply and allow new energies to enter your presence and being. With palms facing upward to face the sky, deeply inhale this most precious gift of the purest air in our solar system. Connect with the vim of the JX that is still present within this sphere. On Chiron, we call this meditation. Allow the vitality that lies within each of our native gemstones to freely escape, joining with the energy of the Latter Twelfstanin. All the knowledge of the past, present, and future to conjoin within our spirit become a part of our collective intelligence. At the count of one, two, three."

Beams of color emanated from every gemstone and moonstone. A fireworks display of light erupted against the late afternoon sky. A familiar twelve-faceted crystal, a stellated dodecahedron appeared high above the circle center, bobbing in a dance with the moonstones of the Latter Twelfstanin. Music filled the air, each instrument playing its very own special song, that very special sound that was unique to each twin. It made them smile.

In that infinitesimal space in time, the knowledge they sought was theirs.

When they each opened their eyes, however, no visible change was evident.

"I'm not feeling too much smarter." It was Thinx.

"Well, maybe it skipped you and came directly to me." Vespers laughed.

Whether the gift of each other's collective intelligence found its way to each of them, no one was sure. One thing was most certain:

although each one of them was still filled with trepidation, they felt more connected, more confident, more centered, and more aligned with their mission to save this planet Earth.

"Hey, Pen, do you think we're on Pangaea?"

"Are you crazy? You are thinking about what we just learned in school, about all of Earth's land mass being one super continent? Is that what is on your mind?"

Nicho continued. "Well, don't you kind of wonder where we are right now. I mean like exactly where we are on Earth right now?"

Pen just shook her head. A minute passed. "So maybe you are right. Where exactly are we? Now, that is something to think about."

"What did you just say?" was her twin's response. Nicho's attention was already off to another question without an answer. It made Pen feel good. "What are you smiling at?" he asked her, puzzled by her grin.

"I am just happy that you're still being you. That' s a constant I can depend on." She gave him an affectionate shove.

Their missions had begun and once again in this moment, they were all together. The doubt still prevailed as to who their enemy might be and how events would unfold. They were learning to live with a promise made without a certainty of outcome, and maybe that was okay.

CHAPTER 17

The Realm of Ahreman

"Maman, why are you not with the twins?" Esme's tone was harsh, almost disbelieving. "After the commotion at the trial with Ahreman and all his melodrama with his theatrical entrance and abrupt exit. He scared all of them. So, why are you still here? Those kids—your grandchildren—will be looking for you. They need you, your guidance, and your help. What could possibly be keeping you here?"

Honora just rubbed her hands awkwardly as she turned towards her daughter.

"I *need* to talk with your brother first. I cannot leave this matter as it stands. I will meet him on his terms, at his domain in space, the Markarian Galaxy 501."

Esme was dismayed, trying to make some sense of her mother's actions. Too many of her decisions as of late were not at all like her. "No, dearest Maman, *please* do not take that perilous journey. Have you really lost your mind? That's what the kids think sometimes, with all your dramatics and flair. Ahreman was outraged about that vote, about what seemed like Gil's betrayal, and not being chosen to lead this mission. Come on, Maman, could you not feel his wrath? The *Sphere* shook from his rage. He can be scary even when he is not totally incensed. You know this; you know him better than anyone."

"Oh, Esme, he handled it much so much better than expected, although he left without a word or a goodbye. I thought he conducted himself quite well, actually. He was always a little more theatrical than you, my dear."

"You are kidding me; you think this is all about theatrics?" Esme said incredulously

"My beautiful daughter, we need to make this right. We must all be in this together, me, you, and your twin. This is all about sibling jealousy, that is all. You are making much too much of the situation. Ahreman never thought that I would toss the Latter Twelfstanin into the ether and beyond. To him, it was just a childish prank; that's all it was on his end. I made a mistake; this is all my fault. Please do not worry so."

Esme was disbelieving. "You're being blinded by your love for him. They, *he* tried to kill you. Have you forgotten?"

"Well now, much worse things have happened, and we made them right."

Esme gave Honora a good hard stare. "Maman, look what he did to that wondrous space he was given. The Algamyth was a most beauteous spot in the Milky Way filled with phantastic cosmic dusk crystals and electrified gaseous elements. The same echo of a piano note's ring was within his very grasp, but he chose a different pathway with his gift."

"No." Honora blazed with anger, her robes turning an ominous shade of indigo blue. "We were not fair to him, ZR and me. We failed him. We tested him to see what he could do; we did not trust him, and he knew it. He was our only son, and we lacked confidence in him. We let him know that we did not have faith in his abilities. We were unfair. To you and Mikai, we entrusted all that we had. We handed over this solar system, in all of its perfection, for the two of you to guard and protect."

"But you gave your son a chance to see what he would do with just such an empty space," Esme countered. "It was a most magnificent and extraordinary cosmos, and you gave to him the opportunity to create his very own sound—his very own piece of the universe to guard and to cherish. Maman, you need to come to your senses." Esme's temper flared as her metallic robes flickered. She waved her arm so quickly her movements could not be seen.

"What did your oldest, dearest friend and comrade Jais say about what Ahreman created? What does he say about how Ahreman caused this black hole to be, to come into existence? Listen to what came to be of his very special piece of the universe that he promised to care for and protect and nurture."

The professor's avatar appeared. He was smiling, glad to be summoned by one of his oldest pupils and dearest friend. With the cobalt blue of the ether to his back, he turned to the celestial blackboard. The Milky Way was the canvas that appeared behind him, a blanket of twinkling stars. With his ionized pointer, he identified an incredible dense spherical object, ominous to view and frightening to behold. He rose high to single out the object.

"'Ahem. Black holes are one of the most dangerous places in the galaxy. It is a region in space and time where the force of gravity is so powerful that no particles, not even light, can escape it gravitational hold.'" The professor's avatar waited for further inquiries.

"Maman, all of this you already know. It is time. There is something you are not telling me, a confidence that you have kept from me for too long. You must tell me what you are hiding, you must. Enough with this family's mystery secrets!" Esme's robes were now sputtering and flashing as she whirled about her mother who remained undaunted, impervious to her daughter's demand for answers.

"At this point, Ahreman's powers are almost second to none throughout the galaxy and beyond. So exactly what is this reason that you need to somehow 'make things right' as you say with my twin? Why would you meet with him in his world and enter the very space where you are the most susceptible to his influence? Where you expose yourself to his domination? Why, Maman, why?"

Honora was very quiet. "Esme, I have been making too many mistakes as of late. It seems like the harder I try to correct them, the more trouble I cause." She looked at her daughter Esme, her eyes filled with admiration.

"You are Esme, Concordaie. You and Mikai, you're the new guardians of this solar system. We could not have chosen better. I was like you, so many many years ago or so I thought." Honora paused and quietly reflected as she continued thinking out loud. "Yes, ZR and I should have passed on—moved on—to the life that exists beyond this one. But I challenged that. I wanted more. Even though we entrusted you and Mikai to complete the mission that was entrusted to us, I was not ready to let it all go. So, no, I did not stay in Varuna. Instead, I came back to the place where I promised not to be. To that very spot where I knew I could replenish my powers, knowing it would deplete the very same environment that we promised to protect. That is all the past. I was selfish, and I took what I thought I was entitled to, but at what cost? I must correct the future, what I think is to come. I must try. I owe that much."

"Maman, what are you talking about? We are all aware of the Tale of the Latter Twelfstanin. Now, you say, there something of greater concern?"

Honora quietly gazed into the heavens that surrounded the great ship. "Esme, how could I not foresee the terrible cost of my mistake? I need to know if I caused this terrible harm and if I can reverse it."

Esme stood by her mother's side, looking into the twinkling abyss. "*Enough!* Now you have put *my* children's lives at risk. No more puzzles. I will not stand down, not if you have put the twins in greater danger than what was anticipated. Let's start from the beginning, the very onset. What mystery secrets have you been holding onto for all this time?" Esme could not even look at her.

Honora took a deep breath, not wanting to further encourage her daughter's simmering rage. "In that singular moment when I created the rip in the continuum of time, there might have been more at risk than the creation of the two parallel worlds. In that nanosecond, I believe the furor of that energy signaled gamma particle beams from the Black Hole to accelerate. My fear is that the rip allowed their ultra-high frequency to escape from the Markarian Galaxy. The destination is Earth; its purpose is to destroy it."

"What do you mean?" Esme gasped. "You can't possibly think *this* is the reason for the hum of discord? I thought, no we *all thought,* the mission was to finally return the Latter Twelfstanin, to restore the hum of harmony—past, present, and future. The dissonance that filled the ears of the Concordaie was heralding the onset of that battle—to put back the gemstones that control the past. Now you are saying that there is another menace that is just as devastating. *You think that ultra-powerful cosmic rays have been hurling towards the Earth for all of these millennia and you caused this to happen. No, Maman, no.*"

Honora met the confusion in her daughter's eyes. "This is what I need to find out. The Latter Twelfstanin constantly changes; sometimes I get a glimpse of what might be, or what might have been, or what could be, or what should be. The future I see is ever changing. The visions, their meanings are elusive to my mind's sight. Your brother might have the ability to stop it or control it. I don't know." Honora now spoke in a whisper.

Esme was exasperated. "Maman, you don't understand what you are saying. How can you tell me that the answer you seek after all of this time is as allusive to you now as it was then? No, you are guessing, trying to right an old wrong, and maybe misjudging what to do. You really don't know, do you? That is what puzzles me most of all."

Honora was dismissive. "Time in time, or time out of time, I know the domain of the black hole is different. The closer you get to its gravitational pull, the slower time moves until its stops completely at the event horizon." Honora was undeterred. "I need to know if the rip in the continuum really caused this phenomena, and if so, why it has not reached the Mrk 501 to trigger the release of those high accelerator particle beams." Honora turned to Esme. "I see that sometimes it's a vision of those gamma particles hurling towards the Earth. I need to know, to be sure if it was my fault or caused by some totally unrelated incident and to know if your brother has a hand in any of this."

Esme softened and looked more closely at her mother's face. Honora now seemed so very old, almost frail.

"Maman, you are thinking in circles. My twin, yes he is most powerful, but he is not omnipotent. That is where you misjudge. However, he is most cunning. He is playing a cruel ruse. I know it. There is trickery here." Esme sounded grim. "Maman, he is always several steps ahead of all of us, even you. He is dangerous, calculating, and formidable—never to be trusted."

"You are too harsh on your brother. His demands for ZR's seat on the Coterie are justified. He feels as his son that was his birth right. Maybe it should be so."

"Papa will never relinquish that seat to him, never. He has passed that privilege to Mikai. This is not your favor to bargain away. Maman, please leave this alone. Your guilt is clouding your judgment. You are underestimating Ahreman, in his desire and in his intent. I am sorry, I know he is your son, but you need to see this more clearly. You are putting yourself in a place where you are most vulnerable, in the very space where his powers are maximized." Esme implored her mother again.

"You need to trust me and my judgment."

"Maman—"

"*Enough!* Enough from you, Esme, as you now sound like the querulous twin. Ahreman's path of destruction is more the result of petulance than evil. He has always felt like he was not treated equitably. There was no real malevolence in his heart. Misguided yes, but not malicious."

"Please, just do as you *promised*—restore the Latter Twelfstanin. Each of us will work together to deal with my brother and these alleged launched particles of destruction. *All of us together, do you hear me Maman—there is a lot of power in that.* Do not go to Markarian 501." Esme's words lingered in the air unheeded.

Honora has just disappeared.

"Ahem. Markarian 501 is an elliptical galaxy located in the Constellation of Hercules."

"Professor Jais," Esme said, interrupting him. "My mother is gone from us." Esme was disheartened.

"No, my dear, she is gone from sight, but not from my mind." He peered disapprovingly over his spectacles. "So, we seem to have forgotten our lessons about the powers of the Quintessence."

～

Honora took flight across the cosmos to her son's place on the dark side of the universe, that very space that he created for himself. Convinced of her son's goodness despite all his wanton behavior, she arrived at the place in space where the gravitational hold was so powerful that neither light nor sound could escape its commanding hold—the black hole.

"Ahreman," Honora whispered.

He turned, his cobalt orbs ablaze. "Mother, I have been expecting you." He spoke ever so softly.

Honora moved to get closer, but in an instant was repelled back by the sheer force of the energy that surrounded him.

"Surprised, Mother? Did you expect a big hug?" His tone was jeering.

"I knew you would come. Once again, you are not where you promised to be, not where you are supposed to be. Aren't those brats waiting for you on Earth?" Ahreman sneered. "You are so predictable, always so predictable."

"Ahreman please, I–I wanted to explain about the vote, about what happened." Honora's voice was soft and appeasing, but she stuttered in disbelief at his words.

"Really, that's the only reason you are here? To see how your beloved son is doing?" A Komodo dragon slithered around its master, moving menacingly close to Honora. She shifted her stance, not sure if she was safe from its venomous bite.

"Afraid, Mother? You never liked certain creatures, did you? All of that farce about taking care and loving all of the creatures, and on and on, just more of your own deceitfulness. Or are you so old now that you really believe the stuff of your own legends or, best said, your own delusions?" He was taunting her, and it was working. "You may wonder why I chose this beast. Think about it, that should be easy. You of all people must know the legend of the Komodo dragon and its boy/girl twins. Shall I share the story? It's quite enlightening."

"No, Ahreman, I did not come here for stories, that I already know." Her voice was tired, very tired. "I am here to make things right."

Enough!" His energy crackled about his presence. "Did you really think I would depend on someone like that weak Earthling Gil to make things as they should rightfully be? He was just a ploy, a mere puppet in the scheme of my plan. You, Mother, your actions, your coming here, that was always in my plan."

He set off a bone-chilling laugh that echoed throughout the surrounding tunnel of emptiness. The giant lizard, too, seemed to sense his loathing and hissed.

"You see, dear Mother, I wanted you to come to me. I wanted to watch you attempt to play mother to me, your only son. To do it in my world, here where I am lord and master." He spat the words out. "Now, you will bend to my will. Feel my might."

"Stop." Honora could feel the bands of gravity that held her at bay. They tightened around her waist and arms. With the wave of his hand, he held her suspended high above him. She felt the bubble of air wrapped tightly around her like a chain.

"Ahreman, what are you doing?"

"What am I doing? What I was born to do—to take your and father's place in the order of things. That is what I am doing," he continued to taunt her. "And you can't stop me. You were a fool to come here, but hubris is and will always be your great undoing." His tone became more malevolent and malicious towards her.

"So, you see, you and I are more alike than you might want to think or consider, dear Mother." His voice was condemning. "We *are* very much alike, you know, you and me. The difference is that you had everything given to you. Everything. Your mission and your tasks were the opportunities that I *never* had. You and father prance about, both of you so sanctimonious. We are all the same, save your precious Esme."

"That is not true. You were given so much more, but you took so much from what you were given. You took the very life out of everything. It's what you would have done to the Earth; you would have taken and taken until there was nothing left."

"Just like you did, Mother, just like you. Why do you think I knew to follow you on your little trips to Earth, to the Imperium. To the very place where you promised not to be. Because I know your nature. Ha! Of course, I know your nature; I am your son."

In his rage, Ahreman was becoming even more unhinged. "See, Mother, when you created that rip in the continuum of time, that is not what caused the gamma particles to leave this Black Hole. That event is yet to happen, now sooner than you may think." He laughed manically. "But, of course, everything is about you, or so you think. So, you came here to do what exactly? Stop me, cajole me, pretend you care about me?"

Honora was speechless with shock.

An eerie bone-chilling chuckle became an echo of terror as Ahreman shrieked.

"You think you know everything? Well, you are not the only one who got a glimpse of the Twelfstanin of Tomorrow. You don't even know what you saw—what you *thought* you saw. Well, Tamzin and Camillus saw the future too. Earth will be destroyed just as it was foretold by your precious Clock." A cruel laugh came from her son's throat. Honora could feel herself weakening at a rapid rate of speed. She looked at her son, overwhelmed with sadness.

"So, Mother dear, how does it feel to have your energy usurped? Hmmm."

Honora now could see his hubris, she saw her son with new eyes.

"How do you think I get all of my power? Did you forget why this place is so dark and soundless?" Drunk with power, he rose to meet her gaze, propelling himself upward, hair and robes widely flapping about his frame. "It's because I need it all . . . I need it all . . . I need it all." His words reverberated about his very presence throughout the abyss of emptiness. Then he disappeared just like that.

Honora tried desperately to be released from her bondage, but to no avail. She was weakened in the moment, knowing that her son took much of her remaining vim, yet her resolve stayed firm.

"Help! Help!" she called out into the ether. "Someone, help me!"

"Ahem. Honora, Honora, this time pay attention." She looked for the voice, but she was completely alone.

"It's Jais." The voice identified itself.

"Jais, Jais, where are you? I can hear you but cannot see you."

"Of course, you cannot see me. I am Quintessence, remember?"

Honora smiled. "Yes, I have been forgetting a lot lately. Thank you, my old friend, for remembering me."

"Enough of that, try to focus. Remember, everything is math. The black hole Markarian 501 will be merging with a small adjacent binary black hole. When they merge, you will have a mere second to do exactly as I say." He paused.

"You and your son never played close attention to my classes. And he, too, has your hubris. If he'd paid attention, he would have realized that when two black holes merge, their combined mass is smaller. So, what that means is that energy is released in the process so the total mass of the two shrinks."

"Jais, please, I am in no mood for a lecture. I am too weak to listen and too pathetic to get out of here without your help. Stop your prattle." Honora sighed.

"You must simply listen, not think. It will waste your precious energy. Get over your anger with yourself; it's in the past. Just follow my directions. Get as close as possible to the event horizon."

"No, not the event horizon. I cannot! I will be forever sucked into its vacuum, destroyed upon contact."

"Stop arguing. You must go to the event horizon but not

beyond it. You must go to the very place where time stops. There is a wormhole in that very space; that will be your exit, and then the cosmic string will take you onward to the Imperium."

"Wormholes—you and your theory of wormholes—as if such things actually exist! *Mon Dieu*, I am in more trouble now then a second ago." Honora shook her head in disbelief. Wormhole theory was one of Jais's favorite subjects.

"Pay attention," the professor continued. "Picture a tunnel with two different points in space-time. They could be different points in space, or points in different times, or it could be both different points in space and time."

"Jais, please, I lack the power and the will needed to find even your wormhole. I don't know if I need to travel a million years into the past or a million years into the future." She was filled with defeat.

"Honora, you of all entities should know about the continuum. Space-time is a mathematical model that joins space and time into a continuum." Jais's tone was admonishing.

"Yes, no . . . I have stupidly traveled to the Hercules Cluster, far outside of our Milky Way. How could I ever traverse some magnitudes of light years and millennia space miles, through a time warp? So much of my power is diminished, so much. Leave me to my own devices here, leave me to what will be my end."

"No, I will not. You are Honora, you are Concordaie, you were chosen, you can hear the sound, and most importantly, you made a promise that you now need to keep. Right now, you're whining like several of those grandchildren of yours. What is the matter with you?"

"Jais, for one who has spent an entire existence just watching and thinking, this seems out of character for you."

"Ahem. Really? First, I would suggest that you stop this childish behavior; it's quite unbecoming to someone of your age. Second, acknowledge that you do not know everything. There are some mystery secrets in this cosmos unknown even to you, my friend. Maybe you should start to learn and understand that. Now, I've had enough. I am now needed elsewhere."

He disappeared.

⟿

"So, exactly where is that Honora lady?

"I wish I knew." Pen was getting really annoyed. "I mean, she *is* the reason we came here, right?"

"Well maybe she's ruining someone else's goodnight sleep." Nicho could not help himself. "Or dream . . . Get it?" He slapped his knee laughing.

Pen rolled her eyes.

"Well, we all know one thing for a fact—and you have to admit this one, Pen—that crazy lady is never where she is supposed to be. Never."

"Nicho," A'dept called out as he approached with his ever-present to do list. Pen welcomed the interruption to her brother's rant as she took a step to let A'dept make his request. "We need your help. As you may note, the sun is dropping in the sky, and we need to set up a glamp, as you say on Earth."

"Camp, it's just called a *camp*. Glamping is something different." Nicho shook his head, exasperated. "So much for all that collective intelligence nonsense," he muttered to himself with a grin, giving Pen a wink. "They would be lost without us here, that's for sure."

About half of the twins went off to explore the new surrounding area. The others who stayed back wanted to create a sense of home and familiarity. Though this new world was strange to the celestials, they knew their minds and bodies were changing due to the pureness of the Earth's atmosphere.

"This is very different for us here on your Earth. We do not have such freedom in our movements in the *Sphere of Comets* or on our home planets. We need to be near the JX that sustains us. What a wondrous feeling for us, to be free to roam." Yejidi smiled warmly. "Thank you for helping us."

"We can feel the changes in each of us too," Excelsia offered. "Just the slightest wafts of your air will make some of us almost superpowered. As much as it excites us, it scares us too. We are yet unaware the extent of our newfound abilities or the repercussions of the possible side effects." She then floated away as soon as she finished speaking.

Nicho and Pen watched the others in awe. Some handled their enhanced abilities better than others. Some acted just like they were given a new toy without restrictions or directions.

"OnyX, you are really good at maps, how about finding a spot for our camp?" Yejidi suggested.

"Right here, X marks the spot," OnyX said, leaning down to draw an X on the ground with his finger.

"Good, let's get started." A'dept as always had the plan on how to build it. "Hey, Domenica, move all of the wood over here." His words sounded like an order, but not his tone.

"Oh, here we go again," complained Domenica, "same old plan."

"Because as Maman would say, some of us are idea people—we have the dream, and people like you—make it happen." A'dept stated and that seemed to be the collective response from some.

"That's like saying you are above the grunt work," said Harm, which earned nods and sounds of approval from some of the group.

Zap! Zap! Zap! Wink was trying to sting Clarity with atomic energy bolts. Skye wreaked havoc, busy whirling up little tornadoes creating tunnels of dust. Some others toiled. Fastidious was being fastidious and watching Domenica.

"You need to be much more precise. Move that wooden beam to the left a bit, no, now to the right. You must follow directions better if this fortress will be completed by dusk."

"Really." A silent volcano erupted as Domenica flung the beam to the ground. "You do it then," she thundered.

Fastidious was so startled, he lost hold of his kendo shinai and toppled over, grabbing at the air to break his fall. He tumbled to the ground, taking the newly built walls of their shelter with him. The booming crash got everyone's attention, and all but one of them scrambled to help their brother. One stayed behind as their golden eyes turned into a flaming red, their dark wavy hair flashed with streaks of blazing orange, and their body emanated heat exacted from the sun itself.

"Cut it out," commanded a voice with a rage unmatched by anything the twins had ever heard before. A moment of stunned silence ensued as they all huddled together for comfort out of fear.

Her display of power not only scared her siblings, but it scared Olympia as well, who was the very source of the inferno. "Hey, so sorry," said Olympia. "I don't know what came over me. Yes, of course, I felt a little irritated with everyone acting so annoying, but then this surge of power just took over. It was wild." She stared at her hands. "It felt great to bask in the sun's rays here on Earth. The heat from my birthplace feels so different to me here; it's like I can't get enough of its warmth all around me." She looked to her twin for affirmation. "Courage, I don't feel like myself."

"Well, just so you know, you don't look like yourself either. We need to learn how to constrain these new enhanced powers and how to control them, not the other way around."

"Well, in any event that was some showing. Wow! Remind

me not to give you or Domenica a hard time." AlexSandra gave an admiring grin.

"I, too, am impressed," said A'dept. "Look, you got everyone's attention. See, they're all quiet now."

"Very theatrical. Can that be taught?" CeSe giggled.

"Let's just get started again; no more acting stupid," Wink said with a wink.

"Already started. This time, how about we build a tree house?" A'dept said with a broad smile, looking directly at Pen and Nicho. "It seems like the earthling thing to do."

This time, everyone was on board, working together, getting their own hands a little dirty. Domenica was so thankful for her siblings' help, she cheerfully took that weighty load right from them, with one fell swoop. The twins from Puzzling Pluto used their power of levitation to assist.

They finished in no time.

"This tree house is gigantic," cried Nicho. "I mean, from the outside it seems kind of small, but on the inside. Wow!"

With a mighty check mark for the completion of their new shelter, it was time to explore the area outside it.

They had each snuck down to the planet Earth before, but each twin looked around them with new eyes, including Nicho and Pen. This piece of the universe was pristine in its splendor and grandeur. It was untouched and pure. The very air they breathed was unlike anything they'd ever experienced, so invigorating to behold. But it was not the majesty of the mountains, or the crystal water in the lakes, or the rolling hills of green or the leaves on the trees that touched the sky, no not just that. It was the new and different lifeforms that were everywhere: the birds that flew across the sky, the fish that swam in the sea, and the various animals that roamed the land. There were even those little things that buzzed around and liked to bite them, particularly Thinx and Vespers.

"Ouch." They simultaneously slapped their necks. "What is that vibration, that low humming sound?"

Pen came walking out of the bushes with a very strange-looking creature. "Look who I found. This little guy is called an alpaca—I usually get them mixed up with a llama, but I am certain this guy is an alpaca. They hum all day, but they never speak; they just hum and hum and hum."

AlexSandra was immediately smitten. "That is our perfect pet, because I will never give him the chance to speak. Come, Alphonso," she called to him. "That is your new name. I want you to meet my twin, Sage."

One by one, each of them found cute little furry things to love. Some flew, some buzzed, some barked, some hopped, some scurried, some swam, some purred, some fluttered, some trotted, some flopped, and some glided, but they all had one thing in common: they all instantly became beloved companions.

"Yes, let's all go home now." Of course, it was Evan and Chance. The twins from the Moody Moon loved being at home more than being anywhere else.

Pen answered more to herself, "Home, that can mean something different to each of us. I want to go home home."

"And I can promise you that you will," Thinx assured her. Pen just sadly nodded. Thinx was becoming a steady companion. "I know what you're thinking; that is why they call me Thinx."

But for Nicho and Pen, their internal battles were just as challenging. Some kindred spirits shared their laments.

"We know how you feel. Some of our siblings show the strengths of the Concordaie, others the leadership skills of the Coterie, but those of the Quintessence, we can feel left out," Thinx said, sympathizing with the Earth twins. "Our gifts are of the world of tomorrow, not yet known. While we watch the others' power grow, ours stays exactly the same. It somehow seems unfair.

You and Nicho were entrusted with the moonstones of the Latter Twelfstanin yet left to your own devices in this mission. Or so it may seem in this moment in time."

Pen tried to smile. "I can't believe how much each of you have changed since you landed on Earth. You are all becoming superheroes, just like in the comic books. Me, I'm just the same old Pen." She felt her role once again blurred into the background, much diminished, while just the slightest touch of her birth planet's air made them almost super.

"That's not true. Just because you cannot see something, that doesn't mean it does not exist." Once again, he started playing with his eyeglasses, checking for smudges. "Some things are right in front of you to see, but there are other things, more important things, that you have to look beyond." After cleaning his glasses, Thinx took several attempts to put them back correctly on his nose and after much fidgeting gave up. "Anybody can see Wink's amazing athletic ability or Domenica's incredible strength or Witt's spell blinding speed, but there are gifts that sometimes we can't see because they come from within. Vespers and I needed to learn that lesson, too."

"At our elementary school, Westfield Friends, we learned that there is a light that shines within each of us." Pen was thoughtful.

"Exactly, everyone has their own unique strengths and abilities. You just have to figure out what that special something is for you, and usually that something is what you like to do the best." Thinx became wistful. "It's like you, Pen. Don't you realize how special you are?"

"Well, no, what makes you think that?" she asked, slightly surprised by the question.

"Well, just think about it. You and Nicho were not only chosen as the guardians of your birth planet, but as the guardians of all of the planets."

Penelope, the fact finder, saw none of that. "How do you figure that?"

"Well, each one of us is only the guardian of our birth planet, except for you and your twin; you were given all of our gemstones, to hold on to and keep safe."

"Hmmm, I never thought about it like that."

"You and Nicho were given that task. For whatever reason, that is another mystery secret yet to unfold. One thing is certain, you were given our birthstones, the Latter Twelfstanin. So, you are the guardians of the birthstones," Thinx said ever so proudly. "Imagine that."

Just then, Pen thought of her mother and felt uplifted. "Thinx, do you know who Nicho and I really are? We are the *guardians of the moonstones.*"

CHAPTER 18

Brothers and Sisters

Although the twins had yet to face their enemy, in this moment, the very thought of defeat was one million light years away. Dusk was approaching, and they all were together in their new camp headquarters—the tree house.

They had discovered that they possessed powers well beyond anything that would have imagined. More importantly, they found a strength in each other that they never thought even possible. They really liked this planet Earth. Its pure air, its natural terrain, its various lifeforms, a climate that allowed a freedom filled with possibilities, and an overwhelming abundance of good feelings.

What was on their young minds in this moment was to learn and play all the earthling games that Pen and Nicho had been telling them about. They wanted to really know what life was like on this Earth as a twelve-year-old and do what twelve-year-old Earthlings do.

"All we are doing is waiting right now, right?" They just looked at each other and shook their heads. It was Wink and Catriz's idea but even A'dept and Yejidi agreed. It was time for a new plan.

"When on Earth, do as the Earthlings do. Who wants to learn the latest dance moves from Willful Mars?"

The Mars twins wore red hairbands with their diamond flashing in the center; more than just for show, they wore the hairbands to keep their hair out of their eyes. Their Marian dance moves looked like hip-hop, or maybe something like gymnastics, but they moved to a terpsichore beat. It got everyone up and moving, bumping, and twisting, and it kicked off the party.

"Tennis anyone?" Olympia would not be outshone.

Resplendent in their signature colors of orange and gold, Courage and Olympia bestowed fabulous gifts to their subjects, even if their subjects were their brothers and sisters. Their gifts of red tennis balls highlighted with gold thread were wrapped in golden foil paper and topped with blazing orange bows. Using reinforced spider webbing, they created a makeshift tennis net and found chalk from a nearby rock formation to line the court. Their ruby gemstones, held in a golden pin worn right over their hearts, glinted as they wacked the ceremonial first serve.

Unwilling to be outdone, the twins from Jolly Jupiter shared their favorite earthling game of soccer. Sage kicked the ball so far into the atmosphere that it almost disappeared, but it was saved by Witt who, with the speed of light, got to it first. Shot blocked. AlexSandra's ponytail was adorned by her new favorite flower, an oleander. Her shiny black patent leather tap shoes showed off her turquoise gemstone that adorned her ankle bracelet; it was a real showpiece. It matched their cyan blue sheaths.

Tien spotted the rosebay immediately. "Hey, you, with the ponytail. That flower, it's poisonous."

"Ugh! I knew I should have stuck with my original choice. Amaryllis best suits my personality. Lucky me, I suppose." AlexSandra would not give her brother one inch of acknowledgment that she made a mistake.

Lucky really, well, sometimes I suppose. "Just give it to me, Tien and I know what to do with it." A far-flung whizzing soccer ball was AlexSandra's way of saying thank you. Tien was unimpressed.

Music and more music could be heard everywhere.

The kids all were happy for once to play their earthly instruments on Earth. The twins from Silent Sedna sang instead of playing the violin. When Domenica and Harmonious harmonized, even the stars seemed to shine a little brighter, and the moon moved a little closer, just to listen. Both wore long green scarves around their necks, kept in place by pins bearing their emerald birthstone.

Ding! went the ring of the triangle. It was time for Fastidious and Tien to share their mystical secrets of the ancient martial art of kendo. "Who wants to be a kendo master?" Fastidious asked. Everyone pushed forward to be the first volunteers. With exact precision, the perfectionists from Clever Chiron moved through the exercises as their siblings attempted to copy the combat stances. Eventually, everyone tumbled to the ground in a massive ball of confusion, laughing and wrestling with each other. Fastidious and Tien were careful not to wrinkle their new deep blue silk garments that perfectly matched their sapphire rings.

After a while, some of the kids started to get tired and wanted to go back inside the treehouse.

"Do you think it's safe for our camp to be out in the open like this? Chance asked, just a little worried.

"You are right," Skye agreed. "Let's find somewhere less conspicuous for our hideout."

"X marks the spot to our new *glamp*." Clarity could not help herself.

With the help of Mysterious and OnyX using their power of levitation, the twins from Serious Saturn moved the treehouse to a safer hiding place, so as not to be detected by any outsiders. A map of its precise location was kept by Witt just in case it was needed for some unforeseen reason. Rope ladders hung down, allowing everyone to climb up, and once inside, each one of them was given a special handmade present: a backpack.

A'dept and Yejidi approached Pen. "We have admired your purse that you wear on your back. We thought that everyone should have one just in case supplies are needed, as it's—"

Pen cut them off, laughing. "Important to plan ahead."

"Yes, it is." The twins from Serious Saturn grinned at her.

"Since we are all here, let's play a game of ping-pong," signed the twins from Dizzy Mercury. All eyes were upon Witt and Clarity who played the game by themselves. Moving so fast, they could not be seen, the whizzing noise, or the echoing breeze of their blazing speed was duly noted.

"I know how to stop them," Wink yelled. "Time to play the banjo." The dizzying twins stopped.

"We waited for you to ask; let get the band going," signed Witt, grabbing his favorite instrument.

The piano joined the banjo, and then the flute, cello, violin, horn, drums, fiddle, sax, percussion, harp, and chiming wind. As first they didn't sound so good; it was a wild and chaotic session. The noise was so loud that the mountains shook, the oceans swelled, and the trees bent, but the longer they played, the better they sounded. Someone set down the beat, and one by one, they each recognized their own timing and rhythm.

It was like Professor Jais said, "everything is about math," and that was especially true with music.

With the appearance of the Evening Star, the night's first light in the western sky, the juggling magicians from Pretty Venus took the center stage. "Tai chi, whirling, or magic tricks, you choose, because we can't make up our minds," Gracious called out. She was wearing her signature gardenia flower behind her ear; its color was the softest white, with an opaline shimmer.

Whirling was the overwhelming choice, and each one tried to outdo the other in the pacing and balance of the movements. As the party moved towards its crescendo, a chilling breeze moved through the nighttime air.

"Ice skating anyone?" CeSe asked.

Using the powerful magical wind of the midnight air, the twins from the windy-blue planet froze the top of the nearby lake. The music of the air current surrounded each twin as they glided upon their icy crystal stage. Excelsis and Skye then shared their gift of magical thinking with their brothers and sisters while attempting to jump double lutzes and axels high above the icy surface.

As the tempo of the night slowed down, everyone moved back to the tree fortress, and Nicho asked, "Who wants to learn to play board games like the kids do on Earth?"

Tien and Fastidious could not wait. With all those rules and regulations, this was their indoor sport for sure.

"How about we play a game of cards?" Pen suggested. She and Nicho could not wait to teach everyone their favorite games.

Vespers and Thinx were the first to sit down at the card table. "We're ready if you are," Vespers eagerly announced.

"Okay, so let's play for a penny a point." Nicho winked at his twin.

"Or a nickel a point." Pen giggled as she winked back at her brother.

"We don't know about a penny a point or a nickel, but we sure do want to learn," Thinx said with a grin. The twins from Wacky Uranus picked up card games very quickly, poker being their very favorite.

OnyX and Mysterious challenged their siblings with a thousand-piece puzzle. "Whoever figures it out first, we have a mystery secret to share," OnyX offered, knowing there would be a few takers on that bet for sure.

As the midnight hour approached, moonbeams played tricks on the nearby lake. It was time for the twins from the Moody Moon to take charge of the night's entertainment. As the full moon surfaced and cast its light over the mountaintops, the Moody Moon's shadows danced upon the water, and Evan and Chance showed everyone how they could disappear in and out of the pools of darkness. Then while Chance played the bagpipes, Evan told scary stories about the dark side of the moon to the mesmerized audience.

"Here on Earth, we like to sit around a roaring fire on the beach and tell ghastly ghostly stories too," Nicho said. "Pen and I always have a contest to see who can tell the best, or the scariest one, and then neither of us can fall asleep; it is so much fun."

The gauntlet was thrown, and once more the games were afoot as they all tried to top each other with wild, creepy, spine-chilling tales. Within the hour, they were all so scared that they could not even think about falling asleep.

Suddenly, the wind made its presence known. It howled and swirled about two figures who seemed to rise out of the midst on the lake's center. Their platinum hair was wild and disheveled, while their kaleidoscope eyes exploded with neon colors. The power of the wind enhanced their voices to an unnerving pitch. Their words were spoken as a divination.

"Beware the time when the moon is not moody."

Each one of the celestial twins stared, spellbound by Excelsis and Skye's words, and all but two were captivated by the prophetic warning. Nicho and Pen just stared at each other.

"That was, like, pretty weird," whispered Pen.

"You think? Don't they know this is just a game?" Nicho frowned. "Just when you start thinking that these guys are somewhat normal, they start to act super weird."

"I'll say." Pen nodded. "They act like we're supposed to pay attention to whatever those two say. Those phantasmagoria moments of theirs are pretty wild, though, don't you think? And those two are already weird enough, even without those crazy-looking eyes. They' re always so somber. They might have superpowers, but they have zero sense of humor."

"Have you ever seen them laugh?" Nicho asked.

"Come to think of it, no," said Pen.

"They seem to disappear a lot, too, or maybe it's more like they are around, watching everything, but they don't want to be seen," Nicho mused.

"Yeah, a lot like Mysterious and OnyX—those two just don't want to be seen, period." Penelope paused for a moment, considering the celestial twins. "Look, Nicho, none of them got to go to a normal school; they've just learned everything from up there in that star thing where they only have Esme and Mikai, and they have each other. That must be kind of boring. I mean, yes, they have that whole universe thing, but it's always just them; they never get to meet or have any new friends. We have our beach, our ocean, and our sky and new friends every summer who are different from our school friends, and we have neighbors, both the summer and winter ones—everything changes for us throughout the year. They just seem to have only each other, and everything seems to stay the same for them. Their whole world might be the cosmos, but even that without the comings and goings of people can make it small."

"I guess you could say they are homeschooled."

"Or maybe its more like star school schooled," Pen said with a smile.

Nicho grinned. "Or spacey school schooled."

"Or outer spacey schooled," continued Pen.

"Yes, but they don't get out much," roared Nicho, cracking up at his own joke, slapping his knee again.

As they made their way back to the camp, they smiled to each other, sharing their enjoyment of one known fact. Nicho and Pen finally felt like they possessed a power that the rest did not, and that felt good.

"Hey, Pen, you are starting to look different to me," Nicho said suddenly.

"You know, Nicho, now that you mention it, you're starting to look different to me too."

"Must be this pure air," he said, flexing his muscles.

"Must be," grinned Pen cartwheeling.

The guardians of the planet Earth started to feel their confidence growing once again. They started to see that they, too, possessed something that the others did not, something that was very important: experience.

~

Fun time was over.

Mysterious, always restless, wanted to check the perimeter of the campsite once more. Everyone else was asleep in their tree fortress, or so she thought. She looked up to see that someone else was awake and keeping watch on a nearby hill. She stealthy made her way towards that person.

"What do *you* want?" asked Nicho with his back still turned to her.

"How did you see me coming? No one ever sees me coming." Mysterious was miffed.

"I don't need to see you coming, I can sense it. You should know that by now." Nicho turned to look at her, his face serious. " You know, I don't like the way you talk to my sister. If you don't trust us, then leave Pen and me alone. We don't need you or whatever help you can offer; you can just keep your superpowers to yourself."

Mysterious was caught off guard by his bluntness. She considered his remarks. "Okay, that is fair. I'd like to talk to your sister. Where is she?"

"Pen is off looking for answers in her own way. She likes puzzles, she is a lot like you actually."

"I know." Mysterious gave Nicho one of her stares. "So exactly what are *you* doing now?"

Nicho was impervious to her attempted provocation. "Doing what I always do: stare at the nighttime sky, looking for *my* answers."

Mysterious took a seat right next to him, just as Pen showed up.

"That Honora is nowhere to be found" Pen announced. "So maybe she will fall from the sky or do whatever it is she does or however she does things. She was supposed to meet us here. She's the reason we got roped into this. Why *we* came to do this. To think it all started with that voice on the beach."

"We just should have ignored her and just gone home. Just walked right back to our beach house and gone to bed. Yep, get a good night's sleep. No wild, zany dreams—you know, the normal stuff. What were we thinking listening to some strange voice? Why? Because it sounded like Mommie, who was right there in the house. What were we doing, leaving Mom anyway? Better yet, we followed and did what she said to do. I knew she was a crazy lady. So, *we* must be crazy too." Nicho was exasperated with the whole situation.

"Oh, stop it, will you? What Honora said was convincing, at least to me it was. I believed her. No, we both believed her." Pen held fast to that knowledge. "Dad must have believed her, too. We are here to get Dad back, period. That Clock, those moonstones from the beach, that Twelfstanin thing—those are all unknown to us. Who knows what will happen with all those unknown things? For the first time, I don't need to know all of the facts. If we get the chance to see Dad, it's worth all this guessing. That is why we are here. You know how I hate not knowing *everything*. You are the one who never cares about facts, you are the one who likes to make decisions based on your feelings, your *intuition*. So, you choose now, of all times, to want to know what is actually going on. Of all the times, you pick now, really? Cut it out!"

"Pen, you are not thinking straight," implored Nicho, wanting her to understand.

"Hey, what's up? I can hear people's thoughts even when I am sound asleep." Witt stirred up a cloud of dust as he walked towards them. Clarity whizzed right behind him and caught a glimpse of Mysterious' face and became alarmed. "What is up with those wild-looking eyes?" Bands of maroon, hazel, and topaz intensely blazed around Mysterious' dark opaque center.

"Stop staring at me! You two always get on everyone's nerves, just buzzing around and around. You never do anything but want to know everyone's business, but you never mind your own. Leave me alone!" Mysterious started to retreat from the group.

By now, all the kids had woken up and started to gather around. Sleep was no one's friend, not tonight.

Beau and Gracious looked uncomfortable at Mysterious' outburst, never wanting to take a stand or divulge any of the secrets they kept hidden in those spinning lockets of theirs. The full play of color within their lockets gave that all away—they were spinning and spinning uncontrollably, loaded with lots of hush-hush stuff.

"Humph! Well, just so know, you are not the only ones keeping mystery secrets, Miss Cloak-and-Dagger," Sage taunted. He could not wait to show off what he knew, too. "I know your little secret because I saw you."

"Me too," signed Witt. *"I know what is going on, too. We told Beau and Gracious."* Witt was signing away almost at the speed of light. *"See, there are our colors, lemon-lime; look at them glow in*

their spinning lockets." Witt got so excited, he unwittingly tripped over his brother Skye, who also had a guilty look about knowing what he knew and was also trying it keep it to himself.

It was Yejidi who turned to leave, shaking her head in dismay. "Secrets, some of you have been keeping secrets! Each of you ignored Maman's words; you should all be ashamed of yourselves." Yejidi then paused to give Skye a harsh stare. "Maman trusted you and Excelsia the most of all of us; you were supposed to know better. You did let not just let us down but her as well." She turned her back on the group. "This mission is doomed; it will never work if we don't work together. Enough of these childish games. If anyone feels they're above the others, then we do not need you, nor do we want you or your help. We can do this alone without you."

Those left out of the circle of secrets felt betrayed and deceived. It struck a despondent chord within each of them. They retreated to their tree fortress, not even turning to look at their siblings who'd kept their secrets to themselves.

For Nicho and Pen, the ugly moment seemed like an eternity, and a sense of dread rose within them. They knew there was a ring of truth to each and every word Yejide had just said. That chance of failure was all around them, it overwhelmed them. Pen had not a clue and Nicho not a thought on how to make all of this right. They had defeated themselves. All the good feelings from the festivities that marked their special night had all but disappeared.

Then, amid the solemnity, came the clear timbre of the saxophone. That sound was meant for someone; it was her instrument, and Mysterious heard its calling. Without making eye contact, she instinctively touched her onyx gemstone bracelet. There was no jolt of power or surge of energy that she could identify, but the stone emitted a feeling of warmth. The distinct vibrations made her safe and told her, "You are protected."

When Mikai gave this precious gem to Esme, they understood

the power that belies its layered bands of chalcedony quartz—at its core, onyx encourages emotional courage. The mere touch of the cool black stone empowered her; the energies emitted from this special stone were for her and only to be worn by her. It helped Mysterious entrust her feelings to her family.

"Hey everyone, come back. Come back please. I'm sorry." She was surprised to hear her own words. This time she made sure everyone heard her voice loud and clear. "Hey, I am really sorry. Please come back." She waited for all her family to return and gather back around, and then she continued.

"Okay, so when everyone was busy building the treehouse, I went off exploring by myself. You know how much I love caves and secret hiding places. This time was different; there was this voice in my head that was telling me to go in a certain direction."

"You, who trusts absolutely no one, listened to some strange voice which told you to go somewhere, and you just followed its directions?" OnyX was incredulous.

"Oh boy, do I know about that voice—that voice is nothing but trouble, trust me." Nicho completely understood now. "Okay, Mysterious, I get it, but no more mystery secrets. We know that voice; it's the one that brought us here. Believe me, somehow or someway, you'll end up doing what that voice tells you to do."

Pen stood strong. "Let's hear it. There are forces that we need to learn to understand. So far, we have only been given direction by Honora."

"You mean a.k.a., that missing crazy lady," Nicho added.

Pen felt back in the game now. "We need to be open with each other. Let's figure out who this other voice is and try to find out what they know." Pen's gift of being a puzzle master was needed in this moment, and it allowed her to seize control of the situation.

"Let's take it step by step." Pen took out her journal from her backpack.

Clarity followed suit, signing, *Just in case you miss something, I promised Maman that I would keep a journal too and write down everything that happens on this mission.*

Mysterious continued. "Well, I just started exploring and found these really big rocks that blocked the entrance to this very narrow cave."

"How did you get through them if it was blocked?" asked Pen.

"Duh, I moved them, of course."

"I thought you were going to try to be friendlier." It was that sassy voice again, as AlexSandra gave her sister a reprimand.

"Okay," Mysterious replied, looking sheepish. "You're right. I was, you know, able to levitate them with my enhanced powers. They blocked—no, they safeguarded the entrance to this labyrinth of spiraling panels of solid stone." Mysterious stopped, taking a pause as she wanted to get this exactly right. "It felt like a cave, but it wasn't a cave—the top was open so I could see the sky. It was amazing. Soft colors covered the walls of sheer rock that soared very high up into the air. Snippets of sunlight came and went, peeking through the various twists and turns."

"You are describing a slot canyon," Pen said, interrupting her.

Nicho nodded. "We just learned about those in our environment class. They are long, narrow, and treacherous canyons formed by the wind and water that forged their way through the sandstone and limestone over the millennia."

Pen shared, "They are very dangerous; sometimes they flood in an instance from water, and sometimes the pathway is so narrow you can't pass, but the most treacherous thing, you can get completely lost in them. I mean forever lost."

Mysterious' eyes now contacted the twin who she felt understood her the most. "Exactly, Pen. Upon entering this maze, all of my senses were heightened. The air felt, no it smelled different, and I could see crystals in my breath as it vaporized, I could also hear the sound of rushing water, but I couldn't tell from where the sound was coming. The echo was soft and subtle, like the wavelets gently splashing on the shore. Sometimes, the echoes sounded like music, but it was disconcerting, because it felt more like a warning than a song. It made me feel afraid."

"What did the cave look like inside?" Pen was now super curious.

"Everything was overwhelming," Mysterious told her. "There were vast spiraling walls that glistened in soft rose and green. It scared me. The illumination of the rocks came from within the minerals of the stone itself, so it looked crystallized. A soft wind felt like a hand at my back, propelling me forward, deeper, and deeper into that unknown space. That voice, too, guided me to go farther and farther into this very narrow tunnel. Then I saw them; they were right in front of me."

"Saw what?" Pen asked.

"The glyphs, the same markings that are on the Talking Panels, they were carved on an imposing solid wall of granite! It was that wheel, the one that CeSe and Skye created for us to see, but this wall was sealed and gigantic. All twelve panels were carved on the circle, and the glyphs depicted within it, right there in front of me."

"Wow!" was the collective response.

"Yes, but it gets even creepier," Mysterious continued. "An invisible force held me in place, stopping me from getting any closer to the panels. Talk about a puzzle! I was not allowed to move past the very point where I stood. Something held me solidly in check, so I turned around and ran out, the very same way I entered."

"But I thought the slot canyon was a maze, how did you know where to retrace your steps?" it was Pen.

"I didn't have to, I was guided right back out, the same way I

was guided to the wall of panels." The Plutonian twin paused. "
I felt too scared to tell any one. I then thought it was a dream or
something that I was just making up in my head."

Clarity's hands moved so fast they were a blur as she signed,
*Is this map accurate? Is this where the entrance to the slot canyon
exists?*

Mysterious just nodded as she made a mark on an area of the
map near their camp. "X marks the exact spot, of that I am sure,
but once I got inside, well my memory became hazy, or maybe I
am not supposed to remember. I don't know."

Just then, the eerie song of the bagpipes filled the air. The
moon was approaching its fullest face. What should have been a
time filled with answers was instead filled with more unanswered
questions.

"Let's start again with CeSe's prophecy." Pen steered the conversation, retaining complete control.

"'You mean, 'watch for the time when the moon is not
moody?'" Evan said as she and Chance suddenly appeared out of
the shadow of moonlight, accompanied by CeSe who also emerged
from the darkness.

"The Moody Moon is your home," resumed Pen. "What do
you think it means? You must have some idea."

"Well, our moon has different faces as it waxes and wanes, but
during the full moon Chance and I are most powerful because—"

"Because you are full faced. A full moon represents the whole,
like this group when we are all together," Pen finished.

"Look," said Nicho, tilting his head back. "It's a full moon
right now."

Every set of eyes stared up at the midnight sky. The moment
of the Fall Equinox, the Harvest Moon, was upon them. That very
singular moment, it had finally come.

Out of nowhere, Professor Jais's avatar appeared right above the epicenter of the Imperium. He announced himself with his characteristic "Ahem."

It was unexpected but wondrous as the celestial wheel appeared in the sky with all the astrological constellations perfectly positioned in each of their twelve homes, divided equally along the orbital pathway of the 360-degree circle.

The professor's ionized pointer directed everyone's attention to the radius of the seventh house of Libra.

"Attention if you please. During the autumnal equinox, the Sun has just begun its transit into the Constellation of Libra, at 00 degrees. During this very particular time, as you can see, both the Harvest Moon and the Equinox are occurring simultaneously. His pointer then illuminated another radius bordering the twelfth and the first house, on the direct opposite side of the circle.

"So, at the very same moment, the Moon has now entered the constellation of Aries at 00 degrees in the first house. Please note that the Sun and Moon are in Direct Opposition in the Celestial sky, see from Libra to Aries. In the study of astrology this is known as a time of awareness.'"

Oohs and aahs could be heard all around.

In the next second, the nighttime visual display disappeared back into the Milky Way, as did the professor and his pointer.

The twins all stayed where they were, staring at the spot where the spectacle of lights had been, some with mouths agape in wonderment. Then came the clash of the cymbal; it was to get moving, fast.

"It's time," Yejidi announced as she and A'dept gathered everyone together as they moved towards the tree fortress.

Both Nicho and Pen lagged back as the others followed Yejidi. They needed to think hard about another set of lessons. Honora's words of caution to them about the Tunnel of Infinity became alive in their minds.

Pen precisely repeated Honora's words. "'Both *in time* and *out of time* exist in a parallel continuum, but the time and space within the Tunnel of Infinity moves mysteriously, but always in conjunction with the stars, planets, and moons. So entry into that space is tied to the moment and placement of the solar system.'"

"That's what Honora said, but what is that supposed to mean anyway?" Nicho countered. "Sometimes I think she just talks in riddles because she does not know the answer." Even Nicho did not feel like trying to intuit Honora's motivations anymore.

"But wait." He bolted upright. "Our time and space moves alongside their time and space just in a different parallel, correct? So, it is all the same. Time and space within the Tunnel of Infinity is not tied to anything because it's outside the very sphere of time and space that affects both parallels. It is of a different realm entirely, where no law applies, or maybe different laws."

"Well done, Nicho, well done." Yep, sometimes, just sometimes her twin could be brilliant—maybe. Pen was listening.

"So, she doesn't know," said Nicho.

"Who doesn't know?"

"Honora, she has no idea. I don't think she really understands that tunnel. The tunnel will open and close at a precise mathematical calculation. It is always all about math, whether in time or out of time; time might exist in a vacuum, but the math still applies. Right. So, what we need to figure out is *how* those rules apply within the realm of infinity. Think about what Dad would say: *the rules of math do not change.*"

"Yep, he would say exactly that," Pen agreed. "So, it's the show of the time-space continuum in that tunnel."

Nicho was exasperated. "You know what, I like her, I really do, or I think I like her, but that lady sure does make a lot of mistakes."

"You mean Honora?"

"Yep." Nicho shook his head with chagrin. "Maybe it is because she is old, but she just gets things all mixed up. I don't think she means it, but she sure does get herself into all kinds of trouble."

"And to quote"—Pen laughed, looking directly at her favorite twin brother—"she is never where she is supposed to be."

"Exactly," said Nicho. "Let's go. It's time."

The twins from Earth started to get ready for their own plan. The time for action was upon them too. As the others were getting ready in their tree fortress, someone noticed their absence.

"Hey, where did Nicho and Pen go?" It was AlexSandra, always keeping score.

Now, it was Beau and Gracious's turn to step up as their lockets started a tell-tale spin.

"They went to fulfill their own mission. They, too, have their own promises to keep, just like we do."

CHAPTER 19

The Circle at Midnight

It was midnight by the great Circle of Stones. All the twins had gathered back at the treehouse, to plan their next move, all but two. Nicho and Pen quietly made their way back to the very spot where it all began, to the Imperium. Their going was not missed, and they had not told a soul they were leaving.

Bands of colors emanated from each of the twelve stones, light beams that spiraled above the apex. An ethereal display of varying shades of green, red, violet, bluish white, and yellow shimmered in a dance of flickering lights that swirled, but the air was still. Whether this was a natural phenomenon or just plain magic was a mystery secret. It really did not matter anymore; it was spectacular to behold. Something was going to happen, they knew it. They could feel the energy building, pulsing, as it grew stronger.

Nicho and Pen moved fearlessly past the giant boulders of the circle, into its very heart. They looked around expectantly, but Honora was nowhere to be found.

The twins wavered with resolve. Maybe she would not come, maybe she was never a part of the plan. But they knew they had to be patient. This was a game of wait and see. So they waited.

"Do you hear the hum; do you hear that perfect sound? It's the hum of harmony." Pen was in awe and happy to share the moment with Nicholas.

"*Wow, finally,* I can hear it now too. Pen, I can hear it all, and it is pretty amazing. Do you feel this energy, the get-up-and-go? I can feel it pulsating through my body. It must be that secret element: JX."

She agreed. "It's not that I feel stronger, it's that I feel more empowered. I feel like I can do anything, and best of all, I am not afraid, not at all. Fearless, I feel fearless and confident."

Nicho nodded. "So now we know the difference between being fearless and feeling fearless. I like the latter."

It was all so enthralling, the sights, the sound, the aura, and the infused vitality. Of greater import, it felt like it was all meant just for them. Finally, after all of the confusion, the learning and realizing that there was something greater out there, this was their very moment. And it belonged only to them. There remained, however, one question on their young minds. Where was Honora? She would never have abandoned them, but what would delay her? What could be of greater importance than this?

"Now what are you doing?" Nicho looked at his sister who was just staring straight up.

"I am looking for that cosmic string. It's got to be here. You know, the one that Honora uses to come in and out of this place from wherever she is. Please don't tell me you were not paying attention again and being super stupid." Pen's mercurial penchant for being annoyed had returned, and it was aimed at her twin. "Never mind, I will look for it, all by myself."

"Pen, it's not a string on a trap ceiling door, it's a portal." *Now who is being super stupid,* but he kept those thoughts to himself. "That is why we can't see it."

"Yes, but it's here, right here, the opening. Remember her story about what happened? That's why we came here. I have an idea. Let's just call out her name and see if she drops out of the sky."

Nicho shook his head. Sometimes even his fact-finding sister had some goofy ideas.

"Well, do you have a better idea? It's the Fall Equinox and the Harvest Moon. Honora told us that the tunnel opens in this very moment, and closes in the same, so she better come right now."

Nicho knew one thing: his sister was right; the time was now.

With a loud and clear voice, he shouted upward to the sky, "Honora, Honora, we are expecting you. We are here waiting at the cosmic string. Better hurry up!"

Pen took a different tactic. "Honora, Honora, come out wherever you are."

Now she is playing hide and seek; my sister is really losing it. Nicho shook his head. "You know what, Pen? You are starting to sound a little crazy like the rest of them."

"So, I will ask you again: You got a better idea? Didn't think so, bro." She turned to her brother with her green eyes ablaze. "Come on, Nic, she would not just leave us. She must be in some sort of trouble or need our help."

In some sort of trouble, yep, that sounds just like the Honora he knew.

Suddenly, from her imprisoned space on the Event Horizon, Honora heard it, his voice. She could hear Nicho calling for her; though he sounded sarcastic, she could still hear his cry for help. It reminded her of the promise she'd made to them, the two who needed her most in this moment. *Come on, snap out of it, Honora,* she commanded herself. *You can make it all right because you know you can and you know you should. These kids need you. Enough!* Honora's unbridled will and defiant determination took hold over her as she gathered all of her remaining strength. *Focus, focus, you know you can do this, of course you can do this.*

It was Nicho who heard the sound of her voice first.

"Nicholas, you both need to listen to me very carefully."

"Hey, Pen, hey Pen! Wow, I can hear Honora's voice in my head. She is talking to me! What do you know, she actually answered."

"What are you talking about? Now who is the crazy one?" Penelope snapped, crazy eyes still afire.

"Shhh, I can't hear her if you keep babbling. She is telling me, no she is telling us, what to do." Nicho looked up at the stars and concentrated on the voice speaking to him from across the cosmos.

"Stay in the very center of the Circle of Stones; remain in place for as long as you can. Stay. The element JX, absorb it. It will raise your JQ. Take it in, fully and completely. You will need all of those enhancements. This is your time, right now in this moment. Be still and know this belongs to you." Honora's message was faint from far across the cosmos. Sheer force of will propelled her thoughts, forcing her to escape the impenetrable bonds of the Black Hole, because she to had promises to keep.

"Honora, we are here, just like we promised. It's the full face of the moon. Hurry up. We are waiting here, right in the very center, staying put." It was Pen's imploring voice she heard this time.

"And soon, I will there be too," was her response.

~

Back at the tree fortress Thinx stepped outside once again to look at the nighttime sky.

"Wow, Vespers, hurry up, it's the aurora borealis! It's right over the circle. This is the first time we'll ever get to see it looking up from the planet's surface; we've only ever seen it looking down from above in the *Sphere of Comets.*"

Everyone scrambled to see it. "Wow." "Double wow." "Hey, can we touch it?" someone called out from the crowd.

Thinx and Vespers just shook their heads. "Sure, why not. Go ahead and try," said Vespers sardonically. She whispered to her twin, "Sometimes even twins who are deemed super, say super stupid stuff."

"Bet that is where Nicho and Pen went," came other voice.

"You *think*." It was Thinx, feeling the very same as Vespers. "Of course, that is where they are."

"Let's hurry up, come on let's go," said one of the twins. "Let's go find them."

"Let's have a race to the Circle and see who comes in first." Catriz threw the gauntlet. Galvanized by her challenge, twenty-three pairs of legs stampeded right over top of her before she finished her sentence, leaving her decidedly last.

"Hey, not fair," she called out as she dusted herself off.

Sage and AlexSandra got there first. But it wasn't the aurora borealis they saw when they arrived, it was a display of colored lighting and energy unleashed within the stone circle, the rays emanating from everywhere. In the very center it looked like Nicho and Pen, but it was hard to be sure with all of the colored static.

Eager to aid their new cousins, they rushed to enter the kaleidoscope of electromagnetic beams but were repelled back by a forcefield. A blinding burst of high energy violet light crackled forth as they neared the stones, sending them flying back.

The rest of the group caught up and saw the dazed twins from Jupiter. They all tried to enter the Imperium as well, but to no avail. All were thwarted in their attempts to enter the space. The interior was off limits.

But maybe not to all.

The twins checked on Sage and AlexSandra, who were only

wounded in pride. Frantically everyone milled about the circle. Each afraid to feint to enter, fearing near electrocution.

"Wait, hold off, everybody!" Tien cried. "We're wasting time. I suspect we use the electricity. Thinx and Vespers are the key!"

"Why do you think we are able to enter that Imperium now?" Vespers and Thinx looked quizzically at Tien.

"Well, we believe that electricity is your element, right? Remember when we first landed inside the Circle of Stones; you both felt that pinching."

"You mean those buzzy things that bit us?" Thinx asked.

"No, not the buzzy things," said Tien exasperated. "Pay attention for once and listen."

Thinx and Vespers focused. "Remember when you tried to touch your amethyst gemstone. You felt a pins and needles sensation when you touched it. There was some kind of static electricity that seemed to surround only the two of you. The electrostatic energy was all around when you were in the circle. So, it stands to reason that you and Vespers must be a part of the energy that is generated in that particular space. It must be so."

"Got it." Thinx nodded his understanding.

Tien continued breathlessly. "We have got to breach into that center arena of cosmic energy."

Vespers frowned in concentration. "Okay, I see what you are saying, Tien. As much as I hate the sensation, it is our element. Let's get into the center, Thinx." Squaring her shoulders and taking a deep breath, Vespers led her brother into the haze of colored static.

～

"We can hardly see you, Honora, you're almost transparent." Pen was dismayed. "What happened to you?"

Honora had materialized thinly and collapsed on the rocky

ground. She studied her hands. "I was almost at the point of nothingness, but I needed to be needed. I needed to be here, and I am. I heard you calling me, Nicholas. I heard your voice."

She inhaled a deep breath, taking in the JX. "This is where it all began, the first of my series of mistakes. Right here, in the very epicenter of the Imperium, within this Circle of Stones." The twins just stared at her, still seeing the crackle of energy that clung to her robes.

"Here is the locus of power," Honora told them. "This is the very spot where all of the energies from the planets, stars, and moon intersect to create the most unique elemental combination within all the galaxies. Here, the oxygen, nitrogen, hydrogen, and carbon mingle and link together with Jxyquium. This is it."

"But we thought that the JX was almost depleted?" Nicho knew he was on to something.

"Well, almost." Honora smiled; clearly, she was holding something back.

"So exactly where were you?" Pen asked.

"I was trapped in Markarion 501."

"A Black Hole, you were in a Black Hole. How did you ever get out?" Pen quizzed, always curious. "Wait a second, how did you get from there to here?"

"Well, let's just say my old friend, Professor Jais, reminded me of few things that time has made me forget."

Honora then looked directly at the two of them, addressing Nicho first.

"There are other forces at play now. You will need to use all of your heightened senses to deduce what is real, what is trickery, who is helping, and who is thwarting your mission. Use your power of the sixth sense and use the fifth element—one of your gifts—but look to your sister for the facts." Then she turned to Pen. "Both of you, keep your minds and your hearts open. Remember this promise, help will find you when you really need it. We have much to do and little time."

"At least we will discover the truth once and for all," Penelope declared, secure in knowing all the facts would be revealed.

Honora nodded in affirmation, then hesitated. "Perhaps." Then, with her theatrics returning, she exclaimed, "The truth, what is the truth? Does it really exist? Maybe truth should remain an elusive concept until it becomes the irrefutable past."

"There she goes again, talking in those riddles," Nicho whispered.

Honora's face told the story of guilt and remorse. "Remember, the tunnel, it will be filled with the trickery of the past, the present, and the future. Do not trust what you see, hear, or surmise."

Nicho looked knowingly at her. He gave her a reassuring smile, seeing all the regret on her still-frail face.

And then what happened happened.

They heard a rushing roar. What appeared to be a shower of meteorites began to rain down on them with a formidable show of force.

"Now what is happening?" Pen pivoted wildly to see the burning objects striking the ground all around her. "A meteorite shower, what else could it be?"

"No, they're not meteorites—look, once they hit the ground, see how the hulls dissipate. It looks like the capsules that brought us here from the *Sphere of Comets*," Nicho cried.

"So, they're like little spaceships," exclaimed Pen as she whirled around to face Honora. "But exactly who is in them? This whole thing does not feel very friendly."

Honora's face revealed her alarm. Esme's words rang in her head, "'Maman, Ahreman is always a step or two ahead, always...'"

"Do you know what's happening? Pen asked.

"Yes, yes, I do." Honora looked grim. "It is Ahreman's Army

of Everters. They must have followed me as I entered the cosmic string." *Of course, they followed me, again,* she said to herself. "This is not friendly, not at all. We need to stop them; we need to stop *this* now."

Pen and Nicho blinked at each other uncomprehendingly. Who could stop these invaders midair? Their minds searched madly for an answer, and then the penny dropped for both of them. They knew there was only one way to stop the onslaught. Then, Honora pointed to a strange coruscation of color moving in their direction. Suddenly, Vespers and Thinx materialized through the violet static into the midst of the Imperium. "This has to stop!" Honora shouted at them. Instantly, they knew what she meant and knew the only two people with the power to do what needed to be done. Pen and Nicho knew the very same.

Turning immediately, the Uranian twins created an electro-magnetic wormhole along the radius through to and beyond the stone circle. "Yejidi, A'dept, make it stop!" Nicho's voice roared above the explosions. "Come quickly into the center! We'll hold the wormhole open as long as we can, but you must hurry," Thinx thundered, his voice blooming though the interference.

"You must make time stop! Make it happen, you have the power, do it, do it now. Make time stop." Vespers' voice too reverberated through the incessant explosions.

The twins from Saturn were galvanized by the cry for help and did not hesitate to leap into the portal that their siblings had created. No amount of planning could have prepared the Saturnian twins for this very moment. They'd never used their unique gift without close supervision. It was a power never to be used lightly and without discretion.

Bursting into the center of the circle, with the wormhole crackling close behind them by inches, they had no chance to consider if they were up to the challenge. The meteor-like crafts were raining down around the small group huddled together. Honora spread her cloak over herself, Pen, and Nicho to try to protect them from the shrapnel that exploded from the impact of the landings. Vespers created a magnetic net over her brother while he held the wormhole open, but protection was limited.

Yejidi instantly reached out to A'dept's hand. They were face to face. In unison, they tore the garnet clasps from their shoulders and touched the two gems together. A massive, rubescent globe pulsed between them where the smaller stones had been. The twins were ensconced in deep ruby light, faces to the heavens, radiant to behold. Raising their hands high, they stuck their palms together in a clap that dwarfed thunder.

"Arrete temps!" Their voices resounded through and around the Earth itself.

And it did.

Time had indeed stopped, but it was already too late. Time would prove once again not to be a friend.

The last meteorites hung suspended, but myriad crafts had hit the ground already, turning into monochromatic explosions of sand. In the midst of the sand clouds fused with silica and minute particles of glass stood menacing figures. As first they were colorless and transparent, much like Honora, but the longer they stayed in the Earth's atmosphere the more their eerie shapes began to take on solid forms.

These were the minions of Ahreman, formed by him from the spent energy that remained after he had extracted the potency of the atmosphere of his domain. They were the waste products of his pillaging. He needed minions and had not cared what they looked like. They were vaguely humanoid in shape, with discernible arms and legs, but these appendages were distorted, misshapen—the spent matter had just been thrown together with no thought of symmetry.

Their skin was so white that they appeared bloodless, with a blue cast around their jaw and eyes. And those eyes were opaque white orbs with a tiny pinprick of a black iris that expanded instantly when aroused but not with defined edge. The black iris burst like a jagged pattern, ragged, and blurred. They were heavily armed with all manner of blades and shields made of Xyzanium, their armor too, just as indestructible. Their feet were talons, gripping and grasping the sand and rocks, making scratching and screeching sounds. But what was most unnerving was the sight of their bare torsos. Their sternums gaped apart with each breath, ribs opening to grasp prey, to envelop it into themselves and consume its energy. Each chest cavity was an iron maiden. Even Honora paled to look upon these abominations, and she had seen Everters before.

The huge figure approached, his face ominous and filled with disdain. Honora recognized him immediately.

"Acerbus, so you are still doing my son's bidding, I see," she called out. Her voice was strong despite the revulsion she felt.

"We have come, old women," the creature rumbled, its mouth a blood red gash.

Honora turned to Nicholas and Penelope. With grandmotherly affection she caressed their cheeks as they knelt next to her. "As you can see, I am needed to be right here, right now, in this place, in this very time, to do what needs to be done. By now I hope that you have come to realize that each of us was summoned here for a special purpose. Each of us chart the map of our destiny through the choices we make. Sometimes we are told of our missions, and sometimes our roles remain hidden from us. There is an invisible bond that connects all things. We are all one. It is the universal string of humanity that holds the entire cosmos together in a bond of connection and purpose. Do you understand?"

Pen heard her words but could not grasp their import. "You are using the first person singular a lot. It sounds like your destiny departs from ours. You sound like this is a final goodbye."

Honora could see her disappointment and sighed. "Pen, remember to keep your moonstones close by your side; they belong only to you. It is your purpose to return them to their rightful place, wherever or whenever that might be. Most importantly, have faith and confidence in each other, and only in those you know you can trust. You can do this, and you will do this. It is time for you to meet your own destiny, as I *finally* need to meet mine."

A familiar lavender mist enveloped Nicholas and Penelope. They could feel the sensation of being uplifted and the tug of floating away from her to a different place.

Honora winked. Her parting words floated upon the midnight air.

"We each have kept our own mystery secrets. Our special missions, yours and mine, were never the same." She looked directly at Pen as the mist closed in. "That is a fact you always knew. You will learn to understand why when what happens happens."

～

"Here we go again. I thought this cloud travel thing was behind us." Nicho covered his trepidation with a show of irritation.

"Guess not," Pen whispered shakily.

The twins knew they were no longer within the vicinity of the Circle of Stones but could not see where they were being transported. Distance, travel, and length of time felt distorted. When they were released from their vapor cocoon, they were confronted with their new destination, with a new adventure. They faced the entrance to the slot canyon, the Tunnel of Infinity. A scene of destruction was before them, with the massive sarsens that guarded the entrance left askew. A sense of foreboding was palpable just looking at the broken boulders that were left scattered and fragmented.

Nicho glanced around and noted, "Well, I guess we should thank Mysterious for paving our entranceway. The boulders haven't been replaced to block our entry. That's one good thing."

Pen did not share her brother's optimism.

"Honora, Honora," she called out her name, knowing it was in vain, but still persisted. The only sound she could hear was the empty echo inside this mysterious dark tunnel. She finally stopped, admitting defeat, and let out a big sigh. "We trusted her, and now she is helping them. Really? What about us? It's like we don't matter. We're all alone." Pen was beyond distraught as she knew her pleas would go unanswered. "Is she completely insane? Was this all a trick of some sort? We're going to die, right here, I know it." Indignation was building inside of her.

Nicho echoed Pen's outburst. "I told you she was a crazy lady, I told you. And another thing, for someone who was chosen to help create this whole universe and be its guardian and whatever she goes on and on about, she sure does say one thing and then do another. I can't figure her out. Now she has got a different mission, so she just drops us here, in front of this labyrinth of walled stones. Thank you so very much." Nicho was flummoxed, and just like his twin, well beyond being just cross.

"We—I am not going anywhere, not inside this spooky cave, or slot canyon or whatever she calls it. I am going to wake up from this dream right now!"

"Me too," said Pen. "I am going to close my eyes, and when I open them, we will be back on the beach and out of this stupid nightmare. This game is over. Think about it, Nicho, this lady who falls from the sky tells us *she* makes some big mistake that we don't really understand and now it is all our problem. Really? She just blunders her way around the universe, past, present, future, and just goofs everything up all the time. Well, I am going to force myself to wake up; this time, I have had enough. I am mad right now, I mean it, I am really mad at everybody."

"Well, look who is finally back: Hurricane Penelope." Nicho was amused; he'd been missing her old temper tantrums. Then he stopped just as abruptly.

"Hey, Pen, your eyes are getting that crazy look again, you know, like the rest of those spacey twins. What the heck? Pen, calm down, you're scaring me. That green is like really green but your gold flecks, well, they look like gold lightning bolts . . . they really look like those orbs like that other guy has. Cut it out."

Nicho gaped as he watched his twin transform before his eyes. Bands of color started swirling around her, hair blew wildly, and those eyes were just getting more and more ominous.

Nicho looked around widely. "Okay, a little help here. I really do need a little help and I need it right now. Okay, come on, come on, we need some help; my sister looks like she is going to explode or something worse, so *help*!"

And then what happened happened, just as Honora had promised them what seemed like so long ago—help will come when you need it the most."

It came in a blaze, a crackle, a flash of sparkling light, and it whizzed right by them.

Penelope suddenly snapped back to normal. "Hey little guy, I was wondering where you went all this time." She turned to her brother. "Nicho, what is wrong with you? You look like you just saw a ghost. What is wrong with you now? I would have thought that you would be happy. Look who just came back."

She pointed right inside the entrance to the slot canyon. "Isn't that your 'broken star?'"

~

Back at the Imperium, a different kind of undertaking faced the other twins. Everyone's confidence was waning at the uncertainty of the task that was before them. It looked grim, as least in this moment.

Acerbus lifted his battle-ax and the electrical charge protecting the sacred centre stuttered and disappeared. "Come in, children," he gurgled, with a sweeping bow, a warped parody of courtesy. The twins, unsure, stayed in place.

Their leader continued, "So, Honora, let us formally thank you. You did it again. All we needed to do was follow you once again towards that now infamous cosmic string of yours. Ahreman said you would be predictable, and you never fail to disappoint." Acerbus was gloating.

"And I can see that my son, he also remains predictable. As usual, he sends someone else to fight his battles for him. You are so right; some things never do change." Honora stayed looking frail and diminutive in the epicenter of the circle, apparently too weak to get up.

"What is your purpose here, Acerbus?" Her voice sounded drained from exhaustion.

"Our purpose should be clear to you; we are here to take over your precious planet. Unlucky for you, and lucky for us, your time has long since passed." He could not help himself from laughing at her pitiful state.

"This Earth is ours. Who is to stop us? These stupid kids of yours? Surely not, and you, Honora. You're so very old and very weak, you couldn't stop anyone. You can't even help yourself anymore."

"You have no right to be here. The Coterie banished you to Eris," she snapped.

"If I remember correctly, you and ZR were banished to Varuna, but that didn't stop you from coming back for the very same reason—you wanted immortality."

"We were not banished—"

Acerbus cut her off. "Oh really? You and ZR always thought that you were better, more perfect than all of us because you were sent here first. Oh yes, the words you use, you were 'chosen.' And yes, you were the most powerful. You were—yes, *were*—powerful enough to contain Ahreman. Yes, were almost omnipotent, but even your powers always had its limits."

Acerbus was eager to continue with his rantings. "My master, he was always two steps ahead of you. Your hubris is and was your undoing."

Acerbus warmed to his theme. "You know, Honora, only you would have the power to escape from the Black Hole. My master knew that you would get out. He not only knew you would get out, he counted on it. But we all also knew how much of your energy that you needed to expend to leave that Event Horizon; you are probably completely powerless at this point."

"Others will stop you." Honora stayed on the ground, allowing Acerbus to talk and talk.

"Who? Your precious Esme and Mikai who stayed behind, hiding in that twinkling home of theirs? What do they call it? The *Sphere of Comets*—their little hideaway. How loathsome must they be to send their children into battle because they are too afraid to fight this battle themselves. I bet they're watching us right now, just sitting there like usual, always watching but never protecting, never acting. You are right about one thing, those two are certainly naïve. That's why you chose them; you would always have control. Oh, and the Coterie, those old fossils, where are they now? Their time is over, from a beyond era, just like yours."

"You will never succeed; I can promise you that. There will be others." Honora still crouched in her same spot, unmoving. While her voice was defiant in tone, her lavender cloak seemed to weigh her down. She seemed to be swallowed up by the folds of her garment. It was as if the might of all that had happened was just too much for her to bear any longer.

Two more Everters approached. Tamzin and Camillus moved to the front of the menacing force and stood beside their leader.

"Hey, you remember us, right?" Camillus taunted, pointing at the lunar twins. "You, the little chubby one, if I remember correctly, you're not so tough. You and your twin are the crybabies, right? So where is your twin, hiding in the moon shadows?"

All eyes turned towards Chance who was visible in the light of the full moon. "Hey, do you still get a tummy ache every time when you get scared?" Tamzin's tone was mocking. Chance cowered, but for just a second. Before he had the chance to retort, his sister Domenica's temper erupted in a blaze that could rival Mount Vesuvius.

"Hey, you," she snorted. "You better leave my brother alone, or you will be really sorry. I'm warning you, do not make that mistake."

"Really, and so what are you going to do about it, huh?" Camillus taunted.

Domenica, with a clarion battle cry, fearlessly responded. With a mighty shove she rushed both bullies and brought Tamzin and Camillus both to their knees. It caught everyone off guard. Then the army of Everters growled with delight as the gauntlet had finally been thrown. They raised their murderous blades. Everyone readied their positions for battle. Their legion totaled in multiples against the twenty-four. The odds were not in the celestial twins' favor, at least not in that moment.

But then a reverberation came from within the Circle of Stones. It was the howl of discord, cacophonic and painfully harsh. The mighty sarsens shook. The Earth trembled. Everyone looked for the cause of the tremors.

It came from Honora—all of it.

Everyone was stunned into silence, as they stared in complete bewilderment. In the very epicenter of the Imperium, Honora grew tall like a towering vine, her hair silver, blowing wildly with the wind that seemed under her total command. Metallic sparks crackled around her, and her piercing eyes changed to the color of blood. She threw off her cloak, and her platinum armor was revealed. Moon beams glinted off her breastplate as she boldly turned to Acerbus.

"Enough! So, you actually think that only you and your band of vagabond warriors are the only ones whose powers grow stronger with each passing moment on this planet? My patience has grown very thin, and my time is even shorter. Your powers, Ahreman's powers, Esme's and Mikai's powers will always and forever be second to mine, and right now, as I speak, second to some others here present." She looked at the twins, her grandchildren. "Come on, let us show them who we really are, eh?"

"I am Honora, I am Concordaie, now feel the power of my true might."

All twelve sets of twins just stood there with their mouths hanging open.

She turned to them and smiled. "So, are you all going to just stand there?"

With a shout, Wink moved first, dashing towards the invading force with a spectacular triple somersault that felled three Everters.

Catriz simultaneously wielded the object of her favorite pastime, as she flourished her sword and shouted out a jubilant challenge: "Fencing anyone?"

The battle to save the planet Earth had begun.

CHAPTER 20

Tunnel of Infinity

They just stared and stared at it, not wanting to make a move.

"Here we go again, just like before," Nicho muttered. The stellated dodecahedron lay just as when it first appeared, resting with two prongs wedged into the sand, the other ten points sitting upright.

"Yep, there it is," said Nicho in an unsure voice.

"Do you think this was the help that Honora was talking about? Just like when we got that letter from Mom?" Pen tried to puzzle this one out.

"*Help*? Are you kidding me? When has she ever helped? Come to think of it, we have been helping her all along, not the other way around. That crazy lady is nothing but trouble."

"Maybe that's just it—maybe we don't need her help—maybe we just need each other. Did you ever think of that?"

Nicho's brows rose and disappeared into that mop of fringe on his forehead. What a thought! He was a little in awe of his big sister.

"Hey, Pen, you really did figure this out. Methinks that maybe that JX gave your JQ a big old boost. Of course, it's still not as high as mine, but you definitely got one big bump."

"Really, is that what you think? Okay, little bro, pick up your star and let's go with your great big, ginormous JQ."

Nicho laughed to himself. Who was really the smarter of the two? That would always be a cause for banter. But he knew one thing for sure: Pen was surely the more fearless of the two. That was a fact.

Meanwhile, they both knew that somewhere, out there, over there, mass confusion ensued on a battlefield of unfair proportions. A trained intergalactic army was waging combat against a class of middle school kids, while they were headed into the Tunnel of Infinity to replace the moonstones that control the tick of time. Pen and Nicho paced back and forth in trepidation at the slot canyon's entrance, worried about their new friends. They had grown very fond of their distant cousins and grappled with not being with them to help. It was hard to not be fighting alongside them; just as it was hard to face their task all alone. But this was their mission.

The Earth twins were not exactly sure where they belonged. One mission was a brutal battle against a formable enemy; the other mission was one of uncertainty. They had to do something but remained apprehensive about doing anything. They were really just plain old scared.

Confidence and uncertainty became interchangeable. Of course, they were in the realm of the Tunnel of Infinity, so emotions, past, present, and future, melded. Focus, that was the key. They needed to concentrate and stay in the present and stay the course of their mission.

"So, let's just take it one step at a time, and see what happens," Pen said, wanting to hear the sound of her own voice.

"Okay, so how about we at least go inside far enough to get my star," Nicho reasoned. "Let's see what happens once we get that far. From there, we'll do as you said, take it one step at a time."

They moved with apprehension; an overwhelming sense of foreboding crept up on them, intermixed with sheer wonderment of the space that surrounded them.

"Wow, look at this canyon!" Pen was enthralled by the moonlight filtering so beautifully through the carved rock formations as they moved deeper and deeper inside the maze-like trail. The shadows painted pictures, silhouettes, and ghostlike figures across every surface.

Whatever was going to happen next would transform the entire order of the universe. At least that's what they'd been told, but right now, in this quiet moment, the mesmerizing charm of the soft hues and imprints on the walls were beguiling and seductive. "How beautiful it all is . . . how beautiful."

Adventure was upon them.

Shades of purple, green, blue, red, yellow, silver, and gold moved along with the flickering shadows within the rock's crevices. The shadows on the stones moved, too, in contrast to the harsh stalwart mineral walls. It was as if the two entities within the sandstone itself were at war with each other. The past and the future were struggling to dominate time. It was both powerful to behold. Nicholas and Penelope could feel the sheer energy that encompassed them and tried their best not to be overwhelmed by it.

Pen clutched her moonstones tightly, as they traversed the labyrinth. She knew that their only chance of finding their father and getting back home to their mother rested with the success of her mission—replacing the Latter Twelfstanin back into the Clock of Perpetual Motion, the regulator of time—at least that's what she thought. *I do wonder Nicho, what is your role in this?* Keeping that to herself. *What could it be?* She knew they were in this together. Again, the thoughts of the ferocious ensuing battle happening nearby distracted her, but that undertaking was for the others to embrace. This was Nicholas and Penelope's time to worry only about themselves and each other. Pen needed to concentrate on where she was and what she was doing in this very place and time.

Slowly they approached the spot where the star rested peacefully, waiting for Nicholas. Pen moving slightly ahead thinking it best to keep it safe with her moonstones. Gingerly she reached down to pick it up.

"Ouch!" she yelped, snatching her hand back.

Sparks of electricity emanated from the little stellated dodecahedron, giving an admonishing warning to Pen.

"Okay, I should have explained myself to you first," Pen said, addressing the miniature star. "I was only going to put you into my backpack for protection. Sorry to upset you." Then she added to herself. *Such a temperamental little star.*

"That's my star, remember." Nicho approached his luminary with reverence. As he reached down to touch it, bright bands of color radiated from each point. Then with a mere touch from its rightful owner, it bounded five feet up from the sand. The twelve-pointed star glowed and bobbed as it circled about them. "Well, hello to you too, little guy." Nicho laughed.

As they continued on into the canyon, the gloom deepened, but the star, its sheer radiance, provided them with plenty of illumination as they moved cautiously through the narrow gorge.

"My very own private flashlight." Nicho beamed. He knew this was the help that Honora referred to, and truth be told, they needed the little guy's guidance.

"So, my little friend, my little buddy, lead the way. Go forth!" Nicho flourished his hand theatrically.

"You're getting on my nerves." Pen could not take his showing off. "What does that mean 'go forth'? Now you sound super stupid again. This place is no joke, and I don't know if I trust that thing. He does not seem reliable the way he just comes and goes."

Pen's mind was on a different pathway. She had read a lot about slot canyons, how they could become dangerous in the blink of an eye. A sudden rainstorm could fill such a narrow space in a torrent of water, engulfing everything in its path. She listened hard for the sound of rushing water, but her senses—like some other things in this strange and bizarre place—were not to be trusted. Everything here was too mysterious and incomprehensible. It all felt downright puzzling, even for her. Pen always needed to trust the rules, and now everything was unfamiliar. *Keep to the facts, Pen,* she told herself. *Just keep to the facts.*

"Remember, September is a rainy month." A familiar voice popped into her head. Why did that bother her right now? Who said that to her?" She shook it off.

Trust was the only feeling she wanted to embrace. She felt confident in the hope of seeing her father; it was that hope that propelled her forward. Despite her youth, Pen was tired of being played and unimpressed with the abilities of those who deemed themselves superior. Her mission was to bring her family back together again. But the closer she got to that place where she needed to be, the more anxious she felt. Her confidence waxed and waned like the Moon.

The slot canyon twisted and turned with myriad tunnels appearing and disappearing. It was as though even the moonlight was playing tricks on them. Nicho had complete faith in his star, and that was his one true guide. Pen depended on something very different.

Honora's words came back to her. "'You may think that some random force brought you to this place and space in time, but you will come to learn that here, there are no such things as coincidences. That is a fact.'"

"Stop banging into me," cried Nicho. "You are making me and Silvio nervous."

"I am listening for the sound of water; everything echoes in this cave, and I'm focusing on not drowning, if you don't mind."

A good thing one of us is, she thought, and then in the very next second, "Hey, who is Silvio?"

"My broken star. I wanted to give him a name." Nicho grinned.

"So, you want to give your stellated dodecahedron a name. Really? That is what is on your mind. What happened to the super high JQ of yours?" Pen sounded incredulous.

"Well, all of your moonstones, they have real names, so why not my little buddy."

"What? There you go again getting on my nerves with stupid stuff. What names? They do not have names." Pen was exasperated.

"Well, they do have real names: at least, names for what they look like. Think about it in astrological order: Crystal, Emerald, Peri, Pearl, Ruby, Sapphire, Opal, OnyX, Turquoise, Garnet, Amethyst, and Iolanthe, all girl names, just saying. So why can't my little star have a name? Look how the moonlight makes him glow silver, so his name is Silvio."

Pen had other things to think about, but she knew that what seemed like irrelevant tangents of thought were mental distractions. They helped her brother compartmentalize his thinking. It helped him to free his intuition. Her mind did not work the same way, but she understood her brother.

Suddenly, Honora's words of caution seemed to reverberate through the walls of crystalized rock. "The Tunnel of Infinity is a dangerous place—always unpredictable and relentless in changing what was, what will be, and even what can be. Learn never to trust what seems to be real, even if it will hurt you deeply." Those words spun around in Pen's mind; they were meant for her. What could possibly hurt her so deeply?

Just then Silvio started to dip and bobble, hitting them both gently on the head to get their attention.

"Pen, it's going to happen, happen real soon."

"I sense it too, Nicho."

They were so close to their destination, so very close to the moment when everything would be as it was before what happened happened. Resolution, a conclusion to all of it was just within their reach. A frission filled the air within the cavernous halls, and now even the moon itself peered down into the narrow canyon, joining in, guiding them to their ultimate destination.

Silvio, too, spun and spun alert in place, signaling that something was upon them. They'd reached the canyon's narrowest point and stopped dead in their tracks. The passage was a mere sliver. *Maybe it was too narrow to pass through*? they worried.

"So how come Mysterious did not mention this? Not one word about this impediment. Not one hint that this trail gets reduced to a slit! I know she can levitate, but she and OnyX are very powerfully built. No way she slipped through this narrow slice of rock, no way."

"Remember, Nicho, this place plays tricks. This rite of passage might be only for us to cross."

"Maybe . . . hey, thanks a lot, whoever thinks this is funny up there, out there, over there, wherever you are." Nicho always used humor to deflect, especially when nervous. Sometimes it worked, sometimes it didn't—like now.

Pen peered closely into the narrow gorge. "Nicho, I can't tell if it tapered more in the middle. I don't want to get stuck."

Silvio illuminated the passageway; the narrowness of the gorge was not their only problem. "Oh no," she groaned. "It looks like more bad news. Wink and Catriz's gemstones are embedded throughout this space. Look at how they are glittering in the rocks. Now what?"

"Oh great, right again, Pen; they are diamonds. We are going to get sliced to pieces if our skin comes into contact with them."

Nicho put his finger inside the gorge to test the sharpness of the gems and pricked his finger. "Ouch!" Going through here is really going to hurt. No way that Mysterious dealt with this, no way. These challenges are definitely just for us. Someone or something wants us to turn back."

Pen reasoned, "We don't know that. Maybe that is the reason, maybe not. We need to figure out if we can safely squeeze through these two torture panels."

"Or we can be stuck in there, like, forever. Or we can die a death of a thousand cuts before we get to the other side. Thank you once again, Honora. I tried to tell you that she was a crazy lady—"

Pen just cut him off. "Not now, Nicho, not now."

"Okay, then let's go to plan B. We give a little cry for help like Honora told us; it worked the first time, right? Silvio came, so let's try it again." Nicho looked upward, thinking his voice would carry. "A little help here, a little help if anyone is listening somewhere out there or in here or over there—a little help if someone pleases." Nicho knew to always be polite when asking for help.

They waited, and waited, and waited some more. Nothing happened, nothing at all.

"So now what? Any more of your bright ideas?" Pen asked.

"Give it a moment, a little patience, *Prudence,* if you please." Prudence was his secret name for his sister, his little joke with himself. What made it even funnier; she never really caught on to why it was so funny.

Silvio agitatedly hobbled and bobbed about Pen, irritating her even more. Then they both heard a familiar voice.

"Ahem." There he was again. It was Professor Jais, no, it was his avatar.

Nicho groaned to himself but addressed the apparition most politely. "Professor, we need help, not a math lesson."

"No, actually this time our lesson is all about geophysics," the professor replied. With a wave of his hand a rectangular panel appeared in the air, filled with various calculations and mathematical equations that covered the entire slate.

Silvio illuminated the professor's screen.

"Well, it sure does look like math," Nicho declared, not wanting to be corrected.

"Ahem, pay attention," Professor Jais admonished. With his ionized pointer he swooshed Silvio away. "Be gone for the moment."

Silvio burned red, letting the professor know that he did not appreciate his attitude, nor his tone.

Jais ignored the little star and began his lesson. "Geophysics is the use of quantitative methods of analysis that deal with the physical prospects and phenomena on this planet Earth. There are different branches of the Earth's sciences; in this case we are dealing with the subject matter of fluid dynamics."

Pen already had enough of the science lesson and the professor too. She wanted facts and wanted them now.

"Look, we all know that this gorge was formed by water— ocean, river, lake, flood, something. Save us all the details on the quantitative analyses of these mathematical equations that we do not understand. Okay?" Her voice reflected her exasperation. "So, let me keep this simple. Is this gorge consistent in the space between these two jagged walls?" The professor just blinked. "Okay, let's try this again. Is the space between these walls consistent in width the entire length?" Still no response. "Let us be clearer: are we going to get stuck and die within this diamond-lanced coffin?"

Professor Jais's avatar gave her a blank look and flatly responded. "That, my dear, I do not know." With that comment he disappeared.

"So much for asking the heavens for help. Now what?" Pen glared at her brother.

"Enough of this. Hey, Silvio, come here little guy. You are about twelve inches all the way around, right?" Nicho coaxed. Silvio started to spin yellow.

Pen thought to herself. *Oh great, now he thinks that thing is his pet.*

"I heard that." Nicho smirked.

Pen stared back at him, but he didn't reply.

"Remember how we held you with two hands when we first met?" Nicho asked, and Silvio was starting to playfully bob up and down. "Go see how wide that passage is for us, will you? See how easy it is for you to fly through it and come right back, okay."

Nicho intently watched his new buddy traverse the narrow slit in the rock back and forth several times. "Pen, I think we have about eighteen inches consistently through to the other side. We might come through a bloody mess, but we will not get stuck. That is a promise."

"I'm smaller than you, so let me go first." Pen eased into the aperture.

"Ouch! The cut diamonds are on the ground, too, I can feel every step cutting through my sneakers." Pen slowly inched her way through the narrow corridor.

"Try to control your breathing. Try to concentrate." He cheered his sister onward.

"Nicho, I can't take my backpack, I just can't. It's too hard to drag it, my hands are all torn up." Nicho reached his hand in to grab it. "Don't worry, let's give it to Silvio. He will make it happen. I trust him."

"Nicho, he is not a person, he is a star thingy." Pen grunted as she wormed her way deeper into the crevasse.

"Not true, Pen, not true." Her brother bristled. "Remember when Esme told us that the *Sphere of Comets* was a living thing. Remember when the heart of that big ship whimpered because of

Ahreman's evil. Remember when Honora told us that everything is a link in a chain, a bond of connectors throughout the universe. So, how about Silvio? He's here to help us. We must trust him. That is as real as it gets, so it is a fact."

She felt like she was in the narrow corridor for an eternity, but slowly, surely, Pen made it through to the other side. She looked back, giving her brother a bloody thumbs up. Cautiously he began inching his way down the narrow passageway.

"Nicho, now what are you doing?"

"I am holding in my stomach and making myself thinner, so I don't get stuck." Pen just shook her head and thought to herself. *Maybe less ice cream would better do the trick.*

"I heard that, and it's been a whole day since I finished mom's pint of Rocky Road. Hey Pen, Rocky Road, get it?" Nicho resorted to humor again, as the distraction helped him forget the pricks and slice of the diamond defile.

Finally, he tumbled out of the pathway with Silvio hoveringly protectively, almost nervously, over him. All three of them, backpack included, made it through that challenge. It had drained them both physically and mentally. Quickly they inspected each other. Other than some wicked looking rips and tears to their clothes, and scratches to their hands and face, the twins were intact.

With that task behind them, they readied for what would lie ahead. Turning to look down the trail, they saw their next challenge. It did not disappoint.

"So, what exactly do you think that is?" Nicho wanted to distract his thoughts from what was plainly obvious.

"Are you referring to that dead end, right in front of us, that impenetrable wall of stone that is blocking our way? Is that your question?" Pen was getting really annoyed again.

Nicho shrugged. "Now what?"

"Don't start calling out for help," his sister snapped. "Not that again. I don't need the professor telling us what we already know. Look at this fortification!"

There it stood in all of its grandeur, a magnificent solid marbled wall. It soared high above them, nearly blocking the sky. Its formidable presence loomed above them, breathtaking in majesty and colossal dignity.

Nicho found his voice first. "So, everything is indeed—"

Pen gave him a sharp elbow. "This is beyond math, beyond physics, beyond science—this is beyond anything I could have never, ever dreamed or even imagined and it's right here in front of us. Can you feel it?" This must be what Mysterious felt even at the start of the trail.

"Well, with her particular energy and her powers, she must have fit right into this place," Nicho mused.

Pen agreed. "That's fact. All of this sheer power and energy holding you in place and it all is emanating from this escarpment. It's a fortification built never to be breached—an impenetrable wall of stone."

"Well, that crazy lady finally did something right."

"Not funny, Nic, not funny at all. Now what?" Pen was starting to feel overwhelmed. "We can't just turn around and go back. We can't just quit!"

The wall of crystalized marble sealed the entrance into the inner chamber that housed the Clock of Perpetual Motion. Honora had created this barricade to bar entry into Omnia Tempus. They knew that somewhere on the other side of that wall was their ultimate destination. They were so close, so very close to success.

Nicho took a deep breath to help himself focus. He instinctively stepped back to get a better look at the barrier of looming stone. He even pushed that mop of hair out of his eyes to get a better look.

His intuition paid off. "Hey, Pen, this wall is not so solid."

"What are you talking about? Of course it's solid." Pen again snapped at her brother, frustration clouding her judgment.

"No, it's not. Take a few steps back and look more closely. You will see what I am talking about, I promise. This must be what Mysterious saw, but she did not get a good look at it. Remember she was held in place, so she could not get close enough to really see. It is not solid, that is a fact."

Her brother delivered on his word. High up, on the rock's face was etched a 360-degree circle. The carving was deeply incised with the twelve colored glyphs. Twelve radii that extended from the center to the circumference measured exactly 30 degrees along the perimeter. In the epicenter was an opening, maybe for a Key of Access of some sort. It was hard to tell with absolute certainty— but that aperture had some purpose. It was no accident of natural formation. Someone designed that orifice with a specific intention. It was another mystery secret.

"That Honora always has more tricks. Why did she fashion an exact replica of the Circle of Stones on this barricade? You think the way she just left us here, she would have left a clue. I like her, but now she is starting to really drive me crazy too." Nicho scratched his head, waiting for their next move to be revealed.

Pen moved very close to the wall, feeling its energy, and deferentially touched the first astrological house, with the red carved glyph. The ascendant on the natal wheel was for the sign of Aries. She remembered that from her lessons with Tien.

A hologram instantly appeared at Pen's touch of her glyph.

"Hi, my name is Catriz," said her avatar.

"Hi, my name is Wink," said his avatar at the same time.

Pen fell backwards, letting out a terrifying high-pitched scream. Her shrieks reverberated around and around the cave walls, the shrill sound bouncing and shaking the very foundation of the slot canyon. The sound was so jarring that it must have penetrated heaven and earth, shifting the equilibrium of everything.

"They are all dead!" she screeched. "They are all dead!"

"Pen, what do you mean they are all dead? Pen, cut it out." Nicho tried to hold her shoulders to stop her from trembling.

"Don't you see, they are trying to talk to me. Look, all twelve signs are present on the wall, all hand carved into the stone to mark their presence here on this Earth. They have all died. Why don't you see that they have all passed on? They are all dead. That is why their avatars are present, to tell us about them, to be a memorial."

Whether this was true or just a trick that Pen's mind was playing on her cognizance, it plunged her into a very dark place. After all that they had been through, this last test had pushed her to the edge. To the brink, to the very place where she might never be able to return.

That scream did not sound like his sister, Nicho thought, no not at all. No one was more fearless than she was, no one. Nicholas knew she carried a heavy burden. That in her mind, everything hinged on her success. It was up to her to get their Dad back, to make everything as it was before what happened happened. Nicho and Pen were always yin and yang. Now he was the one who needed that moment to think, to puzzle this out.

The heavens or otherworldly forces had a very different plan.

"Penelope, Penelope, it's me—Dad." Out of the shadows from within a deep crevice to their left suddenly emerged their father, Reed, appearing literally out of nowhere.

The twins were shocked to see him, momentarily paralyzed by the seeming impossibility of it all. Once the initial moment of disbelief wore off, Pen let out a long-stifled sigh of relief. She was beyond rational thought, responding to the deeply visceral joy at seeing her father again.

"Oh, Dad." She ran to him, crying. "You are here, you are actually here, just like I knew you would be. I just knew it." She flung herself into his open arms and hugged her father ever so tightly.

"Daddy, I followed the facts, just like I promised to do, just like you always told me to do, and that's what brought us right here to you. Dad, we have been worried sick since you and Uncle Gil disappeared. We never wanted Mommie to know how anxious and afraid we really were. We were brave, Dad, just like you taught us. We all pretended like it never happened, for Mommie's sake. We all just acted like you were away on a business trip, like you never went away and left us all alone."

Nicho was oddly still silent, standing back. His fingers moved absently as he started to twirl his mop of hair. He felt he needed to say something, but words failed him. What was wrong? Why did the image of Thinx pop into his head at this moment. Why think of him, constantly fiddling with his glasses, polishing them nervously, putting them on, and taking them off. What was it about seeing his father that would bring these nervous tics to his mind?

Pen looked at her brother, searching for joy in his face. "All we want to do is wake up from this horrible dream and let everything be the way it was before what happened happened," she blurted out to her father.

Now what's the matter with Nicholas? she wondered. Why was he twisting his mop of hair? He only did when he needed to think or when he was worried. Just like their mom, it really helped calm them. Why was he so anxious? Why was he so quiet? Why?

Her father's words interrupted that train of thought.

"We are all together now, finally. I knew you would come to rescue me from this prison," said Reed. "I just knew my twins would come to help me."

"Let's all just go home now, Dad. Let's just go home, okay?"

Pen implored. "I just want to go home to see Mom. She must be worried sick. Let's get out of here."

"We will go home, I promise, but first we must get into that chamber where the Clock is kept and replace those gemstones. Let's put them back where they belong," Reed said, reminding her of her obligation.

"No, Dad, I want to go home. I want to go now, right now. This is why we are here; we only came to find you. I don't care about these moonstones, I want everything to go back to the way it used to be before all of this. I want to go home."

"You made that promise to Honora; of course, you need to keep that promise, you must." Reed's voice was almost pleading.

"But how did you get . . ." Nicho mumbled, still trying to sort out what bothered him, but Pen interrupted him.

"This wall of glyphs, it is impenetrable. There is no way to enter, and this place is dangerous. Please, Dad, let's get out of here and go back home. I don't trust this place."

"Oh, my sweet Penelope, you never understood, did you? You and Nicho have the power to enter this sacred space. Nicho holds the Key of Access, that little stellated dodecahedron. He is Quintessence, he has the right. And you, you were chosen as guardian of those gemstones. So, you, too, have the right. Where are they, your gemstones? Let me see them, sweetheart. I will keep them safe for you." Reed reached out for her backpack. "No more worries, no more angst, I will take good care of them."

Pen instinctively took a step backwards. She had protected them for so long her apprehension was a natural impulse. She paused to collect herself, but just for a mere second, and then slowly reached inside her backpack.

With reverence and affection, Pen retrieved Melissa's letter box. The wood's mahogany surface was warm to the touch and made her feel safe. The carved glyphs now felt familiar to her, too. "Dad, look what I got. Do you believe that Mom got this to me? Do you believe she reached us somehow to help us at the very moment when we needed help the most? I have kept the moonstones inside Mom's letter box, you know, the one you gave her. I am supposed to keep them safe inside until we enter the chamber."

Nicho noticed Reed's hand impulsively reached for the mahogany case just as Penelope removed it from her backpack. Although her reflexes kept it close to her person, she continued to enthuse with her father.

"Oh Dad, I feel so relieved that I don't have to worry about them anymore." She sighed, relief evident in her voice.

"Such an unfair chore for one so young," Reed cajoled. "Just give them to me. I will keep them safe until we enter the inner sanctum where the Clock is housed. Hand them to me now, before Nicho uses the Key of Access that opens up these ancient doors." Reed again reached with outstretched hand to take the letter box. "Whenever these marble panels open, it always causes quite a commotion and—"

"Penelope," Nicho started to speak but remained motionless, his feet rooted to the ground. He saw it now. He saw that this Reed was all wrong. His father had the same mannerisms that Thinx did; they kept their glasses spotless, always cleaning them, taking them on and off looking for smudges that never really existed, and positioned their spectacles in a certain way on their nose. This Reed's glasses were smudged and askew, too far down his nose to be useful for seeing. He watched his father's lips move, but his words blurred in his mind. This Reed was out of sync with the hum of the stars in this place.

Whiz. Silvio flew by Nicho's head, almost hitting him. It certainly woke him up from his current languished stupor. He needed to get his head in this game and tell his sister about this imposter, but his mind, why was it so foggy? His gift of intuition was blocked. His voice was nowhere to be found; he could still hardly talk.

Whiz. That crazy little star flew by him again; this time he contacted with Nicho's forehead. "Stop!" he murmured, his voice barely a croak.

The stellated dodecahedron aimed for its target and shot into the very epicenter of the circle, a bullseye fit.

Click.

A perfect fit of course, he was not just a pretty little star; he was the Key of Access. Once Silvio nestled into the ancient lock, the twelve colors depicted on the carved sarsens spun about in a display of fireworks in and about the ageless catch. Then, the twelve mammoth triangular panels screeched ever so slowly and laboriously as they moved to open. The momentum of the opening was arduous and protracted and grindingly slow. Each passing second felt like an eternity even here in the Tunnel of Infinity.

"Wow," Pen, still holding onto the letter box was enthralled, her attention a bit distracted by the moving stones.

All eyes awaited to peer inside the Omnia Tempus, the inner sanctum that housed the Clock of Perpetual Motion, the regulator of time. As the archaic doors slowly groaned open, another presence made himself known.

"Stop! Stop! Penny Candy, no, don't do it" came a very familiar voice, breathless in tone. "Stop, stop!" Out of the darkness their uncle Gil appeared racing towards them.

"Penelope, that is not your father, your father is inside the sanctum serving as its Sentinel and guarding the Atmos Clock. That person with you is not your dad. Do not give *him* your *moonstones.*"

"Uncle Gil, what are you doing here! How did you get to this place? No one knows how to find it," Nicho managed to blurt out. Shock and fear overtook the twins now, shaking them to their very core. Nicho was still struggling, trying to shake off whatever was impeding his mind, blocking his gift of prescience. It was all happening way too fast.

"Don't give him the stones," Gil repeated adamantly, his voice frantic. "He can't enter the space without them. He hasn't earned the right; he is corrupted. He always needed you and your brother. You were given that power, that mission. The power to enter the chamber and the power to touch the Clock; it belongs only to you, and to your mother."

"Gil Val, you are a liar," Reed hissed. "How dare you come between me and my daughter." He turned his back to Penelope, his countenance changing instantly from angry to coaxing.

"Penelope, I *am* your father. I'm trying to save you, so please, listen. You know who I am. Don't let him trick you again. He is a self-seeking hypocrite." Reed looked over at his brother-in-law. "You know this to be true. It is a fact. He is the one you should not trust. Hasn't he already proven that? Look at me! You know you can trust me. Now, give me those stones," he demanded sharply.

In that very second, all of Honora's words came rushing back to her. "'Remember about the tunnel, it will be filled with the trickery of the past, present, and the future. Do not trust what you see, hear or surmise.'"

She whisked the box under her jacket, hiding it. "What does Mom's letter box look like?" she demanded in return.

"What do you mean, it's a letter box, that is all. Like you said, it was a gift, from a long time ago. Penelope, hurry, the doors are opening. Let me help you!"

"No, it was not just any old gift, it was a very special gift. It was an engagement gift for my mother. My father hand carved all of the glyphs on the mahogany wood himself."

Nicho now finally found his voice. "How did you get out of that inner chamber? You were trapped, and now you are here.

And, how did you *know* about Silvio being the Key of Access?" And now, he, too, regained his cognizance. "And why aren't you cleaning your glasses?"

A look of anger washed other their father's face, and then it began to melt. "You, you are just like that father of yours!" The image blurred and the leering face of Ahreman appeared. "And you, Gil Val, how did you come here to this place?"

"I used your old trick, you know how you always followed your mother Honora? So, I knew you would follow my niece, and I just followed you." Uncle Gil smiled.

The pure energy of Ahreman's raw dark power emerged, creating a ferocious wind tunnel within the narrow slot canyon. Rage emanated from his orbs, the streak of white lightening blazoned across their centers that turned into fiery red globes. Penelope was terrified by the wrath of fury in his face as he advanced towards her.

Her uncle Gil's voice could barely be heard over the whistling power of the rampaging wind. "He can't touch those moonstones unless you give them to him. Hold them close, just like you promised." The cyclone howled and screeched in a chaotic frenzy, echoing around and around, the clatter reverberating off the solid marble walls.

Penelope froze in place and watched as the great panels finally heaved open with a deep resonating rumble and a thud.

"Penelope, get inside, get inside the chamber." A familiar voice called to her, but she could not move. She stood still as a statue. The wind inside the tunnel pinioned her, whirling around her and lifting her off the ground.

"Penelope, come inside the chamber. Quickly, Penelope, please!" It was her father, Reed. This time she knew for a fact it was really him.

"I can't move," she screamed. "These winds have me trapped in this cyclone. I can't get out!"

"Yes, you can," Reed assured her. "You are Penelope, Concordaie, Guardian of the Moonstones. Know that now and own it, in this very place and time. Trust all your gifts, all your powers. Will yourself now. His powers are not greater than yours. Know that, it is a fact."

Pen trusted her father. He was the one person whom she never needed proof to believe. She needed to believe him now, but Ahreman proved too powerful. Did she have powers that lay dormant in her until this very moment? How to reach them? "Come on, Pen," she told herself. "You can do this."

Voices swirled, her mother, Honora, Esme. She focused and steadied her breathing. She thought of her mother, whose presence became very real to her now as she struggled for her life, but no, even that was not enough. None of it was enough.

"No," she screamed at her adversary.

Ahreman deftly moved the cyclone that imprisoned her towards the narrow gorge in the slot canyon; the glint of the diamonds' edges gleamed like spiked teeth waiting to rip her to bloody shreds.

Then she saw her twin's face and heard him. "Think about Mom. Think about how mad I make you when I go into your room and take all of your school supplies and never ask. Think about how I eat all of your food that you make for your lunch, and you don't know it until you are at school. Think about all of the times I take your house key and lose it, locking you out. Think about—"

"Enough," she thundered. Hurricane Pen was back. She could feel a surge of energy like she never felt before. A power within her welled that felt strangely familiar and wonderful. She needed to embrace all of it now in this moment, to let it flow and to absorb every ion of it. Finally, this was what the summons had promised.

"Break free, do it now!" She could hear her father's and her uncle Gil's frantic cries to help her. Everyone was immobile, petrified in place battling the sheer power of the unrelenting vortex.

And then, clearer than any other voice, she heard him; it was Nicholas again, but this time he joined her thoughts, becoming one.

"Come on, Pen, you got this. I know for a fact you got this. Don't be afraid of him; you are fearless. He is nobody compared to you, nobody. He just looks super creepy, that is all. Yeah, he is always dressed for Halloween, but never got asked to go to any parties." In the midst of the gale, she laughed out loud. At last, she stopped questioning his intuition and his out of context thoughts. She trusted it, trusted him, just in the *nick* of time.

Strength surged in her. She thrust fear aside with unwavering courage, it was useless to be afraid. One determined Penelope began to emanate a force of her own, driving the tempest back that held her captive. Her feet found solid ground, and she moved inexorably towards the chamber. The tortuous demise that seemed eminent moments before was no longer her fate. Ahreman, sensing the shift, directly confronted her, frenetically trying to regain control of the gale forces that surrounded her. His arms flailed; though still willing the power of the wind itself in relentless gusts and gale-force currents, she spotted a slight inexactness in his motions. She was Penelope, she was Concordaie, and most importantly, she was not afraid of him, not anymore.

She was indeed fearless, inured to his influences and domination. Ever so slowly, she inched her way towards the opening, to the entrance of the Omnia Tempus, towards her father and his outstretched arms. She knew she could do this and she did.

"Dad, Dad, reach out in one, two, three . . ."

Reed was careful not to step outside the protection of the inner chamber. He precariously extended his hand into the uncontrolled cyclone. "Penelope," he cried. He caught her outstretched hand and pulled her into his arms and into the safety of the Omnia Tempus.

Ahreman screeched. "You fool, you will pay dearly for that mistake, you will pay, I will make you all pay," he screamed at Reed, as he whirled around and turned his attention to Nicholas. "Your very future will remain uncertain into perpetuity, but your son's future will end right here, right now." His face was distorted with blood-pounding rage as he aimed a deadly bolt at Nicho.

Then what happened happened.

It was a sizzle, a crackle, a flash of sparking light, and then a whizzing sound, like that of a bullet, unerring in its path. Silvio launched himself out of the lock with the speed of the blazing comet and the force of a detonating meteorite. The little star then knocked Ahreman right into the sedimentary wall of rock. *Bam!* Dazing him for a brief moment as he slid to the ground. Silvio stayed poised for a second attack, but he stopped a few inches from Ahreman's left orb, threatening in place.

Defeat was now upon him and bitterness oozed from his voice as he growled, "This is a hollow victory, as you will soon come to find out. You will see." The tone of his sinister laugh echoed throughout the canyon. Even in defeat, his reverberating sound was unnerving.

Reed as the Sentinel took command. His voice resounded from within the sacred space.

"Begone! You have no place here. You are unwelcome. Entry is denied, as it was in the past, as it is now, as it forever will be. Go back from whence you came; you are summoned elsewhere as you well know."

Ahreman rose and his body became like smoke, black and

billowing. An eerie sound of rapture's wings reverberated through-out the tunnel. Amidst his bellowing cries of anguish, he was gone.

"There is nothing like a present from the present," interjected Nicho, breaking the silence amid their moment of reprieve. "Thank you, Silvio. You saved my life. And here I thought you were just a little broken star."

Pen glared at her twin. "So now with everything that just hap-pened, the very first thing you do is sound super stupid again. Talking to that thing again, like it's a real person. Another thing, I know he does not like me."

Her annoyance at her brother gave her comfort, it was their familiar banter. She walked over to give him a sisterly shove, and suddenly she saw it. Nicholas followed her eyes—there it was, the Clock. It was overwhelming at first. With eyes wide with wonder, she took it all in. It was not just the Clock, but the breathtaking magnificence of the surroundings that sustained it. Penelope was awestruck. "Like, wow!" she murmured. Mere words could never convey the experience. How could one behold such splendor, let alone try to describe it?

"I know," said her father, "and you never tire of its solemn beauty."

Penelope took a deep breath and stepped forward into the rectangular vestibule. Its walls paneled with what? Was it marble? No, not marble. This stone was more luxurious with an inner glow that exuded a sense of being home, of being welcome.

"It's pure Xyzanium, an impenetrable substance created to protect this chamber. It's used for many different purposes I have come to learn, and it looks different with each of its uses. The only consistency is in its unparalleled strength. Touch it, see how it feels." As the Sentinel for the Omnia Tempus, Reed had learned many of its secrets.

Penelope opened her hand and pressed her palm to the stone, expecting a cool touch. But no, it really was warm, it felt liquid, almost alive. It made her feel comfortable. She remembered the feel of her moonstones on the beach. It was the very same. That moment seemed so long ago.

"Why is it so luminous? Is there a source of light causing these reflections?"

"Come." Reed motioned to Gil to come closer too, but he hung back.

"Reed, I am really sorry." Gil tried to explain as he rhythmically tapped his pocket, his personal tic of unconsciously keeping time to music only he could hear.

"Whatever you do, please no more of that whistling or that tapping, okay? You saved my kids' lives; there is no need to say another word."

Gil looked sheepish as he stilled his nervous hands and followed Reed inside.

For now, you should all see what all the commotion is about," Reed told them with a smile. "Trust me, it's worth it. It's beyond anything anyone could even imagine on this Earth. Heck, beyond anything anyone could even imagine throughout this galaxy."

All three passed through the meticulously carved vestibule. It was filled with numerous glyphs and engravings whose meanings were yet to be discovered, and more importantly, yet to be understood. The patterns continued into the rotunda.

The energy that filled the space spoke to them—*we have been waiting for you, welcome.*

"Honora claims this substance to be the hardest element in the entire universe. It was created to protect this very space. Yet, see the sculpting, it's uncanny. I cannot imagine the master's hand who carved such exquisiteness. The work is unparalleled in its beauty and perception. I always wanted to ask Honora who was this great artist, maybe it was—" Reed suddenly stopped and looked around. "Where is Honora?"

"What? So, you really do know that crazy lady?" Nicholas blurted without thinking. "Oops, sorry Dad. Are you friends with her too? She told us she knew Mom."

Reed smiled. "She has been protecting your mother against Ahreman's spells ever since I left. Yes, she is a great friend. However, she is never where she is supposed to be, never."

Nicholas pipped up, glad to find another who thought the same as he. "Dad, you have no idea. That lady is *never* where she is supposed to be. *Never.*"

"Well, she is always up to something. No one knows if it's planned or happenstance. However, your mother's trust in her was complete." Reed hugged his twins. "She even trusted Honora with both of you."

The small group continued their journey into the inner sanctum. "Oh my, this is beyond anything we could have ever imagined," Penelope murmured. She could not believe her eyes; she was in awe, at a loss for words. The conversation stopped short as they moved from the rectangular vestibule into the colossal rotunda. Finally, the space that housed the tick of time was right there in front of them.

"Where are we, Dad? Are we still on Earth? I don't feel like we are still on Earth." Pen was feeling suddenly pensive.

"Funny you should ask that question. I will let Nicholas answer that one," Reed said, clapping his son on the shoulder.

"You want me to answer?" Nicholas sounded incredulous. "My brain is still fuzzy. At least, I think it's still fuzzy." He looked around for Silvio, not wanting to get poked again.

"You have seen the space and are now experiencing its presence. We are now in a continuum of time and space," Reed continued.

"You mean we are in a void?" Pen was still trying to figure this all out.

"No, not a void, but that is an excellent deduction." Reed loved these teaching moments, especially with his twins as they reasoned out their own puzzles.

"It's not a void because even though it looks like nothing, we can still feel the presence of something. I bet this was what Honora faced when she was sent here, or there or wherever she was sent a long time ago," Nicholas pondered. "Even what appears to be empty may not be so because there is an essence of something."

Reed smiled to himself and looked at his son and daughter. *Yes, they might be twins, but their minds worked so differently and yet in perfect sync.* With a wave of his hand, he motioned the three of them.

"Come closer and follow me. Take a deep breath and try to take it all in."

They entered the circular room filled with the vitality of all that was around it. There it sat, under the very epicenter of the massive domed ceiling—the Clock of Perpetual Motion, the regulator of time itself, the perfect armillary sphere. There again were the twelve Talking Panels, same as they were in the *Sphere of Comets.* Their pulsating coffers rimmed the cylindrical pavilion, their colors vibrant, soft, inspiring, alive.

Nicholas studied it closely. The twenty-four metal circular disks of the Clock looked like gold, no, maybe silver, no platinum, it was too hard to tell. The glint from the metals moved with the forward motion of the twelve rings of the future. The twelve rings of the past stood motionless.

Penelope was enthralled. "Do you hear it? It's the very hum of this solar system's past, present, and future." She felt that music was just for her. She watched the symmetric harmony of the Clock's spheres moving in sync with the orchestra of its sound. There they were too, the twelve gemstones moving clockwise to the future. "Oh, see how they sparkle, the colors so rich."

Whiz. Silvio mounted itself into place. That little stellated dodecahedron snuggled right into the very center of the armillary sphere. He was the star of the present after all. He nested into the clock's interior, making himself right at home for the moment. His center was closed. Nicho had noticed that when the little star was closed, its design was similar to an Atmos clock with a hermetic seal. Just what did Silvio's hermetic seal protect? Nicholas had an idea, but he was not sure. That was yet another mystery secret, an enigma maybe never to be revealed. It was just as complex as the language of glyphs inscribed on all of the panels that surrounded the clock.

How to uncover the riddle of the present? Nicho mused to himself. "Maybe the answers would be deciphered someday. Maybe the decrypted information inside this chamber would provide the answer to every question about this universe. Hmmm, now that was something to really think about."

Penelope now was on her own reverie as she approached the regulator of the past, present, and the future with reverence. "Are you real too? My moonstones are, and they need to return home."

Embracing the comfort she felt in the presence of her family and hearing the hum of harmony, Penelope carefully reached for the letter box. She slowly took it out of her backpack, not yet ready to let it all go. She gently opened the lid. There they were in all of their beauty: the twelve moonstones, all brilliant liquid in color. It must have been the presence of the air and light as each one seemed to come to life, as if awakened from a long deep sleep. They were unhurried to leave the shelter of their little cocoon, but they slowly left their nesting place and dispersed throughout the chamber's ether. Penelope watched in awe. "Oh, look at you, how you glisten and gleam."

Their special hues were so pure, so perfect in their flight into the time and space of the pavilion. If you listened closely, you could hear them hum. It was their most perfect song. Now, they were finally home at last. Pen watched her moonstones take flight, but they did not go back into the clock.

"Hey, where are you going? Hey guys, come back here!" Pen commanded, but to no avail. "Dad, what are they doing? Why aren't they going back into the clock where they belong?" Penelope was puzzled. With minds of their own, they soared high and then higher right up to the apex of the dome and hovered. Silvio, not wanting to miss out on any of the action, flew up to join them, illuminating what looked like an opening.

"Pen, Penelope, look, there it is, wow, look, see the heavens! It's an oculus!" Nicholas cried with delight. "The hole in the ceiling's center, that is an oculus. Can you see it?" Nicholas hollered. "Silvio, come down and get me. Take me up with you to the opening. I want to see the stars more closely." The other three watched in stunned silence as Silvio obeyed.

Nicholas put out his hand, and with an invisible string Silvio took him up to the very place where the Earth meets the sky, to the horizon point. Nicholas looked out upon the nighttime sky. "I know exactly where we are. We are on Earth, and judging by the placement of the constellations—but how, can that be?"

"Is anything here that is just plain old what it is supposed to be? Or does everything somehow become something else?" Pen wanted a real answer.

"Like Silvio, like the *Sphere of Comets*, like your moonstones, like the Xyzanium, like the JX, and so many other things yet unknown, yet to be realized, there exists a living thread of humanity throughout the Universe. Every element becomes a part of the fabric and pattern in the circle of all living things. And then so much more." Reed spoke reverently.

A sudden click echoed into the chamber.

"What was that noise? It sounded like the turn of a key." Reed was taken aback by the interruption.

"It's the movement of the entrance panels to the Omnia Tempus. Reed, you have to get them out of here now," said Gil. "Time is moving again on the other side of the entranceway."

Reed turned to his brother-in-law with mixed feelings. Gil smiled ruefully back.

"So, it's up to me now. I will stay here to take your place. Don't worry, it will be just me and the clock. I can't get into trouble here. Besides, I will have a lot of time to think about some things. Maybe get it right this time. I will not let Melissa down again, I promise."

"What made you change, Gil? Did something happen? What was it?"

Gil started to whistle and then stopped.

"The truth is, I was really afraid of him. I never had my sister's courage, you know that. I got seduced by his empty promises. Then I remembered Melissa's love of these kids and my strong love for them too." Gil then stood straight up. "I know my sister better than anyone. And knowing Melissa, I knew exactly who to be afraid of, no contest."

Then came his charming Hollywood smile. "I never meant to harm anyone, just wanted a little of my old fame back, that is all. I lost my way. But that guy, or whatever he is, he has no idea about what someone will do for love, especially my sister."

Reed gave him a knowing look and patted Gil on the back.

"Okay, Sentinel, you know the drill, right."

"Sure," said Gil grinning. "Nobody in and nobody out."

"But watch this little rascal." Reed said, pointing to Silvio. "This stellated dodecahedron, the Key of Access, the star of the present, whatever he is in the moment—he has a mind of his own. He comes and goes as he pleases, bobs around for fun, but he was good company when he behaved. He uses that oculus like a revolving door. Always up to mischief just like Honora."

"How is it that this star can come and go from the chamber?" Gil asked Reed.

It was Nicho who responded.

"Because Silvio is the present in the continuum of time and eternity, only the present is a constant. What I did not realize is that he is a formidable little secret weapon, too. He has got the full power and might of a shooting star, and he is my friend."

Gil looked at the twins with great pride. "Of course, you figured that out, you are Nicholas, member of the Quintessence, who still needs a haircut. I can hear my sister complaining about that hair in your eyes right now. T'is twin telepathy."

The brothers shook hands. "Remember, tell Melissa I love her."

"She knows that, Gil, she knows."

Reed then looked at the clock and shook his head. "This Tunnel of Infinity is tricky. When things happen here, memory fails us because it's so hard to remember what may or may not have happened. Time, space, place—everything can change."

"Well," said Gil good-naturedly. "Remember only what you want to, the rest is maybe best forgotten."

"Dad, my mission was to free you. It was never about returning the Latter Twelfstanin to the Clock," Pen told him. "Those moonstones can't just be returned; each stone needs to earn its way back into its particular space into the history of time."

"You have become quite the puzzle master, haven't you, Penelope?" he replied. So proud of his daughter.

She looked at her twin. "To tell you the truth, Nicholas helped . . . just a little bit, though well maybe. I just finally learned to listen to him." She grinned.

Nicholas stood strong, and proud, pushing his hair out of his eyes. "And I finally started to pay attention to my fearless twin.

Sometimes the facts are all that matters, not all the time, but sometimes." Nicholas gave Penelope a knowing wink.

"Hey, Penelope, your moonstones are still buzzing around the opening to the oculus. Should you call them or something?" Nicholas watched them hovering with Silvio.

"I don't know." Reed opened the letter box. "I thought they are going back home with us, again."

"Again?" It was Penelope.

Silvio whirred by, burning red hot. He prodded them to get moving by rotating close. Although he did not speak, he was telling them to go and go now.

"Dad, I can feel the shift in the energy. My moonstones have left me at least for this moment." She looked up at them swirling about each other—twelve protons, neutrons, and electrons. There was Silvio right in the middle. She shrugged. "I guess they have their own mission."

Honora's words suddenly popped into her mind—*this is late summer, the rainy season is in late September.*

The gears that controlled the panels made the noise of a sleeping giant waking up from a long slumber. Its signal was clear; it was time to close.

"The Omnia Tempus is readying to seal itself. You need to follow me. Hold tight."

"Dad, I hear it, I hear raindrops. Dad, I can hear the rain. The sound of rushing water." There was alarm in her voice. "Honora warned us about this, the flooding."

"No matter, we have some time!"

The venerable doors that housed the Talking Panels slowly started to close. The thick wall of glyphs would once again remain impenetrable, thick, and opaque to the outside world. Those glyphs that were marked by each of the celestial twins as a way to say hello, we were here once upon a time, were also there to say goodbye.

"Dad, the water, I can hear a whooshing sound!" Penelope screamed.

As they hurried past the inexorably closing doors, Pen dared a backwards glance. She saw her beloved uncle in the narrowing gap, calmly watching them go, tapping his pocket in time to his own music of the spheres and whistling the tune that would entertain him for this particular eternity. He saw her glance and waved as the doors boomed closed. He smiled at her, and she knew all was right between them.

"Come on," Reed said calmly. "Let's stay together, close by each other's side, and know that we love each other. There is a lot of power in that. Besides, we need to get Nicholas home; he is in desperate need of a haircut."

CHAPTER 21

The Battle

Shards of lighting pierced the low murky sky that lowered over the Circle of Stones. This was no ordinary thunderstorm. Energy crackled from the powers beyond nature. The flashing jagged bolts slashed the serenity of the cobalt velvet, competing with the fiery detonations of the enemy. Above it all loomed the full moon of the Autumnal Equinox as she hung, watching in ghostly glory. Such was the melancholy canvas for the battle, as swarms of Everters engaged the celestial twins.

Their situation was not optimal. The twins knew they were outnumbered. Hordes emerged from the enemy crafts before Yejidi and A'dept had stopped time. The fearsome Everters had marshaled themselves into six arrays, six warriors wide and six deep. The twenty-four twins were outnumbered nine to one.

Some who were strong and martial had plunged into the thick of battle and were fighting deep into the fray. The others, those whose strengths lay in strategizing and logistics, converged on the treehouse, now a command post. There were still some, however, who watched from the sidelines.

There was a nervous humming of low murmurs intermixed with screams of pain, shrieks of victory, and cries for help. It all created a rumble. In one corner of the battlefield behind a pile of stones, Witt and Clarity couched and trembled at the discordant sounds. They knew it would not be long before those fighting became tired and made a fatal mistake.

What should we do? Witt signed swiftly, his elegant hands a blur. His mind filled with uncertainly as balls of fire flew overhead. The fury that blazed around them only fueled his confusion.

I don't know, but we need to do something. We need to do it now, Clarity implored.

I know, I know. He paced and paced around in banjo circles. Clarity did the same, trying to take in the enormity of the scene, jumping at every blast and crouching as each shower of dust, dirt, and shards of rock made its way towards them. Faster and faster and faster they went until to the naked eye they were just a lemon-lime blur, almost invisible to the naked eye.

Then Clarity stopped short and used her voice. "This is what we do best! Let's cause some confusion, you know, like we always do!"

What are you talking about? Witt signed back.

"What did Maman say, 'do what we do best.' Well, we spin, and we spin, and we spin around everyone, all the time. We are always everywhere causing mischief and mayhem and drive everyone crazy because we can't keep still. Why not around those bad guys? No one can see us, whether we're coming or going."

Yes. Witt caught on immediately. *The battle has scattered everywhere. We can help by getting the drop on their opponents from behind.*

"Agreed. Diversion, distraction, disorder! That is what we bring. It will give our siblings a real chance to find the openings they need to even up the odds."

Yep. Witt could not wait. *So, we can give them a good poke in the eye, and they won't know what or who hit them because our speed makes us invisible! Or we could even push them or trip them or we could even bite them.*

"Okay, okay, cut it out, that's really too creepy. Let's just go and really make them go insane. It's not like they don't have it coming to them," Clarity said with a grin, using her voice.

Right, besides, that big guy is really getting on my last nerve. Witt sent a glare towards the battlefield as he signed his reply.

∼

Further into the woods, Evan and Chance also watched from afar, worried as usual. In truth, they were worried enough for everyone. Being on the sidelines gave them no comfort, none at all. "We can't just let them fight our battles for us." Evan put her foot down and then gave it a good stomp. "*Enough.*" A bright beam of moonlight responded to her command, as illumination broke through the ragged clouds. It bathed them in their natural element. In its light, they disappeared. As they both used the light of the moon to mask themselves, their intuition, too, soared.

"We can most certainly do a lot of damage if we just disappear right into the fray of that battle," Chance suggested, feeling quite bold. "While we are at it, let's find those little runts, Camillus and Tamzin. I'd love to see the looks on their ugly faces when we pummel them and they can't see us. That will be a story. I can't wait to hear them tell about how they were defeated by an unknown force that no one could see."

"Peek-a-Boo!" who do you think you are calling chubby? And then, *bam!*"

"Everyone will think *they* are the scaredy cats, not us," Evan intuited, while Chance relished just such an opportunity. With the light of the full moon as their spotlight, they went right into the very heart of the conflict.

As O, the lightening bug, buzzed around, she looked for

her masters who were for some reason conspicuously absent. "Hmmm," O thought to herself, "just where is the royal duo? Are they having another temper tantrum because they are not the center of attention?" She knew them better than they knew themselves.

She found Courage first. "Cut it out," he demanded, "stop buzzing in my ear. Hey, you almost poked me in the eye." He swatted to no avail. "We know we are not doing as we promised, but no one is paying attention to our orders." O's lighted tail radiated from yellow to orange, clearly irritated at their reticence to engage.

Olympia hung her head at O's chiding flashes. Her mother's words came back to her mind, and she felt ashamed. "Remember, if you lead with your hearts, all your sibling will follow you effortlessly. Lead by example."

O's glow went from orange to bright red to smoldering white, as she bobbed and bobbed up and down. Olympia looked at her little lighting bug and smiled. "Okay, okay, little one, I hear you."

She gritted her teeth and looked knowingly at Courage. "We need to live up to our names. We have a perfect communication link right here. O can go anywhere and transmit field information in code. Sage and AlexSandra can see it from anywhere. We all know twin code but the Everters don't. He nodded as the sound of a cymbal could be faintly heard in the background.

"And we can really turn up the heat on those bad guys, literally. A little concentrated sunlight and they will lust for shade and water, not blood."

The twins from the Dazzling Sun rose up, tall and regal, summoning O to be their mascot, and to follow. Their battle cry resounded, giving heart to their siblings.

"*We rule!*" and once engaged they did.

Meanwhile another set of reluctant heroes were still waiting to discover their own particular calling. "We will catch germs if we go into that battle. Did you see how dirty those Everters are? They do not bathe on Eris; I am sure of it." Tien grimaced at the thought.

"I think you sound a little scared," said Fastidious looking out over the raging battle. "Well maybe we both are," Tien replied. She loved to tell on herself, it was a Virgo trait. "You know if someone gets hurt, we'll need to concoct the medicine to heal them. So, it's best we stay put right here." It was a feeble point.

Fastidious pondered. "Maman said we are the Kendo Masters of the Universe. Those guys might be more afraid of us than you know."

"Do you think so, really?" Tien said dubiously.

"I think it's time for us to teach them a lesson they will not soon forget." Fastidious rallied himself, limbering up with a few practice swings with his kendo shinai proving his skill.

"Let's go!" Tien and Fastidious launched into the very front lines of the combat zone, making first contact. "Ah-ayah!" No one was their equal as the clang of their unyielding wooden sticks struck the pure Xyzanium shields of their opponents. Strikes so hard that they paralyzed the enemy's hands and arms. One by one, swords and shields once thought invincible, dropped from useless limbs. The twins' kiai, their fighting cry, echoed across the fray, reinvigorating their brothers and sisters.

The night wore on, both sides increasingly became exhausted and weary. The twins still were outnumbered; math and time again were not on their side.

"We can't keep up this pace much longer. We need a real plan, and we need it now." A'dept and Yejidi came straight from the eye of command back to the tree fortress. "AlexSandra and OnyX, you are hurt! We just came from the battlefield, our guys, they will need a break soon."

Inside their tree fortress, AlexSandra, her face grey with pain and stress, gingerly nursed the long gash on her leg with ice. She winced. OnyX too, tried one-handed to wrap a cloth around the wound on his right hand. The bleeding seemed to have stopped.

"Where is my twin brother?"

A'dept turned to her. "Sage is atop the sarsen on the far side, keeping an eye on the Everters' movements. Olympia's lightening bug O is proving invaluable in transmitting his information to the others. She is so tiny, no one sees her skimming above them, and her coded flashes have saved several of us from falling into ambushes."

AlexSandra nodded and looked around the room, annoyed at what she saw. "So, I have a question with an answer I already know. Many of us have risked our whole entire young life fighting to save this planet, save a few. Who might those *few* be?" She paused giving those who were in the relative safety of the treehouse an ill-tempered glare. "Well, I am still waiting for an answer."

"If we really must respond, our skill set is not yet needed." It was quite a dismissive response from CeSe, who also spoke on behalf of Skye. It did not bode well with anyone who heard their remark. The twins from Wishful Neptune put their heads down, embarrassed.

∽

AlexSandra bristled. "Oh, well, how about you two from Wacky Uranus? Do you have any skills that might be needed on the battlefield, or are you still busy just *thinking?*" She kicked a soccer ball right in their direction. It just skimmed Vesper's head but knocked off her eyeglasses.

"That is not funny. We don't want to let anyone down; you know that. Stop with your angry attitude; it doesn't help. To be honest, it never helps," retorted Thinx. "We know what we promised, and we just need time to figure it out. We are sorry. We know you are hurt, and the others are at risk, but we don't quite know yet what to do. It will come, it always does." Thinx went back to staring at the nighttime sky.

～

Frustration drove AlexSandra to continue her vent. "Okay, so who is next?" She looked towards the glamour twins. "Fighting is not the 'in thing' to do right now." She sneered, holding nothing back.

Beau and Gracious knew it was best not to say one word in response. Even though they desired harmony above all else, the battle that was raging nearby was to a deadly finish. For once in their young lives, they cared nothing about what others were doing, or even thinking. They cared about saving their family. They knew they did not have the insight of Excelsia and Skye or the intuition of Thinx and Vespers, or the physical strength and powers of their other siblings. Truth be told, they did not even possess their confidence.

Like the others, Esme's words came back to them. "Do what you do best." It was simple once they started; it came to them all at once. "Juggling!" Beau blurted. The others looked at him as if he'd lost his mind.

"Excuse me?" AlexSandra gaped at him openmouthed. "You want to play at a time like this?"

Beau stood up and looked at the others. Gracious soon joined him knowing exactly what he meant, as she threw the first ball at him. The balls moved hypnotically as if they held a force all their own, moving in perfect synchronization. They added more and more balls at different heights, literally juggling in three dimensions. Faster and faster, they spun, compressing the air surrounding them. They had created a lift, like a helicopter, and began to rise off the ground. They'd invented an aerial screw.

OnyX and AlexSandra tried to kick one of the balls, but the spheres moved too quickly, their trajectory too powerful. They got closer and tried again. Just as their feet neared the orb of the balls' pathway, they were propelled far back. This time both landed on their petards, which was exactly what they deserved. The tension broke, as everyone laughed.

"Look," Gracious shouted, "if we team up with OnyX and Mysterious, their ability to levitate things by sound, coupled with this vortex, this can become so powerful that we can scoop up the Everters and imprison them."

"So, we have a new secret weapon," OnyX offered. He liked the sound of that.

"Yes, we do," said Gracious.

"But how do we get them to close ranks? We need them to be together, side by side." It was AlexSandra, being a Sagittarian, asking one of their famous questions.

"Oh, right." Beau sighed sadly, his enthusiasm collapsing. The balls fell, and Gracious just watched dejected as they clattered and rolled away.

~

Meanwhile, Esme and Mikai watched in trepidation from the Sphere of Comets, *acutely aware of each and every one's actions and inactions. The dawn would be upon them. They could feel the energy of the planets shifting from nighttime back into day. The interplay of power between the sun and moon affected not only the Earth's atmosphere but their children's energy as well.*

Courage and Olympia of course would be boosted by the sun's rays. How to control that force was another matter. Some of their children still were not cognizant of the full extent of their capabilities, and some were overconfident. Time seemed interminable as they worried.

Their twins needed a plan. They needed to create it, and they needed to believe in it. Having faith in their collective abilities would be the key to their success. Mikai and Esme eavesdropped on their whispers and hoped in their judgment.

～

It was Thinx and Vespers' time; they spoke up, grasping at the thread of an idea.

"CeSe and Skye, it's the four of us," Thinx told them. "We have our own mission now, to figure out how to outmaneuver that Everter army. Our best fighters are fighting; even Beau and Gracious have joined the fray. Hand-to-hand combat is not our strong suit, but we need to try harder to puzzle this out. "

Silence was the best response, as they all used their intellect and intuition to reason through this brain teaser.

Adept interpreted their thoughts. "You are right. We need a plan that uses every one of our powers, abilities, and strengths." Yejidi went over to the wooden chalkboard. Only the other night, it was used for recreational puzzles; now the sport had changed to modeling war games.

"Let's list all of our powers and then figure out how to use them together," Yejidi said. "We need to catalogue each one of our special abilities. Then think through the different scenarios on how to use them most effectively."

Adept and Yejidi stood erect by the chalkboard, taking great care to identify each power to be used and how to coordinate the effort.

The list looked like this:

Wink and Catriz—athletic/can split atoms
Domenica and Harm—superior strength/can mimic voices
Witt and Clarity—tremendous speed/superior hearing/
    shape shift
Evanescent and Chance—control the tides/can disappear
    in moonlight
Courage and Olympia—control the powers of the sun
Tien and Fastidious—Kendo Masters/superior intellect/
    thought transference
Beau and Gracious—magic/hypnosis/create aerial vortex
Mysterious and OnyX—levitation/puzzle masters/Reiki
    healers
Sage and AlexSandra—superior sight/powerful legs/very
    lucky
A'dept and Yejidi—stop time/gift of methodical planning/
    endurance
Thinx and Vespers—electricity/electromagnetism/
    prescience/ESP
Skye and Excelsis—telepathy/magical thinking/control
    the wind

The eight siblings pondered the list. The sound of the raging battle centered their thoughts, reminding them that time was running out. The twins went around and around, thinking hard. Gradually the pieces of this puzzle started to fall into place. A plan grew from the idea that Beau and Gracious had planted—now it was time to execute.

"Let's do it." High fives all the way around sealed the mission. They were ready and anxious at the same time. That was a good thing.

Skye set the dominoes in motion; using his powers of mental telepathy, he contacted Courage and Olympia, who were leading the raging battle on the field. Instantly the plan was communicated to them.

"Got it." The sun twins nodded in agreement. They shared the details with Witt and Clarity who sped through the battlefield so swiftly they were undetectable. The message to all was "fall back now!"

Many of the twins were reluctant to obey. "*Lay down our arms?*" Wink and Catriz would have none of it; Domenica and Harmonious the same—the order seemed like nothing short of surrender. But they all had faith in each other and gradually broke off their attacks and retreated to the command center at the treehouse.

The Everters began to cheer, a horrible gurgling sound. "See how they cower; they are weak little children. They know they are defeated." Slowly the hoard, moving as one, made its way to the twins' fortress, seeking to converge on the site.

Beau and Gracious, ethereally beautiful, elegantly moved into the center stage of the battleground, weaving their hypnotic spell. Well-known throughout the universe for their want of harmony, the Everters would never consider them a threat. Their most charming smiles grew more enchanting as they advanced to their enemy. It appeared to the brutish Everters that they were coming to ask for terms of surrender.

"See, they send their ambassadors of peace in the hope that we will let them live. Never!" Acerbus growled to his troops. "They sent spoiled brats to save the universe from us." He laughed smugly. "They will never be true warriors. They have only learned from their sniveling parents Esme and Mikai. Those two, both cowards, are watching their children's failure from their hiding place in that starship of theirs."

The twins from Pretty Venus kept advancing, using every

ounce of their charm, laced with a false sense of optimism to keep the Everters at bay. "Look how beautiful these two little ones are, listen to the beautiful sounds they make as they approach." Acerbus was mesmerized even at the mere sight of them.

So besotted with watching them, the Everters failed to see that some of the twins were no longer at the treehouse. Tien and Fastidious along with Evan and Chance had eased their way behind the rest. The lunar twins wrapped their arms around their siblings and all four disappeared into the light of the full moon.

They rushed back to the Imperium. Their assignment—discover how to access the cosmic string that opened and closed the portal. As the four of them passed through the great sarsens, they slowly looked around into that hollowed space within the great circle's stones.

"Do you see anything?" muttered Chance.

"Who me?" It was Fastidious. "No, I do not."

"Why, do *you* see anything?" It was Evan's turn.

"Of course, I don't." It was Tien. "Why bother asking?"

Chance thought to ask the question in a different way. "Does anyone know what a cosmic string looks like?"

"Ah, nope" was the collective response.

"I think," said Tien bewilderedly, "that it is one of those things, how they say on Earth, 'you know it when you see it.'" The problem was, not only that they could not see it, but that they were also not sure about how to even try to find it. Such ancient knowledge was known only to Honora, who kept that secret safe.

"Okay, let's just try again; it's got to be here somewhere," Evan said encouragingly. But again, their efforts were thwarted. Nothing, there was not even the slightest clue. The twins were frantic. They needed to find that access point of entry for the cosmic string, and quickly.

"So exactly where is Honora? She knows the secret of the

string," said a worried Evanescent. "I thought she was supposed to help us out. Did she just show up again and leave?"

"I think she went with Nicho and Pen. They seemed to all disappear about the same time." Tien was searching for some tangible clues, knowing that something of such great importance would not be in plain sight.

"Nicho sure was right about her." Chance started to hug his tummy. "She is never where she is supposed to be and makes a lot of promises she can't keep." Apprehension started to take over Chance.

"Cut it out." Tien's voice was soft but stern. "Maman told you that your mood affects each of us. You need to control your anxiety, you promised. You both were sent here to help us."

"Our strengths are superior intellect, for noticing detail and clear thinking. We need to focus and not be distracted." Fastidious's tone was much more admonishing than he intended.

"We know it is near the epicenter, most probably aligned with that secret stash of JX. So it is most likely somewhere right above it," Tien reasoned. She lifted her face to the heavens. "Even the slightest clue would help us greatly; can you give us a hint?" She spoke to the heavens without success.

Evanescent dragged her brother directly into the epicenter. "Could you please move to the side and clear the space so it's just Chance and me. Move to your 6th House along the elliptical of the circle." The twins from Clever Chiron nimbly dashed aside.

"What are you doing, Evan?" Chance whispered into his sibling's ear. "Have you gone crazy too?"

"Be quiet and stop acting like a baby. We need to help. It's not fair to the others. We need to dig down real deep. Our powers can't just be that we are intuitive and can slip in and out of moon shadows. Really, that is just so lame. We must have something more than that. And it's a full moon when we are supposed to be our most powerful. So, let's see what happens. Can't you feel that energy? It is right here."

"Come on," said Evanescent. "Stop feeling sorry for yourself. Look at our moon, our home, see her at her fullest face brimming with intensity, power, and might. It's the Autumnal Equinox and the Harvest Moon. All that stuff about how significant it is. Well, it's our home. So why not us? Maybe this is one mystery secret that we, the two of us, can answer."

"Well, I don't know," said Chance, still moping.

Then what happened happened.

The vapor in the air crystalized into a silvery green mist. A moonbeam from their home surrounded them. It was both brilliant and ethereal and filled with twinkling ions of crystals.

"Chance, look!" Evanescent exclaimed, her very breath forming more of the sparkling particles. They danced on the air around her. Evanescent tried to touch them. Chance reached out too, wanting to caress the twinkling dust that swirled about, but it eluded him. He took a deep breath and exhaled. The magical dust flickered and glittered, gradually winding into a funnel up into the heavens. As the twins from the Moody Moon looked upward, they saw it. Within the green silver mist was an ionized tunnel into the cosmos—an opening. It was lit by the light of the Moody Moon, their home. It was small, but with the bright glow an entranceway appeared, and it gleamed. The entrance to the wormhole was discovered. They'd found it.

"Hey, Tien, Fastidious, it's right there." Chance took a little victory strut, in awe at how plainly visible it now was.

"Your greatest gift is that you control the tides, the water, even water vapor. Earth's composition is more than seventy percent water." Tien looked at her sister. "Evanescent, your very name means to evaporate."

"Now it's up to us to figure out the mathematical calculation of the exact placement for the rest of the team. Well done, both of you," said Fastidious.

Chance beamed and then gave a bashful grin looking at the other three. "Don't you dare say it, don't you dare."

Evanescent could not help herself. "Aren't you glad you took a chance?"

◠

Finding the exact placement of the cosmic string was one thing; how to open it in the precise moment in time that it needed to be open, well that was another problem for yet another set of twins.

Thinx and Vespers slipped away, too, and hurried to the circle, going directly to the epicenter. They went over in detail all of Tien's and Fastidious's calculations. Their math was perfectly exact, of course. Now that they knew the exact placement of the wormhole, now the bigger problem—how to open it. The entire plan hinged on that cosmic string activating to allow access into that tunnel. How to create that much energy to trigger that event?

"Hmmm, let's see the twins from Wacky Uranus figure it out; it's their turn now." Tien and Fastidious were completely confident in them.

"Ouch, ouch, ouch!" The electromagnetic rays pinched the Uranian twins once they moved beyond the boulders. Neon currents zigzagged in a frenetic pattern around them.

"Oh, how I hate this pinching!" Vespers did not like the sensation, not even a little bit. She struggled against the shocks.

"Me neither, but this is our thing, so to speak. You know this static electricity thing. Ugh, why can't our powers be like Beau and Gracious?" Thinx grinned good-naturedly. "We could be pretty, not prickly."

Vespers groaned at the pun. "No such luck. Our presence is most definitely causing these electric beams to go haywire. Look

at them frenetically zigzagging. We need to figure out how to control our powers and this static energy." Vespers was perplexed. "It
looks like they are just bouncing off the boulders and us, erratically
without a purpose."

Thinx started to really pay attention. He turned to his twin.
"You know what, I just thought of what to do. It's all counterintu-
itive come to think of it, so bear with me. We need to make it all
go faster, crazier, not the other way around."

Vespers just rolled her eyes; she'd had the same epiphany. "No
kidding, it's about time you caught up."

Thinx loved that he and Vespers need not ever explain to each
other, that they could finish each other's thoughts. They both
preferred that actually. To never ever have to explain themselves;
in his mind, it was for Vespers to understand, and vice versa, not
for the rest of them.

"Hey, Thinx, you know what, bro? I just got a great idea, and
it's a real good one on how to do it."

Beau and Gracious still held the Everters in thrall. Courage and
Olympia waved a white flag of surrender, standing strong in the
battlefield's center. Wink and Catriz, their best warriors, stood
guard by their side to ensure their protection just in case of a
misstep. Acerbus was not to be trusted; he was prideful in his
stance and slow in his gait. He walked with the strut of victory,
still disarmed by the enchantment of the charmers from Venus.

Domenica watched him as he approached the battlefield's
center. Her patience played to her strength as she waited for just
the right moment to show the softer side of her powers. Witt and
Clarity were next to her. Although the conversation between the
armies' leaders was inaudible, too low to overhear, the Everter
army had no clue to that. They were all too focused on Beau and

Gracious doing exactly what they did best. The twins from Venus stood between the troops and their leader, holding the attention of the rank and file, obscuring their view of the "negotiations."

"Arms down." Acerbus appeared in front of his surprised troops. "Everyone stand down. Can't you see we are in cease fire. They are surrendering. All of your arms are to be placed on the ground."

The Everters were startled by the order but began to drop their weapons. They didn't know it was Witt who now stood before them, who had shape-shifted, and looked for all the world like their leader. Domenica mimicked Acerbus's voice perfectly.

The Taurian twin continued, "Those children are all cowards, weaklings; even their leader Honora abandoned them because of their spineless behavior. We are now taking them all prisoner. They have surrendered. See their leaders begging for forgiveness and their best fighters just standing by, awaiting the terms of their surrender. We will not be merciful."

"Get into legion formation now." Her voice thundered, in perfect pitch as Acerbus. They followed orders and formed six tight ranks of six by six.

Beau and Gracious gazed out at the orderly field, smiling their captivating smiles. Slowly they began to juggle; faster, faster, and faster the balls spun. CeSe and Skye sprang to the forefront. Ever so gently they had been coaxing the power of the wind to nudge their army of enemies closer and closer to the Imperium, ever so careful not to alert them. The soft currents seemed a comfort to them as they slowly moved with the undercurrent. Closer and closer they got to the very place where they needed to be.

With a roar, the soft breeze they so enjoyed now picked up to a gust, to a gale, to a twister. Then the suction of the aerial screw created by the twins from Pretty Venus burst into a whirlwind. The Everters were suddenly swept up in a cyclone of air that moved them over to the epicenter of the circle.

Acerbus snapped out of his trance and realized the extent of his folly; the big guy had been duped. A ferocious growl shook the ground itself as he tried to wield his mighty sword towards Olympia and Courage.

"Put that sword down," Honora thundered knocking off his helmet and grabbing him by his hair.

Turning to the twins, she said, "You seem to have things under control here, my dear hearts. If you don't mind, I have a private score to settle here with this one." They could hear Acerbus screech as she dragged him off high into the nighttime sky.

Suddenly, a thunderous clapping could be heard, its sound undeniably recognizable.

Arret du temps.

Time was being slowed down to a complete stop. It was A'dept and Yejidi, giving their brothers and sisters time, the time they needed to complete one more task. The sheer brute strength of Harm and Domenica kept the vortex of wind around their enemy tight. Wink and Catriz fought any stragglers who tried to escape the tunnel of wind, making sure the Everters were imprisoned in the airstream.

Time had indeed stopped, but not for all of them. Some of the twins stayed outside the perimeter of the time stop's reach and dashed back to the tree fortress.

"Everything is math," said Thinx and Vespers, at the chalkboard refining their device. The Aquarian twins stretched a detailed scaled drawing of a catapult. Madly the others hurried to construct the machine, working outside of time. The Celestial Task Masters gave them the space needed to complete the task.

"Clap! Clap! Clap!" Another thunderous clap.

Le temps commence, and it did.

All twelve sets of twins were now in play, set in motion like a finely tuned clock. The wooden apparatus was built to specifications and was ready to go. Now it was up to OnyX and Mysterious, who steadied themselves right outside the circle. Their moment was upon them. They awaited their orders from Courage and Olympia, who led the maneuvers to levitate the giant catapult into place.

Courage shouted. "Now!"

Using their powers of levitation, the twins from Pluto lifted the cyclonic cylinder of the Everter army higher and higher towards the opening of the wormhole.

Wink pointed towards the cosmic string. "Steady! Steady! Steady!" It was all maddening.

The giant catapult was in the exact place that Thinx and Vespers specified. The twins from Uranus were now stationed in the very heart of the Imperium. They depended upon A'dept and Yejidi to follow the mathematical formula they'd laid out. The calculations had to be exact, precise to the smallest decimal if this was ever going to work. The slightest deviation from the drawings would prove to be a disaster.

The twins from Jolly Jupiter readied themselves for launch into the catapult. Right now, they needed every little bit of that luck everyone said was their special gift. Each of them worked so very hard on this plan, this united effort that required the upmost precision in skill, power, and concentration. It seemed so wrong to depend on something so random as chance of fortune, but so be it. One thing they each had in this moment in time was the gift of faith in each other.

The clapping stopped; time was on the move again. Who else but the twins from Willful Mars to take the lead? Wink and Catriz centered themselves and ran towards the seesaw before executing a perfect synchronized triple somersault into the air. They landed most correctly on the other side of the seesaw, catapulting both Sage and AlexSandra high into the Earth's atmosphere. Steady,

steady, steady they soared until they were right under the entire army of those bad guys. Closer and closer and closer they soared, legs outstretched in perfect position.

Using the power of the full moon, Evan and Chance used the moonbeams to encircle the electromagnetic currents, to corral in their erratic movement to help Thinx and Vespers have better control over the elements within the circle. It worked, as Witt and Clarity—now moving at the speed of sound—created an electrostatic doorway. Within seconds a cry went out.

"We found it. We can see the opening. We can see it!" Thinx shouted. Now he and Vespers needed to withstand the pain of the electromagnetic currents. They did not have the power to harness its boundless energy, not yet.

"Hurry up, we can't stand this much longer."

Colored bands of light crisscrossed the heavens, and the static of electricity raged within the circle. All twelve sets of twins stayed the course, awaiting the exact second—the only moment that would spell success. And then that moment came.

Thinx sent a telepathic message to his siblings. The portal to the cosmic string was opening. *One, two, three . . .*

"*Bam!*"

Cheers, hoots, and hollers could be heard throughout the galaxy or so it seemed. The twins were jubilant with their victory. "We did it! I did it! Everybody did it!" It did not matter who or how—*they did it!*

Their moment of celebration was cut short.

A shrill sound pierced the air. The wormhole was a two-way street.

The Everter army was thrust back to whence it came, but a large dark ominous creature dropped from the sky within the very second the portal opened. It landed with a tremendous thud, its hiss menacing.

"What is happening?" Evan screamed.

"You have got to be kidding." Wink was not amused.

"Now what?" AlexSandra was perplexed.

"*What is that thing?*" signed Witt.

"That's Ahreman's pet. It's known as a Komodo dragon," Thinx informed his siblings.

How do you know that? signed Clarity. *Never mind,* she answered herself.

"Is it dangerous?" asked Courage.

"*Is it dangerous?*" Domenica imitated her brother's voice. "What do you think?"

The creature then responded with a breath of fire. Flames flickered from its nostrils, its eyes blood red.

"Be careful," Fastidious cried. "Its saliva is deadly poison."

"I am not worried about its venom. I'm more concerned about being burned to death." Gracious weighed the options and was poised to flee.

"Look at those teeth and claws. They look like razors." Sage pointed, taking note from afar.

"There are sixty of them," Vespers blurted. "Watch out for its claws; they are made of Xyzanium. Its hide is also almost impenetrable."

"Any other helpful facts in this moment?" A sarcastic Catriz was losing patience.

"No, not in this moment." Vespers adjusted her eyeglasses.

OnyX moved in a little closer. "Hey, big fellow, look this way. Come on." The monster responded with a roar, brandishing its weapons.

"Be careful, brother, not sure if this big guy is afraid of that stare of yours." Yejidi, too, moved closer, trying to assess their next play.

"We need a plan." Adept needed to hear his own voice and more importantly wanted his siblings to know their best strength was in the collective. "But first we need to close that portal before we get any more surprises."

"No, not yet!" It was Skye. "No, not yet!" His voice carried a reverberation to its tone that helped carry its echo.

"Spar! Come now, Spar, come to me now!" It was Excelsia. She raised her face and spoke to the sky. A silvery mist enveloped her; ice crystals twinkled in the vapor as she rose to meet the cosmic string. Her platinum hair was wild and flowing. The wind ripped ferociously about her presence as she held her hands with palms outstretched.

"Maman, ready Spar and release him to me. Release him now."

Esme watching at the portal, ever-present if needed, ever vigilant in anticipation of just such a summons. Excelsia using her powers of mental telepathy focused her thoughts, and Esme heard her daughter's voice. With alacrity, the great ship readied. In an iolite pod of cosmic dust, Spar was released from the *Sphere of Comets* hurling towards the planet Earth, along the cosmic string a nanosecond before it winked shut.

Like a bolt of lightening, so magnificent to behold, the horse's pure platinum mane and tail billowed in a cloud of ionized iolite. The steed's armor glinted by the light of the moon; its startling entrance left the twins in awe, breathless with their mouths agape.

Pawing the ground, sniffing the air, and absorbing the JX, Spar became accustomed to the Earth's atmosphere very quickly. The twins watched spellbound as his ears grew sharp-tipped into long sword points.

"Spar's rapier ears are also of Xyzanium. Just saying." Of course, it was Vespers the Aquarian who needed to let everyone know what she knew. "Oh, and his chainmail coat, that too."

Sage and AlexSandra were without words, completely stunned by this powerful creature's transformation. Simultaneously, their eyes looked at their little pet alpaca who quietly whirred in the background.

"Hey, Alphonso, are you really a secret shape shifter? Are you really a menacing super pet, too? Come on, you can tell us, we will keep your secret. We promise not to tell anybody." A low soft hum was his response and then more soft humming.

Flummoxed, AlexSandra felt the need to say the wrong thing. "So why exactly do they get a super pet and not us?" The twins from Sagittarius were still keeping score, no matter what the odds.

Everyone just ignored the two from Jolly Jupiter, save Harmonious whose temper was getting the best of him. "I can beat this monster. I know I can. Let me at him," he recklessly howled.

"No." Domenica stopped her brother. "These two creatures are evenly matched at least in brute strength."

"Maybe so," said Beau. "But this monster's saliva is venomous. It's not fair to Spar, not fair at all."

"No, that would be very unjust." Gracious would have none of the suggestion always seeking to balance the scales.

Fastidious quickly spoke up. "We can remedy that situation and even the odds." He turned to Clarity who was right next to him. "Hurry, if you please, and get the oleander salve that Tien made last night."

"Do you mean that ointment she made from AlexSandra's flower, that lovely pink oleander rose, the one that was poisonous?" Clarity was using her voice.

"Exactly."

In the blink of an eye, Clarity had the potion and placed it in her brother's hands. Tien grabbed it and jumped up on Spar's back. "Easy, easy, this will not hurt a bit. I just need to smother your new shiny weapons with this ointment, that's all, big guy, that's all. Just another second, I will be finished. I promise."

The mighty steed snorted in acquiescence. Jagged crystals of ice formed from the vapor. The others followed this plan without question. Believing in this new turn of events.

It was Skye who made his way into the center of the group who crowded around the great stallion. He spoke gently to Spar as he nuzzled his best companion's nose.

"You need to go for his underbelly. It is the only place where he is vulnerable." The horse shook its head in trust. They shared this quiet confidence. That quiet moment of trust before a battle.

~

Spar quivered, eager to be off to meet his fate, but it was now Excelsia who held him firmly as her twin relinquished the reins. "Give me Wink's sword over there," she said. "And dip it into the oleander salve, too." Skye watched his beloved twin as she began to form the iolite sphere that would encase her. It was not completely impervious but would shield her from glancing blows and protect her from the poison.

How he longed to go with her, but Spar was her special familiar; the two had trained and trained until they seemed to be of one mind. This was her choice to fight, her way of protecting the family she loved so much. Each and every one of her siblings would have taken her place, especially he, her twin.

This summons—this calling was hers to answer.

Shimmering in the pink/blue coruscations of her sphere, she vaulted into the saddle. Spar reared and pivoted in a circle as she saluted her celestial siblings, a formable Valkyrie primed and fearless. Excelsia nuzzled the stallion's nose and whispered into his ear the secrets of battles not foretold. They were of one now, together in this, their fates intertwined.

"I know about these dragons; they are fearsome, of the same mind as their master." Thinx and Vespers knew to stay close, never knowing when some of their boundless fount of useless information might be needed. "Be very careful; their speed and agility is most deceiving."

Spar snorted, nodding his understanding of each word. And then, at an invisible signal from his rider, Spar leapt into the air and shot like a missile towards the dragon.

Gouts of fire erupted from the gaping maw of the beast. Its forked tongue snaked out testing the air, seeking its foe by smell. As CeSe approached, Spar zigzagged hoping to confuse the creature. It was a mistake, as the dragon suddenly rose up on its hind legs, jaws wide to snatch her. The brute was much faster than they had thought; Spar quickly retreated.

That was a little too close. The twins from Uranus swallowed hard, trying to anticipate Spar's approach. *Remember he is Ahreman's pet, and just as dangerous.*

CeSe murmured to her mount, verbalizing what was telepathic communication. "We can't fight it head on." She urged her beloved pet. Her mount disagreed. Against all logic, Spar stood his ground directly in front of the massive jaws. In a blinding move, the stallion spun his forelegs and executed a perfect croupade, smashing his mighty hind legs square under the monster's chin. The dragon responded with a mass of flame.

"No!" Skye cried aloud, wanting to save his twin. Wink held him firmly back, as did the others, as the inferno roared past them, barely missing Spar's hooves by inches. It looked hopeless as everyone realized this foe was far more deadly than anticipated.

Catriz called out. "You need to get him in a pincer movement to get to his weak spot."

It was again the twins from Uranus. "That massive body has lightning quick reflexes. Not easy to get to his underbelly."

Others jumped into action. The twins from Pluto tried to levitate the dragon but to no avail. Time was moving much too fast, and all of them were spent and exhausted by the battle that just ensued with the Eveters.

Then the solution came, from a must unlikely warrior.

"They have a third eye, they have a third eye, and it's right on top of their head." It was Thinx. "He can't see you because it only senses light, but it's the only other vulnerable spot."

CeSe sprang into action with a reverse of tactics.

A horrified gasp could be heard; the heavens took note as twenty-three pairs of eyes witnessed Excelsia leap from Spar's back and hover midair. Her trajectory was slow and deliberate. The dragon lifted up, throwing its head back to gather a fatal volcanic blast at his opponent. Spar was caught in his headlights. The Xyzanium scales glittered; they were impenetrable. What the monster did not see, and did not sense, was CeSe poised directly behind him. Raising the gleaming sword that belonged to her brother and sister from Mars, she thrust the poison-coated spear deep into the soft third eye. It was a perfect tactical move.

Black gore erupted from the wound, spurting high into the air. Spar and CeSe rocketed away, out of reach from the poisonous ichor. The beast bellowed, belching flames, and clawing the air in a futile attempt to dislodge the blade. With a shriek, it crashed to the dust and shuddered one last time.

Lightly, CeSe touched down, her iolite sheath dissipating in a shower of twinkling light. Spar alighted at her side, and she collapsed against his neck. Both warriors were trembling at the strain of the battle, depleted and frayed. After a couple of breaths, she raised her head to find her twin. Skye pushed through the crowd and gave her a hug, not wanting to let go—wanting time to stop, to stay in this moment of being forever safe.

"You did it!" he mouthed, not needing to hear the words.

"No, Skye, we all did it!" She, too, answered without a word being spoken.

Spar whinnied in agreement.

CHAPTER 22

Moonstones

The battle was over. The Earth was reborn, back to the way it was before all that happened happened.

Hills and valleys rose and fell in carpets of green. The water shimmered as it moved from the streams to rivers, flowing at last to the oceans teeming with sea life.

Time moved again.

The air—one of the Earth's most precious gifts with those tiny particles of nitrogen, oxygen, and hydrogen—remained safe and sound, almost perfect, well almost perfect. Some of it, unfortunately, will be forever lost, used wantonly by those unaware of the predetermined limitation of such gifts.

Only one field remained scorched and barren, the sun's powers barely able to pass through the dust. It was where the battle had taken place. To those who come upon it, it will remain a compendium of mystery secrets as to why nothing will ever grow there. What catastrophic events could have rendered this place so infertile? They will speculate and pontificate, but the answers will remain forever carefully locked away.

But this story has a beginning. It started with two who were chosen, were sent on a mission, and were committed to completing it—no matter what the personal cost.

Earth, the third planet from the Dazzling Sun was safe. Victory celebrations were happening all around; it resounded through the universe. The celestial twins were so overcome in the excitement of the moment that they forgot what had been at stake and what might have been lost. In this moment, they wanted to be kids again, and it was about time for them to have some fun and enjoy their well-deserved moment.

"So, exactly where are Nicho and Pen again? *We* saved their precious Earth for them, and once again they seem to have disappeared. They always wander off, doing whatever it is they were supposed to do, or promised to do, or whatever . . ." said a miffed Mysterious.

"Well, I guess fighting is not one of their strengths. They did a good job missing all of it, that is for sure." It was AlexSandra, still keeping her endless tally.

"Well, *we* did it, *we* beat up those bad guys, *we* kicked them right back to whence they came," boasted Catriz, not choosing her favorite word—"I"—showing some maturity.

"Now they can come back and thank us, each and every one of us," Wink continued. "Come out of hiding, Nicho! Come out, Pen, come out, come out, wherever you are." The banter continued with hoots, cheers, and jeers.

Their childish games continued until Chance and Evan spoke up.

"We have a really bad feeling in our stomachs about this, an awful feeling," Chance said. "Something might have happened to them, something bad." He gave his siblings an earnest look; he trusted his intuition.

"Chance is right," echoed Evan. "Where *are* they?"

"The last I saw them was in the Imperium, right before the battle, then they disappeared, just like they always seem to do." AlexSandra paused for a second upon hearing her own words and then started to sound a little concerned. "Well, that was the last time I saw them anyway."

Wink and Catriz spurred the others to action. "They can't be far; let's all get started and look for them. Come on, everybody, let's go."

Witt and Clarity whizzed around and around, looking high and low. Domenica and Harm lifted all the fallen debris from the battle, searching in the destruction for clues.

"We all know they went to look for the Tunnel of Infinity to replace the Latter Twelfstanin. Do you think they are still there, stuck in that crazy dangerous space?" Mysterious knew the territory. "I mean, what could have taken them this long?"

Everyone now was on high alert.

"Our sun is just coming up, it will be easier to find them once it's light out." Rage and Olympia sounded optimistic. Tien and Fastidious did not share their confidence; they just knew that something terribly wrong had taken place. It was a fact.

A'dept and Yejidi brought the map that Witt and Clarity had made to help Mysterious retrace her steps. "Let's get a plan together right now."

$\approx$

Esme and Mikai, too, watched in trepidation from the *Sphere of Comets*. This was a different sort of test for their twins, something they had never experienced. What happened if Nicholas and Penelope were dead? How to explain death to immortals? What could she as their mother say? That there is an emptiness where there was once plenteous. That there is a silence where there was once music. They now understood the hum of harmony and the discord of evil, but how could she explain the presence of just such a loss? For each, it would manifest so differently.

To Beau and Gracious, the flute without a sound,
To Wink and Catriz, a game without a winner,
To Domenica and Harmonious, a song without a chorus,
To Witt and Clarity, a moment without hearing,
To Evan and Chance, a moon void of course,
To Courage and Olympia, to lead without anyone who would follow,
For Fastidious and Tien, to teach without anyone to learn,
For Mysterious and OnyX, a puzzle that cannot be solved,
For Sage and AlexSandra, a story with no one to tell,
To Yejide and Adept, a day without order,
To Thinx and Vespers, a question without an answer,
And to Excelsia and Skye, to never see their reflection.

"Is this where your map would have sent them?" Tien asked. "It looks like a wall of solid rock, in the shape of a puzzle. See how all the pieces intersect." She looked to her sister. "How can this be? X marks this spot. So where are they?"

"It looks like the same place, no, this is the very same place that I entered, but now it is completely sealed up. I don't understand how that could have happened." Mysterious looked to her brother Sage, who spied on her at the slot canyon's entrance. "Mysterious, you are right. It does sound a little crazy, but yes, that's the truth. You never resealed that opening. I watched you as you left that spooky place."

So, exactly who did, and why?" Their voices melded and sounded perplexed.

"Move away, let me look." AlexSandra shook her head, as she pushed the others aside. "This just can't be." Even with her superior gift of sight she could not see through the impenetrable wall of solid stone.

"This is a real puzzle, even for me." Mysterious was still flummoxed.

"Here, let us have a go at that wall; we can knock it down, for sure." Domenica and Harmonious were ready for action. "Mysterious and OnyX, help us lift these boulders by levitating them just high enough for Sage and AlexSandra to give each rock a good swift kick into the atmosphere. Witt and Clarity, shape shift and try to see what is beyond this barrier. It must be a fortification of some sort. Let's knock it down; come on, everyone."

They all tried, but their efforts were to no avail. It was futile. The entrance to the Tunnel of Infinity was blocked. The massive wall loomed up, seeming to laugh at their childlike attempts to knock it down.

A quietness came over each of them as they searched for their Earthly friends. "Well, let's at least clear this small stuff that is buttressed against this blockade of stone." A small pile of rocks still remained clustered up against the cliff face. "We can sift through this debris, maybe find a clue, or anything that will tell us something—even give us a hint." A slight tone of desperation could be heard in Thinx's voice.

A sentiment shared with many of his siblings as they dutifully began to slowly sift their way through the debris. It was an arduous task, as they meticulously swept and brushed up the thick and cloying dust. Searching, hoping for an answer.

"Hey guys," Clarity used her voice. "See over there. Can you please move these scattered stones deep in that recess? Witt and I can at least get a look behind them."

It took but a moment; within seconds, their shocked cries echoed off the great wall, their voices filled with hope and dread as they squeezed through the now-open crevice.

Here, here they are, right here. Oh no, we found them, but lying very still. They aren't moving, Witt signed. He and Clarity kept spinning around, not wanting to think about another word.

The others slowly made their way to the two listless bodies.

"Do you think they are just sleeping?" Beau asked. "Why else would they be lying so still?"

"Maybe they got knocked out in all of the confusion of the battle," Gracious reasoned. "They are almost hidden. Almost . . ."

Echoes of "Do you think? Do you think? Do you think?" Spread throughout the group.

"We were supposed to protect them." Courage and Olympia said it first.

"Yes," agreed Skye and Excelsia. "That was our promise to each other."

Then Excelsia offered an idea. "OnyX, Mysterious, Fastidious, and Tien, you have power to heal. *Do something.*"

The four of them nodded in agreement but hesitated to move, fearing what they might discover, fearing the unknown, fearing to know what they did not want to know.

"Oh, this does not seem right, not at all. I mean it can't be that all of it, everything that each of us had been thought is supposed to end this way. Maybe they are still here with us; we just don't know it." Domenica wanted an answer.

Harmonious agreed. "Domenica must be right; this cannot be the end." The twins from Silent Sedna, always shy and retiring, now took a big leap of faith. "This might be one last test for all of us."

"It is certainly plausible. I mean with this 'in time' and 'out of time,' the past, the present, and the future all mixed up. Maybe their bodies are separated from their minds," reasoned Beau. "Well, it's certainly not implausible." He looked for affirmation from his siblings, and then he did not feel he needed it. "Domenica and Harmonious, I think you are on to something. It's a fact."

"Agreed, since nothing else makes sense, why should this make sense? All of the rules are different, and whatever happened, it happened in that tunnel. So, who knows, anything is possible, anything." Tien analyzed and she, too, felt sure of it.

"How about Pen's moonstones, are they there? Look in her backpack. Are they still in her backpack or not?" Vespers asked, thinking ahead.

No, her moonstones are all gone, Clarity signed. *But we still have ours.*

"Moonstones, that is it. Let's go back to the beginning when we first got here, let's go to that Circle of Stones." Olympia led the way. Harmonious and Domenica followed, gently carrying Nicho's and Pen's bodies. They tenderly placed them in the circle's center and slowly walked away.

Their moment of triumph now felt empty, their hearts broken. Although each one of them was very much aware of their superpowers, they felt in this moment completely powerless. They wanted to believe there was a way back. They wanted to believe that there was hope. They did not want to live another second of this path of uncertainty.

"Remember when we first met Nicho and Pen? We all sat within the Imperium, each one of us in our designated space. We all used our collective intelligence to share all that we needed to complete our task," Tien pointed out. "Now, we need to use all of our collective energies with the help of our moonstones. We should start there again."

Each set of twins took their place before the corresponding glyph. All stared towards the very center of the circle where Nicho and Pen lay, looking fast asleep. Their expressions were peaceful, as though they were dreaming of an adventure in some faraway place.

Tien and Fastidious methodically placed in a circular formation one of each twin's gemstones near and about their earthly bodies to form a straight line with the other twin's matching stone, forming a radii to each matching pair. Just like before, due to the precise placement of each of the twenty-four stones, the moonstones all glowed and then formed a band of pure color within each section of the circle, like the twelve spokes of a wheel.

The presence of the full moon was still evident in the early morning sky, while the sun was just rising in the east. Tien led her siblings in what she hoped was a solution.

"Now let's hold hands and concentrate on the powers that we have, the powers we would like to have, and those that we are meant to have. The power of that JX must still be present. Honora used it to regain her strength; let it help them now, too." *And us,* she thought, *please, and us.*

Forty-eight hands clasped—all hoped and prayed as they tried to focus using their collective energy. Although the sun rays did not yet reach the horizon, Courage and Olympia could feel a new surge of power unlike anything they had felt before. They knew from their recent experience, their newfound powers were not yet under their control, not yet. So they chose to just let the energy flow through them instead of trying to direct it.

Glimmering rays of color emanated from each moonstone, like fireworks against an early dawn sky. This pattern was familiar to them at first, but then the luminosities seemed to take on a will of their own. Shifting symmetrical patterns rotated in a surge of power the twins had never seen. This kaleidoscope moved with such speed and force that flashes of light splintered between the pillars. The power within the circle seemed unrelenting as shards of multicolored light shafts blinded the twins again and again.

Then a preternatural clap of thunder and a bizarre bolt of lightning streaked across the heavens. Then it all stopped. A deathly silence reigned.

The twins rans towards their earthly friends, hoping to greet them again. But nothing, nothing had changed. They'd done everything they knew to do, everything within their powers, and they'd failed.

They looked at each other in disbelief.

"I want to go home," wailed a plaintive voice. No one knew who said it first; it did not matter, all of them— started to cry tears of sadness as they were bereft with grief. Each of them felt so lost. All twenty-four clamored at the sky, hoping their parents could hear their fervent wishes up in the *Sphere of Comets*. "*We want to go home. We just want to go home.*"

"Are you kidding? Yes, well, we want to go home, too, but we mean home, home—where we were before all that happened happened." It was Pen, her voice so matter of fact as she sat up in the center of the circle.

She yawned, and then yawned again. "What is everyone looking at? What is the matter with you guys?" She was annoyed already. "What is up with those crazy eyes?"

"Hey, what happened, did we win?" Nicho had a good feeling about the battle as he too stood up, dusting himself off. His mop of hair fell over his eyes, as he tried to slick it back. *I really do need a haircut.*

Shocked faces turned towards the twins from Earth as a profound quietness overtook the group—save one.

"Where did you go, we thought you were . . ." Sage started to say; somehow the words thankfully would not come.

"Thought we were what?" Pen looked puzzled, but not as confused as the other 24 sets of eyes that just stared at them. She just shrugged and continued. "We went, we went into that crazy

Tunnel of Infinity, that Mysterious warned us about, oh, and that Honora, well she just left us there, *again.* The next thing we were outside, somewhere over there, I think. I don't remember. Everything is a bit fuzzy." Pen gathered herself and looked around as if searching for something; no, she was looking for someone. *"But wait, where is . . .?"*

Nicholas abruptly interrupted his twin. "Oh no, it's you again! You have got to be kidding? You have a lot of nerve!" His look was one of complete incredulity as he just shook his head in disbelief. The crimson dot in his dark brown eyes glowed.

"You really must be crazy and I mean it this time. Just so you know, what we already know, we do not need you, not anymore. Come to think of it, maybe we never did need you. So, you can just go away. Better yet, go away for good!"

"I will ignore your insolence." It was a familiar voice. *I swear these Earth twins really need to learn better manners when speaking to their elders.* She approached with her usual flourish, swirling her flickering robes. Her regal bearing was once again uncompromised.

"We have come to say goodbye." Who else but Honora could maintain such a swagger. "Nicholas and Penelope, this is my husband ZR. You were never formally introduced, but he knows all about the two of you."

Nicholas begrudgingly extended his hand, and then smiled with his heart. His fondness for her, it glimmered through his eyes. For some reason he could never stay mad at her, not ever. Honora knowingly winked at him.

"So, exactly who were those bad guys?" Pen asked, without even missing a beat. Her memory was still foggy and unclear but she wanted answers as she fervently looked around the circle. Who was she searching for? Her train of thought was again interrupted.

"Do you remember when you first looked upon the faces of Mikai and Esme?" Honora asked them, and they both nodded.

"You thought the goodness in their hearts shone in their faces just like a luminary, a light from within. Well, the hearts of those banished to the planet Eris are filled with a darkness; it's the type of darkness that grows within someone who is not happy and doesn't know love. That is who they are."

"Will we ever see them again?" Pen was trying to understand.

"Yes, I am afraid so," ZR replied. "Their evil has no beginning and no end, as is their pathway of destruction."

Nicholas and Pen felt they knew what he was trying to say, even though they hoped he was wrong.

"We don't understand why," Nicho replied.

"Sometimes, it is good not to understand. By the time you learn to understand something, the time has come to learn to forget."

It was another of those word riddles that Nicholas loved to solve. Penelope still disliked them but was learning to just ask the right question to get to the answer. With her green eyes ablaze, she looked directly at ZR and asked, "Forget, forget what?"

ZR smiled. "One can forget many things: how to trust, to love, to laugh, to learn, to hope, to dream, to be happy, and most important, how to live in the present moment. "We"—he looked at his lifelong companion—"wanted to be told things like: What was the purpose for all of it? Why this blue-green jewel was of such importance? Why did we need to pass on? We wanted to know our future. What we needed to learn was how to live, how to thrive in our present, not in our future, and not in our past."

"Did you figure out why?" Pen persisted, ever the inquisitor.

"Yes, we think so." ZR looked at these two newest guardians through the eyes of a Coterie member. He felt gladness and, more importantly, a sense of contentment for the future.

"Now it is time for us to go home." It was Honora, her voice crystal clear and firm.

"Is that back to Varuna?" asked Olympia.

"No, it's time to pass back into the place from whence we came, where we came from in the beginning," she responded but was not making eye contact with her grandchildren.

Nicholas welled up, knowing what those words implied. He instinctively moved the hair out of his eyes as he extended his hand to ZR. This time, not to say hello but to say goodbye. His grandfather then looked directly into the knowing eyes of one who was so young, but yet so old. No words were needed.

"Now we understand what was to be and what will be. We can pass knowing that we kept the ultimate promise to the one who sent us. We trust that you will keep yours, too." Honora struggled for the right words.

"We promise" was the united response, but their deepest thoughts belied the confidence of their words. Many of them wondered just what they were promising. To keep the Earth safe from bad guys. That was an easy task, but what of the other things? All Honora wanted was to imbibe more of this Earth's most precious air and its JX. That could seem harmless at first, but then again, every living thing depends upon its very existence. To learn limitations, to understand abuse, to preserve and protect the future, was that their promise?

Honora and ZR looked at each and every single one of them, and in turn, felt they could read their young minds. Only they knew the enormity of this request and of the insurmountable obstacles that would confront their grandchildren later through the trials and tribulations of their own journey in life.

"Remember, a promise is an easy thing to make but not always an easy thing to keep," Honora said, imparting a gentle word of caution.

Suddenly, the wind started to move. It brought with it the sense of change, the draft of opening one door and the closing of another.

"It is our time to go," ZR announced.

"So, where will you be if not Varuna?" asked Penelope as she moved ever so close to the both of them, not satisfied with the former response to Olympia's question.

Their eternal grandparents gave a wink and pointed to the bright blue firmament above. "Will you promise to remember us?" Honora asked.

The Earth twins winked right back.

"We promise," said Nicholas. "We will remember you every time the stars twinkle, knowing that they are winking at us."

"Or whenever we hear the echo of a piano note's ring," added Penelope.

At that moment, a brightly colored mist swirling with all twelve colors enveloped the elders, and they started to fade.

"*Wait!*" It was Penelope. "Why were we summoned?" Why us? You never answered us, and well, we have a right to know." Nicholas stood solidly right by his twin.

Mon Dieu! These Earth twins never stop with the questions. Will they ever learn some manners? Honora lovingly shook her head in disbelief. It was their time to pass, their time to experience the next phase in their own continuum, and these two finally remember to ask an unanswered question of such magnitude.

A moment of silence ensued.

It was ZR who looked directly at Nicholas. "Well, you reasoned that answer very early on, and yes, you were correct. Would you like to explain to your newly extended family what you have deduced?"

Nicholas cleared his throat and began. "It is because we are all related in the future; well, we are related now too." He paused as Esme's words came back to him. "'Remember Nicholas, time moves differently between our two worlds.'" He steadied himself through his explanation.

"Penelope and I have the DNA of all of you. We have the DNA

of each of the twelve sets of celestial twins. Our genetic code, our DNA is made up of a combination of yours—each and every one of you." He looked to ZR for support. His nod urged him to continue.

"The thought started to meld with me, when Honora told us that she was our grandmother and we shared the same genetic code. Esme and Mikai alluded to it too. It just made sense as to why we were summoned." Nicholas continued on.

"Mom and Uncle Gil, they both have the DNA of only eleven set of the twins. Our Dad Reed, has the DNA of just one twin set—Think and Vespers, the last remaining set."

Like lightening, Penelope piped in. "When our parents got married, and had us, we completed the DNA circle." She looked at the twins from Uranus. "When I first saw your wisteria-colored eyes through your glasses, I knew it was a fact." This puzzle, she figured it out, even if only a moment ago. She smiled, proud of her deduction.

Honora and ZR continued to fade.

"Wait! I still need to know . . ."

"Another time Scholar Pen, another time . . ." Honora's voice was soft, filled with grace and understanding. Each twin watched as they faded and faded into the horizon, finally disappearing into the ether. A multi-colored mist remained to mark their presence here on this Earth. A moment of silence ensued that was inter-rupted by a skyrocket of color that exploded toward the heaven and beyond.

"I am sure going to miss that crazy lady." Nicholas lamented. *But you are never where you are supposed to be, so exactly where did you really go?* As if the heavens read his mind, a light drizzle made an appearance.

"What is this? These water droplets that come from the blue above?" It was AlexSandra.

"It is called rain; and because the sun is shining, this type of rain is called a sun shower. Now, look up above." Pen pointed at a rainbow that arched across the heavens, radiating each one of their twelve colors.

The collective response was euphoric, the twins could not believe their eyes. Nicholas pointed to the blue-green band, the Sagittarian's favorite hue. Sage and AlexSandra, they gave a thumbs up—they understood.

Grinning with amusement, Nicholas gave a sideways glance to Penelope. "That Honora, as always, has one more trick up her sleeve. She always has another play."

"Yes, she always does," agreed Pen. "That is a fact."

Then they could hear her voice, but it wasn't Honora, no, not this time.

"Nicholas, Penelope, Nicholas, Penelope! Nicholas, Penelope!" This time they could hear the difference. This time they knew.

~

From the portal in the *Sphere of Comets*, Mikai and Esme watched their twins.

"Do you think they will ever want to return to their home planets? Or do you think they will decide to live together right there on this third planet from the sun?" Mikai mused.

Esme twirled her hair. "Judging by the sounds of their laughter, I think we know what they would say if we asked them." She paused. "Maybe this was the plan all along. It was in the scheme of each of their uncharted destinies to settle on the planet Earth."

Mikai joined her thoughts as they turned to look at the twelve containers of JX—now safely housed within the *Sphere of Comets*. It seemed like an eternity ago that each twin set had taken their world's supply from their home planets when they left to join their siblings. A chance request at the time. Well, perhaps.

"What seemed like a random interruption in the conundrum of

time and space, maybe was not so unintentional. Maybe Maman's folly was predetermined in the charted heavens, not an indiscriminate act of fate."

All of these thoughts were cast aside for the moment. Esme reached for her favorite flower, an iris, the rainbow flower. Mikai just shook his head. All of this for another time. He too had come to learn about unpredictability, especially when it came to Honora. "So, the loss of the Latter Twelfstanin, does that determine whatever was or whatever will be? Was it fated for all of this to remain uncertain?" He pondered. "Our world of in time seems to hold the constant stasis, but in that other world, what exists out of time, that remains the mystery secret. Maybe that is the course of fate for every living thing and not secret after all. Just the natural order of the past, present, and the future. The way of what is *free will*."

"One thing is most certain, their love for each other has most certainly grown. They have learned how to depend on one another. Maybe that too, was also a part of the uncharted way of things." Esme's heart was filled with motherly confidence; she was so proud of each of her children.

"It's time to say hello. If I remember correctly, this is how all of this started." Esme reached for her twelve-stone gemstone necklace, running her fingers across each one of the twelve gemstones. "Yes, this is exactly how we began in what seemed like another lifetime ago."

With the mere touch of her fingers, those three little words sang across the cosmos. "We love you."

"We love you, too!" came the collective response from each of her children.

In that moment, Esme's necklace beamed more brightly than ever before, and the hum of harmony, it had never sounded so perfect.

~

"Master, we have failed you." Acerbus hung his head in shame. The bruises from his lesson in humility that Honora had taught him were sore.

"You were defeated by a bunch of children and an old woman. So, what say ye, General, to my army?'

"I will accept any punishment you deem so that I may be held accountable for my actions." Acerbus's voice was barely audible.

"Oh, will you?" Ahreman sneered. "I knew you were worthless. Did you think I was not aware of your weakness? You are pathetic. This was all in the plan. Let them celebrate their false victory. Time is on my side."

"At least Honora and ZR have disappeared, this time forever." Acerbus simpered.

"I was never worried about my mother. No, there is another much stronger force than she, a much more worthy opponent has been revealed to me. I will wait. I will wait. Time is on my side."

Ahreman's chilling laughter echoed throughout his sanctuary of darkness. "I will wait." And the darkness became even darker.

CHAPTER 23

The Day After

Sun 01 degree of Libra
Moon 12 degrees of Aries

Melissa woke up with a start, gasping for air.

It was dawn, and the sun's early morning rays were struggling to shine through the pouring rain; she could feel its power trying to reach her. The pitter-patter of the water drops rhythmically echoed on the mica slate roof. It was agitating and unnerving, but it propelled her forward. The steady beat reminded her of something that she already knew she knew.

She was being summoned. She knew that sensation. She'd felt it before.

Melissa willingly obeyed; hurrying to the window, she strained her eyes to see them through the blurred stained-glass.

"Please, they must be there." It was a fervent prayer to the heavens above.

Her head seesawed between feeling foggy and moments of extreme clarity. Something had happened. How long had she been sleeping? A night, a day? Anxiety replaced any calm she had left in her being. Melissa fixed her eyes back to the water's edge trying to control the pendulum of emotions.

"How could I have fallen asleep like that? Why didn't they wake me?" Melissa was filled with rebuke, not sure if she was angrier with herself or with her twins for leaving her behind.

This feeling of remorse, it too, felt familiar. She shook it off. Grabbed an umbrella and bolted towards the screen door. As it slammed shut, it sounded like a thunderclap; the sound only upset her all the more.

Schlepping through the puddles and heavy sand, her surroundings that were always so familiar to her, now felt dreamlike. Nothing was clear, all semblance of lucidity gone, as if her mind were still in a twilight state. This time she would have none of it, she determined as she pushed on, willing herself forward to the surf, keeping her eyes centered at that place where the ocean meets the sand—the shoreline.

"Nicholas, Penelope, Nicholas, Penelope!" Her voice bounced off the water, accompanied by powerful sounds of whipping wind, pounding rain, and crashing waves.

"They have to be there. This can't happen again—no, not again. They have to be there," she chanted to herself over and over. It was pure grit that drove her to her destination, back to the beach where it all began. The panorama that surrounded her was surreal. Cognizant of different realms transitioning from here to there and back, it was like watching an old movie reel that flickers in black and white— with scenes jumbled together, ever changing but still staying the same. Then it came, that distinct hollow sound you can hear on a phonograph, in those very seconds right before the first note of the song. Melissa waited in anticipation of what it would bring. It was not the hum of harmony nor the cacophony of discord that followed, no, it was a void of complete, deafening silence.

She blinked to adjust to the shift in the continuum and refocused with new eyes.

There it was, the Moody Moon's presence still prominent, straining to be seen through the looming storm clouds. With the break of day, the Dazzling Sun's emergence was becoming more prominent in the clear section of the sky. It was that very real moment when both celestial bodies made their presence known in the dawn of the early morning vista. This day, one was shrouded by the storm of the late night while the other was pronounced in the brightness of tomorrow—two worlds, not colliding, just existing side by side. The rain had subsided as a clearness presented.

She spotted two figures by the coast. She caught her breath, could it be them? She looked again. No, they were not her twins, but . . . At first, she thought she recognized them, but then, she wasn't so sure. As she got closer to the water's edge, a sudden calm surrounded her. She knew its source and welcomed its presence.

The early morning mist was rising from the water's edge. It embodied all the soft colors of the rainbow that churned up from the sea. Melissa watched the fog envelope the two people like a cocoon. They turned to Melissa and nodded. The subtly tinted fog surrounded them for a few more seconds, giving Melissa just enough time to acknowledge them. No, just enough time to let them know she knew. That she was thankful. Then they both disappeared. Melissa looked out upon the tranquil sea, her eyes searching, drawn towards the offing—but, they had absconded to the place where they now belonged. A sun shower had replaced the storm and a magnificent rainbow arched across the firmament. It was an affirmation.

"Nicholas, Penelope! Nicholas, Penelope!" She continued, hoping that the resonance of her voice would summon them, bringing them back to her. Of course, it would. Melissa now understood what had happened. She trusted what it would bring.

When she refocused her attention back towards the surf, there they were—her twins. She watched them closely. Nicholas withdrew his hand, and Penelope wiped her face, no, she was wiping tears from her eyes. Over the next few moments, they stared quietly into the absconse at the horizon. *Were they pointing to something?* No, no, never mind, it did not matter, it did not matter at all, they were here now, safe at home. Safe at home with her.

As she approached them, her emotions were mixed with elation and angst. She knew she should be furious with them for going to the beach alone at night, but she somehow knew in her mind's eye and in her heart, they were both exactly where they were supposed to be.

"Nicholas, Penelope," their mother whispered this time ever so softly.

They both slowly turned around and stared at her as if in disbelief. Like they, too, had just been awakened from a deep sleep.

"Mom, where did you come from?" Nicholas seemed skeptical.

"What are you doing here?" followed Penelope, her tone, too, incredulous.

Melissa stepped gingerly and moved closer to them, offering her umbrella. It took but a few seconds, and then came their mischievous twin smiles. Melissa breathed a sigh of relief. Without saying a word, she opened her parasol wide and gathered them to her. It felt good, it felt right. At first, they were silent listening to the soft raindrops splash against the ground and the umbrella. Then, before she could ask them any questions, both Nicholas and Penelope began telling and telling their stories, words flourishing like the rush of the wind before a late summer storm.

"Mom, we went beyond Earth, into other worlds, and we flew in this spaceship called the *Sphere of Comets*, it was a school, and we saw, well, it's hard to describe them, but we made all of these new friends. They were like us, but magical. I think they were angels—" Penelope began.

"*Nooo*, Mom, they were not angels," said Nicholas emphatically, interrupting his sister, "but they each had their own special powers, each one of them. There were twenty-four of them—twelve pairs of twins, just like us."

"I have enough trouble just keeping track of the two of you. Twenty-four?" Melissa replied.

Nicholas heard the pinch of doubt in her voice. "Come on, Mom, there were twenty-four kids, just like in our class at school. That's not so hard to remember, is it?" he insisted. "And they all had the same mother and father. Their mother's name was Esme, and their father was Mikai."

Nicholas and Penelope spoke about Esme and Mikai, the twins' parents, and their grandparents, Honora and ZR. How they were kind and happy, loving to each other, their children, and every creature in the universe. In fact, they were caretakers for the Earth, the planets, the moons, the stars, the sun, and the wind.

"So, Mom, what is your JQ?" Penelope suddenly changed the subject.

"Excuse me?" Melissa asked, caught off guard.

"You know, your JQ, everyone has a JQ. How come you never heard of it? I know mine is very high." Nicholas smiled proudly.

"Maybe so, but it's not higher than mine!" Pen would hear none of that—not now, not ever—even if she didn't know how high hers actually was.

There was another long pause as if no one wanted to actually reply.

"Mom, some of the stuff that happened, well, it gets confusing in my mind." Penelope was first to admit. "I don't remember a lot of it or if it really happened. I just remember snippets, and then I don't. Does that sound crazy?"

"Yeah, it's like some of it, we aren't supposed to remember. Does that make any sense to you? We keep thinking it must have been some crazy dream, but *how* can we both share the same exact dream?" That was her Nicholas, always questioning beyond what was in front of him.

"Just tell me everything," Melissa said. "And then it won't seem so bad because we're together now and we love each other. There's a lot of power in that."

In that moment, the unreal impact of what had actually transpired was crystal clear in Melissa's mind. Then in the next second the knowledge slowly slipped away.

So be it, she muttered to herself. She too had learned some lessons and accepted that these recollections would continue to remain elusive. *Get accustomed to it and learn to live the uncertainty.* Melissa looked down at her twins and was simply grateful to have them returned to her. "I have come to take you home," she stammered.

Their response to her was silence for what seemed like an eternity. They looked different to her; like they were changed somehow. As if they were not her two little twins that she had put to bed the night before what happened happened. Maybe it was a feeling that they were growing up and slipping away from her. Maybe the life that the three of them knew might somehow be changed by what happened while she was asleep. She didn't know.

So she just said it.

Those three little words, that she had intoned to them every night since they were born. It was a familiar mantra, and she had come to depend on the response. With a deep breath Melissa whispered, "I love you."

The words floated on the air. The aria of the violin played ever so softly as the phrase drifted above the ocean's roar and the wind's whispers. Time seemed to stop as she waited for their response.

"I love you, too," they both replied with a wink.

"Hey Mom, did you know that when a baby is born, its star leaves the sky." Nicholas's tone let her know this was a statement not a question.

"And, Mom, when it's their turn to pass on, that very same star goes right back to the heavens, exactly from where it came," Penelope stated with same affirmation.

Nicholas called to her as he bounded ahead, stopped, and then turned wanting to see the expression on her face. "Mom."

"Yes?" Melissa, too, wanted to see the very same on his.

"You are here to take us *home home,* right?"

She smiled and winked right back at them. As they walked through the sand, dune grass, and walkway of the colorful wild-flowers that graced their little cottage by the sea, Melissa spotted someone on the porch.

She was apprehensive at first. "*How could this possibly be?*" But there he was. He was waiting for her, no, he was waiting for them, sitting in her favorite green rocking chair.

As he slowly stood up to welcome them, Melissa could see that pair of wisteria eyes. They twinkled a smile at her through his spectacles.

Penelope leaped towards him.

"It's like I said, we are *all* together now, and there is a lot of power in that." It was Melissa.

While in midair Penelope's response was clearly heard.

"Hey Mom, that's a fact."

THE TALKING
PANELS

Wink and Catriz, "the starters"

Birth Planet: Willful Mars
Culture: Iberian Peninsula—Latinex
Astrological DNA: Aries
Astrological Element: Fire
Platonic Solid: Tetrahedron

Moonstone: Diamond

Signature ID: Diamond at the forehead; wears hats/headbands/ headscarves/tattoos

Favorite color: Red

Pet: A Ruby Hummingbird (Rojo) and a Ladybug (Rue)

Flower: Red Daisy

Food: Lollipops and Pomegranate seeds

Special powers: Can split the nucleus in atoms to create energy, create fire, powerfully athletic and acrobatic

Physical Attributes: Athletic build; berry-colored skin; large warm brown eyes, and thick dark hair both tinged with red; arms always back ready for action; tiny scar around the eyes; male/ female; wink a lot

Favorite Activities: Sprinting, skateboarding, lacrosse, fencing, drawing comic book illustrations of action graphics, playing the drums, and loves, loves, loves to be first.

Personality Traits: Wink and Catriz are wonderful leaders who always need a pat on the back for support. Compliments and encouragement move them forward in a positive way. They can possess a willfulness that can characterize their personality in one word—impulsive. They will use the word "I" a lot, but that is not because they are talking about themselves, it's because in their minds, they are stating a fact. They are very willful, headstrong, and energetic. They love the underdog and people who are kind to them. Open to change and optimistic, they have self-confidence but not as much as they would like you to believe. So again, be mindful to always cheer them on. They can tend to sulk with a childish temper when things do not go their way. Mischievous and winks a lot, easily bored with little patience but have the gift of luck that is shared by their other fire sign siblings (Leo and Sagittarius). A good starter of the action but not a good finisher. They need most of all to understand the consequence of their actions and accept their competitive nature. Then learn how not to be so defensive about the essence of their personality. Aries rules the head so they need to learn how to "think first." Of course, as children they will often trip because they don't watch where they are going. Loves to wear hats and headbands and loves to be noticed, after all they are a fire sign, you know. Catriz does not like to wear a dress unless she is dancing, but always super stylish in the boldest of colors: red. They make for great friends especially in times of need. In classical astrology, think of the key words—I Am.

Domenica and Harmonious, "the doers"

Birth Planetoid: Silent Sedna
Culture: Roman
Astrological DNA: Taurus
Astrological Element: Earth
Platonic Solid: Cube

Moonstone: Emerald

Signature ID: Neckerchief, very long scarf, choker with their emerald pin

Favorite Color: Green (colors of spring)

Pet: A Parrot (Avangelina "Ava") and a Grasshopper (Pimento)

Food: Flavored water ice and green pimento olives

Flower: Magnolia

Special Powers: Strength, excellent memory, mimics voices

Physical Attributes: Thick muscular physique, light brown wavy hair, emerald eyes, olive-toned skin, and a beautiful melodic voice.

Favorite Activities: Singing, sculpting, violin, wrestling, loves scooters and complaining

Personality Traits: Domenica and Harmonious have a quiet sweetness. Their lovable demeanor accentuates their shyness. They love lots of hugs and kisses. They can be patient and resistant to change. They initially say no to things and then eventually come around, so remember to nudge, they will be happy you did. Always need to feel secure, if not, they are unhappy, and then be a little cranky. They can play alone but also like the team spirit and can always be relied on in a clutch. They sometimes take credit for the good deeds of others, but that is only because they find criticism so difficult to accept and seek approval much like Libra. They also believe what others may tell them at "face value," similar to their other Venus-ruled siblings. Domenica and Harmonious can be very funny because they have an uncanny ability to imitate voices. So, they will repeat themselves a lot, telling the same stories over and over again. They complete the trail of unfinished tasks of others through sheer force of will—but complain about it similar to their Capricorn siblings. They can be little hoarders as they keep and collect everything as that suits their nostalgic nature. They can also be very secretive. They do not like to share their food or toys unless they really like someone; they feel a sense of ownership about such things. They will use the words, "it's mine," a lot. They need to accept change more readily. Has a bad temper that thank goodness rarely erupts. They are creatures of habit and love their home. They possess artistic talent that includes painting and sculpture. Taurians love rewards and to be recognized for their good deeds. They love to dress in soft colors of nature. In classical astrology, think of the key words—I Have.

Witt and Clarity, "the informers"

Birth Planet: Dizzy Mercury
Culture: Anglo-Saxon
Astrological DNA: Gemini
Astrological Element: Air
Platonic Solid: Octahedron

Moonstone: Peridot/Titanate

Signature ID: Earrings

Favorite Color: Lemon/Lime, bright colors of summer

Pets: 2 Jack Russell Terrier puppies, Huckleberry is brown/white, Mollydots is black/white, and a Sandpiper (Peep)

Flower: Anemone (the wind flower)

Food: Rainbow-flavored popsicles

Special Powers: Gemstone earrings endow them with super hearing. Speak so quickly (like a hum) that their words can travel great distances, use sign language that can travel at the speed of sound, shape shifting, tremendous speed, morse code

Physical Attributes: Blond haired, pale blue eyed, long limbed, sinewy

Favorite Activities: Ping-Pong, writing, banjo, spin art, sprinting

Personality Traits: Witt and Clarity are excellent writers and should even as young children keep a journal. The problem, they are always doing so many things at once that they forget to take the time to write things down. They move so quickly that it appears that their feet never quite hit the ground. Very nosy (curious) and can gossip but make for wonderful friends, as they are always up to something. Always make other children feel that they are interested in what they have to say, so they have excellent political skills, always quick with a smile. Born with the gift of persuasion whether it is selling an item or an idea. Will always try to outtalk their guardian out of any jam. Extremely smart but because they can't focus or stay in one place for too long, they can misjudge situations; this also leads to a string of unfinished tasks because they are easily bored. They are very clever, very witty, and very smart—very fun and can always be counted on to cheer on friends and family. Because they feel the need to be everyplace and everywhere, they are always late. Love to see new places and meet new people. Have a quicksilver personality They need to learn how to really listen and stay still, at least for a moment. They will succeed in finding out what they don't know because they are always intellectually curious and keep their mind in the game. Their classical astrological key words—I Think.

Evanescent and Chance, "the entertainers"

Birthplace Moon: Perspicacious Moody Moon
Culture: Celtic
Astrological DNA: Cancer
Astrological Element: Water
Platonic Solid: Icosahedron

Moonstone: Pearl

Signature ID: Belt, Belly ring

Favorite Color: Silvery colors of the sea

Pet: A singing Harp Seal Pup (Dwyn) and a Luna moth (Halcyon)

Food: Cupcakes

Flower: Peony

Special Powers: Can disappear into the moon's light, very intuitive, controls the tides and moonlight, most powerful during eclipses, full moons, solstices, and equinoxes

Physical Attributes: Luminescent skin, strawberry blond hair, curly hair, freckles, and silvery green eye (clear colors of the sea), full faced, soft build

Favorite Activities: Step dancing, stage acting, singing, bagpipes, fiddle, golf, swimming, storytelling, drawing illustrations

Personality Traits: Evan and Chance are naturally very funny, gentle, kind, patient, and sympathetic. They can also be very cranky, self-absorbed, and feel a little sorry for themselves. They secretly love the limelight, but sometimes when they are the center of attention, they suddenly turn quiet and need to disappear, to go back home, to brood. They need constant support, encouragement, and harmony. Food is always a good source of comfort. They rarely take a direct route. They worry about everything; this is particularly true if their environment is somehow disrupted. They have a blind spot when they like someone and are always very loyal. They are sentimental softies with a heart of gold with an air of nostalgia—very old souls. They are hard to deceive because they are so intuitive so they can spot deception, but always remember their blind spot of affection. It is very important to these moonchildren that their mother approves of what they do and they feel a complete confidence in her affirmation. Always try to encourage them to be less sensitive. This will protect their feelings from getting hurt. Avoidance of getting hurt may be a deterrent to their success in life. Must learn to trust their feelings more and to use their great powers of perception to help others. They tend to worry about things that have not happened; this projection can cause a distortion on their presence of mind. Whenever they play grown-up games, they always play the parents. Their astrological key words—I Feel.

Courage (Rage) and Olympia, "the leaders"

Birth Star: Dazzling Sun
Culture: Greek
Astrological DNA: Leo
Astrological Element: Fire
Platonic Solid: Tetrahedron

Moonstone: Star Ruby

Signature ID: Pin worn over their heart

Favorite Color: Hot summer colors like orange and gold

Pet: A chubby fleecy lamb (Zoë) who yaks a lot, and an extremely bossy lightening bug (O) whose tail fires up for attention

Flower: Sunflowers Girasoli

Food: Cherry-flavored gumdrops

Special Powers: They have all the full power of the sun and are naturally great leaders. They can transfer the sun's energy and use heat upon their will and can create sunspots.

Physical Attributes: Dark thick wavy hair, dark wide-set eyes with a golden yellow to dark red center, tall and angular with wide shoulders, olive-toned skin

Favorite Activities: Tennis, having parties, acting, singing, cymbals, conducting, discus throwing, oil painting

Personality Traits: Courage and Olympia always bring sunshine into the lives of others. People always know when they enter a room. They are very generous, kind, and open hearted. Vanity and pride are their Achilles heel. They won't accept failure and love to tell others how to run their lives, but do not take advice very well. They possess wisdom well beyond their years, yet they are the eternal children of the zodiac. Born entertainers who love attention but need to know how to share that limelight with others. Even from a very young age they know how to give a fabulous party; it's a part of their DNA. Only the very best will do for them, lavish in their tastes. Needs flattery, attention, and always needs to be appreciated. In other words, they love to be spoiled and will respond with hugs and kisses. Their stuffed animals always listen to their commands as they all possess a kingdom whatever that may be. They are willing to do for others, and if approached the right way will do what is asked but likes to have that dramatic last word. If injured, they strike back quickly but never hold a grudge. Public image is very important, and they know how to get the attention they enjoy. Will always protect a victim or the underdog. Needs to learn how to give from the heart without any expectations—this will help them protect their big Leo hearts. In classical astrology think of the key words—I Will.

Tien and Fastidious, "the teachers"

Birth Comet: Clever Chiron
Culture: Asian
Astrological DNA: Virgo
Astrological Element: Earth
Platonic Solid: Cube

Moonstone: Blue Sapphire

Signature ID: Ring

Favorite Color: Cerulean Blue

Pet: A mouse (Astute) and a Dragonfly (Yuko)

Flower: Star Blue Aster

Food: Triangular cookies with slips of paper with ancient teachings inside

Special Powers: Reiki healing, superior intellect for detail and clear thinking, Kendo Masters, power of thought transference through collective intelligence

Physical Attributes: Tawny skin, shiny straight dark hair, sinewy musculature with an agile build, vibrant sapphire eyes, agile, Fastidious needs his kendo shinai to walk

Favorite Activities: Yoga, cooking, sewing, clarinet, triangle (instrument), mixed media art, kendo, and other martial arts

Personality Traits: Tien and Fastidious even as children are modest, practical, and kind. Their intelligence is well grounded like practical Taurus and fact-based Capricorn, when coupled with their mental agility = excellent little negotiators. They are very attuned to the well-being of the physical body and do not like any form of physical discomfort. They are also very picky about what food they eat. They love a schedule of small tasks because it suits their methodical nature. They are fastidious; this extends to their outer world where tidiness is needed around them. Enjoy making concoctions, whether for culinary or medicinal purposes, reinforcing their need to be of service. They like to have and to carry a lot of small bags in their hands. They are fidgety, similar to their other mutable siblings Witt and Clarity/CeSe and Skye. They are very analytical and ask questions; in order for them to know something they need to know all the facts. They make for excellent teachers who listen and pay attention to the details. They can appear calm but are actually very nervous and can sometimes be hypochondriacs. They enjoy both giving and receiving small tokens of affection. It is important to them that they feel needed. Their obsession with precision makes them detect the tiniest flaw, but this often leads them to miss the bigger picture at times. This attention to detail, however, can make for excellent artists. They always tell on themselves like their siblings Skye and CeSe. They need to try to be less critical; such obsessions may lead to frustration even as young children. They are excellent mimics as they can spot nuanced behavior in others. They make for good friends as they are loyal and patient. In classical astrology the key words—I Analyze.

Beau and Gracious, "the charmers"

Birth Planet: Pretty Venus
Culture: Mesopotamian
Astrological DNA: Libra
Astrological Element: Air
Platonic Solid: Octahedron

Moonstone: Opal—milky white, with their siblings' eleven other colors floating inside the stone

Signature ID: Spinning Locket (where they keep the secrets of others, in particular the other twins)

Favorite Color: Lavender

Pet: Turkish Angora cat (Pari) and a Butterfly (George)

Food: Taffy

Flower: Gardenias

Special Powers: Magic tricks, hypnosis, power of illusion, nymph-like powers, Reiki healing, aerial screw

Physical Attributes: Androgynous, extraordinarily beautiful and exotic looking, cinnamon-colored skin, lavender eyes, dimpled cheeks

Favorite Activities: Tai chi, dancing, flute, juggling, whirling, squash, drawing with pastels

Personality Traits: Beau and Gracious can be calm, sweet, welcoming, charming, and balanced; they can also be annoying, quarrelsome, stubborn, irrational, and shrill. They always have a "bee in their bonnet." They can be underachievers because they do not like conflict for any reason. They like to be a part of the "in crowd." This can cause them to sometimes choose their companions unwisely. If someone has a charming façade they can be easily fooled. They are the incurable romantics. Always have a winning smile, demeanor, and sweet melodious voice. They do best with a partner or a best friend, and if left alone too long can become very sad. They can cause more trouble by choosing to sit on the fence. They love beauty, harmony, and peace at any price. They can be self-centered at times but will never acknowledge even the suggestion of that. They can appear to be indecisive but this is not because they can't decide, but because they do not like to risk the consequences of acting—the opposite of Aries. They find criticism very hard to take. Need to learn that making a mistake is part of growing up and it is okay. Beau and Gracious dress beautifully and truly embrace color, music, and art. Once they establish a routine, they have a fear about any change creating an imbalance. Wonderful at keeping secrets (where they keep them safe in their spinning lockets) and are great listeners and are of course, so very likable. They make for wonderful friends. The classical astrological key words—I Balance.

Mysterious and OnyX, "the investigators"

Birth Planetoid: Puzzling Pluto
Culture: Egyptian
Astrological DNA: Scorpio
Astrological Element: Water
Platonic Solid: Icosahedron

Moonstone: OnyX

Signature ID: Bracelet

Favorite Color: Topaz, Copper, Bronze (fall shades), and persimmon for dress

Pet: A gray wolf (Ether) and a black wolf (Asa)

Food: Popcorn

Flower: Dahlia, the Queen of the Autumn Garden

Special Powers: Acoustic levitation, finds lost things, puzzles, hiding, Reiki healing, can control gravity

Physical Attributes: Intense eyes with an opaque center with bands of bronze, hazel, maroon, topaz; bronze-colored skin; thick wavy bronze and copper colored hair worn sometimes in a ponytail, sometimes worn very short. Male and female can look identical.

Favorite Activities: Exploring, puzzles, maps, saxophone, playing pool, being secretive, charcoal drawing

Personality Traits: Mysterious and OnyX are intense, passionate, and extremely resourceful but most of all enigmatic, and they like it that way. Be warned: never try to pry into their business even as a toddler. They will never show what they think and can easily hide behind their cloak of mystery. That is why it is so important that the guardians of these children from Pluto establish a very close relationship with them at a very young age. So, lots of hugs and kisses help these children share their emotions to overcome their secret fear of abandonment. Strong and powerful music is soothing to them and helps to direct their high-pitched emotion. Their intensity exerts an excessive force that is easily identified by their ability to outstare anyone. They can be courageous, fearless leaders and yet sometimes clingy and are prone to brooding. They never forget a kindness or an injustice. Things that are weird or scary by other children like caverns, caves, and even the sight of blood fascinate these children. They will always be the first to look under a rock or pick up an insect. Love to watch the transformation of things like cocoons into a butterfly and to play "doctor." Superheroes are a special attraction. As children, they seem to become very attached to one special friend, teacher, or family member at a time and can become jealous. Due to their great powers of perception, Mysterious and OnyX solve mysteries, find lost objects, and finish puzzles. They need to learn how to entrust their feelings to others in order to develop their full powers of leadership. It is very important to encourage that independence. They even as young children become nostalgic. Their classical astrological key words—I Transform.

Sage and AlexSandra, "the adventurers"

Birth Planet: Jolly Jupiter
Culture: Mesoamerican
Astrological DNA: Sagittarius
Astrological Element: Fire
Platonic Solid: Tetrahedron

Moonstone: Turquoise

Signature ID: Ankle Bracelet

Favorite Color: Cyan (deep greenish blue)

Pet: Alphonso the very sweet humming Alpaca, and a lucky Cricket named Fluke

Food: Ribbon candy

Flower: Amaryllis (Hot Pink preferably)

Physical Attributes: Turquoise/cyan eyes, dark hair worn in braids, AlexSandra wears her hair in a braided ponytail, long and powerful legs.

Favorite Activities: tap dancing, soccer, pole vaulting, trumpet, and horn, gossiping and painting with acrylics

Special Powers: ability to see far, chart star calendars, very strong legs, lucky

Personality Traits: Sage and AlexSandra are wonderful storytellers who like to speak with the wisdom of the ages. Or at least like to appear as if they have the wisdom of the ages. They are fun-loving, enjoy entertaining, and love to be entertained. Having a good time is a way of life. They have great aspirations for themselves with foresight, optimism, and versatility as their tools. They are very lucky but need to believe in their own luck. They seem to always be in the right place at the right time, but *always* think that the grass is greener on the other side. This explains their both generous and parsimonious nature. These traits can be shared with the other fire signs, Leo and Aries. Can get easily bored, be a little sarcastic and can sometimes put their foot into one's mouth. Very gifted at conversation with a great sense of humor, can sometimes lead to being a little full of oneself. Do not like repeating and will often say, "You told me." They are very likable, a good friend who likes to have a good time but can at times like to "stir the pot" so to speak, with their incessant questions. Good at roaming and exploring new places. They can have a problem focusing because it's hard for them to sit, stay still, and listen. The world is their classroom and not necessarily in a school. They need to experience in order to learn. "Why" is their favorite word and are very nosy like their Gemini siblings, although they will never acknowledge it. Always need to change the scenery but at the same time don't want to miss any action, so they don't like to make any plans too far in advance. These children need to learn how not to jump to conclusions or judge too easily. They are quick to spot nuances in others, but never in themselves. This can lead to lots of unnecessary pouting. Their classical astrological key words—I See.

Yejide and A'dept, "the planners"

Birth Planet: Serious Saturn
Culture: Nubian
Astrological DNA: Capricorn
Astrological Element: Earth
Platonic Solid: Cube

Moonstone: Garnet

Signature ID: Shoulder sling, garnet gemstone clasp

Color: Shades of brown, garnet (strong earth tones)

Flower: Clematis

Pet: A baby goat (Khaya) and an Ant (Guga)

Food: Candy bags

Special Power: Can make time stop by clapping, they have the Key of Access to the Omnia Tempus, the art of methodical planning

Physical Attributes: Mahogany skin and eyes, fluffy hair

Favorite Activities: Tree climbing, wood sculpting, marathons, rock climbing (endurance sports), bass, cello, and percussion instruments, living in their treehouse, wood carving sculptures

Personality Traits: Yejide and A'dept are the Celestial Task Masters and *always* have a plan. They like structure and order and respect and admire history. They are very capable, reserved, patient, and reliable. They will take an opportunity because they are ambitious but never by brute force. Determination and discipline are their tools. Never underestimate their abilities; they will let others talk and go ahead (because they are very polite) but somehow always get there first. Have a great desire for success and respond well to reward and recognition. Their competitive nature rivals their Aries siblings. They love to plan especially from their treehouse that they of course built themselves. They love to control their environment and put things in a certain place and order and do so in a routine sort of way. Although they have an aura of sternness, their seeming remoteness is often misunderstood. They feel that they can only depend on themselves and have great faith in their own abilities. This self-sufficiency masks their sensitive and sympathetic nature. These children stick around when the going gets tough. Although they are the loners of the solar system they really need to be loved and recognized. They have a wry sense of humor that comes on unexpectedly. All children of Saturn are born with an adult sense of responsibility. They become younger with the passage of time. They need to stop thinking that they are the only ones who can do anything right and to start to depend more on others. They, too, like their other Earth sign siblings (Virgo and Taurus) need to listen to themselves—and hear how they love to complain! These children need to be careful not to let their ambition cause them to lose a sense of what really makes them happy. In classical astrology, their key words—I Use.

Thinx and Twilit Vespers, "the day dreamers"

Birth Planet: Wacky Uranus
Culture: Isle of Zhymn, Apex to the North, a future culture
Astrological DNA: Aquarius
Astrological Element: Air
Platonic Solid: Octahedron

Moonstone: Amethyst

Signature ID: Glasses

Favorite Colors: Nighttime sky, magenta, midnight blue, crystal white, cobalt

Pets: Trio of silver foxes who play instruments (Nikleo, Winifred, Theodore)

Flower: Wildflowers

Food: Rock candy

Favorite Activities: Astronomy/astrology, cards, harp, charting, and calligraphy

Special Powers: Electromagnetism, electricity, prescience, sixth sense, ESP

Physical Attributes: Non-athletic, ash tone hair that is streaked with purple, ash-colored eye with a wisteria dot in the center

Personality Traits: Being different is a way of life for Thinx and Vespers as they embrace the concept of live and let live. They always seem to be a million miles away with a strange faraway look in their eye. Usually, they do not like people to finish sentences, as they do not like to finish their own. They already know what will be said and expect others to have that same capability. Tranquil by nature but love to defy public opinion; they like to act erratically through their attire. This shows their refusal to conform—they laugh at the very same people who are laughing at them. They enjoy the company of various people and often use the word *friend*. Love to be invited to everything but doesn't always like to show up. They are above all else *a student of human behavior*. They cheerfully ignore what others think yet feel out of place when not included by their peers. They have an unusual air of detachment especially when preoccupied. Physical hard work does not interest them. They like to create ideas but like Aries not necessarily implement them. Imaginative but does not like the drudgery of the detail and the minutia of management. They are kindhearted and slow to take offense and do not like to argue but do like to provoke. They hate wasting time getting ready for things; they simply want to put on their glasses and go. They enjoy the mental fight not the physical. Will let others like Courage, Sage, Wink, and OnyX carry the sword for *their idea* into battle. They have an excellent memory and can pick up knowledge right out of the air. They are highly attuned to others' thoughts and will blurt out a solution that might seem ridiculous, but since they live in the future, give their ideas some time to catch on. Their greatest weakness is a tendency to inflate their own intelligence and have a "know-it-all attitude." Expect others to overlook their faults as they overlook theirs. Will need to learn how to listen, and appreciate, and give validation to the ideas of others. These children like to use different spelling of their names just because they like to be nonconforming. Their classical astrological key words—I Know.

Excelsia (CeSe) and Skye, "the seekers"

Birth Planet: Wishful Neptune
Culture: Nordic/Viking, "Land of the Midnight Sun"
Astrological DNA: Pisces
Astrological Element: Water
Platonic Solid: Icosahedron

Moonstone: Iolite, a sunstone

Signature ID: Toe Ring

Favorite Colors: The colors of the Northern Lights—ice pinks, blues, violets

Pet: Trumpet Swan who looks at herself in the water (Tuuli), and silver platinum stallion with long flowing mane and tail (Spar)

Flower: Wishing Flower

Food: Cotton candy

Special Powers: Magical thinking, telepathy, *controls* the solar wind, can hear the symphony of the solar system, clairvoyant

Physical Attributes: Platinum hair, willowy, kaleidoscope eyes (pleochroism), can only see by reflection

Favorite Activities: Feng shui, wind surfing, ice ballet, snowboarding, poetry, wind chimes, and painting watercolors

Personality Traits: CeSe and Skye are blind yet see beyond all others because they see by reflection. They can be the forgotten ones who touch all without anyone knowing. More than any other children, they are affected by their surroundings and by the people who touch their life. They are the eternal students like their Virgo counterparts. Lullabies are a great source of comfort. Skye and Excelsia have a mystical quality. They *love* to be in *love* with things, pets, or people. And will say "I love you" very often. They make wonderful friends because they are so warmhearted and sentimental. They like to laugh especially with others; it's almost infectious. They have an air of refinement, elegance, and glamour that seems to envelop them. They can daydream their life away if not carefully guided. A little flattery will always bring them back to reality. Their use of the imagination is delightful, and they tell a story in a dramatic and poetic fashion. So, telling fairy tales and playing dress-up games of make believe is a way of life. The difficulty is in telling whether the story is true or not.

Even though they are very old souls they have a lighthearted exterior. They are flirtatious and changeable, and they love to look at their reflection in a pond or lake. Excellent memory so they make great actors, musicians, and artists. They can radiate enchantment and seem to float across a room like a ballet dancer. Very intuitive so follow their hunches, and they share some of that luck of their Sagittarius siblings. They can be both sympathetic and empathetic to a fault. They need to be careful not to take on other's problems. Extravagance in everything can be a problem. It is important that these children do not let life pass them by because they in fact touch the reality others do not see. Their mutable nature can also cause them not to do in life what they really want to do, so remember to encourage their flights of fancy. In classical astrology, their key words—I Believe.

PANGEA

ROUGHLY 300 MILLION YEARS AGO
THERE WAS ONLY ONE SINGULAR
LANDFORM KNOWN AS PANGEA. THE
ENTIRETY OF PANGEA IS SURROUNDED BY
THE PANTHALASSA OCEAN. THE EARLY
FORMATION FO THE TEHYS SEA CAN ALSO
BE SEEN JUST OFF THE EASTERN COAST OF
PANGEA. DUE TO THE WARMER CLIMATE
DURING THIS TIME PANGEA IS MOSTLY
COVERED BY FORESTS AND DESERT AREA.
THE EASTERN HALF OF PANGEA IS
SLIGHTLY COOLER THAN THE WESTERN
HALF DUE TO THE AIR CURRENTS AND THE
RAINFALL PATTERNS.

THIS MAP SHOWS THE APPROXIMATE
LOCATION OF THE CURRENT
COUNTRIES AND CONTINENTS AND
WHERE THEY WOULD BE DURING
THIS ERA. DUE TO TECTONIC PLATE
SHIFTING SOME
AREAS OF THE LANDMASSES ARE
STRETCHED OR DISTORTED COMPARED
TO HOW THEY APPEAR NOW.

WHERE DID EACH TWIN SET VISIT?

WHERE IS THE IMPERIUM AND
THE CIRCLE OF STONES?

GLOSSARY OF WORDS

Absconse: The imaginary line that exists within the horizon; an escape hatch

Acerbus: From the Latin word acerbic, to be acidic or bitter in tone or manner. General of Ahreman's Army of Everters, father to Camillus and Tamzin.

Aerial Screw: A gift of Beau and Gracious, as they can create a propeller wind when they juggle.

Air: The mixture of gases that forms the Earth's atmosphere, mainly hydrogen, nitrogen, and oxygen.

Amethyst: The fictional moonstone of Twilit Vespers and Thinx; translucent purple quartz.

Amulet: A gemstone charm or a talisman.

Ahreman: Master and Lord of the Black Holes, wants to be a member of the Coterie, son of Honora and ZR, Esme's twin.

Apex: The highest point.

Archetype: Something that served as the model or pattern for other things of the same type.

Armillary sphere: A spherical model of the universe first used by the early Greek astronomers.

Asa: Fictional name for Mysterious and OnyX's pet wolf; in Hebrew the word means doctor.

Ascendant: The point on the ecliptic that represents the east. In astrological terms, it is the calculation of the rising sign or the ascendant at the time of birth.

Asterism: An optical effect appearing as a star in the light reflected from certain crystals like the Star Ruby or a Star Sapphire.

Astrolabe: The planisphere astrolabe was used by astronomers to calculate the position of the Sun, the prominent stars, and other celestial bodies. It can also tell time.

Astrology: From the Greek word astros "star" and logos "speech"; to talk about the stars.

Astrological Chart: Take a moment and close your eyes. Imagine the universe's position in the sky at the precise moment of your birth. Next, chart the exact location of the sun, planets, asteroids, comets, and moon within that very tick of time. See where they reside, in what constellation. This is a snapshot of your astrological chart, a map of all of the energies present at that most unique and special time of your birth. Your astrological sign serves as that prism channeling your own unique energy and light. A guiding hand to help us channel our inner being in response to our environment. Harnessing the energies of our surroundings, our environment which includes our parents, guardians, friends, family, neighborhood, and country. Free will and choice are the constants that allow us to master our uncharted destiny.

Atmos Clock: A clock that has a hermetic seal.

Aurora Borealis: An ethereal display of colored lights shimmering above the nighttime sky. A colorful dance of lights that flicker green, red, violet, blueish white, and yellow. It is created by the sun's energies, Earth's magnetic field and atmosphere.

Autumnal/Fall Equinox: The moment when the Sun's ecliptic pathway is directly above the Earth's equator moving south, occurring around September 22. It is also called the Fall Equinox. The portal to the cosmic string opens during this alignment as well as in the spring around March 20 during the Spring or Vernal Equinox. During an equinox the day and night are of equal length. The portal also opens during the Winter and Summer Solstices.

Black Hole: A region in space where the gravitational force is so powerful that nothing can escape from it. Created by Ahreman who controls the ultra-high-energy cosmic rays that are hurling towards Earth.

Botany: The study of plant life. A botanist like Tien and Fastidious can identify different species of plants and flowers to order to make potions, remedies, and poisons, like a modern-day pharmacist.

Broken Star: A fictional shooting star that seeks adventure; escapes from its place in the universe. In the "Moonstones" adventure series it is controlled by Nicholas. Always in the present time, it is the Key of Access into the Omnia Tempus. Nicho named him Silvio. It is a twelve-point stellated dodecahedron.

Carbon: Number 6 on the periodic table of elements. The basic element needed for life as we know it on the planet Earth.

Catriz: The name of the female twin from Willful Mars. It is taken from the Spanish word for scar, cicatrize.

Celestial Task Masters: The fictional name given to Yejide and A'dept by their siblings because they like to have organization and a plan for everything

Celestial Wheel or Celestial Sphere: The imaginary sphere around the Earth on which the sun, moon, stars appear to be placed.

Chiron: The fictional home of Tien and Fastidious, first assumed to be an asteroid then thought to be a comet when a fuzzy luminous cloud and tail were detected; in Greek mythology, the centaur Chiron was known for his great wisdom as a teacher and healer.

Circle of Stones: A fictional array of large boulders that stand erect in a perfect circle of 360 degrees divided by twelve houses each of 30 degrees. Each boulder is marked by a glyph that corresponds to each celestial twin. The portal to the cosmic string opens and closes in its epicenter during the Autumnal and Vernal Equinox/Winter and Summer Solstice. The Four Fundamental Forces of Nature intersect within the enclave at its epicenter. The atmosphere within the Circle has the purest highest concentrations of hydrogen, oxygen, carbon, and the lost element Jxyquium (JX) that empowers the ancients and carbon-based life. The space within its circumference is known as the Imperium.

Circumference: The edge or perimeter of a circle.

Clock of Perpetual Motion: known as **the regulator of time**. A fictional timekeeper for the universe. It looks like an armillary sphere with twenty-four moonstones: twelve that move clockwise (the future) and twelve that move counterclockwise (the past) with a twelve-point dodecahedron at its center that is hermetically sealed (the present). That is Silvio, Nicholas's broken star.

Collective Intelligence: A power given to Tien and Fastidious that enables them to teach or convey knowledge.

The Concordaie: They can hear the "hum of harmony." They are the warrior class charged with peacekeeping. Honora, Esme, Melissa, Pen belong to this group of people from the "in time" and "out of time" worlds.

Continuum: A mathematical model that joins space and time.

The Coterie: The twelve members who are the ruling class of the galaxy "in time." They are the Council of Leaders who have the power over the four mundane elements of air, water, earth, and fire. ZR is one of its members. The fifth element, the aether or the quintessence, is under the domain of the members of the Quintessence.

Cosmic String: This is the portal in the Center of the Imperium. The energy retained around the Cosmic String is pure with a very high concentration of JX and other elements. Honora knows its secrets.

Dahlia: The Queen of the Autumn Garden, flower of Mysterious and OnyX.

Dark Side of the Moon: Or more correctly, the far side of the moon; the moon is divided into two halves, the hemisphere we see called the near side, and the hemisphere we don't see, which is the dark side or the far side.

Déjà vu: A feeling of having experienced something before, like remembering the future.

Diamond: Wink and Catriz's moonstone; a transparent form of carbon that is the hardest known mineral; when faceted it displays a most brilliant fire.

DNA: The carrier of genetic information, the genetic code.

Dodecahedron: The geometric shape of the *Sphere of Comets* and Silvio, the star of the present. It is a polyhedron with twelve faces. According to the Greek philosopher Plato, the dodecahedron is said to represent the universe. While the other four Platonic solids represent the four elements: earth (the cube), fire (the tetrahedron), air (the octachoron), and water (icosahedron)—it is the fifth element known as the ether, the Quintessence (dodecahedron) that represents the universe, mystery, and higher learning.

Earth: The home of Nicholas and Penelope; the third planet in order from the sun.

Ecole des Etoiles: The School of the Stars is where the celestial twins attend classes; it is housed in the *Sphere of Comets.*

Eclipse: The partial or complete hiding from view of a celestial body when the sun or moon comes between it and the observer.

Ecliptic: The sun's annual pathway, the circle that the sun follows in the celestial sphere.

Electromagnetism: A power of Thinx and Vespers; the interaction of electricity and magnetic fields; one of the forces within the Circle of Stones.

Emerald: Harmonious and Domenica's moonstone; a beryl-colored green by chromium.

Epicenter: The exact center or focal point.

Eris: A small planetoid located towards the outer edges of the Solar System in the Kuiper Belt; named after the Greek goddess of discord and strife. The Everters were banished to this planet.

Esme: The fictional mother of the twelve sets of celestial twins; her name means *as me*.

Ether: Also called the Quintessence. The space above the horizon in the sky. The name of OnyX's pet, the gray wolf. It is the fifth element.

Event Horizon: The space within a black hole where time stops. It is an imaginary line within the hole that separates what can leave that space on one side, and on the other what can never escape.

Everters: The evil ones from the Latin word for "to turn out" who were banished to the planet Eris.

Eye of Command: The position point from where A'dept and Yejide watch the battle unfold; a strategic position to watch and make tactical decisions.

Evanescent: To dissipate like vapor; the fictional name of the female twin from the Moody Moon; the sister of Chance; from the Latin word *evanescere*.

Feng Shui: A power of Tien and Fastidious that they teach their siblings; the Chinese system that studies people's relationship to the environment in which they live to achieve maximum harmony with the spiritual forces believed to exist in nature.

Firmament: A name for the sky or the heavens; the color of a blue sapphire.

Four Fundamental Forces of Nature: Gravity, electromagnetic, nuclear large, and nuclear small. These forces exist within the Imperium.

Full Moon: The phase of the Moon when its surface as seen from the Earth is fully illuminated by the sun as a circle.

Galaxy: Also called the Milky Way Galaxy, viewed from Earth as a hazy band of white lights that is seen in the night sky arching across the entire celestial sphere; it is the home galaxy of the planet Earth.

Garnet: The moonstone of A'dept and Yejide; a dark red crystalline silicate mineral.

Gilbert/Gil: Nicholas and Penelope's uncle, Melissa's twin; the name means *"bright promise, or oath."*

Glyph: A symbol or character that has been carved out in a stone surface; a nonverbal symbol, each of the twins has their own special one.

Harvest Moon: The Harvest Moon is the full moon closest to the autumnal equinox. It appears to glow with a reddish hue and appears much larger than other full moons because it hangs low in the nighttime sky.

Halo Moon: Double ring around the moon. It could mean rain or a symbol of foreboding.

Hercules Cluster: A galaxy outside of the Milky Way, where Markarian 501 resides.

Hermetic Seal: Means something is sealed airtight; named after the Greek god Hermes who was the messenger of the gods. Silvio, the clock of the present, has one.

Hum of Harmony: A fictional reference to Johannes Kepler's harmonic law of planetary motions; Esme, Clarity and Witt, and Penelope can hear the sound.

Hypnotism: A feeling so mesmerizing that the attention of people watching is so completely absorbed that they go into a trance-like state of consciousness; it is a power of Beau and Gracious.

Hydrogen: Is a chemical element with the symbol H and the atomic number 1. It is the most abundant chemical substance in the universe.

The Imperium: The space within the Circle of Stones.

Infinity: Time, space, or distance without limits; A'dept and Yejide have the power to make time stop within its realm.

Intuition: The ability to know something without any reason or proof; a power of Evan and Chance and Nicho.

Iolite: The gemstone of Excelsia and Skye; the name comes from the Greek word *ion*, which means violet; used by the Viking mariners for navigation as a polarized lens to track the sun's position; it also contains the proprieties of pleochroism, a sunstone.

Iris: The rainbow flower, that is Esme's flower. In Greek mythology, the Goddess of the Rainbow, and a messenger of the gods.

Jupiter: The home of Sage and AlexSandra; the largest planet in our solar system and the fifth in order from the sun; in Roman mythology, named after the king of the gods.

JQ: The measure of one's power derived from the five elements: air, water, earth, fire, and the ether—all contained in the element Jxyquium. (JX).

JQ = Astrological DNA Power Rating.

Jxyquium (JX): The lost element that makes the Earth so unique. On the elemental table it's denoted as **JX** without any number. To the ancients, one's **JQ** was a measured source of measured power just as one's IQ that measures intellectual intelligence or EQ that measures one's emotional intelligence. This element **JX** powers the *Sphere of Comets* and allows life to exist on the Sun, Moon, Mercury, Venus, Pluto, Neptune, Jupiter, Mars, Sedna, Chiron, Saturn, and Uranus. Only Earth has a naturally occurring supply.

Komodo Dragon: A pet of Ahreman. When in the Earth's atmosphere it becomes gigantic and can breath fire.

Kendo: A Japanese martial art in which people fence with two-handed swords (shinai) made of bamboo instead of metal; Fastidious is the kendo master of the universe.

Key of Access: It is a small stellated dodecahedron that unlocks the inner sanctum of the Omnia Tempus that houses the Clock of Perpetual Motion/the regulator of time. One must traverse through the slot canyon (Tunnel of Infinity) to reach the chamber. Nicholas and Reed are two deemed worthy to hold the Key of Access that controls the present. It is Nicho's broken star that he named Silvio. The star has a hermetic seal that opens and closes like an Atmos clock.

Latter Twelfstanin: the twelve moonstones in the Clock of Perpetual Motion that controls the past.

Levitation: The act of raising something in the air without visible means of support in defiance of gravity; a power of Mysterious and OnyX.

Mars: The home of Wink and Catriz; reddish in color due to its high concentration of ferrous; the fourth in order from the Sun; in Roman mythology named after the god of war.

Melissa: Nicholas and Penelope's mother, the name means *bee* just like the name Debora.

Mercury: The home of Witt and Clarity; the smallest planet in the Solar system; named after the messenger of the gods.

Mikai: fictional name for *son of the one who was sent;* a derivative of the name Michael. His father is Jais, and they are members of Quintessence.

Moon: Home of Chance and Evan, the astronomical body nearest the Earth; its gravitation pull controls the tides and water.

Moonstones: Name coined by Gil and Melissa for sea glass found on the beach during the full moon.

Moravian Star: It can be a twelve-pointed star usually used on a holiday tree, a stellated rhombic dodecahedron. Sometimes the center is open, sometimes the center is closed.

Mystery Secret: A term coined in the Guardian of the Moonstone story; it means a secret that is a mystery.

Nadir: The lowest point on the celestial sphere opposite the zenith. On an astrological chart it is the fourth house.

Neptune: The home of Excelsia and Skye; the eighth planet from the sun; named after the Roman god of the sea.

Nitrogen: This element, number 7 on the periodic table (N). Occurs as a colorless gas that makes up four-fifths (78%) of the Earth's atmosphere; it is a constituent element of all living tissue and amino acids.

Northern Lights: see aurora borealis. The bright dancing lights of the aurora are actually collisions between electrically charged articles from the sun that enter the earth's atmosphere. The lights are seen above the magnetic poles of the northern and southern hemispheres. Known as Aurora borealis in the north, and Aurora australis in the south. The colors of pale green, pink, red, yellow, blue, and violet can be seen.

Offing: the most distant part of the sea that can be seen from the shoreline; the part of the sea that is closest to the horizon.

Oleander: Also known as rosebay. Is a beautiful flowering plant whose stem is poisonous. Tien and Fastidious are botanists and know how to create potions, medicines, and poisons from plants/flowers.

Omnia Tempus: The chamber that houses the Clock of Perpetual Motion, only those pure of heart can enter its realm.

OnyX: The gemstone of OnyX and Mysterious; a fine textured type of black chalcedony quartz, it can also have layers of different bands of color including white, black, maroon, and brown.

Oxygen: This element combined with hydrogen creates H2O, water. One of Earth's most precious elements.

Opal: The gemstone of Beau and Gracious; it is said that all of nature's splendor is reflected in the face of an opal, fire, and lightening, all the colors of the rainbow and the shades of the seas; they shine and sparkle in a continuously changing **play of color**.

Pangaea/Pangea: A super continent incorporating all the Earth's major landmasses, this C-shaped land mass spreads across the Equator. Terrestrial life could roam from the North Pole to the South Pole; the entire land mass was surrounded by water called the Panthalassa Ocean approximately 300 million years ago.

Pearl: Chance and Evan's gemstone; formed when a small lustrous sphere of calcium carbonate forms around a grain of sand in a mollusk or oyster.

Pegasus: The winged horse in Greek mythology. Spar the pet stallion of Skye and CeSe bears a striking resemblance or maybe that is vice versa. It is also the name of a major constellation visible during summer and autumn in the northern sky.

Peridot: one of Clarity and Witt's gemstones. Its color is yellow-green and sometimes a lime-green to emerald-ish hue.

Platonic Solids: There are five Platonic Solids.

    Cube: Is said to represent the element Earth. The Earth Signs are Taurus, Virgo, and Capricorn.

    Icosahedron: Is said to represent the element Water. The Water Signs are Pisces, Cancer, and Scorpio.

    Octahedron: Is said to represent the element Air. The Air Signs are Aquarius, Gemini, and Libra.

    Tetrahedron: Is said to represent the element Fire. The Fire Signs are Aries, Sagittarius, and Leo.

    Dodecahedron is said to represent the universe/the ether.

Play of Color: It is called opalizing (see opal); the optical effect seen when looking into the face of an opal. When Beau and Gracious are given a secret from their siblings, their color is kept and reflected in their spinning locket.

Pleochroism: Is an optical phenomenon where a mineral appears to change color as it is rotated by a plane of illumination (see iolite).

Pluto: The home of Mysterious and OnyX; it is on average the furthest planet away from the Sun, named after the god of the underworld.

Prism: A glass or other transparent body that is used to deflect or disperse light. All of the colors of the rainbow seem to shine through a triangular prism.

Quaoar: Is a trans-Neptunian planetoid (like Eris) orbiting the Sun in the Kuiper Belt at the very edges of the Solar system; named after the Native American deity of creation.

The Quintessence: A group of seers, they have the power of the fifth element and the sixth sense. They are professors, astrologers, the rulers of the ether. Jais, Mikai, Reed, Nicholas are members. They have the power of mental telepathy. Only they can hold the Dodecahedron, the Key of Access: Nicholas's broken star. They can serve as the Sentinel in the Omnia Tempus.

Rainbow: Occurs when the rays of the Dazzling Sun shine onto droplets of moisture. A multicolored arc of light appears across the sky, starting with Catriz and Wink's color red and ending with CeSe and Skye's color violet. The flower of Esme is an iris, named after Iris, the goddess of the rainbow.

Reiki: A treatment in alternative medicine in which healing energy is channeled from the one to another to enhance vitality and reduce pain; a power of Tien and Fastidious, Courage and Olympia, Beau and Gracious, and Mysterious and OnyX.

Rip in the Continuum: The moment when there was a schism "in time" and "out of time," where the two parallels worlds of in time and out of time were created.

Sapphire: The gemstone of Tien and Fastidious; a clear hard precious stone that is a variety of the mineral corundum; its color, the blue of the Earth and sky.

Saturn: The home of Adept and Yejide, it is the second largest planet and sixth in order from the Sun. Its bright rings are made up of orbiting fragments of rocks ranging in size from microns to meters. Galileo Galilei first discovered its rings.

Sea Glass: Also known as beach glass or called "moonstones" by Gil and Melissa; it is glass found along the beaches of oceans and large lakes that have been tumbled and made smooth by the sand and water.

Sedna: The home of Domenica and Harmonious; a planet-like body in the far reaches of the Solar system belonging to the group of other trans-Neptunian objects in the Kuiper Belt.

Sentinel: one who guards the entrance in the Omnia Tempus, the chamber that houses the Clock of Perpetual Motion.

Shinai: A sword of bamboo.

Silvio: Nicholas's name for his broken star and his best friend. It holds the space of the "present" in the Clock.

Sixth Sense: The ability to sense changes in the electromagnetic field that surrounds the Earth due to changes in barometric pressure. This power is possessed by the Quintessence who protect the hermetic seal on the Clock of Perpetual Motion's time in the present.

Slot Canyon: A narrow canyon that is formed by rushing water. It can be as narrow as three feet in width and 100 feet high. It can also be several miles in length. It can be very dangerous if it rains as it floods. The Tunnel of Infinity is a slot canyon.

Solar System: Consists of the Sun and other celestial objects bound to it by gravity, consisting of eight planets, moons, dwarf planets, asteroids, comets, meteoroids, and interplanetary dust.

Solar Wind: The flow of high-speed ionized particles from the sun's surface into interplanetary space; a power shared by Courage and Olympia/Skye and Excelsia.

Spar: Also known as Icelandic crystal, it is a sunstone used by the Vikings to locate the sun.

Spar: It is also the name of Skye and CeSe's pet stallion. Spar who is he/she is a platinum stallion that can also shape shift into very powerful warrior flying horse like Pegasus without the wings. Spar's ears turn into spikes of spar crystal and can turn the air into ice crystals. Uses the power of the solar wind/air to fly.

Space-Time: A mathematical model that joins space plus time into a continuum.

Sphere of Comets: Fictional home of Esme and Mikai and houses the Council of the Coterie; the _Ecole de Etoiles_ (School of the Stars). It is a large spaceship in the shape of a twelve-pointed star of twelve different colors. It is a large dodecahedron that is powered by the element JX.

Spring Equinox: Also known as the Vernal Equinox. Occurs when the sun crosses the celestial equator moving north. The celestial equator is the imaginary line in the sky above the Earth's equator. Again, when of the two moments in the year when the sun is equally above the equator; the day and the night are of equal length.

Star Ruby: The gemstone of Courage and Olympia; a ruby with a crystalline structure that reflects light in a shape that resembles a star (see asterism).

Summer Solstice: The sun's presence in the sky marks the longest day of the year in the Northern Hemisphere. It occurs on or about June 21.

Sun: The home of Courage and Olympia; the star at the center of our solar system that gives the Earth heat and light.

Sunspot: One of the cool dark patches on the Sun's surface that possesses a powerful magnetic field; a power of Courage and Olympia.

Sunstones: Crystals used by the ancient Vikings to navigate; Icelandic spar is a sunstone.

Tai chi: A Chinese form of exercise characterized by a series of very slow and deliberate balletic body movements; a favorite activity of Tien and Fastidious and Beau and Gracious.

Tamzin: The name means "twin"—brother of Camillus.

Telepathy: Communication directly from one person's mind to another without speech, writing, or other signs; also called ESP or extrasensory perception; a power of Thinx and Vespers, Professor Jais, and Nicholas.

Terpsichoric: From the Muse of choral songs and dance in Greek mythology, Terpsichore. It means to love music and dance.

Tien: Fictional name for the resonance of the triangle's ring, twin sister of Fastidious.

Titanite: Another gemstone of Clarity and Witt; also known as sphene. It's a magical gemstone, of lime-green with flashes of yellow and orange. When faceted, it displays more fire than a diamond, with flashes of color.

Transcendence: Existence above and apart from the material world.

Turquoise: The gemstone of AlexSandra and Sage; a greenish-blue mineral form of aluminum and copper phosphate; the color is meant to bring happiness by mixing the color of the sky and the sea.

Tuuli: The fictional name for Excelsia's pet swan; her name means "wind" in Finnish.

Tunnel of Infinity: A place where time has no beginning and has no end. It is the slot canyon that guards the Inner Sanctum, the Omnia Tempus.

Twin Talk: The secret language shared only by twins. It is a form of gibberish. The sound "gediga" is used between each syllable.

Uranus: The home of Thinx and Vespers; the seventh planet from the Sun; in Greek mythology, Uranus was the ruler of the heavens; its axis of rotation is tilted sideways.

Valkyrie: a symbol of ancient Norse mythology. They are usually depicted as beautiful maidens riding a horse into battle. The name means "chooser of the slain," who led heroes killed in battle to Valhalla.

Varuna: Another trans-Neptunian object in the Kuiper Belt; the sometime home of Honora and ZR.

Venus: Evening Star, the home of Beau and Gracious; in Roman mythology, the goddess of love and beauty; it is the second planet from the Sun and one of the brightest objects in the nighttime sky. Also known as the Night's First Light.

Vernal Equinox: Also known as the Spring Equinox.

Winter Solstice: The day in the Northern Hemisphere where the Sun's presence is the briefest in the visible sky; in other words, it is the shortest day of the year. It occurs on or about December 21. From that day forward, each day the sun is present for one minute longer until the Summer Solstice that marks the longest day of the year.

Worm Hole: a hypothetical link (tunnel) between two separate points in space and time. The points can have two different locations in space, two different placements in time, or both.

Xyzanium: The hardest known substance in the cosmos; its source and composition a mystery secret as it's harder than a carbon-formed diamond. It looks like crystalized marble because of its smoothness. Its shell cannot be penetrated. JX is only stored within containers (cube, dodecahedron, octahedron, tetrahedron, icosahedron) made of this substance. Xyzanium makes up the walls that guard the Omnia Tempus.

Yejide: A Nigerian name that means *in the image of her mother.*

Yoga: A system of breathing exercise and postures based on Hindu principles.

Zenith: The point of the celestial sphere that is directly over the observer, the highest point on the celestial sphere. On an astrological chart it is called the mid-heaven.

Zhymn/Isle of Zhymn: The fictional home of Vespers and Thinx. It is a place of the future that is yet to be.

MOONSTONES: WINTER SOLSTICE

Sun 00 degrees of Capricorn
Moon 00 degrees of Cancer

I t was the third week in December, and the sun, moon, planets, and stars were preparing for their annual nighttime display during the winter solstice. It was the shortest day of the year in terms of the Dazzling Sun's presence in the daytime sky and the longest presence for the stars that twinkle in the sun's visible absence. On Earth it was the time of Yuletide celebration, and everyone was preparing for Christmas, Hanukah, and the Festival of Lights. A surprise early winter storm descended upon the small town of Longporte. A layer of crystal snow blanketed the beach; even the waves of the ocean wore icy peaks. The season of fall had left them, and so had the memories from their adventure. The season of winter had truly begun.

From their second-floor dormer window, Nicholas and Penelope sat quietly watching the horizon and the gently falling snowflakes. Waiting and waiting, ever vigilant, hoping for something to happen. By this time, they wondered if their adventure was all just a dream. It seemed so, anyway. Tonight, would be the Full Cold Moon, another rare occurrence for any stargazer. Would it bring something extraordinary?

The house was filled with the scent of evergreens. Downstairs, the freshly cut blue spruce was ready to be decorated with all the lights and the ornaments that had been handed down through generations; they were the family heirlooms.

"Hey, guys, come downstairs and help us finish decorating the tree," their mom, Melissa, called to them. They left their post to join in on the holiday fun.

"Who wants to put the star on the top of the tree?" their dad, Reed, asked.

"I will," Nicholas volunteered. His father handed him the tree topper. It was a Moravian star that had been in their mother's family forever. It still looked brand new. Nicholas held it reverently as he admired it.

Just then, Penelope flew past him, almost knocking him over into the fireplace.

"Hey, do you see the burning logs that you almost knocked me into?" he griped at her.

Penelope had no time to respond. She was a blur as she flew past the screen door onto the front porch. Nicholas recovered his balance, gently put down the ornament, and followed his twin. That was his custom.

"Did you hear it, did you hear it?" Penelope asked excitedly. "It was the sound of the French horn! Something is going to happen. I know it!" She scurried about their front yard, dancing through the flurry of snowflakes. The crystal droplets swirled around them in a frenzy. This was no mere snowstorm; no, this blizzard was special. Someone was sending them a calling card.

Then what happened happened. It was a blaze, a crackle, a spark of flashing light.

"Nicholas, look," Penelope shrieked. "It's Silvio. He's come back; he has come to visit!" She could hardly contain her excitement. She ran over to him. He was sitting on the ground, with three points hidden in the snow. "Look, see how he is perched? Just like the night we found him on the beach stuck in the sand, but now he is stuck in the snow." Penelope went to touch him, then instinctively held back as he blinked red. Penelope was exasperated. "This little star is so annoying; he won't do anything unless it's for you, Nicholas. I still think he doesn't like me."

"That's because he knows how bossy you are, and he has a mind of his own," Nicholas told her with a smirk.

Different colored light emanated from the little stellated dodecahedron, Nicholas' broken star. The twelve points all twinkled in agreement. Nicholas went to pick him up, but Silvio playfully bounded forward, almost hitting Penelope in the face.

"Cut it out." She took a swat and missed.

Then the little star bobbled at their eye level and graciously opened his portal. The twins looked inside and smiled. What they saw made them both wink.

Onward . . .

ABOUT THE AUTHOR

Debora Russo Haines is a native Philadelphian, who currently resides in Princeton, New Jersey. Her young adult fantasy work draws inspiration from years spent studying the art of astrology and raising her girl-boy twins. Her writing reflects her many passions, including playing music and stewardship of nature. Her fascination with flowers and gemstones inspired the aesthetic of *Guardian of the Moonstones*.

Before tapping into her creative ambitions, Debora practiced law for more than twenty years at the City of Philadelphia's Solicitor and Managing Director's Offices, where she led litigation matters that affected the implementation of civil rights statutes. In her spare time, Debora serves as a trustee for nonprofit organizations that support art education programs for children.

She believes there is no such thing as a coincidence and that every encounter, blessing, and trial has a meaning and a message. Debora's favorite place to write is the Jersey Shore. Sea breezes and salty air are her favorite elixir, and she often takes midnight walks with her Jack Russell Terriers by the water's edge, listening to the ocean waves' hum of harmony.

Made in the USA
Columbia, SC
30 October 2022

70189148R00241